Poised

CALUMET EDITIONS

Minneapolis

First Edition June 2024
Poised. Copyright © 2024 by Cheryl Bailey.
All rights reserved.

No parts of this book may be used or reproduced by any means, graphic, electronic, or mechanical, including photocopying, recording, taping or by any information storage retrieval system, without the written permission of the publisher except in the case of brief quotations embodied in critical articles and reviews.

This is a work of fiction. All of the characters, names, incidents, organizations, and dialogue are either the products of the author's imagination or are used fictitiously.

10 9 8 7 6 5 4 3 2 1

ISBN: 978-1-962834-15-5

Cover and book design by Gary Lindberg

Poised

A NOVEL

Cheryl Bailey

CALUMET EDITIONS
Minneapolis

To my mom, Cynthia, the strongest person I know. I couldn't have done any of this without you.

And to my patients, forever my real professors. Thank you for trusting me with your medical conditions, yes, but also with your stories and inner lives. As you so often showed me, cancer can be funny.

"You own everything that happened to you. Tell your stories. If people wanted you to write warmly about them, they should have behaved better."

—Anne Lamott

Glossary of Terms
(in the ridiculous world of medical education)

Medical Students: Very driven college grads who ace the MCAT test, interview all over the country, and get that blessed admission letter. They can't wait to spend four years studying for careers as physicians all while paying big bucks for the privilege. "Fun-loving" won't be your first impression of this crew. Medical school requires memorizing boatloads of facts, dissecting a human cadaver, and doing breast and rectal exams ON EACH OTHER. When they graduate at twenty-six they are doctors in name only. You *definitely* should not trust them with anything medical yet.

Match Day: Every graduating medical student finds out where s/he is going for residency on the same day in March. Most match with a spot in their top three choices. A few don't match, but that's a whole 'nother glossary.

Internship: This is the first year of residency. An intern is also called a scut monkey, or PG-1, which stands for post-graduate year one. Scared and exhausted, interns are mostly learning how to accomplish mountains of "scut work" for their medical team—checking lab results, updating notes, and pre-rounding on sick patients. Nope, don't trust them with anything medical.

Residency: These young doctors are PG-2s, 3s, et cetera, up to PG-7s for many surgical residencies. During the 1990s, interns and residents spent every third night in the hospital "on call," up all night answering pages, going to see sick patients, and performing surgery. Regardless of how brutal the call night was, they put in a full day's work the next day. And although the TV shows make it look like they're all having sex in call rooms, residents are mostly too damned tired. Salaries pay for an apartment and a shitty car. After the three to seven years of internship and residency, they get a real job, unless they want to subspecialize, in which case they apply and interview all over the country to get a coveted...

Fellowship: A one-to-three-year post in which physicians learn the extra skills needed in that specific field, do medical research, present their department's work at conferences, and usually write a thesis. These are your cardiologists, pulmonologists, gynecologic oncologists, etc. Finally, they can hone their craft and do the work they've been killing themselves to do--they might even dare to have more collegial conversations with their immediate superiors. Yep, you can ask these guys about your wife's hernia or that thing on your neck now.

Attending or **Staff Physicians:** These folks have gone through all of the above and are now in the position to teach all those other people. They've earned the title Professor, Residency Program Director, and Fellowship Program Director, depending on how many scholarly articles they can publish and their skill at office politics, of course. Some high-powered academic programs thrive and develop great reputations for being a teaching hospital. Others eat their young.

Private Practice: In the rest of the country's hospitals and clinics, most of the physicians are not in a teaching role—they work in private practice. This is what the rest of the world calls "a job." They take their own call without the buffer of medical underlings, now using their phones instead of the beepers which only doctors and drug dealers relied on for decades.

Patient: Someone who is ill who manages to get to a clinic, hospital, or helicopter pad in hopes of a doctor helping them. As physicians go through training, they encounter hundreds of scared human beings with medical conditions that need attention. The passion that simmers in every doctor is the desire to help the patient in front of him or her. They can't seem to help themselves. That's good to know, isn't it?

Novel: A fictional representation of everything above. That means stuff is made up. Of course, some parts of fiction are true. You'll have to decide which is which.

Prologue

An unbearable tension filled the room. Surgeons worked fiercely to save the patient, shouting for sponges, sutures, and the like. An assistant dabbed sweat from the main doctor's forehead to keep drips from falling into the sterile field. Blood, surely too much of it, was splattered all over the green linens.

"Joe, do something, dammit!" fired the anesthesiologist as the beeping of the ventilator added to the chaos. "I can't keep him going much longer! You've got to stop the hemorrhage!" He noted the worsening vital signs while squeezing an IV bag to pour more volume into the dying patient.

"I've got it! There's the bleeder, right there. Clamp!" Dr. Joe Gannon arrested the bleeding, sweat beading along his brow, his every gesture perfection. Everyone in the room sighed. The audible pulse slowed, comically too fast in response to the intervention, and the male surgeons exchanged glances of mastery across the OR table.

"Shelly! Honey, I've called you to dinner three times now. Turn off the TV and come eat." Catherine stood, dish towel over her shoulder, shaking her head at the sight of her lanky nine-year-old daughter sitting cross legged on the living room floor, rapt as the scene from *Medical Center* played out. Shelly still didn't appear to have heard her mom, who leaned over to turn the TV knob.

Shelly was startled out of the drama by her mother's movement. "He did it, Mom. Dr. Gannon saved that man's life. That's exactly what I'm gonna do." The girl adjusted her octagon glasses and stood, wrinkling her nose as she met her mom's gaze. "Except with less sweating."

CHAPTER 1

Pretty Shoes

Pretty shoes would do her in. Shelly Riley suspected she had poor taste in clothes--and knew she had no money--but hoped her skirt and top murmured "professional," whatever that meant. Nylons, of course, and the only pair of size eleven dress shoes she owned. They weren't comfortable, but at least they fit her long, skinny feet.

She made a pot of espresso in the aluminum Italian pot she'd used since medical school, just as her roommate Evie had taught her. The electric stove coils glowed hot red, threatening to melt the pot's black plastic handle. She deftly lit her first cigarette of the day off the edge of the burner. With a deep inhale, she wondered where she could hide the Altoids mint tin holding her Marlboros. She didn't have her white lab coat yet, and doctors never carried purses around the hospital. Shelly wanted to stride into the Powell Cancer Center with confidence, which would be hard to pull off juggling all the crap she needed for the day.

The pot chirped and sputtered on the stove, filling the little kitchen with the aroma of coffee. Shelly poured it into her favorite mug with a spoonful of sweetened condensed milk and stirred. She perched on the arm of her sagging sofa and savored that first sip of hot espresso, always the finest part of the morning.

She was finally here. It had taken four years in Minnesota for medical school. Another four years in Massachusetts for her OB-GYN residency, and she almost hadn't gotten a fellowship at all. Shelly could remember the kick in the gut when she found out she hadn't matched. She'd schlumped around the hospital wondering what the hell to do when she graduated in June.

Then the surprise call from Kentucky University Southeast came with a sudden opening. Shelly grabbed it, ecstatic and a little desperate to prove herself. Months later, here she was, in a little rental house in southern Kentucky, ready to dive into the gynecologic oncology fellowship—the final step. It had taken for goddamned ever.

Shelly was determined to impress them on this first day. She supposed there'd be loads of paperwork and a boring orientation, though the office had provided no information. She'd called a couple of times during the last few weeks, but Arlys, the senior secretary to Division Chair Dr. Farber, had only offered, "Just show up for five-thirty morning rounds, doctor. Second floor, Powell Cancer Center. They'll show you around then." Shelly could handle it. She had her most grownup outfit on, and she was ready to go.

* * *

The second she opened the door of her air-conditioned rental house, a wall of humidity blasted the energy right out of her. She tossed her purse into the hatchback of her 1989 red Ford Festiva and folded herself into the driver's seat with a *clink* from the flimsy door. Shelly loved her car despite its utter lack of modern features or power anything. She'd bought it her last year of medical school.

"Huh," the salesman had grunted, "you remind me of the clowns getting out of the tiny car at the circus, you being so tall, you know."

She rolled down her window, pushed in the cigarette lighter for a quick smoke, and squinted at her folded road map. She'd inked a circle around her house and an X through the hospital campus. Yesterday's dry run of the route had only taken about seven minutes. Her lead foot could make it faster.

She felt and drove like a young maverick on a new adventure. Every stop sign obeyed was a small traffic triumph, and every wrong turn avoided, a miracle. As she squealed into the hospital lot, Shelly noticed several cars completely covered in a thin silver wrap to protect the paint from the heat. Strange. She understood scraping ice off a windshield in January or jumping a dead battery during a cold snap. *Summer* was not an enemy in the Midwest.

She surveyed the hospital building, drab and unremarkable in multiple shades of concrete. With only fifteen minutes to find her team, she hustled into the hospital lobby and toward the elevator. *Nope--I'm not getting locked in a stairwell on the first day.*

The elevator doors swished open, and as Shelly entered, her heel lodged in the space between the elevator and hospital floors. She was stuck, and the doors batted at her sides. Panicked, she dropped her items in the elevator, slipped her foot from the shoe, and bent to extricate it. Her lighter skidded across the floor and nearly doing the splits she blocked it from falling into the crevice with her stockinged foot.

Before she could get her balance and stand up, the doors swooshed open to reveal a twenty-something phlebotomist in a hurry to start his morning blood draws. He nearly pushed his cart of needles and test tubes onto her leg as she struggled to gather her other shoe and the cigarettes ejected from the Altoids tin. "Morning," she squeaked.

He muttered "Good grief" at Shelly as she strode out into the Powell Cancer Center, tucking her shirt in and tossing her hair back.

In front of her was the ward clerk's semicircular reception desk, covered with charts and papers. She could see the woman's purse handle peeking out by her feet. *Deep breath.*

"Hi, there!" Shelly smiled at her. "I'm the new gynecologic oncology fellow, Dr. Riley. I'm supposed to meet the team for rounds at five-thirty?"

"Oh, Lord. It's July the first, isn't it?" the clerk drawled. "I forgot all you new doctors would be coming in this morning. Well, we're awfully glad to have you! The team grabbed the cart and they're setting up at room 201, just like always." Her girth flowed as she stood, pulled down her blue-green blouse, and walked around her desk to point the way.

Shelly hesitated. "I wonder if you'd do me a favor--I have my keys and some other things in this little bag. Could I stash it here at your desk until I get my lab coat?"

The woman nodded with a grin, reaching under her desk to pull out two drawers. "This here is the 'Leave my stuff alone' drawer, and this one here is the 'Help yourself to some candy' drawer, and I believe everyone knows the difference between the two. Just tuck it in here, and it'll stay safe. The senior fellow, Dr. Mackey, keeps his brief case here too. Lord knows who'd steal it, the thing's so beat up." She offered Shelly a peppermint from her drawer.

"I'm Bernice."

"Thanks for the help." Shelly confided, "I have no idea what I'm doing."

Bernice gave her waist a gentle squeeze and whispered back, "Well, I like the looks of you. It's about time they got themselves a lady fellow!" Her firmness gave Shelly a boost. "I believe you'll be fine. Go on, now. Get to your rounds. And don't forget your little sack at the end of the day!"

The humidity, elevator mishap, and dress shoes be damned. She'd made a friend, and it was only 5:25 a.m.

With a tilt of her head, Shelly gave herself a pep talk and hustled over to the small group assembled outside of room 201. She pondered her growth from the other first days in college, medical school, and residency. She was ready to conquer these last two years of training. *More* than ready.

It was so early that the overhead lights were dim, and the hospital hallway was quiet and calm. The group was collecting itself, and Shelly scanned them like a detective at a crime scene. There were three residents in long white coats and blue scrubs plus two med students, identifiable by their shorter coats and panicky demeanor. She assumed the man with salt and pepper cropped hair was her senior fellow, Ken Mackey, dressed in business casual with a pressed white lab coat. Ken had just finished the year Shelly was about to start. He'd be her lifeline.

The head nurse on the night shift, in a dark orange set of nursing scrubs, came down the hall, drying off her hands. Shelly noted all the high strung, nervous faces with a smile. Same energy, just different stages of medical training.

The reliable scent of fresh coffee filled the air and Shelly assumed an aide had put a pot on to brew for the night team getting ready to document their shifts. Someone had gathered the patients' charts together on a wheeled cart in order by room number.

Without a white coat, she stood out like the foreigner she was.

Except for the intern, also brand new to this hospital, all the others knew the drill, knew each other, and knew the schedule for the day. Shelly did not. *Jesus, wait 'till I open my mouth...*

"Well, hey, there! You must be Shelly. I'm Ken Mackey, and I'm tickled to tell you that as of this very second, I just became the *senior* fellow. Glad to have you aboard." Ken greeted her with a handshake and a grin. "You all, this is the new fellow, Dr. Riley," he nodded to the rest of the team. "You found us just fine, then? Orientation all done?"

"Glad to meet you finally, Ken." Shelly smoothed out her flat midwestern tones. "No orientation yet. Arlys just told me to come here at five thirty. I'm sure she'll find me when she gets into work, and I'll get my tour and everything."

"Well, good." Ken flashed an impossibly bright and enigmatic smile.

Shelly gauged him for warmth since she'd need Ken's help to get up to speed. Knowing how intensive this fellowship was reputed to be, Shelly supposed he was sizing her up, too. One weak link would hurt everyone in this hectic life of medical training.

They all greeted one another around the wheeled cart stuffed with patient's charts. It was plain that she was the only northerner as they introduced themselves. Shelly's Minnesota speech was blocky in comparison to their swing. *Great,* she smiled to herself, *I'm going to fall for a whole new set of accents.* During her four years of residency in Springfield, she'd loved the voices of western Massachusetts, words like "The Vinyid" and "lobstah" occasionally needing translation.

She inhaled and nodded. "Good morning, everyone. I'm Shelly Riley, originally from Minnesota, as you can probably hear." She appreciated their jaws didn't drop to the floor. "I finished my residency in Massachusetts and drove down a few days ago. Got most of my stuff put away, can't wait to operate, and I'm happy to be here." Shelly grabbed a piece of paper from the back of a chart to jot down names. Memorizing had never been her strength, and her stomach started to ache with first day jitters.

The intern, or first year resident, was Dr. Angie Decker. Her wrinkled scrubs and nervous twirling of her hair gave the impression she was somehow already behind. Shelly noted the massive spiral book jammed into her lower left lab coat pocket. The "Washington Manual of Medical Therapeutics," lifeline to interns, was a guide to nearly all medical scenarios and emergencies, with algorithms for tests and treatment. Everyone used their "Wash Manual" in the first year. By June, each page was stained, dog-eared, and memorized. Angie also had about twenty pens, an enormous stethoscope, and notecards in her other lower pocket. Yep, the jury was out on her medical chops, but Angie seemed dear.

"Y'all, keep our pager numbers on a note card in your upper pocket, so it won't get creased. We keep a couple of the Onc textbooks in our residents' room—you can share those, and I'll show you which chapters to start on later today. Do y'all have the code to get in there?"

This was the third-year resident, or PG-3, Patricia Quinn, already giving pointers to the med students in the gentlest manner imaginable. Shelly could have listened to her recite the phone book just to hear that smooth, friendly lilt.

"Do you live close by, Patricia? I mean, did you grow up here?" Shelly had the sense that she was not a city girl.

"Oh, no, Shelly, my family is from eastern Kentucky, pretty rural. I'll surely meet people from my county on this service. This is the closest hospital to those little towns, and we all sort of know each other, in a distant way." *Serenity's a good fit for an onc service*, Shelly thought.

Meanwhile, a pale white-blond woman with angular features and round glasses marched back to the cart after answering a page at the wall phone. She paid Shelly no mind.

"We'd better get started. Cases in the OR begin soon." Carmen Reese, the chief resident, appeared to be no nonsense and efficient.

"Okay, a few ground rules to start out the rotation," Ken explained to the team with a Tennessee-touched voice. "The med students and intern get the cart ready at room 201 and preround with the list. Check with the night nurses about any problems, look up last night's labs, and make sure you know who's being discharged today. Get a prescription pad so we can write scripts as we go. You check in with Carmen, your chief, throughout the day, and she'll make the daily assignments in the OR. You all exchange your beeper numbers now. Sound good? Well, good."

Ken's accent put two syllables in words Shelly thought had only one. Heads nodded; yawns were stifled. This was bread and butter post-op and oncology hospital care—checking surgical wounds, copying labs and vital signs, and making follow-up appointments for patients being discharged that day. Ken's several additional instructions concluded quickly, and by five forty-five a.m. they were off for her first rounds of her first day of her first year of fellowship.

Her feet already hurt.

BRODER SIGURD
(née Thorsen)

Born Bergen, Norway, April 11, 1913 Died March 30, 1964, aged 50, of cancer.

Graduate of Saint Paul Central High School where she met the love of her life, Paul Lawrence Broder. They married in St. Paul 1935, and were blessed with children Paul Jr. (Felicity), Catherine Riley (Matthew), and Bertie. Survived by her sisters Eudora and Lenore, husband, children and infant grandchildren Shelly and Chris Ann. She is predeceased by her sister Gladys.

Sig was a positive influence on her family and friends. She was a wonderful cook and baker, and her friends treasured her recipes, especially her famous Christmas sandbakkels and krumkaker cookes. Sig was also an expert homemaker and bridge player. She never forgot a card.

The end for her was tragic and too early in life. Her strength, faith and courage never wavered, but she wished for more time with her little grandchildren.

Services at Lauderdale Heights Congregational Church, April 3rd at noon, with luncheon to follow.

CHAPTER 2

Poised

With Ken's guidance, rounds moved along well around the circle of hospital rooms. The intern tucked the last chart into the rack with its red plastic flag indicating doctor's orders. Carmen assigned tasks for the morning scut work, the tedious but critical task of tracking down bloodwork, X-rays, and prescriptions. Shelly spied the small room with the coffee maker, confirming the earlier aroma of a fresh brew. Aching for a cigarette, she hustled down the hall to grab a cup before going to the OR with the others. She met one of the nurse's aides there, chatted briefly, and returned to the front desk to find…no one.

The docs had left. Bernice held her purse and was applying a fresh coat of lip balm, awaiting her day shift replacement.

"They headed down, doctor. Dr. Mackey said to tell you to go ahead and meet them in the OR. Oh, and here's your little bag. Have a good day, now. I'm off to bed," she chirped, the scent of peppermint wafting from her. "Glad to see you got your orientation!"

"Thanks, Bernice. Um," she stammered, "can you point me in the direction of the OR?"

"Why, sure! Just down the stairs to the main floor and head down the long hallway. I believe there are signs along the way. It's a hike, now. Bye!" she called, waving Shelly off. Was it her imagination that Bernice muttered, "They're gonna eat that girl alive…"?

Shelly realized she'd better glom onto the blob of white coats until she knew her way around. She sped past the elevator banks where she'd done her early morning splits and instead ran down the stairs, her dress shoes slick on the speckled, glittering staircase linoleum. She instantly loved the ancient scent of that old stairwell, its wooden handrail rubbed smooth by the thousands of physicians' hands that had used it to balance their fierce pace, much as she did that day. This was the original part of the hospital, and she liked that space, those ghosts, those echoes.

Following the signs, she hurried to the corridor labeled SURGERY and found the women's locker room. Shelly walked into the messy space, large yet cramped. Most of the lockers, plastered with photos of kids, dogs, and weddings and secured with a padlock, were occupied. Shoes and plastic operating room clogs were tucked under a couple wooden benches. Shelly grabbed her size of scrubs from an open shelf and changed as fast as she could.

"Damned nylons," she muttered. "Damned shoes." How could she have imagined that the first day would be anything but a normal surgical oncology service, with case after case in the OR? What had she been thinking? Shelly would've killed for a quick smoke.

She hung her clothes, the cotton blouse already wrinkled, in an empty locker. She tucked her bag with her keys, lighter and cigarettes behind them, and donned a pair of blue paper shoe coverings and a disposable blue bonnet. She ran to the bathroom, a cardinal rule before scrubbing in any operation, knowing it may be hours before she had the chance again. The toilet aroma hit her hard. The ineffective bottle of hospital issued odor blocker in the stall was no match for so many employees. Shelly exited, and around the corner saw "Surgery Control." They would help her.

"Good morning! I'm Dr. Riley, the new gyn onc fellow," she offered.

"Whatcha need?" The woman behind the desk, back to Shelly, never took her eyes off the huge white board hanging on the wall. Patient names, surgeons, operating room numbers, and procedures made up the simple graph. The woman was adding a new case in blue marker.

"Um, I'm new, and I'm here to operate this morning, and I wondered if..." Shelly trailed off, hoping for help. "I'm looking for the gyn onc rooms?"

The woman turned around and sighed. "Rooms two and four, like usual. Like for the last twenty years. You know, y'all need to get your orientation in your own department. I'm not running this board *and* teaching you how to operate *and* keeping this shit show afloat all at once." With that, she pointed to her right, picked up the ringing phone, and took a patient chart an orderly had just rushed up to bring her.

Shelly realized the conversation was over, gave her a whopper of a smile, and headed in the direction of the abruptly pointed fingers. Surely she could find rooms two and four without a tour. "Thanks for all your help!" she called.

Shelly skittered along the OR corridor, her dress shoes more treacherous in their paper covers, and ran smack into her boss rounding the corner. Dr. Theodore Farber was the most senior attending, the Chair of the Division, and former President of the Gynecologic Oncology Society. She remembered him from her interview months earlier, and from his icy stare in the university brochure. He was distinctive, older, but his age was impossible to guess. He kept his silver hair cropped short, his six-foot frame lean and fit in fresh scrubs. His bony angles brought the image of a bird to mind. A raptor.

"Oh, my gosh, I'm so sorry Dr. Farber. I was just coming to find you and the others to get the cases going…" Shelly was mortified to have nearly bowled the man over.

"Well, hey, there! Shelly, is it? You made it all right, then. Did Ken get you oriented?" *Dammit all to hell. What exactly do these people think the word orientation means?* She'd been in the hospital for two hours, seen about twenty patients, sent three of them home from their surgery, was about to operate on a total stranger, and no one had shown her a thing! Despite her unease, instinct took over.

"I'm learning the ropes just fine, Dr. Farber. No problem."

Lines crinkled around his eyes. *Ding*—right answer. A fellow had told her years earlier, "You're there to protect the patient from the attending, and the attending from the patient." She finally understood there would be no orientation. Her game plan now? Stay alive and figure out the details with Ken at the end of the day. She masked and walked Dr. Farber into room two, reveling in the familiarity of the operating room, the beeps coming from the anesthesia equipment, and the glorious smell of surgical life. With the welcome whiff of fluorinated gases and alcohol pads, Shelly felt at home.

"This fellowship is very well respected, you understand. I'm proud of our national reputation. You'll meet up with Arlys and get all your paperwork done this week—she said some things are missing." His tone a bit cooler tone than she expected, and Shelly was puzzled at being deficient already.

He cut off his welcome speech and he searched the room. "Ken?" he called to no one in particular. Dr. Farber opened the door for her to leave. "Shelly, you'll probably be down the hall for Dr. Boldon's case."

Cocking her head at the sudden eviction, she took the hint, wandered around the hallways, and found OR four. Shelly pulled up her surgical mask as she entered her surgical home for the next two years.

The patient was asleep and prepped, with the scrub tech sitting by her sterile back table. The tech regarded Shelly with neither malice nor warmth, and nodded. There was an anesthesia resident at the patient's head, adjusting lines and checking vitals. The circulating nurse was reaching into a cabinet, heard the door open, and turned to Shelly.

"You must be Dr. Riley. We are *so* excited you are here, aren't we Velma?" Velma, the tech, barely nodded again.

"Doctor," she said.

"I'm Kit, your team's nurse. You'll have to put up with me and Velma for the next couple of years, I'm afraid. Dr. Mackey just called into the room to tell you to go ahead. He'll be getting started in room two. You should find him after this case."

"Glad to meet someone who knows what's going on, because *I* certainly don't." Maybe she should have held back such candor, but there was a sense of trust with these two ladies. She went on, "I walked into Dr. Farber's room and he practically pushed me out the door."

Kit and Velma exchanged glances, and Kit offered, "Well, Dr. Farber usually gets the senior fellow. I think that's all there is to that. Now. Here's the patient's chart—you'll want to know all the details for Dr. Boldon. He probably won't pimp you on your first day, but you never know."

Ah, yes, pimping. The charming tradition of older doctors asking pointed questions of the junior staff about important anatomy landmarks, or the name of a particular surgeon who invented a technique, or the constellation of symptoms that accompanied a disease. It could be a good way to learn, she supposed, but mostly it made people afraid. Shelly assumed she was done with being pimped now that she was a fellow. In fact, *she* would have to find a way to teach the med students and interns.

She read through the patient's chart, and found the surgery was for a huge fibroid uterus, causing unmanageable bleeding and anemia. The patient was thin and healthy--great first case for her fellowship. No devastating news to relate to the family, and no worries about dismal pathology reports. She ran through the important caveats for removal of this big a mass. *Okay--keep the ureters in view the whole time. Get the bladder down early. Tell anesthesia ASAP if there's bleeding.* She was ready.

"I'll give you the basic tour before you scrub," Kit said. She'd finished the patient's abdominal prep, painting orange -brown iodine solution over a large swath of skin, trying to keep the drips from staining the floor. She showed Shelly the cupboards where clippers, scrub solution, catheters, and dressings were kept. Kit then walked her to the scrub sink outside the room to get started.

"But Kit. No one's here! Where's Dr. Boldon? Where is *any*one?"

Kit said quietly, "This is your case, Dr. Riley. Dr. Mackey gave you the go ahead, and Dr. Boldon will expect you to tee it up and proceed as if you don't even need him. Plus, we'll talk you through it, and Velma could do this case with her eyes closed. You'll be fine." She didn't wait for a reply, simply walked back into room four and let the door swoosh behind her.

All these years dreaming of being the surgeon in charge, but now she was shaking. Hell, she'd acted like she was in charge since halfway through her intern year. Why was her mouth dry, and brain sluggish? She stood at the scrub sink, half of her trying for calm steady breaths, and the other half desperate to run screaming to the parking lot and drive home to Minnesota. As she'd done hundreds of times, she took off her watch and rings and attached them to her pager. She scrubbed her fingers, hands, and arms, and told herself in a loud inner voice to *get it the hell together* and act like she'd been there before.

Clean hands up, she backed her way into the room with her ample tush and held out her right hand for a sterile towel.

"Doctor." That had been the only word out of Velma's mouth so far. Shelly was fairly certain that if she dropped dead at that moment, Velma and the Control desk nurse would shoot dice over her watch and rings as the morgue was gathering her body. Nervous, she put on the sterile gown, then gloves as Velma held their bases open wide and still for the hands to slip in.

She grasped the sterile paper tag attached to the gown's belt and offered it to Velma.

"Dance?" Shelly joked to the tech as she whirled around. Velma, silent, pulled the tag with a jerk, and Shelly tied her knot in the front of her gown to complete the sterility. She stood at the patient's left side.

"Okay to start?" Shelly peered over the sterile sheet at the anesthesia resident.

He nodded, "Ready."

Shelly prayed for some sort of approval from Kit. "I should really go ahead?"

"Yes." Kit exuded confidence that Shelly was capable. "Dr. Boldon will be here in twenty minutes. I paged him while you were scrubbing."

"What about the chief resident?"

"I was sort of wondering where Carmen was, myself. This is the type of case the chief usually does while the fellow advises."

Shelly stood there for a second, pondering her choices. The *beep* of the EKG and the *swish* of the ventilator were the only sounds. She thought back to her med school days when an attending screamed at the chief resident for starting a surgery without him. "How dare you touch my patient without my permission?" he'd blustered.

The very next week Shelly watched him chew out the same resident for waiting for him, yelling as if she'd made the gravest error imaginable. Shelly recalled the chief's bewildered question, "Dr. Wilcox, what do you want me to do?"

"I want you to operate, for God's sake. What the hell do you think you're here for?"

Screw it, thought Shelly. *What the hell am I here for?* "Knife." She held out her right hand. She was about to operate on a patient entirely by herself, with no supervision. She wanted to vomit.

And for the first of what would be hundreds of times, Velma replied, "Poised," and slipped the knife into Shelly's open palm. Beautiful. In appreciation of her perfect instrument pass, the flutter and fear subsided, and muscle memory kicked in. There was just no better dance than a tech and surgeon who worked well together. Anticipation, the right firmness, and confidence in the instrument's delivery to the surgeon's hand, the quick and dexterous movement of suctioning, the automatic adjustment of the overhead lights all showed perfect concentration.

Velma stood at the ready, suctioning, dabbing with gauze, as Shelly operated. The tech planned for every call, teaching her new surgeon the names of the instruments she'd need to use in this program. At times, Shelly would call for a clamp and Velma would put something else in her hand, name it, and say, "Dr. Boldon likes you to use this. They call it 'The Way,' and you'd best stick with it when they're around." Teaching her, keeping her moving, and anticipating each step—exhilarating. Shelly didn't dare break the spell by complementing Velma. Somehow, silence was best for this scrub tech, and Shelly would have to figure out how to acknowledge her perfect precision. She wanted the feeling to last forever.

Shelly was almost halfway through the case when Dr. Boldon walked in.

"How's it going, Shelly? Are Kit and Velma getting you oriented to 'The Way?' They're just about the loveliest ladies in the hospital, I must say. No better way to start my morning, surrounded by you beautiful women." The surgical flow broken, Shelly watched him rub his hands together. "Well, let me scrub to see how you operate." He handed over his watch, ring, and pager, leaving the room for the sinks. "Put the radio on, would you, dear? It's too quiet!" they heard before the OR door closed completely.

This was her second meeting with Dr. Brian Boldon, the head of the whole OB-GYN department. She'd had a brief interview with him when she'd arrived as an applicant and recalled her first impression then. *Slimy.* He was not a gynecologic oncologist, but he occasionally found patients better suited for the oncology service than standard OB-GYN. Dr. Boldon came back in, arms up and elbows dripping on the floor, making small talk with Velma as he was gowned and gloved. He sidled up across the table and proceeded to watch.

"Go ahead, Shelly. You're probably a better surgeon than me, dear, since I don't operate much anymore. Just those pesky C-sections, you know, and then running the department, and doing clinic, of course. Just move along, and I'll assist." Shelly felt more relaxed, her confidence building as she stitched and tied knot after knot, sutures cut by her attending. They removed the enormous fibroid uterus, big as a volleyball, and sent it to the Pathology lab in a sterile bucket on wheels for an instant reading, or frozen section.

"This lady is going to feel a thousand times better," Shelly said, making small talk as the two surgeons, total strangers, irrigated the abdomen and cauterized little bleeders to prepare to finish the operation.

"No doubt, God willing," Dr. Boldon agreed. "She's been dealing with heavy bleeding and pelvic pressure for years. Even though I'm sure it's benign, her quality of life will be massively improved. I'd recommended a hysterectomy with one of the gyn onc staff, but she was just insistent that *I* do her surgery, since I'd delivered her babies." Shelly must have just imagined that his chest puffed up a bit.

Kit answered the ringing phone. "Pathology's on the line." Into the mouthpiece, she told him, "Go ahead, Dr. Steele, I have Dr. Boldon here."

The man's voice carried through the OR on the speaker phone.

"Brian? Frozen section here is a benign leiomyomatous uterus, weight 2400 grams or so. Big one, eh? The endometrium is clean, so I didn't freeze anything there. Anything worrisome in the abdomen?"

Dr. Boldon answered, "Chris, good to hear your voice. Now that the mass is out, everything else looks healthy. Thanks for weighing it. The family always wants to know that, once they hear it's not cancer. Say, how's your lovely wife? I heard she took a bad fall."

"Aw, better, thanks. She broke her leg in two places, so the cast will be on for a while. No more lawn mowing for her for the summer. Okay, gotta go—I have two more frozens to read."

Dr. Boldon held Shelly's gloved hand for a moment, then broke scrub as Shelly started to close. "Chris and his wife hike all over the state," he explained. "Last weekend she tripped on a tree root. Her ankle got stuck and her leg kept going. Took them forever to get out of the woods and back to their car. You'll meet Chris at Tumor Conference--best pathologist in the hospital."

Thanking everyone as he stuffed his soiled sterile gown and gloves into the bin, Dr. Boldon told Shelly, "I'll talk to the family, and you get her note and orders tucked in. Good case—you have a nice touch. Welcome aboard, dear. Stop by my office anytime," and off he went.

Shelly took a huge gulp of air and blew it out with an audible sigh. She grabbed Velma's hands across the table.

"Okay. Honest opinion. Do I live to see another day?"

For the first time in the case, Velma gave a genuine grin and said, "I believe you just sailed through the first ring of fire, doctor. The others will be hotter, though, you understand?"

Shelly released her grip on the tech's hands and danced a quiet jig at the bedside. "Crap, I'm sweating in places I didn't know could sweat. Thank God the first case is over. I appreciate your help, Velma."

Kit adjusted the radio settings. "Closing music, Dr. Riley? You won't operate with him much over the next two years, but that was good feedback. Keep it up and you'll be just fine."

Waves of relief passed over Shelly as she removed all the moist packing that had been keeping the bowel out of the surgical field. Velma and Kit started the sponge and instrument count while Shelly closed the fascia of the patient's abdominal wound. Taking great care with the giant needle and wiry suture, she moved to keep from gouging herself with each "bite" of the sturdy deep layer. The final step of reapproximating the skin edges was a much finer process, and Shelly's favorite part of surgery for its rhythmic, meditative nature. She picked up each skin edge and laced the tiny needle and suture through the dense connective tissue below. Shelly stood back to admire her closure.

"Very pretty, doctor," Velma approved. Shelly pulled off her OR gown and gloves, pushing them in the huge trash bag Kit had wheeled over, while Velma rinsed off the old scrub paint and blood, using gentle pressure to cover the incision with a sterile dressing. The volume increased in the OR, with the radio turned up and more chatter amongst the staff. Once the soiled paper drapes were off and the patient was extubated, they transferred her to a hospital bed Kit had brought in, on anesthesia's count.

"One, two, three," the anesthesiologist called from the head of the OR table, and they slid the woman onto the hospital gurney. The patient, moaning and groggy, pulled at her oxygen mask. The odor of exhaled fluorane gas from the anesthetic passed through the space.

"Thanks, all," Shelly said, as she grabbed the chart from Kit's desk. Catching herself before leaving the room, Shelly realized she had a dilemma. "Kit, I'm kind of stuck. I don't know any pager numbers, and I've got to do the paperwork the way Dr. Boldon wants it done. Can you find Carmen's number?"

"Of course! I've got the list right here," and wrote down the number. "Frankly, that was just the strangest thing today. Usually there are five different people in here vying for a chance to operate. Still, it was a nice case. Hope the rest of your day is just as good."

Seeing Shelly hesitate at the door and spin to ask another question, Kit took down her mask, smiled, and said, "The Post Anesthesia Care Unit is that way—all the way down the hall and turn left." Kit walked over to her. "Don't go to his office alone, Dr. Riley," she whispered. "And you didn't hear that from me." Shelly nodded, grateful to them both for giving her a chance and making her look good. Poised, indeed.

She strode through the halls, eventually finding the PACU. Here the patients from the entire OR were in various states of recovery from their recent surgeries, some snoring, some sitting up and answering questions from the nurse. She entered a small alcove with three cubbies, all equipped with a phone and desk, one with an old Styrofoam cup half filled with cold coffee, all with a whiff of old body odor.

Shelly paged the chief resident.

The phone rattled in a minute, and Carmen's cool voice was on the line.

"Carmen, this is Shelly. I'm a little stranded here. Can you give me a template for the post-op paperwork for the staff? I've got the orders and the op note to do, and I'm sure Dr. Boldon has preferences."

"Well, the fellows usually take care of training each other. I'm sure Ken would be happy to walk you through it."

My chief refusing me on day one? Hell, no. "I'm sure you're right. Ken's scrubbed, though, and I really want to chart the way Dr. Boldon expects it to be done. Can you come down now so we can polish it off? I'm by the main desk in PACU, in the dictation room. Thanks, Carmen!" And she hung up.

Shelly muttered, "If she doesn't show, I'm screwed." She introduced herself to the clerk, who put down the thick paperback she was reading and managed not only to find Shelly's dictating ID, but a cup of truly horrible coffee and a pen for her as well.

Staff physician at the top, Ken and me next, then the chief resident, and down the line to the younger residents and med students. Shelly pondered the medical hierarchy. *Here I am, having just done my first surgery of my fellowship, and I'm begging for help with paperwork to avoid getting embarrassed.*

As Shelly started a brief narrative of the surgery in the progress notes, she was surprised by an overwhelming urge to cry. She felt ridiculous, somehow. Tall, single, with a flat Minnesota accent that was foreign sounding amid these lyrical southern voices. Why did Kit warn her about not being alone with Boldon? Why did Farber practically kick her out of his room? She blinked over and over, blew her nose, and charted.

Out of the corner of her eye she recognized Carmen's blond hair and thin frame walking into the PACU. "My savior! Thanks, Carmen. I know you're scrambling to get the service organized. I'll just need a quick tutorial."

She didn't respond, but perhaps the tension lightened in her a bit. Carmen was all sharp points in elbows and chin. That voice, though. *God, these people sing when they talk,* Shelly thought. Despite her prickly body language, Carmen sounded like an angel.

"I have lists here of the way the different attendings like their op notes and orders done. We pass them on to each other, and change them when we need to," she said quietly. Next a pause. "I should have given them to you this morning. I'm sorry about that." She faced Shelly directly, no apology in sight.

"Thanks. I must admit to feeling a little deserted. First, I almost ran over Dr. Farber in the hallway. Quite a chill in the air in his room. Then there was no one in Dr. Boldon's case except me, and he's not even a gynecologic oncologist. He must've mentioned that ten times while he was scrubbed. Is he a big part of our surgical load?" Shelly shifted her chair so there was room for them both to reach the chart.

"Gosh, no. He only finds big operative cases a few times a year. Maybe since it's your first day. You know you'll be on your own for the most part in his cases, right? That's what we residents like."

"Because you get to do more," Shelly answered, nodding. "Good to know. Well, I appreciate these papers, Carmen. It was a benign fibroid uterus. Huge, though. Had to dissect out bladder and ureter, but she should do well. I can take it from here, and frankly it'll take me less time to do the paperwork myself than teach it to an intern. What's next in the OR?"

The ice was broken. She was a stranger, clumsy and nervous, but Carmen seemed to accept Shelly as her own fellow. They spent the next fifteen minutes going over the day, Carmen grateful that Shelly offered to take some of the day's tasks. The women took a minute to exchange little nuggets of their lives, finding they were both single, with boyfriends who lived out of town.

"Just the way I like it," they agreed, laughing as they voiced the sentiment together.

The rest of the day was hectic and tiring, but without major problems. Shelly assumed the staff intentionally booked a lighter surgical caseload than normal. The fellows and residents were very green on this first day of the academic year. Savvy patients knew to get their procedures done earlier in the summer, avoiding all the new residents on July first. Ken finished his surgical cases in the other operating room and found her in the PACU.

"You survived!" he said, plopping down in the squeaky rolling chair next to her. "Why don't you all get changed and I'll show you our office."

Shelly walked to the staff changing rooms with him. She removed her scrubs and groaned to see a run in her nylons from heel to thigh.

Ken brought her up to the fellows' space on the third floor. There was a closet with some spare lab coats without names, and she grabbed one, grateful to have a place for her papers and "mints." There were a couple other desk cubbies there, and she could hear nurses talking to patients about chemo symptoms and other medical items. Space was at a premium.

"Let me give you the rundown of your next two years with three bosses in one minute, okay?" Ken used a low voice, leaning so only Shelly could hear. "You just operated with Boldon, so I'll start with him. He's the head of the whole department. Not the brightest bulb, frankly, and the other two are pretty cranky about it."

Shelly interrupted, "He seemed pretty lowkey this morning. Didn't even come to the OR until I was halfway through the case."

Ken nodded his head, "He's always off somewhere, trips for conferences, meetings all over the country, and not trained for the radical stuff we do. Don't count on him for much support. That's the best advice I can give you."

"Understood. Then there's Dr. Peter Cardinal," Shelly said. "I met him once at my interview. I've heard he's an absolute stud of a surgeon."

Ken laughed. "I wouldn't use the word 'stud' for him—he's your fellowship director, for one. Directly in charge of us and our requirements for graduation. He's also extremely religious. Born again, and you'll hear about it. The only time I *ever* heard Dr. Cardinal swear was when I asked him why he kept pestering me to check a certain patient's NG tube. He finally told me he'd had a patient years ago whose NG tube was taped to her nose too tightly, and it scarred her nostril when they pulled it off. He told me, 'Ken, behind every doctor's obsession there's a fuck up!' Lord, I about fell over when I heard that word!"

Shelly smiled, though she reminded herself to watch her own foul mouth. Dr. Cardinal had been lovely to her the day she had interviewed, though his short stature meant uncomfortable surgical days ahead for her, bending to his height. "He lives on a farm, has a wife and a boatload of kids, and..." Shelly remembered.

"What *you* care about is he's famous for painful teaching rounds, which he starts around 7 at night by saying to one of us fellows, 'Let's go check in on a couple folks.' That's code for 'go to the bathroom now, because you won't be going home for the next two hours.'"

There was a third staff surgeon, of course. Shelly had an uneasy rapport with the head of the department, Dr. Ted Farber, since this morning in the OR when he'd wanted her out of his OR as quickly as possible.

"What about Dr. Farber, who I practically knocked over this morning outside OR two?" Shelly wanted more details on him. "Those icy eyes--he seemed to panic seeing me there. Kit thought it was because he's division head and always gets the senior fellow."

"You got it," Ken agreed. "Farber's an east coast transplant. He married a local, *very* wealthy woman, and has lived here for the last thirty years. Good surgeon, stuck in his ways, not real involved with the post-op care. He's got this odd habit of stretching various body parts while he's talking to you. We'll all be in a circle listening to him on rounds when he'll suddenly make this maneuver like he's trying to stretch some back tendon, or favor a torn Achilles' heel. I can't decide if it's a distraction or if he's in pain. Anyway, he's our ultimate boss. We just plain *always* make him happy. In fact, we'll head to his office now and get you set up with Arlys, his secretary."

She swallowed. Dr. Farber had the demeanor of an absent-minded professor, but Shelly had seen him skewer speakers at national conferences if their papers had weaknesses. There was a blade in that silver tongue, and she didn't want to be on the receiving end of it.

Ken brought her through the hallway to Dr. Farber's office, the air heavy with a floral scent. The head of the division's door was closed with Arlys seated in guard position at the large desk in the foyer.

"Well, hey, Arlys," Ken sang out, "how are you?"

Arlys was beautiful. That was a fact. Lustrous, shoulder length deep red hair, perfectly curled and styled, she was the type of woman who'd applied her foundation, eye liner, mascara, and lipstick with precision every day of her life since the seventh grade. Hell, she probably wore a girdle.

Shelly figured Arlys regarded women like her with disgust. A blob of all-purpose lotion smeared on her face that morning, a quick dab of deodorant under each armpit, and Shelly's daily cosmetic routine was complete. The enormous run in her stockings, which she tried to hide, was clearly just frosting on the cake.

Shelly remembered Arlys from her interview months ago, when the secretary had picked her up at the airport. The car's interior had been heavy with the deep floral perfume Arlys favored, and Shelly had tried to breathe through her mouth to escape it. Even then, she'd felt she was tasting the thick, artificial fragrance that stayed on her clothes as she got out of the car minutes later.

As Arlys had driven to the hospital on a busy anchor road in town, going about fifty miles per hour, they'd passed a Black man standing at a streetlight, waiting for the green to cross. Arlys had locked her car door. The soft *click* on all four doors in the car had stunned Shelly. *It's like that, eh?* she'd thought to herself. Now, months later, the perfume and the *click* came rushing back.

"Well, now, Dr. Mackey, aren't you blessed to be the senior fellow?" she smiled. "You just let me know how I can help you with your senior year. And Dr. Riley, I hope you're finding everything just fine?" Her stare lingered on Shelly's legs. "I haven't had a chance to order your lab coat, yet, but I'll surely get to that this week or next. I wanted to see your size, of course. You're *tall*, aren't you?" she added disapprovingly. "Here's your beeper—Dr. Keyes just turned it in last night." She pushed the pager over her desk to Shelly.

"Great! I haven't felt normal without a pager on my waistband for the last couple days. Thanks, Arlys," Shelly smiled, and tried to tuck her blouse in better as she placed the beeper in front of her right hip.

"I'll put some papers on your desk that need your signature by Monday, doctor. Salary, car identification for the lot, that sort of thing. I'm sure you already stopped by the Security office to get a photo ID, isn't that right?" Somehow the purring voice alarmed Shelly to stay vigilant.

"No, ma'am, I didn't know I should. Ken, do I have time now before rounds?" His pager was going off, probably from Carmen wondering where they were.

"I'll walk you past there on the way to the Powell. We'd best go, to see if we can catch them. Bye, Arlys, you all be good!" Ken called and hustled them out the door. When they were out of hearing range, he confirmed Shelly's intuition, whispering, "Do *not* piss off Arlys. Meet us on the Powell when you're done."

Dropping Shelly off at Security, he hustled down the hall to get evening rounds underway while she had her photo taken. Seeing no mirror, she fluffed her hair, flat from a day in an OR bonnet and a headlight, and smiled for the camera. She watched the badge in horror as it came out of the machine, but one glance at the guard and she knew it was one try per customer. *I've been waiting for god-damned-ever for this job, and I'm gonna spend the next two years with a picture ID like a Dairy Queen cone.* A tuft of hair stood straight up in the middle. Her surgical mask had etched a crease on each cheek like an old scar. Was that old blood on her forehead?

There was no point in protesting. She clipped the ID badge on her borrowed lab coat and found the Powell Cancer Center. The pretty shoes tore at taut blisters on the sides of both feet. She wandered around the patient care circle until she came across the team. Same cast of characters from five-thirty that morning and same cart. Patricia hid a yawn as the intern Angie presented the next patient's case. The speed of her words was only slightly more remarkable than her twang. Shelly missed half of what she said.

Ken nodded at her bewilderment, saying, "We'll translate later."

They checked on each patient over the next hour, and Shelly had the chance to talk to the lady she had operated on just that morning.

She smiled when Ken introduced her. "Pleased to meet you" the patient said, then coughed at the effort and held her pillow to her abdomen.

Shelly took a moment with her to explain the surgery, describing the huge fibroid uterus. The woman sighed when she had heard the pathologist had called in, right during the operation, to say that it was almost certainly benign.

"That'll never get old," Shelly remarked to Ken outside the patient's door. "That look of relief when they hear they don't have cancer."

The next patient was to be discharged the next day and needed a pain med to take at home. Shelly handed the prescription pad to Angie, saying, "Poised."

Ken smiled. "Velma got you oriented today, then, did she? Good for you."

I must have walked ten miles in my "pretty" shoes, Shelly thought. *The boss's secretary hates me. The chief resident doesn't trust me as far as she can throw me. I haven't peed in nine hours. I'm dying of nicotine withdrawal. And I can't understand a word coming out of this little sparrow of an intern's mouth.*

Shelly laughed out loud. *Only 729 fourteen-hour days left before graduation. Good for me.*

CHAPTER 3

Bite me!

Uff da, Shelly thought, reverting to her Nordic background's epitaph. She wobbled down the stairs with an armful of scrubs and stepped out of the Powell Cancer Center. After the sterile comfort of the air-conditioned hospital, the wall of humidity smothered her. She noted a buzzing, pounding sound. Frogs? Crickets? Her northern senses left her clueless.

No matter. After the hours of performance anxiety, painful footwear, and intense concentration, all strength fled. She didn't know how she'd find her car and drive the three miles home, but nylons weren't going to be part of the trip.

She loped to the little red car, unlocked the door, and kicked her shoes inside. With a quick motion, she pulled down the offending hose and threw them on the passenger's seat. Sweet relief flowed as her blisters escaped the rub of the shoes. Shelly flicked her lighter to the tip of her Marlboro, taking a grateful, deep pull on her first cigarette since the morning.

Off she went, shifting, steering, and smoking her way home. Fatigue blinded her to the landmarks along the route, and a couple wrong turns prolonged the trip. She drove up to her rental house, the windows dark compared to the cheery, lit homes surrounding it.

Day One, and everyone survived. Her patients, her staff, and Shelly.

Well, they weren't exactly *her* patients yet. No one had asked how long they had to live. No one had seen enough of her to get past that northern accent to believe in her, but that would come. The patients were the whole reason she was there.

She tumbled into the house, arms balancing her purse and scrubs. She felt for the light switch, banging her hip in the search. The glare on that empty, awful living room reminded her how foreign she was to this part of the world. Many of her emptied boxes were stacked in the vestibule, a musty symbol that she owned little aside from clothes and books. She'd find a department store over the weekend to buy something to hang on her walls. Dinner was a couple pieces of deli meat from her fridge as she sunk onto her couch. What a day! And the instant replay was set to start in about seven hours.

The next two years were going to be filled with days like this, often harder. Well, wasn't this exactly what she'd wanted? Shelly took a millisecond to realize that if she did not immediately get her sorry ass off the couch she'd fall asleep right there, miss the alarm, and be late for morning rounds. She turned on the porch light, locked the door, and showered. Tumbling into bed with crisp yellow cotton sheets was heaven. She set two alarms for 4:45 and 4:50, verified "a.m.," and was out in no time.

This daily routine became homey and familiar within a week. Like the rest of the working world, Shelly watched for little omens amongst the morning habits to predict the day's mood. The elevator waiting and open for her? Good day. The favorite parking spot, the one next to the huge truck to shade her little car, already taken at the crack of dawn? Bad day. Her favorite housekeeper stopping to chat about her crazy kids? Good day. Gas tank switching to "E" as she pulled in for a twelve-hour workday? Freaking miserable day.

During her first month, Shelly attended a welcome breakfast with the hospital's residents and fellows. She listened to Department Chair Boldon, the doctor she'd operated with on her first day, going on about "We're all a big, happy family," and "Your hard work does *not* go unnoticed." She'd heard more rumors about his oily personality from Carmen who warned Shelly to keep her distance. With his perfectly white coat and too-dark black hair, he swaggered back and forth as he took thirty minutes giving his own career accomplishments.

"It's a great honor to welcome you new physicians to our program, and to see the rest of y'all's familiar faces again. What a joy it is, an absolute *joy*," he emphasized, "to preside over this wonderful family of ours. If any of you ever have a problem, I invite you to come right to my office and let me know all about it. I'll close that door, and we'll just get right to solving the problem. We'll just nip it in the bud, y'all, that's what we'll do," and he grinned.

"Yuck. That's one guy I'm definitely not confiding in," one resident next to Shelly whispered.

At any rate, she settled in enough to remember most names and titles and started to get the hang of the fellowship. She connected names with characteristics or mnemonics to keep everyone straight. Since Dr. Cardinal was religious, she imagined the red-gowned cardinals at the Vatican. For Dr. Farber, she thought how *far* he'd come to settle in Kentucky, and added the *brrr* for how icy he was. Boldon? She didn't need help there—his name stuck in her head with alarms and sirens going off anytime he was mentioned.

Shelly was responsible for Dr. Farber's Monday clinic. One look at the reception area suggested damned near every woman in the state was scheduled to come see him at one o'clock. They came with suitcases packed, all sorts of extended family, and a strong scent of tobacco. Even with no OR time available, the patients were just told to come on down for an operation, and that's what they did. Each Monday afternoon at one there was a lobby filled with patients and their worried family members, hoping for answers, praying it was all just a big mistake, and looking for a place to smoke while they waited. Shelly wished she could join them, feeling frazzled by trying to keep so many patients and their stories organized in her head.

She arrived early for her second Monday clinic, and cleared a cluttered desk of extraneous charts, prescription pads, and Styrofoam cups. The center of the room was surrounded by patient exam rooms, and the doctors trying to finish their morning clinic obligations were at various desks, scribbling in charts and speaking into handheld dictaphones.

Overhead pages and beepers added to the pandemonium. Like every public space in a residency program, a whiff of old pizza hung in the air. She cruised a couple empty rooms for dated newspapers and scrounged up the section with the crossword to do later.

Shelly perused the clinic schedule for patient names, diagnoses, and ages. Ten people to see in the next three hours, all with huge abdominal masses or cancer. She started to prepare the first chart by filling in the pertinent facts she found in the stack of records paperclipped to the front. Every record started with the "H&P," the History and Physical. The nursing assistant arrived and started tidying up.

Shelly saw Donna, Dr. Farber's nurse, walking across the clinic in her plastic clogs and bright green scrubs. Shelly guessed the nurse was in her fifties, but her freckled face and Olive Oyl body lent a younger vibe. Her decades of running this clinic prepared her for anything.

"Hey, Donna. I'm Dr. Riley, the new fellow. We met last week?"

"Of course I remember you, Dr. Riley. Ready for another full afternoon? Dr. Farber might be a little late."

"No problem. I just started the H&P on the first chart I saw." Shelly paused, then decided to enlist Donna as an ally for change.

"I wondered if we could look at the charts the week before to make some plans before they come here on Monday. We could even give people different appointment times, so they don't all come at once. I also noticed last week that a couple of the patients really didn't need to get admitted to the hospital." Shelly could see Donna's amused expression.

Donna let her finish with the suggestions, then put her bony arm around Shelly's shoulder. "This is how Dr. Farber has done his clinic here for twenty years, darlin', and he won't be changing anything. I know it's disorganized. Lord, I tried to convince him of both ideas you just had, seems like a million years ago. But Dr. Farber wants it done this way, and I'm afraid that's what we're all stuck with. Good try, though," Donna added with a grin.

This system makes no sense, protests newcomer.

We've always done it this way, states old timer.

After that clinic, hectic and exhausting, she took Ken aside before evening rounds and told him, "You should see it, Ken. The department calls *every new patient* and tells them to pack their bags, come at one o'clock, and plan to get admitted to the hospital. We've got six admissions, and two of them don't even have an OR time assigned yet. I tried to talk to Donna about it, but…" Shelly realized she was not giving Ken much of a chance to respond.

"Wait, what'd you say to Donna?" Ken stopped writing and looked up from the chart he held.

"Well, just that there's gotta be a better way." Shelly paced in the hallway, trying to keep her voice down. "I mean, they were all in the waiting room together talking to each other and found out they all had a one o'clock appointment. Some of them drove three hours to get here, Ken. It was chaos. This one lady was pretty hot about it—she's in the last room. You'll meet her on rounds if they got her transferred up here by now. We just finished seeing the last person, it's almost seven, and I haven't even dictated a single note." She admitted, "Ken, I'm not sure I can remember them all correctly. What if I blow it?"

Ken sighed. "Well," he started, "I get you're frustrated, but let's just say that system improvement is not on your top ten list of things to do as a first-year fellow. Dr. Farber has done clinic like that for forever. That's how he did it when I was a med student, that's how he did it when Dr. Cardinal was a resident, and that's how he'll be doing it when you're gray-haired and retired. Because believe you me, that man is never going to stop seeing patients, he is never going to deviate from 'The Way,' and he is never going to die. No one can even tell how old he is. And remember what I told you about his secretary Arlys?"

"Don't piss her off," Shelly said, looking down. She would have killed for a cigarette.

"Right. Same for Donna. Maybe more so. Either one can ruin us, so…" he trailed off. "Efficiency is a losing battle, okay? Let's round."

Rounds always started at 5:30 a.m.--always at room 201--and finished around eight o'clock at night. Patients having surgery the next day were "tuned up," so they were at their best for the operative challenge. There were also x-ray rounds in the afternoon, meeting with a radiologist to look at all their patients' films.

Perhaps more exhausting than the endless rounding was the labored, rote practice of medicine. The smallest of symptoms from a patient, whether it was heartburn relieved by a burp, or chills in the paper-thin gowns and blankets, resulted in a page to the intern. She then did a fierce evaluation, coming to see the patient, day or night, writing a full note in the chart and ordering a myriad of tests that brought indigestion into a possible heart attack.

There was *damned* sure a full CYA sentiment in force. The ripple of pages would go up the chain of command, and the chief bundled inquiries to the fellow once or twice a day. The medical students and intern spent hours a day copying notes from previous admissions, writing discharge orders, regurgitating information to one another, and dealing with endless duplication of effort on all fronts. Shelly felt flummoxed by all the energy her team expended every day, covering their asses on inane details.

Shelly had been on the receiving end of medical education for nine years now, in three different institutions, and none of those systems had the same lost-in time feeling she experienced here. Even Memorial Oncology Hospital in New York City had a more forward-thinking manner, despite the traditional vibe that often comes with a celebrated institution.

As her frustration built, she tried simple suggestions.

"How about if we split the patients to lighten the load on rounds?" was met with silence. After listening to the intern present her *third* evening call evaluation of burping and dyspepsia as a chest pain work-up, complete with an EKG and bloodwork to ensure the patient wasn't having a myocardial infarction, she asked with exasperation, "How many MI's have you diagnosed this month, Angie?"

"None, I don't believe," she said, a little worried look on her face.

Shelly felt bad for her, seeing that Angie took the question to mean she should be finding more actual heart attacks. "I'm just saying," Shelly continued, "that the incidence of post-op MIs in our population is low. We only have twenty patients on the census right now. If fifteen percent of our patients are having postop chest pain, but no one is having an actual heart attack, maybe we need to tee them up better for acid reflux. You know, head of the bed up, order the acid blockers on everyone post-op, ask them in the pre-op area if they get a sour stomach?"

"I didn't mind getting paged," Angie assured them. "No problem!"

"No, no, I know you're not complaining. But the cost of these worthless tests, Angie. And the poor patients get woken up, night after night, poked for bloodwork, thinking it might be something serious when all they said was they had heartburn?"

One morning, rounds stalled when Patricia, the third-year resident, or PG-3, reported an evaluation that had kept her up for most of the night. As Patricia recalled, the night nurse Frances had answered a call light. She found the patient had pulled out her IV fighting a pile of cheap, thin blankets.

With all her flailing, flecks of blood stained the sheets, and the now worthless D5 ½ normal saline solution was hydrating the floor. Patricia recounted the story.

"Miss Katherine, what in the world?" Frances had exclaimed, quickly putting pressure on the wrist where the IV had punctured skin.

"I'm so chilled, it's like to kill me!" had answered the elderly woman. "I can't rightly get warm, and I got tangled something fierce in this here pile of sheets!"

Patricia continued her presentation in the same sweet accent as the nurse and the patient, and the root of the problem became clear. Apparently, that room's air conditioning was stuck on full blast, maintenance had known about this but hadn't fixed it, and the admitting department kept assigning it because no one had marked it closed for repairs. What was more, the bed was directly under the ceiling vent, putting her in a constant, freezing draft.

Knowing they were running late, Shelly interrupted, "But Patricia, why did *you* get called? This sounds like a maintenance issue."

"Well," Patricia cocked her head, as if that question hadn't occurred to her, "maybe the nurse thought Miss Katherine was a little confused. If patients complain, she usually calls us to make sure they're all right."

"But why all night?" Shelly persisted.

"Well," again Patricia struggled to account for why she, a twenty-nine-year-old physician, needed to spend hours in the middle of the night addressing this non-medical situation, "Frances knew I was in a call room just down the hall, and figured I could help her get things settled down. Ms. Katherine was pretty hysterical by the time I got there, sayin' she was in the middle of a frozen twister!"

The med students on the team snickered.

"She lives just a little way from where my family lives, Dr. Riley," Patricia added. "That makes us like kin." The med students erased their smirks.

Ken tapped on the door while the team barged in without waiting for a response. Miss Katherine was tiny, piled under a mountain of blankets, only her creased face poking out at the top. The room was freezing. Patricia said hello and introduced everyone, they inspected her abdomen and the dressing on her long, midline incision, and made chitchat about her bowels and bladder during the exam. Shelly could feel the draft on her face, strong enough to blow her tobacco scented brown hair over her shoulder.

Lips pursed, Shelly unlocked the hospital bed and pulled it four feet toward her and the window.

"Are you out of the frozen twister now, Miss Katherine?" Shelly started the conversation with the patient.

"Why, lord, yes, I believe I am. That's a heap better. I was ready to run outta here, last night, I was so chilled! The only thing that kept me was this nice young gal doctor here, Dr. Quinn. She is the most darling person I could know."

As she began to cry, she continued, "Dr. Quinn knows where I'm from, see? And I got scared last night, what with the machines beeping, and the blood everywhere, and the twister durned near freezing my nose off. I didn't mean to cause trouble. I can't rightly thank you enough for sitting up with me 'till I got myself settled, doctor," she finished.

Patricia had taken hold of her tiny soft hand and nodded, "I'd do it again, you know that, Miss Katherine. We'll get you home right quick!"

Her assurances were the most loving thing she'd seen since starting fellowship. Admiration for Patricia passed through everyone in that room. Even Shelly's crankiness was swept away on the freezing twister. Off they trudged, Patricia quickly wiping her own eyes as they continued rounds. Shelly asked the med student to call maintenance and get that room's ventilation system fixed, wondering again how this academic hospital could rely so heavily on the backs of her and her younger peers.

The real problem with the craziness for Shelly was that no one else noticed it. When she suggested that one isolated low-grade temperature four hours after surgery did not merit a complete set of blood tests, cultures, and antibiotics, cool silence ensued. When she protested that daily painting of surgical incisions with betadine was counterproductive to healing, Ken warned her against challenging Dr. Farber's insistence on that practice.

Shelly had the sense that she was completely, utterly alone in her assessment. It stunned her that she could be so wrong, but these folks marched to one anthem, and Shelly couldn't even hear the beat. And they were so good-natured about it all! The duplication of effort, the ridiculous hours, and the endless inefficiencies were invisible. Nothing fazed them, from the medical students to her senior fellow. Not a single complaint. Shelly was losing her mind.

* * *

One scalding day in mid-August, Ken and Shelly had finished most of the day's work. Rounds were done, and the patients were "tucked in," meaning all issues, labs, and tests had been addressed. They were sitting in their third-floor office, and Ken had one more phone call to make before they could go home. They never left until both fellows were done.

Shelly waited in her cubby, taking the time to change into a fresh lab coat and filling in the crossword puzzle while he talked to the patient who was being difficult. She didn't understand his explanation about her biopsy results and was keeping him on the line. Shelly surmised the woman didn't have cancer and needed no further treatment, but the patient was not having it.

Asinine: A seven letter word for someone who enjoys the drama of a health issue and is keeping <u>my</u> exhausted behind from a hot shower and cozy bed.

Shelly became more impatient as Ken went over the results several times. It was maddening, really, to hear him go over miniscule, irrelevant details so calmly and courteously, when it was clear the conversation was going nowhere. Fatigue accentuated the frustration, with both fellows knowing the whole dog and pony show would begin again in nine hours. She grasped onto the lilt of his quiet voice, hoping that his latest way of explaining would get through to the patient. Mostly, though, she was thinking how ridiculous it was to see a thirty-eight-year-old surgeon have no ancillary help with getting routine, benign results to patients.

"Well, ah, yes, hmm, hmm, I understa…Yes, Ms. Peters, I under… Well, all right, then, all right." The voice on the other end was yelling now.

Honest to God, Shelly was ready to take the phone from him, say firmly, "Well, Ms. Peters, we don't seem to be able to explain this, and it's very late. We'll have the clinic call you in the morning and make you an appointment so you can come in and discuss it further. Good night, now!" and hang the hell up. She was about to stand up when Ken finally wrapped up the call, murmuring encouraging words to the still talking Ms. Peters, and hung the phone up with a sigh.

That's when he did it. He cracked. He gave Shelly hope that she was *not* living in the Kentucky version of the Stepford Wives. He declared to the blessedly silent phone in front of him, "Bite me."

Shelly jumped up from her rolling chair and looked over his cubby wall. "I knew it! Good Lord, you're an actual living breathing human being! I just knew there was a real person in there," she said with a grin.

He *did* realize that it was now almost nine o'clock and his young daughter had long been in bed. He *did* know that they had not stopped working for fifteen hours. Dare she dream that he also knew half their chores were duplicated efforts, or doable by a nurse, medical assistant, or secretary?

"I was starting to think all of you just loved to stay in this hospital three-fourths of every day. Honestly, I look at you all during rounds and wonder if anyone has moved their damned bowels in the last three days, because *I* sure haven't. You've just been afraid to show yourself to me—no faith, man. I'm your best ally!"

"Well, we've got to keep up appearances, Shelly. You can't get aggravated by all the little frustrations—you want to finish and graduate, right? So, keep the smile on your face and motor on. That's all you can do, I swear."

He leaned over the cubby wall, and confided, "You know when I knew this place was impossible? At the end of the year buffet, when they threw a little congratulation-type party for last year's fellow Brent Keyes. He was a good guy, I mean, but he had no life--never left the hospital. He pushed back from the table and said, I shit you not, he said, 'These have been the best two years of my life!' I almost sprayed the Coke right out of my nose.

"Right then, I knew, while all three staff just cooed from being admired. Naw, you gotta just knuckle down, smile, and get through it. This is the only way to the career we want, and three people hold the key to that last door. Don't rock the boat, envision the goal in your head, and try not to blow it. There's *no changing* this place, ok? Believe me–it's not worth the effort."

As if already regretting so much candor, he grabbed his disgraceful briefcase with a defeated sigh and said, "Let's hit it. I'm pooped."

"How in the world I'm going to be able to keep my mouth shut for two years? It feels like for god-damned ever," Shelly told him as they headed out. "I'm mad all the time."

Although it wasn't much, Shelly felt they were now compatriots, and this gave her strength. "Bite me!" became her fellowship mantra, mouthed under her mask in the OR, or used with abandon recounting her horror stories on late phone calls to Evie. When whispered under her breath on rounds, just as she exhaled, she could let her fury meet the universe in a silent, albeit cowardly, way.

CHAPTER 4

Snapshot

"The days are endless, and the years pass in a heartbeat," Ken told her in her first month.

As the summer months passed, Shelly's endurance grew. She made a happy nest of the modest rental house, splurging on sage-green throw pillows and a rug large enough to cover most of the bald spots in the living room carpet. The small footprint of the place was perfect for her, one bedroom for sleep and a spare room with a futon and desk.

The layout was logical, with a galley kitchen and pass-through window encircled by the living and dining rooms. She never used the oven with her feeble cooking, and the dining room, nested in the space off the kitchen, was a catchall for her medical journals, lab coat, and purse. The stale cigarette smell lingered, since Shelly kept the air conditioning on and windows closed. She ate meals on her couch, feet up, plate balanced on her chest. The telephone cord reached almost everywhere in the living room, good for talks with her med school roomie Evie, her boyfriend Robert back in Massachusetts, and her mom in Minnesota.

Timing the phone call to Robert was hard. She was bone-tired at the end of the day with little energy to expend. When she moved to Kentucky after residency, they'd decided to leave things open-ended. That was Norwegian-American for "I'm too much of a chicken shit to break this off." As she'd pulled the Festiva out of her driveway back east, waving goodbye, she sighed away all the weight of years of obligations she'd tried to meet. Shelly felt wicked relief to be back on her own, not constantly trying to change Robert's melancholy nature from pessimism to something more tolerable. She'd ignored Evie's gentle questions about when she was going to stop running away from relationships.

"Look, Evie, either I have terrible taste in men or my career sucks the patience right out of me. Maybe both, I don't know. I figure he'll eventually stop calling, and I'll find Prince Charming when I get a real job back home."

Feeling that the miles between them would lead to the obvious result of a breakup, she listened by phone to Robert's stories "…and the boss is such a prick. I'm sick of this place. I don't care that the money's good. The guys don't even stand up for…" that she'd heard so many times before. He'd never quit his job. She was clearly staying in her program for the next two years. Problem solved, with zero courage on her part to level with him, and less than zero insight into the fact that for Robert, the relationship wasn't over.

* * *

The first time she had a couple free hours she hustled to Sears to buy a lawnmower, feeling like a real grownup. For four years in Massachusetts, she'd lived in an old brownstone apartment building, four flights up, with no elevator. It was exciting to have come up in the world of medical trainees. Space, grass, even the ratty shed in the backyard made her feel closer to being a doctor in charge of her life. The salesman tried to get her number as he walked her through the inventory.

"I don't need a riding mower," she laughed, thinking of her tiny yard.

"Well, I'd be right happy to come on over and mow it for you, if you like," he crooned. God, if he'd really meant *just* the lawn, she would have agreed. She bought the standard mower and extricated herself from the home appliance Romeo.

"Don't forget ole for the two-stroke engine. And gas! Regular gas!" She waved at him as she left. "Ole" for oil. She could listen to him try to sell her stuff all day, and it was nice to be flirted with again.

* * *

Back at the hospital, Shelly became more confident with the workflow. There was a comfort in the hallway outside room 201, and the second floor Powell started to have a familiar smell to Shelly, antiseptics and sprays mingling with flower arrangements and family members' perfumes.

Her responsibilities grew, especially when she took over all the tasks related to the patients being admitted for chemotherapy. Ken handed her a little black book on afternoon rounds, bowing and saying, "It is my honor and pleasure to officially proclaim you, Dr. Shelly Riley, the chemo doc. Lord, have mercy, have I been waiting for this day." The residents and students clapped as Shelly took the book and thumbed through the pages.

"I'll help you, of course," Ken said. "We get about six to eight chemo admits a week, and most of 'em come from the staff's clinic. Chemo's so much better than when I was a med student, you all," he addressed the rounding team, morphing into teaching mode. "That IV ondansetron has made all the difference in the world for these patients, so they have practically no nausea at all. Before some brainy scientist invented that medicine, people used to puke non-stop. Even puked at home at the sound of the clinic nurse's voice when she called to set up appointments. Who knows the main side effects of ondansetron?"

He riffed on that, going over the drugs they would usually prescribe, and asking the residents about toxicities. Shelly listened and learned, too, since she had precious little practical experience with writing chemotherapy orders. As she leafed through the chemo book, she saw lab results, tumor markers, and other data for each patient.

She told Ken her worries later, up in their little office. Taking care not to heard by the others, Shelly twirled her telephone cord as she confided in him.

"I never wrote for chemo during residency, Ken. What if I screw up a dose?"

"It's scary at first," he agreed. "I made Brent check every single order I wrote for a month, I swear, and we looked at tumor markers together. I'll do that with you, too, don't worry. Dr. Cardinal's always on top of his chemo patients. He'll call you from clinic to tell you if he wants the dose changed or the regimen altered." Ken didn't go any further.

"And Dr. Farber?" Shelly prodded.

"Well, it's more like we catch the doses or the tumor markers on Farber's patients," he admitted. "We sort of run their care, and you'll have to call him when you think we need to change something. It's great if the patient is on a clinical trial. Maddy is the clinical trial nurse, and she'll check your orders—she's wonderful, by the way. Have you met Madeline Hayes?"

Shelly shook her head.

"You'll love her. And the way you go on about our accents? Lord, wait 'till you hear Madeline. She's the thickest of us all. She knows her patients backwards and forwards—you'll hear her talking to them if you're ever in our office before the sun goes down."

Off they went, rounding, painting surgical wounds with betadine, stomping in and out of patient rooms like a bison herd. When the team came upon the hospital door of a chemo patient named Paulette Gibbs, Ken showed Shelly her entry in the chemo book. Carmen started her presentation.

"This is a healthy eighty-one-year-old with her first recurrence of ovarian cancer, here for chemo number three. Her past medical history reveals mild arthritis and the cancer. Her only surgery is the big tumor debulking she had here two years ago. Review of systems negative aside from losing her hair after the last chemo. Minimal nausea. Vitals are good, her exam is unremarkable, but her creatinine is up to 1.3. It was 0.9 last admit."

They discussed her labs and decided on a safe chemo dose. The med student rapped on the door while opening it. The patient was sleeping, an IV running in her arm and lights full on. A younger woman reading a book in a corner chair looked up when the team entered.

"Ms. Gibbs?" Carmen woke the patient with a touch on her shoulder. "Remember I said I'd be back with about six more doctors? Well, here we are."

The most glorious smile Shelly had seen in her life overtook Ms. Paulette Gibbs's face as she awoke to a crowd of white coats surrounding her bed. A small portable radio played church music at her bedstand.

"Well, my good Lord! I thank you for bringing me these young doctors! Why, hello there, Dr. Mackey. I'm pleased to see you again," she beamed at Ken, and reached to turn down the music.

"Hey, yourself, Ms. Gibbs, how are you all doing this round of chemo?" Ken responded with an equally large grin. It was impossible to be glum in the presence of this woman.

Her bony hands clasped her chest, "I'm doing fine, yes, fine, indeed. I'm hoping this chemo knocks this old cancer down a notch. Of course, I'll come if the Lord wants me, but I've got lots more things I'd like to do. I'd appreciate y'all keeping me alive a little while longer!"

"Well, we're going to see to that now, Ms. Gibbs. Your tumor marker dropped quite a bit, looks like, so Dr. Farber wants to give you the same meds, if you're feeling alright. We'll decrease the dose a bit because of your labs today."

"It's working then?" Paulette sat up a bit in the hospital bed. "There's no real way for me to tell. I sorta feel the same as I did when that CT scan came back and Dr. Farber said the cancer was growing again. That CA125 of mine was over 3000! Can you imagine? I believe that's higher than the first time."

"Yes, what was yesterday's CA125, Dr. Mackey?" The younger woman set down her paperback to write in a spiral bound folder labeled *Mom* on the cover. "I'm Paulette's daughter, Mary Beth."

"Good to see you again, Mary Beth, I remember we've met. The number is down to 1864," Ken saw in the chart, "and that's after only the first two doses. I like that, Ms. Gibbs. That's a good response." Shelly marked this value in her little black chemo book, keeping to the format she saw from Ms. Gibb's previous treatments.

Nice drop, Shelly agreed. She might get another complete response from this chemo, which would translate to another six—nine months of good quality life before another recurrence. Even with her limited experience, Shelly knew the advanced cancer would eventually come back in such a way that chemotherapy would no longer work. She was glad Ms. Gibbs wasn't there yet. She looked forward to spending more time with this lovely woman.

With more direct questions about her symptoms, the team nodded and laughed as she answered invoking the Lord, her great-grandson Red, or her long departed husband in the replies. She'd lost her hair again this go-round and had searched everywhere for her wig.

"Mary Beth, here, was the one who finally found it," Ms. Gibbs giggled. "Red got hold of it somehow and had it tucked in his toys, right secret-like. He liked to put it on his stuffed bear's head and call her the 'gate-gama' bear, 'cause he knew it was mine! Lord, I wish my husband could see our precious Red. He would have loved him up something fierce. It keeps me young, I swear, having Mary Beth and Red at home with me. Couldn't have prayed for a better daughter. Show the doctors Red's picture so they can see why he's named the way he is."

Paulette's daughter reached for a photo in her purse, holding it up for Ken to admire. "I'm tickled with my little grandson, Dr. Mackey. He just turned three. And I'm the lucky one, Mom, no doubt about it."

After they left her hospital room, Ken pointed to the chemo book and told her, "Ms. Gibbs is yours, now."

Rounds done, Shelly and Carmen walked the chart rack back to the back room on the Powell the residents had appropriated for charting.

"I've noticed extended family living under one roof with several patients already, but why did Mary Beth look weepy during the "gate-gama" story?" Shelly sat and pulled out a chart.

"Mary Beth's daughter, Red's mom, is a drug addict. She's almost never home. Mary Beth takes care of her mom *and* her little grandson, Red, who wonders why his momma is always gone. That's a lot of strain to bear."

Shelly was a big fan of extended families, having grown up with her divorced mom, her grandpa, and her aunt. She wouldn't have had it any other way, but she'd never had these kinds of issues to cope with in her tribe. "I'll bet the little guy will be fine, with these women raising him," Shelly mused. "What about Red's dad?"

Poised

"Oh, you know. Just an SOS." Carmen said, charting away while they chatted.

Shelly shook her head. "SOS?"

"Source of sperm. You didn't say that in Massachusetts? The guy was never around much, I guess, and moved back to Virginia before Red was even born. That's where they think Red's mom is, though I don't know if she's even still alive. Of course, the daughter doesn't tell me this. It's all from Ms. Gibbs.

"I swear when she gets admitted one of us ends up in her room for hours at a time, just listening to her tales, or getting advice. She pays attention to all of us—the nurses and nursing assistants, too. Paulette Gibbs is the kindest person you'll ever know, Shelly. She says after every story that 'it's all in the Lord's hands, but that doesn't mean He couldn't use a little help now and then.' It'll be hard to lose such a wonderful woman."

Shelly rifled through the chemo book, reading names, cancer stages, and tumor markers. There were various results highlighted in yellow, and an occasional red cross at the end of a page.

"You know what that means, right?" Carmen looked over Shelly's shoulder. "That's a secret sign that the patient died. I overheard the fellows talking about it years ago. They didn't want it too obvious in case any other patient or family member saw it."

By now they had replaced the charts and packed up for home. Carmen paused, then admitted, "I don't know how you can choose it. Oncology, I mean. These ladies are almost all…well, they're just so *nice*. But I only see them for two months out of their entire lives. Just a snapshot," she finished.

"Yes," Shelly wondered how best to put it without sounding morbid, "but I like being with them for all of it. Even for the hard part at the end. I mean, I know what's ahead for Ms. Gibbs, but…" again she halted. "I can make it easier for her than it would've been without modern medicine. We have better nausea meds, better pain meds, Hospice," Shelly trailed off. "I try to *really* be there and explain things, so they can prepare. Plus there's a certain kind of patient who touches me. They tend to be like Ms. Paulette--they're impressive just by be-

47

ing themselves, while they deal with a crappy diagnosis. For me that's what oncology is all about."

"I don't know. This is my last time on service, and in four years I've never been able to listen to you fellows have 'the talk' with patients about Hospice without leaving the room to cry, Shelly. The thought that they're leaving us to die at home with their family just slays me."

Shelly pondered her love of oncology, and how easily she stayed in the room during the difficult stories or the intense family conferences with a dying relative. "I remember this pastor telling a story from a home visit he'd done," Shelly recalled. "The lady was dying, hospital bed in her living room, catheter in her bladder, room freshener trying to cover bad smells, all the medical stuff. You can envision it, right? She was ready for the end to come. She saw the sun coming through a glass crystal hanging in the window, and said, 'Ministry. It must be a difficult joy.' I wrote that phrase down to memorize it. For me, that's the exact definition of oncology. A difficult joy."

Carmen nodded. "We all gravitate to the types of patients who suit us, I think. You've found your calling, Shelly. Frankly, I've never been very comfortable thinking about death. It scares me so much that I don't like to ponder it."

"I like the dragonfly story. The nymphs in the bottom of the lake notice that one by one they vanish. So they make a pact—the next nymph to go away will do everything possible to come back and tell the others where they've gone. The following morning a little nymph goes to the lake surface, molts, and sees the gorgeous surroundings. She can't dive into the water despite trying over and over. A mature dragonfly flits over to see what she's doing, hears the explanation, and counsels her wisely that the life mystery is for each of us to figure out. The little creature will never be able to inform her family. Instead she should revel in the day at hand and enjoy the memory of her loved ones as she explores the beautiful new world she's entered."

Carmen sat back in her chair. "That *is* nice. Not super religious. A realistic parable. I've never imagined that a potentially wonderful thing could happen after death, maybe even surrounding us while we live."

Shelly agreed, "I like thinking the next place is just a dimension that we can't appreciate with our human senses." She checked her watch with a yawn. "Now that we've solved that dilemma, we'd better go. See you in the morning, Carmen. Thanks for the chat."

They trundled off to the parking lot, craving their precious hours of sleep. Shelly wondered if the initial prickliness she had sensed from Carmen was simply a defense mechanism. She felt a warm and caring physician under that cool demeanor.

That's the good thing about eighty-hour work weeks, Shelly thought. *Plenty of time to get to know one another.*

CHAPTER 5

Homefront

Shelly loved the Olive Garden. Really, *really* loved her nearby "It'll be ready when y'all get here, Doc!" Olive Garden. She would call in her usual, lasagna with a big salad and a couple squishy breadsticks. When she rolled the Festiva up to the curb after a brutal day, the brown bag marked "DOC" with blue magic marker took up ample room on the counter and the aroma of buttery garlic bread made her smile. If she called on a Tuesday, it was usually Chet who made it a point to be available for walk-in customers. He'd flirt and hustle and flatter Shelly until she laughed her way out the door.

"Chet, I've gotta go, and I've told you a million times I've got a boyfriend!"

"You keep telling me, Doc, but I never seen him. If you were my girlfriend, *I'd* do the lasagna pickup. Wouldn't make you come out in the dark every week to get your dinner. We can arrange for special delivery, you know," he crooned.

"You don't have delivery, Chet, you nasty thing. Have a good night, now, and get back to your post!" The other workers smirked and shook their heads at Chet's banter. Shelly was sure his routine got a workout several times a shift, but it made her feel more at home, and less a stranger.

She'd stretch two nights of dinners from the Olive Garden order. She found a nice Kroger nearby and got friendly with the deli staff. Shelly liked grocery shopping late at night, a habit she'd gotten into with Evie during medical school. Sometimes the study hours they kept led to midnight discoveries of no food in the house.

Shelly's cooking skills were paltry, and she continued her disgraceful dietary habits from all the years of low income, long hours, and free pizza during the day. The occasional heroic attempts at recipes from the Better Home and Gardens cookbook her mom had given her usually turned out…well, different from the picture.

She hoped to supplement her diet with a restaurant meal now and then. She met a married couple who might be good dinner companions. Like Shelly, Mona and Henry were new to town, infertility medicine and endocrinology for Mona, and anesthesia for Henry. They hadn't worked out a time yet with three insane work schedules.

"You're oncology, then?" Mona had sidled up next to her during a department meeting in the auditorium their first month. "Balls of steel, I assume!" Her grin flashed a welcome sign of cordiality that warmed Shelly to the core, though with an unplaceable accent.

Shelly chuckled. "Yep. And you're ready to get anyone and everyone pregnant, all over Kentucky?"

"That's the basic idea. When IVF works, it's the most gratifying thing in the world. It changes my patient's lives. The tough part is when we can't make a go of it. Yeah, those are the conversations I've got to learn to smooth out, isn't it?"

"Life-changing is right. In oncology we call our big conversations 'the talk.' Any time I tell a patient the chemo's not working, or the scan is bad, I remind myself her life is going to be completely upended. I guess we only really learn by doing it with guidance. That's why we're here, right? To polish us into the final gem of a specialist?" Shelly hoped she didn't sound like a blowhard. "I can't place your accent, Mona. You're clearly not a native Kentuckian."

Mona nodded, "You and I are both outsiders. I was born in Windsor, Ontario, but my folks are Scottish, so my accent tends to throw people. And you're from the Midwest, I heard? You sound like all the newscasters at home."

"Yep, Minnesota. Just think of me as a southern Canadian. Say, I'm not much of a cook, but I love to eat. Maybe dinner out sometime?"

"Sounds great. My husband Henry is the chef in our house, so if we can't get to a restaurant, he'll whip up a nice meal. We can relax and compare notes on the department. Good to meet you, Shelly. I'll leave a note on your desk with some dates."

The remainder of the home front was good, except for a minor battle about the shed in the backyard she was waging with the rental company. It was sturdy enough for her new rake and lawn mower. Its main problem was the paint, chipping off in scabs every time she opened the door. The color was an unfortunate, gastrointestinal shade of brown, which even her neighbors noted.

Ernie and Corinne Michaels, a married couple in their mid-70s, lived next door. They'd been absolutely tickled to hear the shabby rental house was occupied by a young single doctor. That sounded like peace and quiet to them, and they welcomed her over in her first couple of weeks to have a drink on their patio.

"We call it the Crap Cabana, if you want to know the truth," Ernie told Shelly, as they gazed upon the sullen, turd of an out-building next door.

"Oh, hush, Ernie," Corinne gave her husband's thigh a swat. "It's not that bad, but the color's a little drab, now, isn't it? We don't mind, Shelly, we're just so happy to have a nice, responsible young gal living next door for the next two years. We never know who's coming next. There hasn't been anyone there for a couple months now. A truck would pull up and a fella would mow the lawn now and then, but that's about it."

"Poopy Palace is another favorite of mine, when I've had a bourbon or two," Ernie chuckled. "But Corinne likes the Crap Cabana best, 'cause it reminds her of our trip to Mexico a couple years ago. We had a little beach hut, and she called me her cabana boy," he added, as he rubbed her knee. Shelly laughed in agreement, telling them she'd pestered the rental office a couple times about the shed but would try again.

Shelly wanted to feel proud of her little rental house, and the shed ruined the curb appeal. She tried a quick call the next morning between cases in the OR, reaching a girl who sounded about twelve.

"It looks like poo," Shelly told the rental agent. "The paint's all chipped and worn, and the thing is an eyesore."

"Ma'am?" the young woman on the other end was confused.

"My shed looks like poo," Shelly exaggerated the words. "It's in the back yard of my rental on Pikes Creek Road, and I want to paint it. I told the man in the office when I signed the lease and he agreed to bring over a couple gallons of paint. This is the second time I've called, too. I'll do the work--I just need the brushes and the paint. And *not* the color of poo, please, all right?"

"I truly am sorry, but ma'am I just don't follow the poo part," she stammered.

Good grief. "The Crappy Cabana in my back yard is painted the color of shit, miss," Shelly raised her office whisper voice as much as she dared so the PACU nurses wouldn't hear her making a personal call. "The neighbors call it the Poopy Palace. They're complaining. I can't sleep from the haunting color seeping in the windows at night. There's a glow from back there. I've begun to hallucinate that it smells. Get me the paint and I'll stop pestering you. Can you promise me? I'm hanging up now." *Poor thing. I should have been clearer in my poo description.* Shelly smiled to herself. Time to get back in the fray and get pummeled.

Still, the paint skirmish was a sweet distraction from the increasing chaos of Shelly's work life. Day after exhausting day, she saw patients, operated on patients, and told the staff about patients. She'd always been clinically strong, but in this new fellowship role, with these bosses, she couldn't shake the idea that she wasn't very good at her job.

On rounds, the staff lobbed medical questions of her and the residents with the apparent assumption that she knew all the answers and had taught the others. Shelly grew nervous when the attending became irritable, feeling responsible for those younger residents and students to know the subject matter.

"Where do you find the inguinal nodes during a groin dissection, Patricia? Medial or lateral to the femoral artery?"

"Medial, I believe, Dr. Cardinal," Patricia responded.

"You believe or you know? What percentage of nodes will be positive by stage?"

The group was silent. Dr. Cardinal smiled, but everyone on rounds knew they could be pummeled at any second with a wrong answer. Shelly couldn't answer and felt ashamed of her ignorance.

"This should be automatic, really, and the fellows should have gone through it with you. We have that dissection tomorrow, remember. High expectations, Shelly," Dr. Cardinal singled her out with a distinct sharpness to his voice.

When she operated, always her strength, there were digs at "East Coast suturing" or comments about her asking for an instrument the attending didn't want used. "I've reminded you enough times about 'The Way,' Shelly," Dr. Farber chided her. "Let's keep those other instruments you love so much out of the picture, shall we? Just ask for the scissors, and Velma will hand you the Metzenbaums if you need them. No need to be picky here."

She kept quiet, always, knowing better than to verbalize the comments roiling about in her head. *Where else should I be precise if not in the OR?* she thought. She tried to project confidence, but it felt false as the weeks went by. If she was firm, she was told to lighten up. If she changed to cheery, a quick frown showed a casual attitude was unwelcome.

Once the university resumed in September, Shelly had to enroll in a statistics class, a standard fellowship requirement. Arlys paged her one afternoon to tell her the brochure had arrived, and she had to sign up that day. Ken was puzzled at the urgency when she came back to the rounds cart. He took her aside into the coffee alcove as the team moved on.

"I'm sure enrollment was open before today," he said. "The first-year fellow has to do this every year-- they signed me up automatically. You go to the class on campus once a week. I have years of notes and old exams to pass on to you for studying."

She scooted to Arlys's office to sign up for the class. As she approached the doorway, she overheard her talking to Dr. Farber.

"You know best, doctor. She just doesn't seem as, well, *competent* as your other fellows have been. I know how much our reputation means to you. I wonder if she's up to the task?" the honey dripped from Arlys's voice.

"Yes, she's a..."

Shelly didn't want to hear his reply. She knew no other solution but to barge in and act innocent.

"Why, hello, Arlys," her voice a bit too loud, she steadied herself and glanced at the secretary chatting with Dr. Farber. "Good afternoon, Dr. Farber. Hope I'm not interrupting, but I've just raced up to get my statistics class firmed up." There was no reaction from them to indicate concern over their previous conversation having been heard. Dr. Farber nodded to Shelly and retreated into his office, while Arlys found the paperwork.

And that was that. Shelly left her boss's office, stunned enough that she wondered if she'd imagined the whole thing. Why in the world would Arlys find her incompetent? Maybe she should have waited a beat to hear Dr. Farber's reply. Sweating but with a mouth as dry as the papers she'd just signed, she made it to rounds in time to hear Ken's intro to a patient.

"This lady, Ms. Maxine Riner, is kind of special. 'Tetched,' we say. We're not gonna go barging in on her like we do to everybody else. She's been admitted for this chemo so many times. Remember her, Shelly? She lives alone, not much support, and she always wears that clear plastic shower cap."

"Oh, yeah, I remember." Shelly was jolted from thinking about the Farber episode and nodded at the recollection of the eccentric little woman. Ms. Riner was usually in a threadbare housecoat and hospital issued socks. "Like she doesn't realize we can all see through her cap to know she doesn't have any hair. Sweet lady."

The team took a quick glance, then another, then stopped, cart and all, as Shelly opened the door to Maxine's room. Standing there in all her splendor, Ms. Riner was dressed in a one-piece jumpsuit, leopard-patterned, with sling back pumps and a come-hither red wig. Large false eyelashes fluttered with each blink. The effect was extraordinary. It no doubt entered the mind of all who saw her that a prostitute must have taken over the room of the innocent Maxine Riner.

"Well, hey, Dr. Riley! Hey, you all. Coming in for your rounding?" Ms. Maxine moved around the bed with her IV pole for support and reached for a flat paper box. "It's my birthday tomorrow, so I thought I'd wing it up a little for y'all and make some cupcakes. I'm not going to eat one today-- I'll get the chemo in first and see about trying one in the morning. Do you like my hair?"

Shelly's mouth dropped. "Ms. Riner, I have never seen anything like it! You are a vision." The whole group descended on her, taking bites of cupcake and offering her best wishes for the day. Shelly shook her head at the difference between Ken's description, and the real person in front of them. There was no predicting anything in medicine.

"You young'uns, I'd like you to think on something, if you don't mind. We have no idea how much time we've got in this world. Not one bit of an idea." Ms. Riner shook her head, fanciful wig somehow staying in place.

"So, be sure to do right by everyone today, you hear? My pastor did a funeral last week, it was real nice. He said our lives are all about what we do with our dash. You see what he meant? The little dash between the birth date and the death date on your gravestone, see? Your dash." Maxine looked off as if she could see her own headstone.

"I believe he's right about that, and I decided right there to make my dash count for something. Maybe it's making you some cupcakes today. Maybe I can come up with something even bigger, I don't rightly know. But I want to live up to my dash, and this durned cancer is my alarm clock."

Shelly, so fond of this little woman, thought about the advice.

"That's a great lesson for each of us, Ms. Riner. Thank you. And your cupcakes are delicious! The nurse'll be in shortly with your chemo. We'll see you in the morning." As the group exited, Shelly turned to get one more look at the astounding transformation of the dear Ms. Riner. "You do my heart good," Shelly told her as she left, thinking *you cannot make this shit up.*

Shelly and Ken finished rounding and headed back to their offices, chatting quietly in the staircase as they made plans for the rest of the week.

"Ken, I overheard Arlys telling Dr. Farber I might not be as competent as prior fellows. And I guess I do feel kind of dumb at conference with some of the questions," she started. "I've just never heard some of these things. Like rounds with Cardinal. I didn't know exactly what percentage of nodes…"

"No, no," Ken stopped her on the stairs and put his hands up, raising his voice. "Don't let him into your head like that. Those facts will come over the year, and Cardinal just forgets that you're only two months into fellowship. Meanwhile Farber has asked the same questions for ten years, so everyone but you and Angie has heard 'em a hundred times. He thinks they'll be on the Boards." Ken exhaled and put his hands down. "Sorry. I just hate that they're picking on you. The job's hard enough. Which leads me to one thing, though…" He squirmed. "Has anyone mentioned the additional clinical opportunity the first-year fellow gets to enjoy on one Saturday a month?"

Shelly shook her head. "I don't follow you."

"The department has an agreement with the Planned Parenthood clinic in town for the fellow to see patients one morning a month. It's not bad work, I swear." Ken saw Shelly's mouth gape open.

"Are you shitting me? I have to do another clinic on Saturdays?"

"Just once a month. These women don't have insurance." Shelly liked his emphasis on the *in* of insurance, despite being pissed at what he was saying.

Ken continued. "So we evaluate their abnormal Pap smears, do some colposcopy, sometimes a cryotherapy or a biopsy. Bread and butter clinic. They have a great nurse who talks you through it all, and the patients are so appreciative. If it weren't for our killer hours, it'd be nice, actually." His voice trailed off. Ken knew damned well there was no sugar coating more clinical work on top of an already brutal schedule.

"Let me guess. I get a plaque."

It was Ken's turn to gape. "You *do* get a plaque! How'd you know? And a pitiful stipend, too. Dang, I'm impressed you guessed about the plaque. Anyway, it's next Saturday. I'll get you their phone number and the address. It'll be fine, I swear."

Poised? Who was she kidding? This latest addition to her workload, ordered by doctors who thought she incompetent, was inevitable. Shelly was numb to the idea of even more clinical hours weighing her down. It was as if there were a finite supply of fellowship and resident energy, and the goal of the department was to deplete every ounce of it by graduation. The maximum amount of pain had been titrated long ago, on many other bent backs.

Shelly nodded to Ken, using his phrase in defeat. "It'll be fine."

As Ken had predicted, that first Saturday morning clinic at Planned Parenthood was fun.

She could take her time with the patients and the clinic nurse guided her throughout the morning. They'd kept the clinical load light, Shelly felt sure about her medical decisions, and there was a pleasant sense of service that she'd rarely experienced. Although she would never have *asked* for more work, having a grateful set of patients and a chance to regain a little confidence might not be so bad.

The week after her first Planned Parenthood clinic, Shelly was assigned to Dr. Cardinal's surgical case. Aside from the table being too low for her to stand straight, she'd had decent learning experiences in the few cases she'd done with him. Shelly made sure everything was set in the room, knew the patient's history cold, and went out to the hall while adjusting her headlight on her forehead.

Dr. Cardinal was already scrubbing, soapy water draining into the sink. She was about to make the requisite fellow-to-attending small talk, when he turned to her. "How does it feel to be a baby killer?"

She almost dropped the sterile sponge in the sink. The accusation had to have something to do with Planned Parenthood, she assumed, but *what in the hell?*

"Dr. Cardinal, I have no idea what you're talking about." She tried to keep her voice calm.

"You go off to Planned Parenthood, where they kill babies. That's what I'm talking about," and he left her, his scrub complete, to push back first into the operating room. Shelly continued washing her hands and forearms, unconscious of the motions. Her thoughts were traveling a mile a minute, but she saw no solution aside from going in to do her job, staying cool, and not reacting.

Kit was pulling the back of Dr. Cardinal's sterile gown down as he moved to the patient's side.

"Let's start," he said. "Anesthesia is ready?" A nod at the head of the table prompted the med student to make the vertical midline incision.

They started without Shelly. She was quaking, furious, in the corner of the room, arms held up so the water would drip onto the floor and not contaminate her hands. Because the case had started, Velma had less time to get her gowned and gloved, fitting her in between instrument handoffs.

"Poised," she murmured quietly. Her pet phrase didn't embolden Shelly like it usually would. Velma sensed her fury, trying to get Shelly's attention. She moved her surgical tray and guided Shelly into position at the table. "Here, Doctor. Take your place."

Your rightful place, Shelly reminded herself, in a commanding inner voice. *You belong here, and he's trying to shake you. Don't let him.*

The case went on, and Shelly was silent. Dr. Cardinal chattered away, making political remarks, referencing various 'secular humanist' personalities he detested, peppering his monologue with medical questions of the student and resident alike.

"Really, that's the problem with the America of the '90's," Dr. Cardinal asserted. "Godless people making godless decisions have landed us in this brutish secular world, where no one has peace or meaning in their lives. There's no morality without that sacred touch."

He pivoted to clinical conversation, lobbing an easy question at Shelly, which she answered without embellishment. She kept her head down, the headlight pointing into the surgical field, as she focused on her job.

Fury refined her focus on the surgical field to the point where she could sense every capillary and nerve to avoid. It was as if she could hear the red blood cells swooshing through the patient's blood vessels. Her hands moved and stitched and decided which tissues would answer to her, and Dr. Cardinal had no choice but to follow, suctioning and cutting suture as she operated. She was perfect.

When it was time to close, the usual procedure was for the fellow to take over as the staff thanked everyone and left the room. Dr. Cardinal smiled at Shelly and said, "Now you take care of this patient, you hear?"

"Of, course, Dr. Cardinal," she answered. *You awful man.* "As always."

Only after he was out of sight, having stopped to rinse his hands at the scrub sink, did Shelly's shoulders relax. She gripped the sterile sheet and took a moment to blow out pent up air. The room remained quiet. No one threw out any choice words, even though the staff was out of hearing range. They recognized there was to be no joking, though no one had any idea what had just happened. Velma quietly congratulated Shelly on a nice case. "You were on fire in there, operating like you've been doing it forever. Everything all right?"

Shelly shook her head, knowing that she needed to process the morning's events on her own before talking this through. "Keep me honest, Velma. You're the glue that holds these rooms together, you and Kit. Just keep me honest." The head games were just beginning, she realized, and she would need all the help she could get to stay sane.

CHAPTER 6

All I Need

The vibrant, confident young woman was being drained away, day by day, week after impossible week. When in the company of the attendings, Shelly showed less nerve and more timidity. She was hyperaware of slip-ups and felt unhinged at conferences when a trivial medical question could be hurled her way to answer at any moment. She was afraid. She tried to read the pertinent medical journals, but none of the details stuck, and she could never recite the data the way Ken did.

"Dr. Cardinal may think I'm a piece of shit," Shelly told Ken during one of their late nights finishing up paperwork in their office. "But I'll have you know I got good grades in high school, played the flute and saxophone in band, starred in plays, and basically had the time of my life. I must've peaked in high school."

Ken laughed at her candor, leaning back in the cheap office chair with his arms up, hands cradling his head. "Ah, high school—good memories. I was top in my class, too, but I was more a jock, I guess. I grew up with a single mom, since my dad died when I was young. She never wanted to talk about him. If I asked, she'd just shush me and tell me the Lord has a plan, or some such thing."

He paused, flipping the key chain in his desk drawer back and forth. He heaved a sigh and continued. "Anyway, not much else to my life story. When Janelle and I met in college I knew she was the love of my life. Corny, right? We got married in med school. I'm in awe of her every day, watching her keep our wild child Briane under a little bit of control. I love my family, Shelly. Getting through this fellowship is partly for them."

Shelly thought about his story and wondered if they were so terribly different. "College and med school were hard. I had to work my butt off to hang on to B's, and I would have failed histology if my roommate Evie hadn't dragged me into the lab before the final exam and quiz me on slides until I knew every single one. Still, I felt like I'd entered the real world. There wasn't a day that went by when I didn't learn about *something*: relationships, race, feminism, science, literature. Intoxicating! Plus I discovered sex, which was fun. Are you shocked, Ken?"

He chuckled. "Nah, I'm just laughing to think of how different you are from the last fellow, Brent, that's all. I'm not sure he ever *said* the word sex, let alone had it. In fact, we never talked about a single personal thing in our lives, Brent and me. The whole year was strictly business. Surgery and chemo. Wounds and white counts. Kinda sad, when I think about it. One thing's for sure, though. The attendings never ragged on us like they do you. I'd give you advice, but I don't see anything you're doing that's so wrong."

Ken snapped his fingers. "I can't believe I didn't think of this sooner! I have no control over the attendings, but I can show you a hideout. Dr. Hazel's office, right this way." Ken crossed the row of carrels and gestured to a door that Shelly had barely noticed in their bland office space, opened it, and reached for the light.

"Every resident and fellow has needed Dr. Hazel's office at least once to decompress or escape. There're some rumors that it's been used to fool around in the middle of the night, too. It's like stepping back into the 1970's. I swear I can feel the goodness of Dr. Hazel come to me in here. He's retired, but he was in charge of this whole place for so long they let him keep the office. I've only seen him here twice, I think. Cardinal says he was one helluva surgeon."

Shelly nodded. The stale aroma was not unpleasant, and Ken was right to point out how much it felt like time had been frozen in that space. Matching chairs with celery colored upholstery were on the left, and a sagging burnt-orange sofa hugged the wall to the right. Dr.

Hazel's desk grabbed the lion's share of the attention, its deep wood shining from the overhead light. A little green desk lamp perched over the tidy piles of unread mail and journals, the brass chain waiting for a tug to let a reader settle in for a comfortable hour or two.

"These are so old," Shelly said as she explored the diplomas and portraits, leaning in for a closer look. "I think this is an original oil. What a cozy place, even with this massive old desk taking up half the room."

"He doesn't mind us using his office, and he never locks the door. I hope having a little escape pad helps. Stay as long as you want, but I'm heading home. See you in the a.m." Ken headed back through the shared door, closing it behind him.

Shelly sat on the couch, tucking her legs up and wishing she could have a cigarette. Dr. Hazel's office cocooned her into musing about her path to this Kentucky fellowship program. Medical school had been a much different experience from college. Aside from markedly less sex, what passed for learning was rote memorization. The lecture hall had been filled with young adults who were *made* for the kind of data spewing on subsequent tests that Shelly's brain could not fathom. She'd rebelled against it for the first couple months but found obstinance a very destructive impulse if she wanted to graduate.

Her brilliant roommate Evie Hallstrom tried to demonstrate how it was done. She showed her how to take notes from the lecture, and how to intuit the main points that would surely be on the test. She gave her hints on mnemonics, inventing little phrases with letters that would trigger the agents in the Krebs cycle, or the names of the bacteria they were learning. Evie also told Shelly to stop staying up so late with her other friends or getting dinner before study sessions.

"Fewer breaks to dance to Aretha Franklin and more library time, Shell," Evie suggested, frustrated with her roomie's feeble brain. "Learning's just not supposed to be that fun."

Shelly passed the first two years of courses, and grudgingly learned to memorize a bit more efficiently, but sparkled when her clinical rotations started in the third year. As soon as she began to interact with real patients, to see the diseases she had studied, and to try her hand at the real practical part of being a doctor, her heart sang again.

She loved the hospital, loved the nurses and all their asides to her when no one else was listening, and loved the nursing assistants, who performed punishingly strenuous work every shift.

But the day she walked into an operating room was the day Shelly Riley found her direction. Doctor? Yes, she had wanted that since she was in elementary school. Surgery? It called, braying and insistent, informing her that she needed to get going on her knot-tying skills, because this was her home. She melted into surgical rotations, commiserated with the residents, and felt grounded for the first time in her medical training.

That's a good memory, she thought as she pushed up from the couch. Shelly crossed the room to run her hand along the back of Dr. Hazel's swivel chair, wondering if he'd had the same revelation that he was meant to be a surgeon.

She'd found the specific path in her fourth year of medical school. A senior surgeon in charge of a complex gynecologic oncology case was unharried, comfortable allowing the junior staff to do most of the procedure, yet entirely in command. Paul Simon's *Graceland* played during the whole case. And the cherry on the top was that the surgeon was a woman. Capable, female, *and* cool--that settled it. Shelly imprinted on her like a gosling seeing its momma for the first time, and her career was sealed.

Despite a learning style not conducive to rote memorization and standard medical education, Shelly matched in residency. She worked for four years to have a résumé worthy of acceptance into one of the handful of gyn-onc fellowships in the country.

Her glee was palpable from a surprise call offering her a spot after she had initially failed to match. Her fellow residents threw her a party, complete with champagne, presents and a card from them all. One of the naughtier residents wrote, "Congratulations--now you can enjoy yourself 90 hours a week!" The grueling hours, every third night call schedules, and years of sleep deprivation would finally end with her last two years of training.

Yet here she was. Her sassy vitality was seeping away, and she was starting to believe it was her fault. The criticisms were always offered with a smile, to the point where she thought she was imagining things. A resident might make an obvious error, but a brutal comment would single her out for not having trained them better. A lengthy case for one attending might go beautifully in her hands, but the other staff would chastise her for poor time management if it made her late for rounds.

Shelly had lost track of time in her hideaway, memories of better days entertaining her far longer than she intended. She turned off the lights after a quick survey of that friendly room, so close to her own unpleasant office, glad to know it would be there for her in the future.

Bad news awaited her at home. A notification that she'd failed the end-of-residency standard exam was in a pile of otherwise unremarkable mail. She collapsed onto her couch, crying as she read the form letter over and over. *Oh, no. Please God, no!* She would have to retake the test and pass to stay on in fellowship. "If you should fail a second time, your fellowship director will be contacted to discuss next steps…"

Deeply embarrassed, she first planned to schedule the retake without mentioning it to anyone. Cigarette after cigarette, she couldn't even call her mom or Evie to admit her failure.

Shelly remembered being waitlisted for medical school, but hadn't really doubted she'd get in. Didn't match for fellowship, but one happy phone call kept her on track. This test, though. It was the precursor for continuing in fellowship. Her stomach churned as she paced her living room floor and smoked. After contemplation, she realized the news would reach the fellowship director, Dr. Cardinal. Surely the humiliating result would be better received coming directly from her.

The next day, Shelly found a way to slip into his office for a quick chat. The room could not have been more of a contrast with Dr. Hazel's cozy time capsule of an office. Empty aside from medical journals and texts teetering in pile after pile, the austerity suited him. What looked to be framed diplomas were stacked against one another on the floor, intended for the walls years ago. A large blue Bible had some prominence on a bookshelf, and a plastic human anatomical torso spilled its organs onto the corner of his desk.

Dr. Cardinal took the news with no obvious alarm, dove into her studying and learning methods with very detailed queries, and made a specific plan to pass the next test. He collated a stack of papers together on edge, *crack, crack, crack,* stapling them together with a brusqueness that reeked of displeasure. "I'm not sure you really understand how to study, Shelly. We have high standards in this fellowship, you know. I expect you to make this happen. I can't really say what's next if you fail. Again."

"I'm so sorry, Dr. Cardinal," she said, looking for a tissue to wipe her nose. "I didn't think it'd gone poorly. Please let me keep this to myself. I don't want the others to know I failed." She hated begging, but she thought being direct was her only option. He agreed to clear her schedule enough to drive up to Cincinnati for the test. Shelly resolved to use his study methods and nail the exam.

The days flew, and the late August air was a tad crisp on the morning drives into work. One day, during a long surgery with Dr. Cardinal on a woman who would not have long to live, what had previously passed for teaching more resembled an attack. "I don't know if I can count to a thousand, Shelly, but I'll have to learn with you, because this must be the thousandth time I've told you how to tuck the moist laps in the upper abdomen. The minute the field changes, I can't see a thing. This isn't rocket science, you know."

"I'm sorry, Dr. Cardinal. She's been getting light and bucking the packs out so we've had to repack several…"

"Fine, fine. Always excuses. Let's get on with it, shall we? I'm sure the rest of the team would appreciate that." Dr. Cardinal had never demonstrated his method, but Shelly didn't dare to ask given the tension. *If a sneer had a sound, that was it,* she thought. When the surgery finally ended, Dr. Cardinal left the room while the remaining team members started the abdominal closure. Shelly monitored the residents, but her mind wandered toward how she'd explain the woman's medical situation to her during the hospital stay. The poor prognosis would be a surprise, and the patient would need help to learn about the disease, cope with the shock, and somehow move forward.

As Shelly was reflecting on how to manage the future interaction, the medical student shocked her. "Why do they hate you? I mean, anesthesia struggled to keep her paralyzed, and even apologized for letting her move and buck. The packing coming out isn't your fault."

The wonder of a surgical mask, aside from keeping a field sterile and allowing a fellow to mouth "bite me" without the attending seeing, was its capacity to hide emotions. A student had openly stated the obvious, in a way no one else had done since Shelly started in July. And her words, offered innocently, nearly knocked her down. Her life, and her training, was being scrutinized by total strangers, who came to the same conclusion as she had.

They hated her.

"Well, they don't *hate* me, exactly," Shelly sputtered. "Of course I should know how to pack the abdomen. I guess the feedback is meant to help me grow as a surgeon and oncologist. We all need constructive criticism," and she fell back on the platitudes that had run through her head for months, processing the insults and humiliations. The mask hid her flushed cheeks, pink with embarrassment at being found out as an imposter by a med student. She fought the urge to rip off the sterile garb, tumble out of the room and splash water on her face.

"It's not you, Shelly," Carmen observed. "I call it the Capable Breast Syndrome. They just don't know what to do with strong women, so they get flustered and try to kill us, one way or another. I'm quiet, so they leave me alone for the most part. But you? You're lively, I guess is the word for it. You have a lot of energy and pizazz and want to be a part of the solution to make things better. Well, they don't think a solution is needed, because they like things the way they are. Nothing you can do about it except graduate. And then move."

That was the longest string of words Carmen had ever put together in Shelly's company.

The patient's audible heart rate beeped from the monitor in the background, the only sound in the room, pounding a steady beat as Shelly tried to focus on a reply. The incision was closed, dressing applied, and Shelly acted nonchalant as she gathered up her things.

"Thanks, everyone, for not hating me, and all," she chirped. "I'll just take my capable breasts out to PACU and do some paperwork!" Trying to make light of despair, a favorite coping mechanism, wasn't cutting it at that moment.

Shelly managed to finish the day. She made a game plan in her head about when she could get up to see the post-op patient the next day without the whole crowd, to talk her through the cancer and the surgical findings. She dragged herself out to the car after rounds, not even having the heart to call in a Tuesday night lasagna at the Olive Garden and flirt with Chet. When she pulled into her driveway, her despair was deeper than ever. While her key turned the lock, she heard the phone ringing, and she lunged her way in to grab the call.

"Hello?"

"I quit my job in Springfield, and I'm moving down to be with you!" Robert's voice was gleeful, a decidedly unusual phenomenon. "God, I can't believe I did it! My sisters had a hundred-dollar bet I'd never follow through, but I went in there today and gave my two-week notice. Betsy's gonna rent my house, so it'll stay lived in and all, and that'll take care of the mortgage..." Robert kept talking, while Shelly closed the door, dropped her things, and slumped to the floor.

All I need is Robert here to really complete this shit show, she thought. *All I fucking need.*

She put the phone down on the ground, hearing the tinny voice on the other end continue, and grabbed an ashtray. Cradling the phone again, she lit a cigarette and settled in on the ground to battle this out.

"Still smoking, huh?" He finally stopped to hear from her, after dropping his bombshell. "I was kind of hoping you'd have quit by now, working in oncology and everything," he added.

"No, Robert, I didn't quit. In fact, I never intended to quit. Fellowship is a pretty stressful situation, and smoking is the only happy part of my day." She took an especially loud drag for effect. "We've got to talk about this move," Shelly pleaded. "We'd decided to cool things for a while see how the first year went, Robert. I can't believe you quit your job. You had so much seniority, and those good benefits."

Shelly regarded her little rental house living room, peaceful and quiet, her only space to be completely alone. She could smoke without offending anyone. She could watch whatever TV station she wanted. She could eat dinner, sprawled on her couch, with no thought of propriety. He couldn't come. She simply could not share this space with Robert.

"I told you I didn't want to be responsible for disrupting your whole life for me. If it didn't work out, remember? I'd feel so guilty. Your whole family is up there!" Gesturing wildly with one hand, she rapped the back of her head on the wall. *Ow, dammit.*

"I know, I know. But I sat here, after I watched you drive away from me in June, and I thought about how brave you were. You moved into an apartment with your mom when your grandpa got married. Another state for college. Atlanta for the summer after you graduated. You came out here to Massachusetts when you finished med school. You leap into things, Shell, and treat everything like an adventure."

Shelly had not heard anything approaching such thoughtfulness in him before.

"I admire you for that. I want to try to live my life," he searched for the phrase, "not so scared, you know? If I don't try something new now, with you, I'll never do it. I'll live in the same stupid house and work the same stupid job and complain about all of it for the rest of my life."

"That sounds like something your sisters would say," Shelly told him. "Did they compare you to your dad while they were at it?"

"As a matter of fact, that was *exactly* what Betts and Carla said, in separate phone calls," he admitted, "but I know they're right. Now or never, that's how I see it. And if you don't want me, I'll leave. I'm just asking you to give me a chance. Let me see if I can cheer up a little. I actually got kind of excited to get to see another part of the country. There are caves by you, did you know that? Some of the biggest on the continent. And mountains with good hiking paths."

"Robert, I work like a gazillion hours a week," Shelly butted in.

"On your weekends off. I know I'll be on my own Monday through Friday. Besides, I've gotta find a job, too, so that'll occupy me during the week. I can fix stuff, and I can help you paint the back yard thing, what was it, the Shit Shed, did you call it?"

"Ernie calls it the Poopy Palace when he's drunk." Shelly laughed. She stamped out her cigarette and stood. "I call it the Shit Shed just to you. I'm trying to watch my language."

"Yeah, right. I'll bet that lasts about five minutes," Robert chuckled too. "Then you've made another friend and you let it all hang out. That's okay. That's why people like you."

She could feel him smiling, and knew he was laying out on his ratty plaid couch looking at the beautiful view of maples and pines on a ridge out his back yard. No shitty outbuildings for Robert. His place was immaculate, and his ability to fix anything was only outdone by his strong work ethic and desire to keep his home handsome.

"Not everyone likes me, it appears." She told him what the student had blurted out in the OR, and how everyone had gotten quiet. "It was pretty obvious that they all know it's true, but she startled me by saying it out loud. No one admits anything *out loud* down here. They just insinuate, and infer, and in general make a person feel like shit without actually telling me what the hell I'm doing wrong!" It helped to unload her exasperation with someone who knew her.

They talked like that for another half hour, Shelly pacing and yawning, Robert telling her what he'd done for the move so far, and what was left. He regaled her with all the filthy things he planned to do to her lean, hungry body the second he pulled into town, which she enjoyed. He reminded her about their first date, when after a long day's autumn motorcycle ride through the beautiful northeastern countryside, they had ended up back at his house. One romantic thing had led to another, and they'd stumbled, embracing and disrobing like a bad romantic movie, to Robert's room.

"I tried to be funny by jumping on your bed and telling you I was playing hard to get!"

Shelly remembered the bounce that never came. SLAP!

"Yep, I had the waterbed filled pretty tight, didn't I? God, I could hear you land. I thought you were going to be paralyzed, and I'd have to push my beautiful girlfriend around in a wheelchair for the rest of our days," Robert reminisced.

"Hmm, once I got over the smack on my entire back, *and* the mortified feeling that I had just made a fool of myself, I seem to remember a very nice evening," Shelly agreed. There'd been fun times with him, she realized. It had been easy for her to highlight the difficulties while she was alone and dealing with so much. Their small talk continued until she begged off to drag herself to the shower and then blessed sleep.

Apparently, despite her best made plans, she still had a boyfriend. She hung up the phone, rubbed the back of her head, and tried to process what had just happened. *Jesus, I just agreed to Robert moving in*, she wondered. *What the hell?* As she got ready for bed, she gave herself a firm talking to about rules for his appearance. He was a melancholy man, always seeing the absolute worst possible outcome in all scenarios, gloom and doom on his every horizon. She was a Pollyanna, sure that with enough effort and good intentions, things would work out for the best. Despite her best efforts to stop trying to change him, she did her damnedest to try to change him every single time. She was suffocated by his negativity.

That stops, she scolded herself. If she didn't like the life approach he had, she'd recognize it, be firm, and ask him to leave.

Right.

Cheryl Bailey

CHAPTER 7

Weeks, months, or years?

Shelly battled on, taking the weekly statistics class, operating, seeing patients in clinic, and rounding. A September heat wave simmered the day Robert arrived at Shelly's door, truck packed to the roof. They sweltered as they found places for his clothes and tools, eventually tumbling into bed, showering, and heading back for more cuddling and sleep.

"I can't believe I'm here," Robert murmured to her, Shelly's head cradled in the crook of his arm. "It's like we were never apart."

The home vibe started off well from Shelly's perspective. Robert cooked nice meals, preparing something simple and tasty for her to eat at the end of her fifteen-hour days. He was trying hard to be more upbeat, though a cheerful Robert was decidedly unnatural. She had to admit the sex was brilliant. He was a generous, knowledgeable lover, and in the bedroom he could escape life's worries and relax in joy.

With the full workdays and new events at home, it was hard for Shelly to puzzle out the brutality of medical training. Why did she keep coming back for more punishment, day after day?

The patients, of course. The patients were the answer. They were the magic and sustenance that pulled doctors into a workaholic life, always finding one more patient who needed to be seen. The years of training before becoming "real" doctors made physicians masters of delayed gratification. Shelly craved the clinical interaction, turning on all her positive energy when she sensed a medical situation in which she could help.

The salvation Shelly needed to keep from falling apart came at a most desperate part of her fellowship, in the form of the remarkable Faye Colgate. Faye arrived for the one o'clock Monday appointment in Dr. Farber's clinic, knowing something was amiss in her abdomen, and that she'd need surgery. She'd driven over from her little town of Red Rock Falls, just south of Bowling Green, KY, where she owned and ran a dress shop. She and her mom listened carefully to the consultation, while her friend Carrie took detailed notes, occasionally getting clarification on a point and jotting it down.

"I'm healthy as a horse, Dr. Farber," Faye told them. "I want you to remember that while you're at work on me tomorrow. Take out everything I don't need, y'all. I don't particularly want another crack at this surgery thing. Oh, and the folks at home would love a look at my appendix or my gallbladder. If you could send me home with a souvenir, I'd appreciate it."

The group chuckled as they opened the exam room door, Carrie shaking her head.

"I'll need to tell everyone back home," Carrie told Shelly in the hallway, as Faye was getting ready to disrobe for the exam. "Faye acts like this is just a little nip and tuck, doctor, but I'm hearing you say it's quite a big surgery?" They both heard Faye and Donna's laughter coming from the exam room.

Faye's mom Sissie nodded and added, "'Twouldn't be Faye without the laughing, now would it, Carrie? I believe she'll be laughing while y'all are operating on her tomorrow, Dr. Riley!" Sissie's voice was light, and Carrie gave her arm a squeeze in support.

Shelly knew Faye was forty-five years old, never married, no kids, and lived with her mom. Shelly was thinking the older woman appeared to be in her eighties when Sissie read her mind.

"She's my only child, and I had her right late in life, you know. I never could get pregnant, Dr. Riley. My husband Gabriel and I were married for eighteen years, and my monthly came just like clockwork. I'd cry sometimes, at the sight of it. We just took to Jesus for comfort, figuring he had a plan, and he didn't mean for us to be parents." Carrie put her arm around her, evidently having heard the story before and knowing it was hard for Sissie to tell it.

"Well. One day I woke up real tender in my belly. And it looked swollen, you see, and right hard. I told my husband, 'I believe I have a tumor, Gabe.' And by now you know, it wasn't a tumor. It was Faye!" Sissie's face glowed, triumphant in the memory, and Carrie smiled with her, pure delight in knowing her beloved friend had this dream of a mother.

Shelly laughed with Sissie. "The tumor was Faye! What a story, Sissie. I don't think I'll ever forget it."

She ushered them to the lobby and went back to examine Faye Colgate with Dr. Farber. Faye had a lively wit, and managed to ask them, feet in stirrups, if she should have her friends bring the team of doctors anything to eat after her surgery the following day.

"They're great cooks, doctors, and they'd be pleased to do it," she offered. She chattered during most of the uncomfortable part, exhaling with pain. "Y'all know just where to push, now don't you?"

"Did Ms. Colgate just offer to cater lunch on the day of her operation, Dr. Riley?" He appeared to relish the clinical interaction with this patient, his face actually registering something bordering on warmth. "I'm honored by that offer, ma'am," he said as he washed his hands. Shelly could see a hint of a smile on his face reflected in the mirror over the sink. "But we'll be fine. Go ahead now and get dressed. Dr. Riley will come back to go over all the details, so everything goes perfectly tomorrow." Pointing to his heart, he added, "I'm going to make sure of that."

* * *

Faye had a bad cancer. Memorably bad, and the case took hours. The surgeons worked companionably, counting on her youth and good health for Faye to recover from such an extensive operation. The tumor scattered throughout her abdomen ranged from grains of sand to golf ball-sized masses, and it was everywhere. Resecting all the cancer required loops of intestine to be removed and resewn, belly fat to be released from attachments to healthy surfaces, and hours of inspecting each step to avoid damage to vital organs. Still, even with aggressive surgery followed by chemotherapy, she would eventually die from this cancer. Shelly, holding the loops of malignant bowel in her hands that day, knew Faye's future. It broke her heart.

With the huge surgery done, and a long hospital stay ahead of her, the team cleaned her skin and woke her from the anesthesia. "On my count," the anesthesia resident instructed, after he had gathered all the cords and IV tubing. They glided her to the waiting hospital gurney. When Faye's body was in position, nurse Kit covered her skin with warm blankets, and Ken accompanied her to the PACU.

Shelly thanked the OR team, while the housekeeping crew came in nonchalantly to sweep and sanitize, preparing for the next soul. She stepped out for a quick slug of coffee and a cigarette, then popped a mint in her mouth and went to the waiting room to talk to Faye's family.

While Shelly scanned faces for the elderly Sissie, the volunteer announced "Faye Colgate? Ms. Faye Colgate?" She was taken aback when damned near the whole room stood up to come to the consultation room.

With a nervous smile, Shelly cleared her throat and told them, "It's usual for just the close family to come to this little talk."

The entire group, about twenty people, stayed planted, and Carrie answered, "We *are* close family, Dr. Riley. I'm afraid you're stuck with all of us."

Okay. These people are not fooling around, Shelly thought. Faye's mom Sissie came first, and everyone got her seated and settled. The rest found their own space in the tiny conference room, some perched on the arms of the chairs, some on the floor, the men standing in the back. Shelly tried to address Sissie at first, but felt so flustered by all the bodies she finally blurted out, "Who in the world *are* all you people?"

They laughed, bless them. The tension lifted, they kept laughing, and eventually cried as they introduced themselves, and said how they knew Faye. Each was a dear friend, and each claimed Faye liked him or her best, pestering Sissie to confirm it. They included Sissie in their narratives, clearly adoring her. It was like story-time in a big southern family, every person adding to the tale, which always led back to Faye. Shelly was so captivated by the lyrical voices and the singular way they had with their stories, that over fifteen minutes passed before she finally snapped out of the spell. She hadn't told them a thing about Faye's surgery and her terrible prognosis.

That's when she felt it, like the snap of a wristband, a slap in the face. The *shitdammit* moment of oncology. When a wonderful person and a horrible cancer intersect, the oncologist knows that some seriously bad events lie ahead. Shelly would be the source of information and strength for the dear patient she'd just started to know.

She'd seen all the patterns of avoidance or blaming or alcohol that doctors used to cope with the inevitable hurt of losing a patient. Some put up a shield of professionalism that never cracked. Shelly, though, felt called to dive right in, connecting as much as possible, and hoping to keep the patient's humanity front and center. *Shitdammit,* she thought. *All these grand stories, all this hilarity of Faye, but I've gotta lower the boom.*

"I'd like to go over the surgery with you now." She projected more confidence than she felt. "It was ovarian cancer, as we suspected. The masses on Faye's CT scan were all cancer, and there was a lot of it. The surgery took so long because we did everything necessary to remove it all."

The positive energy in the room shivered and vibrated. There was still strength there, but it was no longer funny and audacious. Focused on loving their Faye, the entire group now hung on Shelly's every word, as if hearing it wholly, not missing a single syllable, would help her. Knowing everything the doctors saw, what it looked like, and how they took it out became critically important.

The group had smart, pointed questions, and let Shelly's answers resonate while pondering what else they needed to know. It was beautiful, so many people packed in love in that small space. She thought of bees in a hive, thrumming with energy, and devoted to the larger purpose of helping heal their queen. Shelly said goodbye, glad that these folks were going to be in her life for a bit, and took a deep breath to clear her head.

Wow! Intense group, she thought as she hustled back to the OR for the next case.

Dr. Farber was there, and Shelly recounted the power of the family conference to him. The rest of the surgical cases went well, and Shelly felt a grudging shift in his confidence in her ability after Faye's enormous case. The drama of a young life, now on a collision course with ovarian cancer, and that remarkable posse of family and friends sustained Shelly for the rest of the day.

Faye's recovery in the hospital was uneventful. She was funny, lively, and *never* alone in the room. These folks lived more than two hours from the hospital, but someone from her town was always there.

A couple days after her operation, Dr. Farber and Shelly visited her room together to go over the pathology report and the postop plans. After a couple lighthearted comments on the food and the gas pains that plagued her, Faye took the news of her cancer with a quiet face. She nodded at the details of the staging. "Do I still have some time on earth, Doc? And how much does Sissie know?"

Dr. Farber was plain about the fact that chemotherapy was the next step but did not get much more specific. He made his exit, having managed to avoid giving a firm answer.

Shelly remained in the room, she and Faye watching Dr. Farber's back as he closed the hospital room door. Faye cleared her throat and began. "Now I want the truth, Dr. Riley. So many people depend on me in Red Rock Falls. If I'm to keep my dress shop open, I need the truth to make plans. He couldn't tell me, but *you* will, I just know it. Weeks, months, or years?" It was the only time Shelly had heard no joviality in her voice. "I realize you can't say for sure, but weeks, months, or years? Let's start with that."

What a good way to think about a cancer prognosis, Shelly thought. "If everything goes the way it usually does, you should have years. And we hope to enroll you in a clinical trial that just opened—it'd be state of the art chemo, and you fit it perfectly. Madeline Hayes is our protocol nurse, and if I know her, you two will be best friends before you leave this hospital. She'll come by today to talk you through it. I'm going downstairs right after we're done here to talk to the pathologist about adding special stains so you can be enrolled."

Faye's face was so different when she was serious, Shelly realized. Powerful somehow, as if she were transitioning from wit to philosophy.

"This cancer snuck up on me, Dr. Riley, but you know what's funny? I'm not surprised. I've always had a feeling my life wouldn't be long. No idea why, and I never told anyone about it, but honestly, I'm truly not surprised. You can see how blessed I am to have plenty of people to help me get through whatever y'all want to throw at this cancer. Let's just keep the life expectancy part of it between you and me, all right? Sissie'll never ask, and I'd just as soon keep it that way for her."

They talked a bit more, and Shelly outlined the expectations for the three weekly chemo sessions. Side effects, likely outcomes, and total hair loss led to wisecracks about sexy wigs and painted eyebrows from Faye.

"Did you make the incision straight?"

"Yes, Ms. Colgate, I'd taken a liking to you, so I made a nice line for you instead of my usual wavy incision. You haven't looked yet?"

Shelly felt guilty to recognize that she was already looking forward to Faye's chemo admissions, as if they were social visits. She showed her the wound and talked to her about the care she'd need at home, grateful for Faye's snazzy observations. When a crowd of visitors from home came in, Shelly excused herself to buzz down and see Dr. Steele in Pathology.

She dashed outside for a cigarette, greeting the group of assorted workers and nurses relaxing in the shelter. She popped an Altoid for the familiar tobacco-peppermint mix on her breath. Reentering the hospital, she took the stairs two at a time, curving around the ivory basement corridors. Passing barely marked maintenance and custodial offices, a left turn led to the Pathology office. Its cramped anteroom was stuffed with an oversized desk, piles of hospital forms surrounding a secretary taking calls.

Shelly mouthed, "Hi, Claudia," and nodded as the clerk waved her in, passed the shelf where specimens from the OR were deposited, and walked into the main pathology lab, chaotic with activity. Technicians were cutting open organs, dictating detailed descriptions into microphones, and measuring various pieces of tissue.

She peeked at the current tray of bits and pieces in specimen jars, thinking nothing of it, and looked across the room. Dr. Chris Steele, her favorite pathologist, looked through a microscope and dictated a report on the phone. The smell of formaldehyde filled the room, even the little cubby where the pathologist of the day examined tissue sent down from the ORs for "frozen section." Just the sight of him improved Shelly's mood.

"John, I'm looking right at it. It's not malignant, I'm telling you. Send me another piece if you're so sure because all I'm seeing is granulomatous tissue." Shelly could hear the loud reply echoing through the operating room's speaker phone. "All right. I'll tell Claudia to be watching for it. All right. Later." He clicked to hang up.

He saw Shelly and motioned for her to come in.

"You bloody surgeons think you know everything. You realize that don't you? Then you yell at *me* when I tell you you're wrong. That's my life, in a nutshell. The only thing that gets me through the day, and I do mean the *only* thing, is knowing that your lives are one hundred percent worse. Here, I pulled those slides you wanted to review. Claudia said there's something to add for a clinical trial?" He pointed at the stool in front of him.

"Thanks for doing this, Dr. Steele. Yeah, it's a panel of new stains on Faye Colgate's case. They want them quantified on the tumor cells," Shelly sat at his invitation, looking into the teaching scope he'd set up as she spoke. "What was the specimen you were freezing?"

Dr. Chris Steele was Shelly's favorite pathologist because despite bemoaning his daily life, he obviously loved every second of his job. His voice lifted with enthusiasm and he peered into the microscope.

The two looked through the current frozen section, Dr. Steele teaching her the details in the slide of inflammatory, though not cancerous, tissue the surgeon had sent down. The pain of Shelly's inadequacies, real and imagined, vanished when caught up in Steele-world. They moved on to Faye Colgate's case, and he walked her through the specimens systematically, outlining his approach to every case he read.

"Gotta do it the same way every time. I learned that from your boss. Remember Cardinal's saying?"

Shelly grinned. "You mean 'You suck at your job and are the worst fellow we've ever had?' Or 'Behind every obsession there's a fuck-up'?"

"The latter. And stop ruminating about what they think. I hear you're great in the OR and do everything like Ginger Rogers—smooth like Fred Astaire but backwards and in high heels. Though your filthy smoking habit, evident from the stench of your clothes, is ridiculous. Find a better addiction."

"I know, I know. A smoking oncologist. I started because I thought I looked cool, and it helped me stay up late to finish papers. Now I like it too much to stop."

"Nonsense. You're afraid to try to quit. All right, back to the case," Dr. Steele peered down the binocular scope. They worked amiably and planned how to meet the clinical trial's requirements. Shelly checked her watch.

"Okay. Enough time escaping reality and learning from my favorite medical geek. I've gotta get rounds going. Thanks again, Dr. Steele. You brightened my day," Shelly flattened herself against the door as a pathology lab technician brought in another frozen section for him to read.

"Go stamp out disease, Shelly," he said, reaching for the slides, head already buried in his scope. She whistled as she left the Path Lab.

Faye had recovered nicely over the ten days in the hospital. Before she was discharged, Shelly popped into her room to be sure everything was teed up for her clinical trial enrollment.

She was jolted by the sight of Faye's contorted body, apparently attempting to get her right leg over her head, in her hospital bed, wearing a standard issue gown, IV fluids running. She did not appear to be successful.

"What in the world are you doing?" Shelly exclaimed, sharp and unprofessional.

Faye burst into laughter, looking like an eight-year-old who had just been caught pilfering candy. Her friend Carrie, standing at the window, shook her head, trying not to giggle.

Faye's mom Sissie slapped her thigh and declared, "I told y'all she wouldn't like you lifting that leg o' yours up over your head, Faye!"

Her maternal love, so obvious even at their first meeting in clinic, was more relaxed now that she knew she'd be bringing Faye home to heal. This was a mother who'd been telling her mischievous daughter "I told you so" for over forty years.

Faye dared Shelly to stay cross with her. She lowered her leg, saying, "I just wanted to see if I could," with exaggerated innocence on her face.

Silence in the room.

Shelly snorted. She didn't mean to, Lord knows, but she just lost all her composure with these ladies. She snorted, and that hurt her nose, so she let go and guffawed. By now Carrie was laughing so hard she couldn't breathe, Faye was shaking and holding her abdomen with a pillow, saying, "Ow, y'all!"

Sissie just smiled like a queen who had seen her subjects in this predicament before. Her daughter, her beloved, causing waves of happiness and joy around her. Once they quieted down, Sissie said, "Well."

Shelly eventually learned that word could signify any number of things when it came out of Sissie's mouth. Sometimes "Well," meant "I am done talking about this—time to move on."

At other times, it just expressed pleasure. That day, when Sissie's daughter was up to her usual shenanigans, despite having a horrible cancer diagnosis and an unclear future, Sissie knew Faye was back. Maybe not entirely, since she couldn't get her leg over her head yet. She'd do it eventually, though. Sissie was sure of that. Today's "Well" was one of pleasure and love.

I agree, Sissie. "Well," indeed.

CHAPTER 8

How Hard Can It Be?

Autumn arrived, but October blistered miserably with humidity and unseasonable rain.

The only bright spot for Shelly was getting a "Congratulations—you passed" letter after retaking her final residency exam, and she proudly left a copy on Dr. Cardinal's desk with a thank you note for his help. She'd felt a flicker of hope that she could move forward with more confidence as the junior fellow, but the test results did not put a stop to the sharp criticisms or the disappointed headshaking from the staff. Weekends became a much-needed time to reset her brain, convince herself that the future was hers, and deal with her live-in boyfriend.

Shelly and Robert painted the back shed, making a singular improvement by that small effort. He had kept the yard immaculate, hedges trimmed, and lawn mown. As they scraped and toiled, Robert spent the hours pointing out the deficiencies in the construction, implying the builders were idiots. Shelly's mind drifted with the smell of sweat and paint.

"All I want to know is why we're wasting our time working on a rental property..."

"*Fenton Green*, Robert, that's why. We're elevating this little rental house with the elegant yet saucy tones of *Fenton Green*, and I will hear nothing more about it. You even have a little splash of it on your cheek."

Shelly left him, pissing and moaning, to have a cigarette on the front stoop. She doubted he would even notice her absence. Robert never needed an audience to complain. His overall glum personality hadn't changed, and in fact the job search had been a challenge that made him more insecure than ever. Shelly sighed, sweating and smoking, knowing full well that she had been spineless and deserved her miserable state. She was right back to resenting his every move, and should never have agreed to his coming down to live with her. From outward appearances, it was a sweet set-up, but for Shelly his presence was an invisible cloth over her mouth, smothering her to death.

She stabbed out the butt in the old conch shell she kept tucked by the door for just that purpose and had a brilliant idea. The massive chestnut tree in the front yard was bearing fruit in a big way. Mowing around all the nuts that had fallen on the grass was a royal pain, though the squirrels grabbed many of them. The spiky outer burrs were too sharp to pick up barehanded. She rummaged through a kitchen drawer to find tongs to lift the nuts into a container. Corinne next door had told her they were safe to eat once they were roasted. How hard could it be?

She put her harvest on a cookie sheet, dialed the oven up to 400 degrees, and checked on Robert through the screen door. She wandered out to see if he'd settled down.

"Where'd you go?" irritation coating his voice. "Smoking again, I suppose."

"I took a break. You were getting crabby, and my scrawny arms were sore. I need to work out or something. I shouldn't be so puny at my age," she commented.

"Well, I think it's pretty much done," he said. "I'm sorry I was cranky. I just hate these rental companies making the tenant doing their own upkeep, is all. Still, I've gotta admit, it looks a helluva lot better. Ernie came over and said he's gonna miss the Crap Cabana."

As they were rinsing off the paint brushes, a sudden gunshot rang out from the front of the house. Shelly instinctively fell to the ground, scanning for the source. She dropped the wet paintbrush on her thigh as she went down.

"Jesus Christ!" Robert yelled. "Who's shooting?" He raced to the front of the house.

Poised

"Robert, be careful! Don't go out there!" Shelly hissed, following him despite herself.

They saw nothing, sidling around the garage, Robert muttering, "I knew I should've brought my gun. Betts said to leave it because you'd get so pissed at me that you'd shoot me with it." Making jokes helped with the nerves they both felt, and they made their way to the front, furtive and tense, seeing nothing. Shelly was sweating still, but now more from fear than the heat, when two more cracks rang out.

"What the hell?" Robert said, when suddenly multiple pops were heard. "That's not a gun, and it's coming from inside."

"Oh, my God, it's the chestnuts." Shelly ran in the front door when more explosions reached their ears. "I put the chestnuts in the oven to roast them--surely they're not supposed to explode?" She turned the oven off, jumping back when the last of the nuts broke free of their burr, startling them both. "They smell nice, don't they?"

Robert gave a relieved laugh.

"You've got to be kidding me," he said when he turned on the oven light. Chestnut detritus, nuts and powder littered the whole oven. "You put 'em in whole, didn't you? Didn't notch the bottoms? Jesus, Shelly, they're under pressure, so they pop. You gotta cut an 'x' in the bottom before they get heated up. Here I thought someone was on a rampage…"

Shelly moved to open the door, when Robert blocked her. "Careful—there might still be some cannons in there. Leave'em till they're cool." Shaking his head, Robert said, "Would it kill you to think before you act?" Shelly flinched at his tone and stormed into the bedroom, muttering "Bite me."

They fell into a pattern of Shelly getting up in the dark and going to work, Robert applying for jobs during the day, and then making a meal he could eat at a normal time and heat up for Shelly when she limped in late that night. When the weather cooled off, they turned off the air conditioner to let in the night breeze. Shelly's best sleep was always with a window open, a habit that Robert liked.

"I don't know the birds in this town," he said one Saturday morning, listening to the chirps outside. "I don't know the trees either and that's saying something." He'd been a naturalist back in Springfield, his childhood on the farm in western Massachusetts spent outdoors as much as possible. Suburban life was never going to be a comfortable fit for him.

Shelly came home one late Friday night when he announced, "I have a job. I'm gonna sell cars. Training is Monday, and straight commission from then on. I like the vehicles, and I think I can steer people right, so…" his voice trailed off, and he waited for a reaction.

Shelly dropped her purse and keys on the dining room table and collapsed in the chair.

"Selling cars?" In a million years she couldn't have come up with a job less appropriate for this man's taciturn, peevish personality than sales. Especially car sales.

"On commission? Gosh, Robert, that's a bit of a surprise. I assumed you'd go for pipe fitting, you know, use your job experience and all," her voice wandered. *Don't be negative—he needs an 'atta boy' after this last month of looking,* she told herself. "Well, how hard can it be? You know every single make and model of car and truck out there. If it's a good product, they should sell themselves." Shelly used all the energy she could muster to sound encouraging.

"Yeah, I think I'll be good at showing the features to the customers, comparing models and all. They told me not to assume anything about the customer by how they dress. They had a pig farmer come in, dressed in overalls and not smelling too great. They treated him right, he knew what he wanted, and he paid in cash that day. Pulled out wads of dough from his pockets. Don't judge a book by its cover, they told me."

Robert heated up a plate of food for her, and they chatted about the location of the training to start the next week. Shelly's pager went off, mid-bite of a succulent pork chop. She recognized the number, grabbed the phone, and wolfed down another bite of food. She had a feeling she'd be heading back in, since it was the second floor Powell calling.

"Dr. Riley here," she answered, chewing while the ward clerk searched for whomever had paged her. *God, I don't have the strength for this man's misguided...*

"It's Angie, Dr. Riley," the first-year resident, more breathless than usual, brought Shelly back to the present, "and it's a little bit of a mess, here. I wasn't sure what to do and Carmen said to page you. She's covering Labor and Delivery and can't come over, so we thought maybe you could help." Angie gave a scattered story of a lady who had come to the hospital with lots of drainage after her recent surgery with Dr. Cardinal.

"Slow down, Angie. Who's the patient?"

"It's Irina Jacob. Remember her? We just sent her home last week. She didn't come to the ER 'cause she really doesn't have the money, and, well, she said she trusted us on the Powell." Angie sounded worried. "There is a smell, Dr. Riley. I think it might be bad, and I didn't want to put her through an exam and not know what to do with what I find."

"Let me stuff down a couple bites of food and I'll be there in about ten minutes. Can you get her into the exam room on the Powell? Make sure there's an exam light, culture swabs and a path specimen bottle with her labels."

"Yes, I'll do all that. She looks right scared, Dr. Riley, otherwise I wouldn't have called you," Angie was on her last weekend call on service, and the night was starting badly.

"No, no, you did the right thing." Shelly sighed. "Just get her ready. And don't let her eat or drink anything in case I need to sedate her. See you in a flash."

Robert slumped, dejected at the interruption. "Going back in? That's okay. I'll tell you the rest of the new job stuff when you get back."

Oh, boy. In the space of two minutes Shelly had entirely forgotten about Robert's new job. "Yes, you can fill me in later." Shelly threw her lab coat back on. "I'll be back."

Driving back to the hospital, Shelly's energy surged as she made a mental checklist of priorities during the evaluation of the patient. Angie had ordered bloodwork, so that should be ready by the time her exam was complete. She might need a CT scan, depending on what Shelly found.

Ken and Dr. Cardinal had performed Irina Jacob's surgery, but Shelly remembered the patient from the days of hospital rounds. She was a malnourished bird-like woman from a rural eastern part of the state, in her mid-60s, and notably modest. Shy, even, with a whisper of a voice. Ms. Jacob had an extensive surgery, massive blood loss, and despite transfusions had remained weak and pale throughout the whole stay. She was only about two weeks from surgery, a precarious time when infection, blood clots, and wound healing issues could crop up.

Shelly strode onto the floor of the Powell Cancer Center, lights already dimmed for the evening, and found Angie at the ward secretary's desk, cradling the phone with her shoulder, scribbling notes and answering a page. She motioned that the patient was ready in the exam room, so Shelly nodded and made her way there.

She tapped on the door, "Ms. Jacob?"

There she was, laying down on the cold exam table, covered in blankets which Shelly presumed Angie had found for her. Still she shivered, her neck strength feeble when lifting her head at Shelly's entrance.

"Ms. Jacob, I'm Dr. Riley. I met you a few days after your surgery with Dr. Cardinal. Dr. Decker told me you're doing poorly? And she mentioned there's some drainage." *And was Angie ever right about the odor,* Shelly thought. There was a pervasive smell that she recognized as tumor. It enmeshed itself in the still air of the tiny room, heavy and foul. This was not a good sign, so soon after a big cancer surgery.

The cachectic woman nodded, a sadness on her face, as if she knew something was quite wrong. "It was all right at first, when I got home from the hospital," she started, "but last night the fluid just poured out of me, real sudden, while I was in bed. At first, I thought I wet myself. I'm sorry to talk of such a thing, Dr. Riley," she said, gazing down.

"Oh, my goodness. Please don't worry about that!" Shelly touched her thin shoulder, careful with the move on such a frail body. "Tell me everything, exactly how it happened. Nothing you can't say here." Shelly urged her to continue.

Once they had finished the history, Shelly helped her get ready for the exam. What she saw was dreadful, with all the odor and fluid being caused by necrotic tissue, old clumps of dead cancer, eroding through her where her normal skin should have been. Barriers had fallen. Her frail body was being consumed, and Shelly could see there was precious little to be done about it.

"It's all just the cancer back already, isn't it?" Ms. Jacob's voice was resigned. "I saw some flecks of something come out of me. It wasn't just water; it was something more solid. I figured it was the cancer coming right back."

"I wish you were wrong, Ms. Jacob. I was hoping it was just a little loose stitch from surgery, but you're right about the cancer. We can't really fix this. We'll need to get you started on chemo right away."

"No." Firmer now, the patient continued. "No, ma'am, I'll not be taking chemo, Dr. Riley. This has been a hard life, and I can feel it slipping, I swear. I believe I'll just be with the Lord and let Him decide things."

"But Ms. Jacob," Shelly started to protest, "chemo might buy you a little time, maybe control the growth of this tissue coming out." Shelly believed what she was saying, but could see that Irena Jacob was no longer listening, and that her mind had been made up.

"I don't believe I have too much time left, Dr. Riley." She whispered. "I'm ready, I swear," as the tears began. "Lord, I am so tired and ready, y'all can't even know. I just wanted someone to look and make sure I wasn't dreamin' or such. No, I believe I'm going to heaven, doctor, and I'm going to start the journey from my own little house. I'm not afraid, not one bit." A brave smile, teeth decayed and brown, as she started to swing her legs over the table to get down.

"Wait, Ms. Jacob, I have a pair of paper undies you can go home in---it'll catch the drainage better and keep your clothes dry." Shelly, kneeling on the linoleum floor, helped her get the undergarments up her rail-thin legs, and then pulled them up over her saggy tush while the patient hung onto the bed for balance. Out of the blue, Ms. Jacob clutched at Shelly, sobbing, and hugging her for dear life.

She cried, "Thank you for caring, doctor. I knew y'all cared about me every minute I were here, and Lord that helps so much. I dearly appreciate that, I do." She sniffled as she gathered her composure and calmed down.

"I don't believe a man doctor would a helped me on with my underpants," she laughed even as she continued to cry. "Lord, I've been blubbering like a baby ever since the surgery, like I'm using up all my tears before I go. I'm glad you could be the one to see me tonight, Dr. Riley. You've got a special touch, and not just because you're a lady doctor. You've got a way that lets a person say everything they need to say. That's a blessing to your patients, I can tell you that. A real blessing. I just know you are going to be a real wonderful doctor to a lot of people."

Shelly cried on the way home, wondering how that impoverished woman, with decaying teeth and cancer destroying her very body, could manage to comfort *her. Being blessed by Irina Jacob is why I went into medicine. If Carmen could have been there, she'd understand the pull. Sometimes, even just a snapshot is enough to see glory.*

The encounter left her quiet when she reached home. She didn't go into detail about it with Robert, who launched into his car sales job description practically at the sound of the key turning in the lock.

"I forgot to mention the salary. Now they only give you a little idea about how they figure…"

He failed to notice her mind was elsewhere, as Shelly wondered about the fate of Irina Jacob, and Faye Colgate, and the hundreds of patients she had cared for in her brief career. She could have tried to describe to him the sudden gripping embrace of a dying woman. She could have gone into the medical details of how she knew the cancer was incurable. Nothing would have done it justice, anyway, and she didn't have the energy to try. She had just been blessed by someone who was on her way to the next place, and that was going to stay with her for a long time.

"Good, Robert, that sounds good," Shelly murmured. "Off to bed for me. I'm woofed," as she headed to the shower.

As they nestled in for sleep, Shelly realized that Thanksgiving was around the corner, and she'd invited Ken, his wife, and their little girl for dinner, even before Robert had called to tell her he wanted to move.

"How's that sound? We can make the bird, dressing and potatoes, and they can bring pie and a veggie. Ken said they were going to have dinner alone, since their families are traveling this year, so I thought it'd be nice to cook it together."

"Have you ever done Thanksgiving dinner before?" Robert asked, "I'm thinking of the pie incident with my family."

"Oh, my God, I'd forgotten about the fresh apricot pie. I was trying to impress your parents, but I forgot to mix the sugar and flour with the fruit. Everyone took a bite and tried to keep a straight face." One of the little nieces had said, "This pie sure is sour," and the whole family erupted at the pure honesty, including Shelly.

Robert came from a huge family, two sets of twins—"numbers seven and eight, *and* nine and ten, if you can believe that" the story always went—and each of them had been lovely to her. It was clear that they were rooting for Robert to find someone who could steer him toward gladness. It was also clear, though, that Robert favored his father, and inevitably they would both start a grumpy, pessimistic phrase at the same time, commenting on the futility of whatever anyone was discussing.

"Good grief, you're both like Eeyore," his sister Betsy had said. "You think so much alike identical words come out of your darned mouths at the same time. Don't you ever get tired of being so crabby?" and she'd walked off to clean dishes, or shake out a tablecloth, just to be free of the sight of them.

Shelly shook herself out of her Massachusetts memories. "Well, I haven't done the whole meal, exactly, but how hard can it be? Turkey goes in the oven, I can use my mom's dressing recipe, and I know how to make mashed potatoes. I even have a baster. It'll be fine."

She shifted in the bed to face him. "Robert, I'll just be so damned glad not to be working, the food won't even matter. We'll round early like usual, and the census will be low since no one wants their surgery around Thanksgiving. I'm looking forward to meeting Ken's wife, Janelle. And their little girl Briane—wait till you see her. She looks like a little Shirley Temple in the picture on his desk, blond ringlets, dimples, the whole deal. It'll be like a day in the life of normal people.

"I could really use a happy moment." Shelly tried to be direct. "This fellowship has been taking a toll, and the lady I saw tonight…" Angie's page to come to the hospital that night irritated her and she felt guilty for that. She thought about what Irina Jacob's life was going to be like over the next few weeks and imagined the family coping with her death and funeral. All her patient's dreams had vaporized, and for this one evening, she and Irina were the only ones in the world who knew that.

"Just one happy moment, okay, Robert? Let's try to make a wonderful memory of Thanksgiving in a new town."

"Well," Robert cuddled her warmly, "happiness is not exactly a condition I'm familiar with, you know. I'm a grump, Shell. That's all there is to it. I'm trying to be more upbeat, but it's just not my nature. I'll give it a go, though. And who knows? Maybe car sales are right up my alley and I'll transform into a real charmer. Don't give up on me yet, okay?"

Shelly regarded this fine, fit man of hers, arm behind his head. She shelved the memory, kissed him well, and reached up to turn off the reading lamp.

"It's a deal, Robert. Carpe diem, though, my crabby boyfriend. Every day could be our last."

"And everyone thinks *I'm* the pessimist. G'night, Shell. I'll see you when you get home."

JACOB, IRINA K. (née Havlik)
aged 63, passed peacefully October 26th

She was devoted to Jesus, and her family knows she was welcomed into heaven and feels pain no more. Cancer was the cause.

Predeceased by husband Edwin, and infant daughter Myrtle. Loving children Samantha (husband Dan) and Francesca (husband Charles) will welcome friends and family to the house for a light dinner after the service at Church of the Savior at 3 p.m. this Saturday. Pastor Callay will officiate. Arrangements by Richardson Funeral Home.

A special thank you to Dr. Shelly Riley for her tender care of our mom at the end.

CHAPTER 9

Just a Hillbilly

"Remind me why I'm going out there with you?" Robert whined as he backed his pickup truck out of the driveway for their Saturday afternoon jaunt to Dr. Cardinal's farm.

"He's got some machinery that needs fixing, he's interested in you because you grew up on a farm, and he wants to make sure I'm not a lesbian, I think," she laughed. "How the hell do I know? He's my boss, and to turn him down is verboten."

Shelly was more than a little curious about the motives, too, since things had been decidedly frosty after the "baby killer" episode at the scrub sink and her failed residency test. Robert's comment reminded her of the surgery when he reveled in the gory details of the national meeting his church group had just held.

"It's just God's natural order that men are the head of the household, Shelly, and women are to obey. And really, the men have the harder job in a marriage." He had finished cutting and clamping a pedicle for Shelly to tie off and continued. "The man is responsible for providing for the family and ensuring the wife is content."

Wanting to barf, Shelly had kept her mouth shut. She'd stayed on guard, and always, *always* prepared for his cases.

When Dr. Cardinal had suggested she bring Robert out to his place for a look at the farm, she was immediately alert for whatever sabotage he had planned. Nonchalant, he said he had a few pieces of equipment he could use a mechanic's opinion on, and he'd overheard Shelly's comments about Robert's uncanny knack with machines.

"C'mon out, it'll be fun!" he'd urged. Shelly very much doubted that, but she admitted to a great deal of curiosity about the man and his home.

"What else do you know about him? Might give me a better idea of what I'm getting into," Robert's question jarred Shelly back into the present as he drove. "Dr. Cardinal is the super religious one, I remember you telling me, and he's got like a hundred kids. Isn't he the one who tells his patients on Sunday morning rounds that if they need him, he'll be in church with his family?"

"Yep, that's him. He's supposedly brilliant, Robert--I mean off-the-scales brilliant. He was a chemistry major in college, I heard, and he reads constantly. He's got a photographic memory and understands the material."

"All you doctors are brainiacs, as far as I can tell. You're every bit as smart, Shell. You're just normal about it." Robert shook his head. "When Betts was trying to fix us up, she said you were the great equalizer in the hospital. You could talk to the janitor, or her when she was your scrub tech, or the old fart doctor who was in charge. You just treated 'em all the same."

"That was nice of her to say." Shelly had good memories of Robert's sister Betsy, partly because she was one of the best scrub techs in the hospital. Shelly had laughed when Betts asked her to meet her brother with the caveat, "If you have any sense at all you'll say no and run for the hills."

"So, what's the conflict? You've never had trouble with all the smart people around you before," Robert wondered.

"Well, there's the female thing. You know I'm the only woman they've ever chosen, right? They prefer their fellows to be married men, with kids in tow. Extra points if they're military--then the government pays the salary."

Shelly shook her head in irritation. She continued, "Then I failed that bloody test from residency, so I'm sure he thinks I'm a dope for that."

Shelly thought about the things she'd noticed about Dr. Cardinal, especially when he didn't know she was paying attention. "It feels like he's putting on a show, trying to be this academic surgeon. When he's alone--reading his journals, learning, thinking--I think he's happy. I snooped on him in his office one time, and he was totally absorbed in a textbook. Mesmerized, really, and relaxed. The rest of his obligations, like handling surgical complications, or interacting with scary liberal Amazons like me, or caving to the head guy who doesn't want any innovations in the department, well, those things are not his forte."

Her voice trailed off. "There's so much he has on his plate. Maybe he's just stressed, and he takes it out on me because…" Her logic failed her.

"Right," Robert piped in. "You stopped because you can't come up with any reason for you to get the brunt of it. Does this Dr. Cardinal jump on Ken the same way he does you? In fact, do any of them? No," he answered himself. "You said they even treat the med students with kid gloves, if you're around to attack."

The land was much hillier now, and Robert gave the truck a little gas to meet the rise. The mid-October vistas were gorgeous, still a lush green but with a hint of autumn drought at the crisp field edges. Sweet horse farms dotted the landscape, their fences keeping the thoroughbreds safe in their spaces, yet able to run. The scent of freshly mowed grass crept into Robert's truck, completing the rustic effect. Shelly knew nothing of racing, but even she realized they were no ordinary animals when she saw those rippling auburn muscles.

"I think this is the place," Robert said. Iron gates flanked the long driveway ahead. "I checked the map before we left, and I remember this big curve in the road." He turned into the farm. "If he tries to convert me, I'm outta here!" He smiled as he said it, already appearing more at ease than he had been for months. He knew exactly where he was, cruising down the dirt road, watching a farm dog come running to greet them, barking and yipping.

"Yep, gotta have a dog on a farm. Hey, Shell." Robert grinned as he and Shelly hopped down from the truck. "What if I like the guy?" Belle, the beagle Dr. Cardinal had mentioned in the OR, was all harmless wiggles.

"Hey, there, girl, hey girlie," Robert patted her as she promptly lay on her back for a belly rub.

Dr. Cardinal came out shortly after their arrival, wiping his hands with an old towel. "The welcome committee approves!" he called. "That's Belle, our beagle security system. You must be Robert," he warmly greeted Robert with an open handshake, pulling him to the barn in the same motion. "Let me show you around, and Shelly can finally see what keeps me occupied when I'm not pestering her at the hospital," he said.

Wow, beware, Shelly thought. *He's being friendly!* She reminded herself to stay alert but relished seeing Robert so obviously in his element.

"If you do a good job on these tractors, maybe Shelly's probationary period will get shortened, eh Shelly?" Dr. Cardinal smiled as he led Robert away. "Make yourself at home, now. We'll be back in a little while."

Shelly shook her head, hoping her torturer would give some glimpse of his alter ego to Robert so he could verify that she was not imagining things. She watched them wander around the out-buildings, Robert petting the tractors, appearing to commiserate about the known defects in one model, the poetic beauty of another. Belle wagged her tail and stayed close, not to miss a thing.

While Robert toured the equipment, Shelly enjoyed the beauty of the outdoors. She found a redwood glider and closed her eyes in the autumn sunshine, daring to relax. Dr. Cardinal's wife of twenty years, Melissa, came out to greet her with a sweaty glass of iced sweet tea, saying "what a pleasure" and "how nice" like the wife of a workaholic can do. Shelly stopped gliding so Melissa could step in and sit across from her.

"Peter tells me you're not married?" she stated, voice inflection up.

"No." Shelly held up her left hand and wiggled her naked fingers. "Robert and I have been dating for a year and a half or so, but we're not talking about getting married at this point." She elected not to elaborate further. "How about you and Dr. Cardinal? Were you together for long before you tied the knot?" She took a sip of tea.

"Well, in our tradition, we had a pretty regulated courtship, I'd say. Our families were heavily involved, and if we wanted any privacy at all we knew we'd have to marry," Melissa gazed at Shelly to see if she caught her implication. "The kids started coming when Peter was in his last year of medical school. We were so lucky he got the residency and fellowship here, so we could be close to my parents. They were a big help when Peter was working those long hours."

Shelly searched the face of the woman across from her. "You must have your hands full, taking care of your kids and the farm," she started. "Were you in medicine, too, when you met Dr. Cardinal?"

"I was not a so-called 'career woman,' if that's what you're asking. The Lord called me to motherhood when I was very young, Shelly. This life suits me well, and Peter's a great provider."

"We're both lucky, then," Shelly nodded. "I've never really thought of it in those words, but I guess I was called to medicine when I was young. It's great to know what you want early in life, don't you think? I was positive I wanted to be a doctor in grade school. I'd fantasize about it while I watched those medical TV shows. Someday I'll get married and have kids. Just hasn't felt right yet."

Melissa pondered that, quietly adding, "Well, no offense meant, but you're not getting any younger. You don't want to miss the chance to start a family soon before it's too late. Motherhood is a full-time job, Shelly."

Thinking fast, Shelly agreed. "Same with fatherhood, don't you think? Parenting is forever, that's for sure."

Melissa tilted her head, ready to comment. Then she cast a foot over the glider's edge to slow it, and stepped out.

"Very nice to have met you, Shelly. I hope you're able to last in that long, difficult fellowship. Not everyone does," Melissa offered, meeting her gaze, "and you've only just begun." She disappeared into the house.

Stung, Shelly watched her walk away. Even the guy's wife finds a way to tell me I'm unworthy, accompanied with a smile, some sweet tea, and a pitiful look.

If it were a stranger's home, she could have stayed at the handsome farm all day, walking the land and playing with the barn cats.

After the ominous warning from his wife, though, her skin crawled with the same sense of danger she felt in the hospital. She was ready to get out of there. Rising from her perch, she saw the men walking toward her, both with hands in their pockets, talking and nodding at one another.

"Well, it took Robert all of thirty seconds to fix one of the tractors," Dr. Cardinal told Shelly. "He popped the hood, tightened the choke lever, and it started like a dream. The other one, the one he calls "the beast," will need a little bit more work and some parts. We made arrangements for Robert to get what he needs and come back to patch it up. He's got a lot of know-how, Shelly."

"Glad to hear it, Dr. Cardinal. I know how good he is with mechanical things. Ready to head out?" she hoped Robert could sense she was eager to go.

"Sure thing. Thanks for the work, Doctor. It feels good to be back on a farm, I've gotta say. I'll get the beast purring for you once we get the parts. See you around," Robert gave a little wave as Belle escorted them to the truck.

Shelly sighed the tension away as soon as both doors clumped shut. She shook off the notion that even Dr. Cardinal's wife was in on the torture. "You look pretty content, Robert, admit it," Shelly remarked as they hopped up in the cab, making their departure and waving as they drove off. "You ooohed and ahhhed. This is what happiness feels like, honey. You should make a note of it."

"That was pretty good, I agree," he said. "I haven't seen that beast of a tractor for twenty years, but once I tune it up it'll run forever. If he can find the parts, that is. And if I don't screw it up," he added. Shelly shook her head. Robert was tapping the steering wheel in time to the song on the radio.

"Well? Are you gonna tell me what he said?" Shelly smacked him on the shoulder. "Jesus, Robert, this guy is my nemesis–spill it!"

"Not much to tell. We mostly talked about football, I guess. He told me about this Asimov kid quarterbacking at the university this year—golden boy, can't seem to miss. Most of the time we talked about the beast. He knew more about the engine than I expected, I'll give him that." Robert steered away from the farm back to the little rental house, left arm cradled out the driver's window, right hand on the wheel. "Mostly football, though."

"Mostly football," Shelly repeated, shaking her head again and watching the complex, mysterious Dr. Cardinal fade from her side mirror. "The guy's destroying my confidence at work, invites my boyfriend over, and makes small talk about football for a couple hours. Evil incarnate, I tell you. I can't hate him if he's nice to you. I'll bet that's his game plan."

"I don't know, Shell. He likes the team's chances for the division title, he knew all the players, and he loves his tractors. That was literally it. I hate to even say it, but the little guy kinda grew on me. I like his beagle, too."

"Maybe I need to brush up on the team. Except for the fact that I have no interest in following university football in my ten minutes of free time each week. At least I know you'll do a great job, and I appreciate that, Robert. Really."

"You do? Maybe I'll get a little reward, then? Like a boyfriend bonus?" Robert gave a genuine smile, changing hands to steer so he could reach around Shelly's shoulder.

"I think that could be arranged," Shelly agreed with a grin. "Home, James, and we'll get to work on that!"

With Robert's spirits briefly lifted, home life for Shelly felt stable. Warm, even. Her other universe in the hospital was an alternate reality, the difference between an elegant dining room in a five-star restaurant and its frantic cooking stations in the kitchen. The hectic pace of life flew at the hospital, with gobs of facts, worthless fluff, and critical knowledge being crammed into her brain. The rhythm compressed the days into weeks: early morning rounds, day-long surgeries and clinics, weekly conferences, and x-ray reviews in the dark with an exhausted radiologist eager to go home.

Shelly absorbed the barbs of veiled critiques, followed her chemo patients, and celebrated when their tumor markers dropped. She completed the awful statistics class with a passing grade. She'd been a good surgeon during residency, but the sheer volume of cases in fellowship maximized her dexterity, and most importantly added volumes to her medical judgement.

Before their rotation ended, Shelly had a quick session with each resident about their performance. She was most struck by the transformation in Angie. No longer the disorganized sparrow of an intern, Angie had stepped into the role of physician, making plans with confidence and eagerly assisting in the OR.

"Angie, you've really grown. They say medical training is like trying to drink from a fire hydrant. But your admission notes, your presenting on rounds, *everything,* improved. Can you tell?" Shelly huddled with her in their makeshift office on the Powell, tuning out the overhead pages and trying for a little privacy. They swept journal articles and texts off the swivel chairs to sit in the cramped space. She moved the trashcan outside the door to rid them of the aroma of yesterday's take-out.

Angie nodded, "I was never so scared in my whole life, Dr. Riley, as I was to start my residency on this rotation. You and Dr. Mackey made it, well, definitely not *fun,* but survivable. No offense, but it's probably the worst of all the intern rotations. Still, I learned so much."

Shelly remembered how she felt that first morning at the chart rack, not knowing a soul.

"Yep, we were both newbies that first week. Even though it's scary to start your internship on the hardest rotation, the rest of them will be easier. I look forward to hearing good things about you from the other services."

They finished up the formal evaluation when Angie hesitated. "I saw you cut out the obituary on Ms. Jacob, that lady I called you in to see that night? How awful—she died so soon after that visit."

Shelly nodded, picking up the newspaper notice. "It's a habit of mine, since residency, I think. I read the obits every day, and sometimes I even cut out the ones that touch me. Can you imagine? Total strangers… That reminds me to bring this up to my little box in my office. I knew she wouldn't live long, but it caught me off guard, too. I wish we could've done more. She was just so sure she didn't want chemo."

"I didn't understand that word *née.*" Angie pointed to the top of the obituary. "Why's that there?"

"'Nay', it's pronounced, Angie. Not 'knee.' It means 'born' in French. They put it there to tell people women's maiden names, the names we're born with, since childhood friends reading the notice might not recognize the married name."

Angie sat and pondered this, puckering her mouth with another question. "Why do we have to change our names, anyway?"

Shelly's bristled. "We don't *have* to, Angie. I'm definitely not changing mine. For one thing, if men don't have any desire to change their names, why should we? For another, all the licensing and Boards and accreditation would take forever to make the change. I'm going out with the same name I came in with, I guess. Maybe I'll write my own obituary. "Shelly Riley, née Riley" will make my point."

"You're brave, Dr. Riley. That's what the residents like about you. You just keep going even though..." Angie caught herself. "I'd best get moving, then. Thanks for everything!" she called. Shelly smiled to see her Wash Manual thudding on her thigh as she scooted down the hall, still inexperienced but not so afraid.

As her first batch of residents moved on to their next rotation, a new team lumbered onto the second floor Powell, landing at room 201. Shelly's first thought on seeing the three new trainees, all stocky and male, was that the starting lineup for the football team Robert and Dr. Cardinal had been discussing had arrived. Angie's tiny frame contrasted with Burt O'May, the incoming fourth year, or chief resident. He was a huge, chain-smoking transplant from West Virginia. Carmen had filled Shelly in on his background. His whole family were coal miners, with his dad ill from lung disease. As the oldest level resident, he took Carmen's place as the leader on the service.

Burt's size was intimidating, but his personality was hilarious. Afternoon rounds began in Radiology with a review of the next day's cases. The first CT scan on the illuminated board showed an enormous abdominal mass.

"Go ahead, Burt, tell us what you see here," prompted the radiologist, knowing that even the impossibly eager, utterly inexperienced med student couldn't miss the watermelon sized tumor on the image.

"Well, 't'aint normal," Burt said, with no emotion.

The whole crew burst out laughing with this understatement.

"Care to elaborate, Burt?" Ken prodded.

"I believe we'd best take that bugger out in the morning!" he added, eyes squinting with smoker's lines, trying not to laugh himself.

Rounds continued, with Ken shaking his head. "You all are hopeless, Burt, I swear, but you're so damn big I can't bother you about it or you'd like to kill me." Their lightheartedness continued for the rest of rounds.

There was nothing light-hearted about the third-year resident, or PG-3, Luca Dragavei. He was a fire-breathing, fact-memorizing doctor who could not wait to tear into the OR, or a textbook, or the cold pizza in the residents' lounge. It was all the same to him. Luca was like a WWW wrestling star sharing a body with a freshman college student who just discovered poetry. At times he was just too much to handle. "Idle down, Luca" became the team's mantra, and they used it often to help him realize a situation required a little spritz, not axes and fire hoses and a call for reinforcements.

"I finally get to meet you in person, Shelly," he said on their first morning rounds. His booming voice likely woke every patient on the Powell and the two floors above them.

"Hush, now, Luca, it's five in the mornin'," Ken chided him. "You all are gonna need to idle down until the caffeine has seeped through my veins, here!"

Luca grinned. "I hear you're a northerner, and a *female,* no less." He turned his head secretively to his right and his left. "*And* you're shacking up with another northerner," again checking both ways, "*and* you smoke, like this galoot of ours Burt! I told my wife Samantha about you. She wanted me to watch over you as soon as I was on service. I just know y'all are gonna rattle some cages around here. Hoo, boy, this'll be fun!"

Shelly was bowled over by this hilarious young man, an accent stronger than her morning espresso, and a sense of humor she knew was right up her alley. "Why, thank you, Luca, for your protection. It's not a mafia, thing, though, is it? Do I pay dues so you won't break my fingers?"

"Naw, naw, nothing like that. But we both have to watch out for this little bubba, here, our fearless intern," he nodded to Dick Edsel, the intern on their team. Dick was indeed another enormous man, probably 6'2", 260 pounds, and with a baby face that must have served him very well getting out of trouble.

Dick grinned, and in elegant, Queen's English, bowed and stated, "Hello, everyone. I am thrilled to be on this service and am ready to learn and serve as your manservant."

This time it was Shelly who shook her head at Ken. "Looks like we've got some live ones, here, eh? Let's motor, boys. Times a'wastin'!"

Shelly grew attached to her "boys" in only a few days, and they accepted her directions with ease when she ran rounds in Ken's absence. These young men were familiar to her, reminding her of earlier medical friends. Her male colleagues in residency had been especially solid in their admiration for her badass reputation in the OR, deferring to her for second opinions and difficult cases.

Shelly and Ken corralled their team along corridors, through surgical cases, and into the patient rooms on the Powell for hours on end. Each morning after rounds they would hustle down the gleaming steps of Shelly's favorite stairwell, Luca talking at the top of his voice about the last medical tidbit he had read about the night before. Inevitably the hulking chief resident Burt would mutter under his breath, "Will you shut the fuck up, Luca?" The erudite Dr. Edsel, mere months into his medical training and loving every second, tagged along at the rear with pure pleasure. Shelly had a hard time staying serious with some of their nonsense. At least they snapped to when the hour was late and everyone wanted to get home. It became, as with Shelly's first set of residents, a well-run service.

One Monday morning on rounds, she introduced the team to one of her favorite patients, Kristi Bohannon, who would be coming in for her five-day chemo regimen. They prepared the admission paperwork, and Shelly reminded herself to check her labs early that morning to get her IV meds started on time.

Ms. Bohannon had an aggressive cancer but showed an excellent response to her complicated chemo recipe. She'd probably be cured if she could tolerate the fatigue and low blood counts that accompanied the regimen. This was her fourth course of chemo, and her tumor markers had plummeted to near normal. Shelly smiled when she saw her name on the planned admission list.

Kristi's personality was tranquil. She'd go along with all the questions from the admitting department, nursing staff and med student, settle herself in her hospital bed with her homemade quilt, and let the meds do their job. Everyone called her Ms. Bo, and she took every piece of news and every uncomfortable procedure with stoicism. She never talked much about herself. Shelly knew she was from a rural part of the state, hours away. She came alone, and usually had a book in her hands when the team made their rounds.

Occasionally there were delays in a multi-day chemo cocktail, even so much that the patient would have to stay an extra day. That's what happened to Kristi Bohannon that week.

"Dr. Riley, we have a problem up here," the day nurse Francie explained when Shelly answered her pager. "You know Ms. Bo in 232? The chemo admit on course number four? Well, we got a little behind on the infusion Tuesday and Wednesday, so she's going to get day five in the middle of her Friday night."

"That's okay." Shelly finished her orders in the PACU and closed a chart to hand off to the clerk. "She lives far away, so going home Saturday morning should work out just fine. Safer drive, anyway."

"That's the problem," the nurse said. "She wants to speed up the infusion. And she said she's leaving AMA if you won't do it."

AMA, against medical advice. Those were fighting words, so out of character for the sweet, always agreeable Kristi. "Buy me a little time, Francie. I've got one last case of Dr. Farber's in the OR and then I can buzz up there to talk to her. In the meantime, call the pharmacist for me, would you? See what they can come up with safely if we speed things up. And tell Ms. Bo not to worry—I'll figure something out."

Shelly performed the minor procedure in less than an hour, then scooted up to the second floor Powell to find out what the big emergency was. Francie waved her down to tell her that the pharmacist would have a plan in a few more minutes. She knocked on the door of 232 while barging in, like usual. Kristi Bohannon avoided eye contact, sitting up in her hospital bed.

"We got behind on your infusion, I hear," Shelly said with a smile. "And you're threatening to walk out on me, too! Something happening?" Shelly felt the foot of the bed to make sure Kristi's feet were clear and nestled in to sit down.

"There is, Dr. Riley." Kristi pulled at her top sheet in distress. "Lord, I feel so awful, having the nurse page you and all. I just...well, I just realized this morning that they were behind. By a lot. And I have just *got* to get out of here by Friday. No way around it."

"Might I ask why?" Shelly was impatient to cut to the chase so she could start trying to schmooze Ms. Bo out of it.

"Well, you know all the fuss about that boy Karl Asimov who quarterbacks for the university? He's in the papers non-stop. Radio, too. They think he's good enough to go pro."

Shelly had no idea why she was talking about football, but she'd heard of the golden boy who was leading the local team to an unbelievable season. He was everyone's topic of conversation in the hospital. Even Robert and Dr. Cardinal had been talking about the studly QB from this season's team.

"Sure. Same last name as the science fiction writer. Is he from your town or something?"

"Nope. Their big game is Friday night, here on this campus. And Dr. Riley," she said, now staring at Shelly, "every time that Karl passes the football? It's my boy Ham who catches it."

The fierce look of love on her face when she said "my boy Ham" captivated Shelly. Mouth firm, swinging her legs off the bed, this woman meant business when it came to her son. She'd heard parents talking about their kids and realized the adoration was intense. Still, she shivered at the great love Kristi Bohannon had for her teenager. Shelly was convinced--somehow Shelly had to get this woman in the stadium on Friday. Ms. Bo simply *had* to watch her boy run a pattern and catch a touchdown pass in the cool southern night.

"Understood. I'll figure something out for you, I swear—the pharmacist is working on the details right now. But why didn't you tell me earlier? Maybe we could have made up time during the week."

"I didn't want to be a bother, I guess. I just kept thinking it'd be fine."

Shelly pondered this, a woman sacrificing her life-saving chemo to see her son.

"Tell me about him, will you? Is he smart? Always into sports?"

"Oh, Hamish is a brain and a half, I swear. He's taking his hardest classes in the second semester, when football is done. He loves school. We always knew he was a fast runner, Dr. Riley, but we had no earthly idea he'd have this amazing chance to show off his stuff." Ms. Bo paused, then smiled.

"They're the best partners, him and Karl. Ham says he *knows* when the ball leaves Karl's fingers, even though his back is turned and he's hightailing it down the field. He can just feel it, he says. It's really something to see." Her face glowed at the thought of her boy, running down a beautiful green field, fans cheering, enraptured by a perfectly thrown football.

They kept talking. Kristi was a college graduate, had lost her husband Logan to some awful lung disease he'd contracted in the coal mines, and she'd worked her butt off to support her family. Shelly even offered her rather meandering romantic path to her current boyfriend, with no firm plans to have kids herself. She surprised herself, giving personal information away to a patient, but Ms. Bo appeared comfortable with the conversation.

"I'm just a hillbilly from Pike County, Dr. Riley. My two others are grown and married, and I live for that youngest boy of mine. I'll do anything in the world to get him what he needs. Anything. You'll know exactly what I'm talking about when you have kids one day. My only regret is that my husband died before he could see Ham in college. Logan loved throwing him the ball when he was little, and he'd be plumb filled to bursting to see him play for such a big school now. I like to think he can see it all, from wherever he is."

Francie popped her head in, motioning for Shelly to leave the room to speak to her, and giving Ms. Bo a big grin of reassurance.

"Thank the Lord, she can do it, Dr. Riley. The pharmacist can start everything early enough to get her out for the game! I'm so tickled. I'm gonna bring this up at our next nurse meeting, too, to make some sort of system to keep on top of these multi-day regimens. We should have caught that."

"Wait, you knew about the game? That she wanted to get out to watch her son play football?"

"Oh, hell, Dr. Riley, they call him Hambone! Her boy is the star of the university, after that quarterback Karl Asimov! You didn't know Ms. Bo is his mom?" Francie toodled off, shaking her head in disbelief. "I know y'all work too hard, but *everybody* knows Hamish Bohannon."

BOHANNON, LOGAN
(3/26/49 – 8/18/93)

Extraordinary husband, son, father, uncle, and friend. Lover of music, dinner parties and his beloved holler. He was known to take an occasional sip of moonshine.

Logan worked the mines his whole life, and his lungs paid the steep price. Despite fatigue from his illness, he managed to adore his wife Kristi and sons Patrick (Eileen), Kelso (Carla), and Hamish every second he breathed the mountain air. His trusty hound Beasley was never far from his side, and mourns him, as do we all.

Logan's life was lived with vigor and honesty. He would want us all to savor today's miracles, take a walk in the mountains, and have a sip, just a sip, of something strong in the night. We treasure every second we had with him. He walks with the angels now. Service Saturday 8/21/93 at The Living Light Church, 620 Alabaster Road. A light lunch will be served at the church.

CHAPTER 10

I Left My Heart in San Francisco

The weeks before Thanksgiving were consumed by the hospital for Shelly, and the job training and first few days on the car sales floor for Robert. He struggled with the small talk with customers, as Shelly thought he would. Each day was a little darker, and she grew edgy, wanting him to get his first sale to take off some of the strain. He found the money portion of the car selling business repellant.

"It's a racket, I swear. No one should ever pay the sticker price…" and off to the races he'd go, detailing the back-room guys and their attitudes towards customers as marks to gouge.

Thanksgiving Day came, with abbreviated rounds. Shelly pushed aside survivor's guilt of not being on call for the holiday, reminding herself of the countless times she'd been the one staying at the hospital for the day. Once home, she washed and salted the turkey, planning for a couple hours cooking time, and got it in the oven around early in the afternoon. The first blunder.

"Hmm, Robert. I wonder if we should have put it in a little earlier. Well, the little white button will pop out when it's done. Let's peel potatoes and have them ready to boil."

Ken and Janelle arrived, with their little girl Briane ringing the bell about eight times for fun. Shelly opened the door, and everyone hooted and hollered their "Hey, y'all!" and "Nice to meet you" as they came inside. Ken and Shelley exchanged a glance of disbelief at impending leisure.

"You really think we can open a bottle of wine?"

Ken laughed, saying, "We brought two! Dr. Farber swore he would be the fellow of the day and that we would not be asked to come in. For. Any. Reason. Believe it or not, we can actually unwind a little."

"Mom said a store-bought pie would just have to do," announced Briane, causing Janelle to look down with a chuckle. "And I'm starving!" The child jumped up and down, curls bouncing, as if she were a firecracker about to explode. Shelly passed her first impressions of her to Janelle.

"You have no earthly idea," she whispered, leaning in toward Shelly like they were old friends. "Hell on wheels, with a mind of her own. It's what we love about her best, though. You always hear the truth from Briane."

"That's right," Briane confirmed. "And I'm surely hungry!"

Shelly whispered back to Janelle, "Well, my culinary skills leave something to be desired, and I'm afraid I only put the turkey in a little while ago. I am also afraid that I am a pitiful, 32-year-old female with no kids, and I don't have a clue how to entertain Briane."

This made Janelle laugh aloud, admitting, "No offense, Shelly, but I assumed that'd be the case." The next load out of their car was an entire laundry basket of games, books, cassette tapes topped off with a change of clothes. "I never come to anyone's house without hours of stuff for her. Otherwise she'll be up in your face, asking to go to the neighbors to see if they have anything better to play with. Lord, she's bold!"

"I like you right off the bat, Briane, and I declare us friends for life. Now let your dad open this wine while we get you settled," Shelly said, thrusting the bottle at Ken. "Robert, can you show Ken the glasses and the corkscrew? We have exactly twelve hours to relax!" She looked at her watch.

"And about six hours before we get the food to the table," Robert smacked her on the tush.

She nodded. "Y'all, my heart is in the right place, I swear, but there's a distinct possibility that I operate better than I cook. The house doesn't even smell like anything except my cinnamon spice candle, though maybe I shouldn't admit that before we eat."

"Well, here's our first toast," Ken said, raising his glass of red wine as they all grabbed their own. "To Dr. Shelly Riley, Expert Taker of Shit, First Year Fellow Extraordinaire, and Keeper of the Chemo Book, for hosting this Thanksgiving dinner. And also for, I believe, just saying 'y'all' for the first time in her entire life!"

They all laughed and sipped their wine.

"Ha! I think it did just slip out," she agreed. "It doesn't sound right, coming out of this mouth. And by the way, how come *you* don't say y'all, Ken?"

Janelle took the narrative of this story, clearly having discussed it before. She gazed at Ken, swatting him on the shoulder while she shook her head. "He unlearned 'y'all' in medical school, Shelly, 'cause he wanted to sound professional. It's just so much a part of him, though, that he had to have something close. So, it's 'you all' for everybody, like there's always a crowd."

They went on like that, hearing quiet confirmations about old embarrassing stories, or chuckling at work tales that weren't too gross to be shared. Janelle was smart and put everyone at ease. She left at times to check in on Briane, who'd set up a pretend forest, complete with ogre, bears, and for unclear reasons a hotel, in the spare room. Robert was stiff, and not particularly forthcoming with stories to add to the conversation. Shelly knew he could never meet the gentle banter without souring the mood.

Hours passed, and Briane came into the living room, put her hand on her hip, and said, "When is that dumb turkey going to be done?"

They laughed, warm with their rare taste of liquor, and Robert gave a thumbs up from the kitchen where he had just opened the oven door. The plastic button had popped at last, and the flurry of carving the bird, heating side dishes, and gravy-making began. Shelly was relieved to smell the succulent humid fragrance waft on her face.

"Well, the bird *looks* gorgeous," she proclaimed. "No promises, though."

When food was passed, and tasting confirmed it was all edible, if late, Shelly looked around at the agreeable gathering around the table.

Briane was squealing with delight at her dad's terrible jokes, while Ken hooked his arm on Janelle's chair, pleased and relaxed. Robert, though, sat at his place, stabbing the meat, exuding a sense of not belonging. Anger, almost.

Shelly was not naïve. She knew relationships were a lot of work. But the misery that overtook her during her one shot at a festive and social meal stiffened her resolve to break free.

You said you'd end it if things didn't change, she reminded herself. The contrast between her emotions and the happy connections between Ken and Janelle made her decision obvious. It had only been a few months, but she knew that she would have to ask Robert to move out. Their guests left after dinner, Briane sound asleep in Ken's arms, thanking them and praising the delicious meal. By this point in their relationship, Shelly knew Robert's ugly mood was best left alone. As they silently cleaned up and fell into bed that night, she promised herself to be single by the new year.

* * *

A tiny glimmer of excitement in Shelly's work life was the annual conference for the whole surgical sub-specialty. There were presentations to make, publications to discuss, and old friendships to rekindle. Academic centers prided themselves on getting their fellows to attend, since those with the best fellows were noted by the others with admiration and jealousy. Shelly couldn't tell which was the higher motivating factor.

The week after Thanksgiving, Arlys paged her to say she'd be allowed to travel with Ken to the winter conference in San Francisco. Any break from the grueling hospital routine was welcome, and Evie lived there, so a quick coffee or dinner with her might be a possibility. Since vacations were frowned upon by the administration, this thrilling news signified a mini break from the workload.

She got home that night with a lighter step, and Robert noticed her good cheer immediately. "Well, what's got you so smiley? Ten-pound tumor removed?" He was surlier than ever, with life as a car salesman not panning out to be his dream, and precious little else to change his mood.

"No," she answered, trying not to feel deflated, "though I did take one helluva big mass out this morning, now that you mention it. I got a call from Arlys that they were letting me go to the conference in San Fran! She certainly kept me waiting until the last minute. I thought for sure I'd have to stay behind and keep things afloat while they were all away. Dr. Farber's going to stay back and round with the chief resident in the afternoons. I'm so excited! I might even be able to meet up with Evie—I'm going to call her tonight."

Shelly took off her coat and shoes, throwing her purse and lab coat on the kitchen table.

"I remember the time I flew out to California when her twins were a year old. I told her I'd watch the kids while she ran some quick errands." Shelly laughed as she perched on a dining room chair to face him. "I had no idea how to take care of *one* toddler, let alone twins with a telepathic demon language." She smiled at the memory.

"The kids watched their mom shut the door, looked at me, and then at each other. Within seconds one was in the stereo cabinet, the other one was in the fridge, *literally* inside. Even her dog got in the act, snarling at me and baring his teeth. I'm glad we all made it. And that was the best contraceptive plan on earth, let me tell you. Twins? Never! I don't know how your mom could have handled two sets of them."

"Hmm. Well good for you. I guess I'll just stay here and stare at the walls. I sold another car today, but I don't know if I'm cut out for this job. So unpredictable." He stood up from the couch, arms folded.

Shelly thought about how to respond. Too happy or too sad, in his opinion, would make him even grumpier. She was an old hand at threading the needle of Robert's moods, but it was a burden she just couldn't take that night.

"Robert, that's something you're going to have to figure out for yourself. The way I see it, though, if you're a car salesman, and selling a car doesn't get you excited, then maybe it's time to think up a different plan."

Shelly stood, lit a cigarette, and exhaled with force. "I suggested counseling in Massachusetts. I suggested trying an anti-depressant.

You declined, remember? So now we're back in the same routine as last year. You're crabby, you're resentful, and I'm at a loss for how to help you. And Robert? Sullen is not a good look."

"Really?" he sneered. "Well, pardon me if I'm not as perfect as you, Shelly. I've been keeping the house nice, doing damned near all the cooking, and trying to make a new career stick. And I'm sorry, but some things just don't come as easy to mere mortals like me." He turned his back and sank into the couch, facing the TV and turning up the volume.

"Give me a break, Robert. You'd have to cook and pick up after yourself at home just like you do here, and you knew what you were getting into. I even warned you not to come. Well, I'm sick of it. I have enough of my own shit to deal with. I'm going to take a shower and call Evie," and she strode off to the bathroom.

This is on you, you know, she fumed as the hot water pummeled her sore shoulders and neck. *This is exactly how you felt in Massachusetts, and you let him move down here anyway.* Tears streamed down her face, mixed with shampoo. She had been spineless, and knew she had to do something about it, but didn't have the strength to confront the issue head-on. That made her even more irritated, because she projected such a confident outer appearance, and liked to pretend she was direct and honest in all things. *You're just full of shit,* her inner voice taunted. *Total imposter, and you're miserable because <u>they</u> see right through you.*

She fled the home scene early the next day, arranged the flights and hotel for the conference while at work, and allowed herself the thrill of fantasizing about hotel sheets and drinks with friends. When the day came to go, she and Ken had perseverated on every detail imaginable about the hospitalized patients and what might go wrong. They left Burt with a list a mile long.

"If Faye Colgate comes in, call me," Shelly said.

"We'll page you with a number to call back each night," Ken added, "to run the list and see if there's anything else to go over."

Burt made a shooing gesture, "Would y'all just git? I can handle three days without the two of you asking me about every damned path report and tumor marker. Just git, now!" and he turned his considerable girth to the resident's room door, cocking his head to add, "Don't get too drunk at your fancy conference happy hours. Oh, Lord, who am I kidding, you two probably don't even know how to drink. Just git!" And with that, Ken and Shelly looked at each other, and laughed their way to the airport.

The conference was a smash, though Shelly would have listened in rapt attention to a dental convention speaker describing a new flavor of floss, so hungry was she for a chance to rest, learn, and process new information without being shamed or mocked. She went to every plenary session, moving often in the huge ballroom to avoid the freezing drafts or chatty audience members distracting her.

She was thrilled to see two of her three mentors from residency on the second day. Dr. Kirk Norman, a gruff but beloved father figure to her, had been delighted to help her get a fellowship. At her interview, he'd squinted and told Shelly he'd be willing to train her and get a fellowship. "Are you ready to do a hell of a lot of work for it? I've got about twenty papers I haven't finished, and original clinical research to put together. Plus I've got to cut, you know. You don't cut, you don't pay the bills." She was captivated, and ranked his program first, and squealed when the mail came with the acceptance letter.

The other attending, Dr. Rhonda Devlin, was younger and less experienced, but a devoted teacher and professor. With her sharp Boston accent and red hair, Dr. Devlin notably and vigorously clutched her own body parts when lecturing. Shelly nearly died during a Devlin lecture on breast surgery, when the intern next to her started silently counting the times she grabbed her left breast while presenting. They all adored her.

Shelly lied admirably when Dr. Kirk Norman mentioned she looked too thin. "I'm cutting, Dr. Norman. Remember? We don't cut, we don't pay the bills!" He nodded at her recall of his quirky comments.

"Did we do right by you, Shelly? Did we get you ready for fellowship?"

Hmmm. What's the right answer to that? "Well, Dr. Norman, I was certainly prepared for the long days. I get a lot more sleep as a fellow, so that's a blessing. The residents are good. No major slip-ups so far." She made small talk, diverting them to the gossip about the others back in Massachusetts.

Dr. Cardinal saw them all standing together, and sidled up to them, oozing charm. "Well, hello, Dr. Norman, and Mrs. Norman?" his voice rose, not recognizing Dr. Devlin.

"*Doctor* Rhonda Devlin, Dr. Cardinal, pleased to meet you," her nasal pronunciation "CAH-dinal" catching him off guard, reaching out a hand to shake. "I wouldn't be Mrs. Kirk Nah-man for all the tea in China."

Dr. Norman shuddered in agreement at the thought. "We hope Shelly's meeting your expectations. My department enjoyed having her, and we were just telling her how we missed her enthusiasm and skill." Shelly could have kissed them both on the lips right there, grateful for praise that brought her back to a medical world she'd inhabited with so much pleasure.

"She's doing fine, aren't you, Shelly?" Dr. Cardinal, not missing a beat as the lights in the ballroom dimmed, looked like he couldn't be prouder of her.

"Lecture's starting, and our things are over there," Dr. Norman pointed across the room. He directed her, "Be good now! We'll find you later and take you out for dinner tomorrow. Deal?" Shelly nodded as they ambled back to their seats and the room became dark. To her surprise, Dr. Cardinal stayed with her, taking an unoccupied seat and settling in for the next hour of talks.

At the end of the lecture, the audience applauded as the lights came up. Dr. Cardinal stretched his legs for the break. "How are things with Robert, if you don't mind my asking? He did a nice job with the tractor repair at my place."

"Well, relationships are a lot of work," Shelly answered, trying not to sound miserable. Even the tiniest of reasons to think there was a chink in her armor, especially something so emotional, so female as an impending breakup, was ammo Shelly refused to give him.

"Hmm," he said, softness in his voice. "That's definitely true." He paused. "There should be a lot of joy, though, too. Quite a bit more *joy* than work, I'd say." And with that, her tormentor, her judge, put his hand on her shoulder with a reassuring grip. "You were an English major in college, weren't you? I'm sure you remember Thoreau writing in Walden something like, 'Go confidently in the direction of your dreams. Live the life you have imagined.'" He stood to move with the masses of attendees to the coffee break area. "I always liked that quote."

Shelly sat motionless in the ballroom chair, hundreds of physicians streaming around her, all chatting with new and old friends. When was the last time she had felt real joy with Robert? Unqualified, comfortable happiness had probably only been the first few infatuated dates, and she knew it. The rest of the time had amounted to the losing game of trying to smother her own distaste for his pessimism and gloom.

The truth of it hit her at once. To be a grown woman, a strong and honorable adult, it was time for her to face reality, and take ownership of the future she wanted to build. She had to end the relationship as soon as she returned.

She saw Evie that night, and they ate vegetarian Japanese noodles at her favorite eatery. The aroma of savory broth filled the cozy nook. Settled into a booth and surrounded by bonsai and tapestries hanging on the alcove's wall, they talked about fellowship woes, special patients, and relationships.

"You're supposed to slurp ramen, Shelly," Evie counseled her. The fragrance of the noodle soup nourished her, and the sound of her impeccable friend sucking the thick and ungainly noodles into her mouth did Shelly's heart good.

"How do you tell the difference between nitpicking in the OR versus constructive criticism?" Evie wiped her chin with the thick cotton napkin. "Because I'm feeling it, too. I get this sense that I'm not up to par, somehow, all while I'm just drowning trying to keep up. And frankly, I think I'm at least as good as the other fellows."

Shelly nodded. "For one thing, the other fellow notices it. He's told me a few times that they were never like this to him. In fact, once Ken made a terrible mistake in judgement. I'll spare you the details, but he shouldn't have operated on the patient, and she died post-op. You know what the staff did? Brought him to the office to ask him if he was okay and told him everyone makes mistakes. If that had been me, Evie, they would've fired me.

"Then there's the discrepancies I see every day. Cardinal told me my posture was bad in the OR. 'You can't look confident if you're slumping...' or something like that. The guy's literally six inches shorter than me. I have to bend over to operate, right? No one else who's tall on the team gets the posture comment. Farber told the *med student* how nice it was to have someone 'with such good hands and who was teachable.' He literally moved my hand from the field to let the med student throw a stitch."

Evie shook her head. "Sounds bad. What about the third attending—the guy who's not really a gyn onc?"

Shelly thought for a moment. "Dr. Boldon? I get a bad feeling about him, to tell you the truth. Oily. He's not around much, with all the admin stuff he has to do, but a couple people have warned me not to be alone with him." Shelly shook her head. "Not exactly reassuring."

Shelly and Evie finished their ramen, comparing notes on their impressions of training. It was a relief for both to have an outlet away from work and family, and they parted with plans to call each other more often.

"It's good to have you to talk to, Shell," Evie told her during their goodbyes. "Helps me realize I'm not crazy. Call me later, and safe trip home." She headed downhill for her bus, as Shelly walked for several blocks, up and down the iconic hills of San Francisco's streets, and entered her hotel feeling lighter than she had in months.

* * *

The next day's lectures were more of the same, and Shelly's brain was starting to fatigue. The dinner out was fabulous, and Dr. Norman and Devlin bickered with one another just like they had done in her residency. They ate oysters and steak and drank a ridiculous amount of wine, with Shelly begging off so she could pack for the early flight in the morning. She felt nourished, replenished, and ready for whatever lay ahead.

The bedside alarm went off like an explosion in Shelly's head. Catching a taxi with Ken at the front of the hotel, he cocked his head and told her, "Lord, Shelly, you're green!"

Shelly winced. "Don't talk so loud," she whispered. "I drank an entire bottle of red wine last night and I'm trying not to hurl."

He laughed, knowing how it felt to have others pay for an extravagant meal. Saddled with debt, doctors in their thirties still acted like paupers because, well, they *were* paupers.

"I'm glad my seat is nowhere near yours. You all keep your hurling to yourself, now, hear? We've gotta hit it hard when we get home!"

They arrived after a quick transfer to a puddle jumper in a neighboring city airport and grabbed a cab to drive straight to the hospital.

"Farber needs one of us in room four," Ken said, looking at his pager, "and there's a Gold Surgery case going in room eight that one of us should scrub. Wanna flip for them?"

Shelly thought a moment. This would be a good time to test the waters and see if Dr. Farber would tolerate her presence now. It was getting closer to the end of Ken's second year, and the head of the division was going to have to trust her at some point.

"Would you mind if I take the Farber case? I need him to see my winning ways, since you're going to bail on me in a few months and leave me to manage this shit show on my own," Shelly said, hitting him on the shoulder. "We can trade if you hear him wailing for you."

They dropped their suitcases in their respective locker rooms and hustled into the ORs, no longer thinking of the flight, or the airplane food, or the conference. Shelly read through the chart, verified the procedure with Kit and checked in with Luca, who was helping get the patient's body positioned properly.

"Good conference?" Luca hollered across the room with a grin. "What did y'all do at five thirty every morning in that posh hotel when us peons were rounding? Roll over and ring for room service?"

"Who says I'd gotten back to my room by five thirty?" she asked with fake innocence, dropping her pager, watch and rings on the desk where Kit sat shaking her head.

"He's been *impossible* with no fellows reining him in these last couple days, Dr. Riley," Kit said, loud enough for him to hear.

"I need a vacation, Kit," Luca protested. "Now that I think on it, I need a conference in Antigua, that's what I need!"

"You need a spanking, Luca, and you know it. The law is back in town, son, so time to straighten up and fly right!" Shelly adjusted her headlight and walked out to scrub. Back in town? That was for sure. No more time away for the next six months at least.

She started the case, with everything going as expected, when the travel, rich food, and red wine caught up to her. Shelly felt drops of moisture on her brow, unacceptable when leaning over an open abdomen.

"Can we lower the temp in here? I'm roasting. Kit, I hate to act like Chad Everett, but I need my forehead swabbed." The nurse came to help as Shelly stepped away from the surgical field for a moment.

"We all know that's why you went into medicine, Dr. Riley." Luca regaled the room with a story she had told them once on rounds. "You saw an episode of *Medical Center* when Dr. Joe Gannon came strutting out of the OR, wearing scrubs and a surgical cap, looking all handsome and official, big medical doors swinging open, worried family waiting for news. But the important thing was, he had sweaty armpits. And you just thought, *Dang! That's what I want to do for a living!* I mean seriously, who decides their career based on sweaty armpits?"

That was it. The image of the smelly wet armpit tipped Shelly over the edge, and she knew it was a choice of *where* to throw up, not if. Still tethered to the headlight source, she started to panic, not knowing if she could free herself quickly enough to get to the scrub sink. "Kit, help the doctor!" The authority in Velma's voice alerted Kit to move quickly.

Kit took one look at Shelly's face, unplugged her headlight, and got her out the door in seconds, just as Dr. Farber was walking in. Shelly ripped off her gown and gloves, gasping the cool air in the corridors, and threw the headlight on the floor. Cool water on her face snapped her out of the wave of nausea, and she could lean over the scrub sink and take deep breaths while the horrible sensation passed. *Oh, my God, I was seconds away from throwing up on his shoes,* she thought to herself.

"Why, what is it, Shelly? Is it cramps?" Dr. Farber's befuddled look aggravated Shelly even more.

"No, Dr. Farber, it's not cramps. It must be a GI bug, I guess,

Poised

from one of the meals at the conference." *Yeah, like the one last night, accompanied by an entire bottle of a Seghesio Zinfandel from Sonoma.*

"I already feel better, sir. It was just a wave, and I thought it was best to step away. Just give me a second," Shelly really did feel better, and had cooled off quickly. "I'll be back in about ten minutes, Dr. Farber. Luca is in there now, and Ken is scrubbed in that Gold Surgery case in eight." She didn't give him any time to protest, striding away to the women's locker room where she could change scrubs, sit with her head between her legs, and compose herself. Soon she returned, finished the case, and felt back to normal, for the most part.

She waited for Dr. Farber to leave, then remarked while she was closing the abdomen, "I'm *not* pregnant, if anyone was wondering."

"Well, that's good, because we all were," Velma admitted.

"Too much rich food at the conference, and an early flight, is all," Shelly explained. "Thanks, by the way, for clearing the path so I could avoid making a mess in here, Velma," Shelly said with appreciation.

"No problem, doctor. I haven't seen that color green in quite a while, I'd have to say. Not since my husband got hungover on our honeymoon, I believe!" The whole room laughed.

Shelly assisted Luca in closing the incision and had a grim thought. Only one thing could be worse than nearly puking on Dr. Farber. That was going home to ask her live-in boyfriend to move out. Yet that was the next task at hand, and there was no way of getting around it.

She drove home, saw light from the TV on in the living room, and unlocked the front door.

"Decided to come back after all, eh?" Robert neither turned his head nor got up from the couch.

She leaned the suitcase on the foyer wall, sighed, and answered, "Must be a really good program, Robert."

He pushed the off button on the remote and turned in her direction. "I know you want me to go. I've known it for a while, and I got mad about your trip because I knew you'd realize you're better off without me out there. That's what happened, isn't it? Came to your senses?"

He looked beaten down, but not sad, exactly. More like resigned to the facts, and already moving on. He pointed to some newspapers, marked with yellow highlighter. "I've looked at a couple apartment rentals here, and I think I can make it work, with what I've saved, and the paltry salary I'm earning. Maybe you want to go with me and look on Saturday? Thought you could be my reference." He kept looking down.

Shelly fell to the couch, looking at his face, and wishing there were another way. "I just can't do it anymore, Robert. Our personalities don't mesh, and I can't go on trying to change you. Neither one of us is going to suddenly become a different person." She added a couple trite phrases, finding those that came to her tongue had truth to them. Robert agreed it was for the best, though it hurt like hell. Then he surprised her.

"I'm not sorry I came down here, Shelly, and I'm not sorry I tried my best with you. I know I'm a grump, but these last few months have given me a little courage to keep trying things out. You're always telling me 'Carpe diem' because of all your cancer patients, but I already knew that life is short. I just get in a rut and feel scared to branch out. You helped me be a little brave, at least this once. I'm not sorry about that at all. In fact, I'm kind of proud of myself!"

Somehow, they sorted out a plan going forward, without tears or outbursts. Both felt that the break was inevitable, and Shelly felt relief at the decision to separate. As she thought about Robert staying in town away from his family, she knew she'd have to fight the urge to be his savior. It had been nice to have a companion, but it was time to move on.

"You have to find friends, Robert. Seriously. Don't be such a horse's butt about letting people in your life. And now that we've decided our entire futures, I've gotta shower and hit the hay."

With the miserable conflict no longer eating at her, she slept well at last. In the morning she found Robert asleep on the couch. She went about her espresso ritual in silence, slipping out at the usual time. She shut the door on another relationship, failed and painful. She felt the tiniest pang of guilt when she realized how much she was looking forward to living alone again. Dr. Cardinal was right about living the life one imagined. There really was no other way. Brave or not, alone or not, she had things to do that she couldn't resist.

Off we go to the next chapter, she thought, lighting a Marlboro and starting up her little red Festiva. Let's see how much these capable breasts will piss them off today!

"Go confidently in the direction of your dreams."
  Thoreau.

Shelly Riley, née Riley

Born March 1962, died ...
Shelly was proud to keep the
name she was given at birth.

blah blah blah

Shelly's career as a gynec-
oncologist was a blessing. She adored
her patients, and she hoped they
could tell.

You know how obits always say
send money instead of flowers? Nope!
Send lots of flowers, come tell funny
stories at her funeral, and have
a wonderful time. Then — give to a
charity to help others. Be nice to clumsy
people. Adopt a dog. All of that
would please her. Don't waste time
mourning her — you have to make the
most of your dash.

CHAPTER 11

A Glorious Rising Indeed

It was Eastertime, and Shelly's mom Catherine was flying down from Minnesota for a week. There would be home cooked meals, evenings to catch up on news from home, and Shelly hoped to sneak out early one night to treat her mom to dinner at a nice restaurant. She knew two things from phone calls from her mom over the last few months. The first was that she would not visit Shelly until Robert was no longer living with her. The second, from her tone of voice and her pointed questions, was that she was worried about her only daughter.

"I've heard springtime is glorious there. We could find a church and go to Easter Sunday services, if you don't have to make rounds," her mom told her on their last late-night call. "I thought I'd make a batch of spaghetti when I get there, so it'll be ready for you whenever you get home. Maybe we could go to the grocery store the next day? I'd like to see what the stores are like in Kentucky."

Shelly smiled to herself, hearing the excitement in her mom's voice. Oh, boy. The menu was being planned, so she meant business.

"That sounds delicious. Maybe your beef burgundy another night?" Shelly could hear her mom dragging on her cigarette just as she was doing. "And we'll have a fancy dinner out, too. I'll definitely drive you around on the weekend, so you can see the horse farms. It'll be so fun, Mom. I'm glad you can come!"

Shelly sprawled out on her couch, lighting another Marlboro. They chatted about events in Minnesota, where her family lived. It sounded like all was well, aside from mild concerns about her beloved grandpa's memory. Catherine Vedman had adjusted to life as a widow, having lost her husband to a heart attack when Shelly was an intern. Shelly hadn't known the man well and didn't see him as a stepfather. Still, he'd been good to her mom during their ten years of marriage, and his death had caused Cath a good deal of misery.

"I don't think there is a single Episcopalian in town except me, Mom. I'll snoop around and see what I can come up with. You'll love my little house. Cute neighborhood, super close to the hospital. You can have the futon or my bed – I'll make sure both have clean sheets."

Shelly relished having something to plan for, something joyful, outside of work. The hospital had become more miserable, knowing Ken would be gone at the end of June. She felt worse than ever with her bosses in the department. No matter what she tried, her efforts fell flat. The biting, almost savage comments directed at Shelly on rounds, in the OR, and in clinic were taking a toll.

Her latest burden was the original research paper that all fellows were expected to complete to graduate. Given the number of quality labs at the university, she assumed she'd be welcomed to do cutting-edge scientific work. Instead, the staff members informed her the paper would be a clinical review on ultrasound results from the department's large database. Shelly was deflated. Her peers had already published numerous papers from that information. No one in the academic world would care about a reworking of the same, tired theme coming from her university, but it was obvious that this wasn't her decision to make. She spent every free moment printing out ultrasound reports, getting other articles from the medical library, and trying to understand what her data showed.

"Well, I know one thing," Shelly confided in Mona, also a first-year fellow in reproductive endocrinology. She had popped over to Shelly's one evening for a whisky and a chat. "I didn't retain a thing from my statistics class! Thank God the department statistician is helping me. The computer system's not meant for extracting the information I need, so I'm doing it all by hand. It's a slog."

Mona shook her head. "Honestly, Shelly, your program is brutal. My paper's supported by the whole division. The secretary, the program head, and the lab director meet me once a week to go over progress. That's the only reason I'm so far along. They keep me motivated and give me protected time every other week. You should complain," she recommended.

"Complain? To tell you the truth, it never occurred to me," Shelly answered. She blew her smoke out the open screen door, the spring air wafting in to freshen the winter's accumulation of her cigarettes. "It'd be an admission of failure, and they'd fire me. The continents would shift. Sirens would blow citywide emergency alerts. Can you imagine, the only woman fellow, unable to hack it? Nope. Gotta muscle through it and get this paper done. Then defend it at Boards."

Shelly sighed, trying to gather her thoughts. "It isn't even the paper, Mona," she admitted. "It's the sense that I'm subpar, somehow, and don't deserve to be here. *Nothing* improves their terrible impression of me. I've been cheerful. I've been quiet. I even got a little lippy last week, trying that out for size. Dr. Farber caught me in the hall, rubbed my back in that creepy way, and asked how the patients were. I said, 'Well, they all have cancer, Dr. Farber,' and kept walking. I mean, he doesn't actually want any patient details, anyway, so…" Her voice trailed off.

"I'm sure that endeared you to him," Mona giggled. "You never swear in front of them?"

"Oh, God, no. I don't let a speck of the real me out in front of them. Sometimes I'm myself with my clinic nurse Anita, but she works with Cardinal and Farber, and I don't want to put her in the position of defending me to them." Shelly shook her highball glass to dislodge the ice, taking a sip. "Mona, you're the only one I even dare let on to that I'm suffering. You're my lifeline, and I know you'll keep quiet. Or, of course, I'd have to kill you!" They laughed.

"Well, it's been noticed in my division, I'll just say that. My superior told me he couldn't believe the way you were treated. I get the feeling my docs are afraid to make waves, though. Your department has a lot of power around here."

That stunned Shelly. She was relieved that it wasn't her imagination. Still, if others noticed, and found it repellant, why the hell didn't they help her? *Oh, shut up,* she thought. *You're a grown woman. Handle your own damned business and quit complaining.*

"Even Ken notices things are bad for me compared to him. But--Mommy's coming to the rescue," she admitted sheepishly. "Ken's going to try to spell me, just so I can catch my breath. Mom will clean everything and I'll eat my worries away with her yummy dinners."

"Well, let me get home," Mona said as she drained her glass. "I'm going to relax and call *my* mom now that you made me think of it." She looked at Shelly and squeezed her shoulder. "Be well, friend. You're made for this work. I just know it. The patients love you, and the residents think you're great. Keep your eyes on graduation. We'll find a spectacular way to celebrate on that day."

"Good advice, Mona. I didn't expect such emotional torture, though. You know we'll be thirty-five years old by the time we finish our training? We've lived almost half our lives and we're still emotional infants."

"Doctors are the best in the world at delayed gratification," Mona agreed. She gave Shelly a big hug and drove off in the night.

* * *

Sleep came in fits that night, and the week was murder. One bright spot was the chemo admission of Paulette Gibbs. Her tumor markers kept responding, and this would be her last course of therapy for now. Shelly went back to chat with her after rounds, yearning for some comforting stories from the lovely woman. Ms. Gibbs was tucked under a quilt in her usual room on the Powell.

"Things are better at home for my daughter Mary Beth. Her girl Ruby finally got in touch, and she admitted she'd been using drugs and carrying on. It's so sad, and hard to believe when I think on her as a child. She's in a rehab house where she had to promise not to drink or use any drugs. So far, she's been able to keep her wits about her. Mary Beth said Ruby just burst into tears on the phone, asking about her son Red." Paulette dabbed her eyes.

"I don't rightly understand why these things are like poison to certain people. My grandpa was a terrible drinker, and we were all so afraid of him. That must've been seventy years ago, Dr. Riley, but

I can still feel the terror that man caused. Do you doctors know why some people get attached to certain chemicals?"

Shelly shook her head. "We don't know very much about addiction. Sometimes you can see it run in families, and sometimes not. We don't have too many ideas on how to help, either. Your granddaughter's lucky to have found the strength to quit, and a safe place to get healthy. What's little Red up to?"

They chatted for a few more minutes, both relishing the warmth. Shelly got up to go, and verified the details of Paulette's dismissal the next day.

"I'll be glad to be strong for Easter services, Dr. Riley. My church does it up like nobody's business, I tell you. The whole altar is covered with Easter lilies. Pastor Frankson gives the liveliest sermon, and Jeremiah Hayes plays trumpet every year." She chuckled, adding, "Truth be told, he's not very good, but he likes to do it. We all offer to the Lord what we can." Shelly figured that was about as naughty as Paulette Gibbs could be.

"Ms. Gibbs? I hope I'm not out of line, here, but my mom is coming to stay with me for a week, and we wanted to go to church that morning. Would it be all right if we joined you?"

"Oh, Mary Beth and I'd be so tickled if you'd come, doctor. It's All Praise Methodist Church, if that suits you, right here in town. You'll just love our pastor, too. He can really help you feel the joy of the day. I'll write down the address of the church right here. Easter will be at 10:30. Make sure you're a little early. We'll have some special food downstairs after. Oh, Lord, wait 'till you see the hats, Dr. Riley."

Shelly grinned. Now she had a church for Easter, her house was clean, and she was feeling almost light-hearted. As usual, she left Ms. Paulette's room in much better spirits than when she entered. She left the Powell to grab her purse in her office when she saw her intern, Dick, making his way down the hall. He was shaking his enormous, cherubic head.

"How are you, Dr. Riley?" He had his usual smile, baggy hospital scrubs, and a white lab coat slung on his arm. "I'd love to share an important fact I just gleaned from Ms. Josten, our patient in 215. Do you have time for a story?"

"From you? Of course!" Shelly laughed. Dick's quirky personality was pure pleasure. "I have nothing to race home for. Come regale me in Dr. Hazel's office, my decompression chamber."

She showed him into the rarely used office, flipped on the lights, and headed for the chair. She motioned him to the couch. "Welcome to the '70's time warp, Dick. I'm listening."

"See the address?" The couch sagged under Dick's weight as he leaned to show her Claretta Josten's patient ID stamp on his three-by-five index card, where he kept clinical notes. "This little town's very close to where my grandparents live, Dr. Riley."

"Dick, you can call me Shelly. Dr. Farber is fast asleep by now, so no formalities required," Shelly urged.

"Well, then, Shelly." Dick leaned back on the couch, arms clasped behind his head, and continued. "This area of the state is gorgeous, hilly country, with people whose kin have lived there for what they think is forever. Everyone knows each other, and there's a little of the Hatfield and McCoy kind of personalities at times."

Shelly nodded. She was becoming familiar with these eastern folks, each of whom took a "nerve pill' and a "pain pill" as well as inhalers for their terrible emphysema, even at young ages. Poverty was a big issue, as was drug usage and heavy cigarette smoking. Family loyalty and pride was powerful. The hospital's social workers never arranged for nursing homes because the family members wouldn't hear of it. They always found a way to care for their dear one at home.

"Some of them make moonshine from a still, and they keep that hidden. And many of them grow marijuana, which they keep *very* well hidden. In fact, there are raids from time to time, with agents flying overhead to find the pot fields. Well, it seems Ms. Josten is quite the marijuana expert!"

"I must be thinking of the wrong patient, Dick," Shelly said, pondering his story. "I thought Ms. Josten was the 86-year-old with a partial bowel obstruction. She was getting better, and we were going to send her home in a couple days?"

"The very one," Dick agreed, "which is why I was shaking my head. This tiny, elderly woman just spent twenty minutes giving me a primer on how to maximize the THC in your pot. She knows how to hang it upside down, when to harvest, how to dry it, you name it. She said, 'I'll deny every word if you tattle on me, now, doctor! And you'll never find my plot, I gar-antee that, if you come looking!' She just slapped her leg and laughed, and said she can't wait to get home. Getting high helps her pain."

"I'd never think to ask an eighty-six-year-old if she smokes pot! Good story, as always, Dick. You are pure light on this service, you know that? It's fun to watch you and Burt and Luca bat at each other, and still get the work done. I know we don't assign you to the OR much, but Ken and I are trying, I swear. Rules are pretty rigid here, and interns are always last to play."

"It's my great pleasure to be on your service, Shelly." He paused. "I'm going to be truthful with you. We think you're fabulous. I've meant to find a way to tell you that for a while. Don't let the workload," again he paused, "or anything else get you down. We're on your side. Well, I'm not sure it's an advantage to have Luca on your side, but you get my drift!"

Jesus, even the fresh intern knows I'm in the shitter.

"Thanks, Dick. I'll keep my head up. My semester of statistics is done, my thesis is coming along, and I can turn the chemo book over to the new guy in exactly two and a half months. It's gonna be a piece of cake from here on out, right?" *Because it could not possibly get worse.*

* * *

Another week flew by, and her mom arrived from the Twin Cities for her first look at Shelly's new home. Cath would catch a cab from the airport, and neighbors Ernie and Corinne would let her into the house and have coffee with her. While Shelly was taking care of business on the Powell, the ward clerk found her and motioned to her to come.

"There's a special delivery here for you, Dr. Riley, and you're not going to believe it." They made their way to the curved desk in the front of the station to behold a massive wicker basket, overflowing with goodies.

"Well, hey, Dr. Riley, I'm Thelma, the one who talks too much." Faye Colgate's dear friend giggled as she admitted her distinguishing characteristic. "I was coming into town for a furniture warehouse show, you know, to get a feel for what's new to add to our store? Hoo, boy, they have some beautiful bedroom sets, I'll tell you.

"Y'all are not going to believe this, but the trend this year is gonna be *walnut*, looks like, and brass for whatever reason. I always think brass looks a little cheap, but that's just me. Oh," Thelma paused and refocused. "Faye said your mom was coming down from Minnesota and set us all to making a little care package. I'm the one who can't rightly cook, you know," she blushed, "so I made her this little piece of jewelry here." She held out a card and necklace made of lovely wooden beads.

"And, Lord, Faye went and made her German Chocolate cake." Thelma sighed. "You know *none* of us look good when we're up against her specialty. I packed that in the center, and it didn't get too smashed, considering the way my husband drives. I thought I was about to meet my maker this morning, I am *not lying*, the way that man takes a corner…" Shelly and the ward clerk were laughing out loud by now, enjoying Thelma's stream of consciousness, and marveling at the pile of treats stuffed into the enormous basket.

"My God, Thelma, how much food is in there? Not that I'll let you take a single thing away. I want to leave work right now and dive into this basket in privacy. My mom'll be so impressed, I can't even tell you."

Shelly looked at her watch. "She's probably in my house by now—her plane should have landed a couple hours ago. You're the absolute best," Shelly wrapped Thelma in a hug. "All my love to the ladies back home. Tell Faye and Sissy we all say hi, promise?"

She joked to the clerk, "Guard this with your life! I'll even share a piece of Faye's cake if you keep it from Luca and Dick."

Shelly finished her remaining work on the Powell, rejuvenated, and broke away from the surgical cases in the afternoon to call home, thrilling at the sound of her mom's voice.

"Riley residence," Cath answered.

Poised

"Mom, you made it! Did Ernie talk your ear off about Robert? I'll bet Corinne made a cake or something." Shelly was surprised at how happy she was to imagine her mom puttering around in her house.

"You're right on all counts. They're a delight, and they love my accent. I figured out the TV, I unpacked my things and I've got a book so take your time. Dinner'll be ready when you get here. Thanks for getting all the fixings for the red sauce—it's simmering on the stove right now."

That was about right, Shelly figured. Her mother was an independent Norwegian, forced to fend for herself when her awful husband Matthew left her and infant Shelly without warning.

Cath's mother died a painful death of metastatic cancer the next month, and Cath stayed home with her newly widowed dad and toddler Shelly. She entered nursing school, insisting to the administrators that she was perfectly capable of graduating. Yep, her mom was a tough cookie who'd have no trouble making herself at home in another city and getting dinner on the table.

Shelly finished work, buzzed home, and opened the door to the lovely smell of her mom's spaghetti and garlic bread. Her little table off the kitchen was arranged with a festive salad, two place settings, and candles. Cath, enjoying a Winston and *Jeopardy*, turned around on the couch to greet her beloved daughter.

"Mom!" she hugged Cath tightly. "So glad you made it. I see the table is set--novel idea, using the dining room table to eat a meal. It's usually a journal and lab coat holder when I'm here alone. Flight okay? And dear lord let's catch up while we're eating whatever is causing that unbelievable smell…"

The mother and daughter sat and enjoyed their meal together, with comfortable back and forth conversation.

"The house is darling, Shelly, and I love your neighbors. Ernie said they are having me over for happy hour every afternoon when you're at work. They're *very* proud to have you as a neighbor, by the way. Except for the exploding chestnuts--they still think you were a trifle dim on that one. Seriously, they couldn't say enough nice things about you. Ernie was sad to see Robert go, but Corinne knew it wasn't meant to be."

"God, Mom, you guys really sorted out my life, eh? Well, it's been great having them next door. I can rely on them for anything. Ken's taking the weekend, so we can tour around tomorrow, and then one of my patients invited us to her church for Easter."

Shelly remembered the gift Thelma had delivered that morning. "And look what that special patient Faye and her friends did for you." She heaved up the massive basket onto the living room coffee table. They admired all the treats, and both were sated with Cath's cooking and Faye's cake by the end of dinner. Her house smelled delicious, looked tidy, and almost felt like home.

* * *

The next morning, they drove around the area, places Shelly had never had the time to investigate until then. The April morning was cool without the dreadful humidity of summer.

"I'll show you the horse farms, Mom, and there's a cemetery I want to see. My nurse Anita told me the dogwoods and magnolias are gorgeous there in the spring." The lime of the unfurling leaves displayed their fresh growth. Birdsong accompanied their tour, and the stunning springtime views of grass and trim horse farms replenished them both.

The hours flew as they admired the countryside. Shelly kept chattering, eager to appear nonchalant and confident in front of her mom. She grew quiet suddenly when she realized her meandering had led her right past Dr. Cardinal's farm. She swallowed, and pushed in the car's cigarette lighter.

"All right, fess up," Cath said as they drove past the farm. "I know you're unhappy, and I don't think it's Robert. What's eating at you?"

Should I? Shelly wondered. *I'm a grown woman. I can't burden her with my stupid feelings of inadequacy.*

Yet out it came. For the next couple of hours, she unloaded as she drove. She pulled over once to cry, sobbing out some of the stories that struck her the hardest. Calling her out in rounds. Criticizing her surgical technique while praising a medical student who could barely keep from contaminating himself in the OR. Failing the residency test. Baby killer. Sighs. Keeping her from scheduling requirements until the last minute. On and on. When more collected, she stopped so they could peer at historic sites, flowering redbud trees, and horses standing in magnificence, hooves deep in already mature grass. They eventually headed into a restaurant the residents had recommended. The packed parking lot prepared them for the crowded interior, tables filled with people holding animated conversations between forkfuls of their meals.

The hostess seated them in a booth, the table spotless and centered with two cruets of vinegar with peppers floating inside. "Enjoy your dinner, ladies," she said, flourishing the menus. "Everything's good here, but most folks like the 'meat and three' choices in the main section."

Shelly finished outlining the various insults and trials she had experienced over the last year. "I'm perpetually confused, Mom, because the nurses and the residents all seem to think I'm fine. I haven't made any clinical mistakes, and I love these patients. I just can't catch a break. It seems they assume I'm going to screw up in every situation, and honestly, I feel like that's exactly what they want. Now why would you want your trainee to fail?" She told her mom about Carmen's "capable breasts" theory, and they laughed.

"Sexism, Shelly. And it sounds like the religion may be a problem—you don't have the same sense of hell and women in their place that they do. Plus, you're different, honey. You've always been a little exuberant, true, but that shouldn't be the barrier. When you were in ninth grade one of my neurologist friends at the hospital agreed to let you shadow him for a morning. You talked to every single patient. He predicted you'd be an oncologist."

The waitress, a short red-headed girl with a pen tucked behind her ear and another she was chewing on, had already refilled their water glasses. Starving by now, they forced themselves to stop talking long enough to decide what to order. The waitress came over again, catching their cues from across the room that they were ready.

"What can I get you ladies?" she asked, her pen hovering over her light green notepad.

"I was thinking about the lamb fries," Shelly said. "What are they, exactly?"

"Ma'am, 'em are lamb testicles, and the small order is six, I believe. The large is more like ten. Comes with soup or salad."

Shelly tried to not react. "Lamb testicles? I'll, um, I'll pass. What else is good?" They ordered cocktails, and Shelly introduced her mom to crackers with pimento cheese, a delicious and fattening pale orange spread. After the appetizers they dove into steaks, greens, and corn pudding, all tasty.

"Home awaits," Shelly pushed herself away from the table with a groan. "I've eaten more in the last twenty-four hours than I have all year. Don't forget Faye's basket still has some goodies, Mom."

"You should've had the lamb fries, Shelly. No guts, no glory. Let's get home so I can get a good night's rest before Easter. I'm excited to go to church down here."

As Shelly headed the Festiva for her little house, her mom at her side and Robert no longer her lover, she felt relief from having leveled with Cath. At least she wouldn't have to put on a show for the rest of the visit. *Maybe Mom will think of something I can do to improve the situation,* Shelly hoped.

"It's good to have you here, Mom."

* * *

Easter Sunday began as a beautiful sunny morning, cloudless and crisp. Shelly wore her outfit from her first day of fellowship, along with the pretty shoes, hoping she'd fit in with the congregants of Paulette's church. They arrived ten minutes before the church service was to start.

The wooden altar was plain, and bare. There was no cross, and not a flower to be seen. "What's the deal?" she whispered to her mom, shrugging her shoulders. "She'd said the church gets all decked out for Easter." Just then she spotted Ms. Gibbs and her daughter Mary Beth. A darling little boy, hair the color of spun gold, perched and wiggled on the pew next to Paulette.

"Are you the doctor from Minnesnowta?" he exaggerated the name with glee, and showed a mouthful of missing teeth. "It's Easter Sunday and I'm-a have a caramel roll after church," he declared.

"You've gotta be Red—your great-grandma talks about you all the time. And this is my mom, Catherine. Thanks for saving us a seat,

Red," Shelly scooted in with the family. Ms. Gibbs was resplendent in an elegant ivory dress, a large antique brooch on the lapel of her matching jacket. Her feet, puffy and swollen, were stuffed into glittering gold slippers. Paulette's fine hat, purple with ivory and pale green ribbons, was one of many adorning the ladies that morning.

Paulette saw Shelly glance at her edematous feet. "Lord, Dr. Riley, they were so swollen this morning I thought I was going to come on into church barefoot!" she told to her doctor. "These slippers of mine are the only thing I could stuff them into, but the Lord doesn't mind. Now, get ready. Pastor Frankson will come in and get your blood up. You won't want to miss a thing," and she took Red's hand as they leaned back to watch the front of the church.

At exactly ten-thirty, a woman ran up the aisle of the sanctuary, exclaiming, "Did you hear?" She looked left. "Did you hear?" Now right. Still running to the altar, she announced, "He is risen! Christ is risen! The Lord is risen, indeed!"

And with that the place went wild. Women from the altar guild rushed in from the side entrance and quickly dressed the wooden table with linens of ivory and gold. An army of men in their Sunday finest brought armfuls of lilies and hydrangeas, bracketed with enormous deep green palm leaves, placing them all over the front of the church. The organ pealed from the back, its massive pipes reverberating in the chest of everyone present.

As Paulette had promised, old Jeremiah's trumpet spurted and strained from the choir loft, hitting a good eighty percent of the tones, Shelly guessed. And the people stood, joy on their faces and hymnals at the ready, belting out the first hymn with the dazzling choir. They swayed in time in their matching purple robes, surrounding the congregation.

Shelly sang along, and eventually told Cath, "The Methodists really know how to put on a show, Mom. You'll have to get your fellow Episcopalians to up their game." Shelly's heart was glad, and she was rejuvenated enough to keep her chin up, report to work the next day, and take whatever they wanted to throw her way. At least for now.

CHAPTER 12

July the First!

Only a month left for Shelly and her nurse Anita to have their weekly Tuesday laser clinics. After July first, that job, plus the Saturday Planned Parenthood clinic, and importantly the chemo admissions responsibility, would all pass on to her incoming junior fellow, Walter Dooley.

Shelly couldn't wait.

"Anita, are you ready for some laser action?" Shelly strode into the clinic for her first Tuesday morning patient, tripped on the carpet edge, and hissed a quiet *shitdammit*. Her nurse Anita was steady, kind, and one of Shelly's biggest fans. Anita had grown up and raised her family in town, earned her registered nursing license at the university, and basically knew where *all* the bodies were buried.

"Oh, Dr. Riley," she scolded Shelly's muttered profanity, "you know I'll be praying for you this Sunday. When are you coming with me to church?"

"I tried out the Methodists on Easter, Anita. Did you ever meet Paulette Gibbs? Ovarian cancer, older lady, lives in town? She's on her first recurrence, but she just finished course six and got a complete response. She invited us to her church, and my mom and I loved it."

Anita shook her head, "Dr. Riley, I need you to come and worship at my place. You know, Black people have relied on the church for everything. Religion, yes. But safety, too, and community, and fellowship, and joy…" Her voice wandered. "It's just the most wonderful place in the world, and I *know* you'll love the music. Promise me before you graduate?" Anita was serious, and Shelly agreed to set a date.

"I'd love to, to be honest. I just don't want to stick out."

Anita laughed, "Oh, you'll stick out, Dr. Riley. But you'll be welcomed with open arms. I'd be so glad to introduce you to my family, too. You know I've never asked any other fellow to my church."

Shelly had felt Anita's care over the last few months, as her spirit felt increasingly crushed, and her confidence lagged. "I appreciate that, Anita." Shelly, seeing no one close by to overhear them, took a chance.

"You see everything. Tell me the truth--am I inferior to the fellows who've come before me? Am I lacking something? Not as smooth, or as smart, or something else? The attendings just don't seem to trust me, and they *definitely* don't like me."

"I wondered when you were going to bring it up," Anita's gaze strayed to the far reaches of the room, as if gathering her thoughts, "and here's what I've come to think. You're a strong woman, Dr. Riley, and that just rubs some people in this department the wrong way. You don't ask permission to step in and do the things your job requires. Why in the world should you?

"But I think they expect a woman to beg a little. Act more grateful to be here, instead of acting like you belong here. Which you do, by the way. Deep down, they think we women aren't as capable as men. That's what they've been told their whole life, and when they're faced with someone so independent, so forward as you? Well, they lash out, and blame you for your audacity."

Anita pursed her lips. "I have a little experience with being found lacking, just at the sight of me. Oh, Dr. Riley, it's a big world out there. This town is not the only place, I promise you, where white people don't appreciate the color of my skin, or where men don't trust a young, confident woman like you. It happens *everywhere*. Your job is to figure out how to thrive despite those who want to block you. And don't forget to help the ones who come after you, now."

Serious talk over, Anita stood and reminded her, "Okay, then, we've got six lasers. And I made my world-famous turkey tetrazzini for the clinic at lunch. You ready, Dr. Riley?" A firm look, a nod of the head, and Shelly knew she had nothing to complain about.

"You're a great nurse, Anita. And your turkey tetrazzini is the most delicious thing I've ever eaten, with enough butter and sour cream to give me a heart attack. I'll miss you and this laser clinic in July. By the way, did you know July the first is right around the corner?" She stood up too, pronouncing it Joo-lye and smirking.

"Yes, doctor, you've told me a hundred times. You're just raring to give that old chemo book to Dr. Dooley, aren't you?"

"I can't think of a better man for the job of chemo doc than the good Walter Dooley. I will hand it to him with pomp, I tell you, pomp and circumstance, and kiss his married mouth on the lips on Joo-lye the first."

Always wise, Anita chuckled and responded, "You're going to miss Dr. Mackey."

* * *

June flew, and Ken snuck away for a second interview at a practice he coveted in Florida. Shelly kept her fingers crossed for him, admiring his skills and work ethic. He'd been a steady presence for her all year and cared about their patients just as much as she did. She'd miss him something fierce, and hated the idea of having to share him with the department for his going away party.

"I'll bet Walter doesn't say 'bite me' on the phone to his patients," Shelly twirled the phone cord at her desk, waiting for Ken in their office after another late night. "And he doesn't drawl, he doesn't say 'you all', and he's not pudgy around the middle. Plus, *he* has procreated the way one is expected to do in this department, and you've only produced Briane. I admit your daughter is magnificent. Still, I find you utterly inferior to Walter and I will not miss you. Not one bit." Shelly poked at Ken, expecting a biting come-back.

"Well, Dr. Riley," he said, arching back in his swivel chair and grinning, looking for all the world like a man without a care, "I'll point out to you that I have more hair than Walter. I'm ten years older than him and I *promise* you, with all those kids, he'll plump up by the time he's my age. May I remind you I will be on the sandy beaches of Florida in a few weeks, on my Wednesdays off? I'll feel the ocean breeze rifling through my luxurious-for-my-age hair and ponder your pitiful existence. I will pray for your soul, I tell you, I will pray on my knees that you survive this last year and get your paper done. Because freedom awaits, doctor. It's within your grasp."

They both laughed, and Shelly avoided eye contact with Ken so she wouldn't tear up. She knew this was as close as they'd get to telling each other how shitty the year had been, and how grateful they were to one another for not making it worse.

"Seriously, Shelly, I've known Walter for years, before I came here for fellowship. He's a good friend, and an unbelievable surgeon."

"I've heard that from everyone. Sounds like he's Dr. Farber's golden boy, wouldn't you say? He gushes when he talks about him. I'll *never* get a gush out of any of the three of them, you know that. I'd be happy with a "Hmm, that didn't suck…""

Ken hesitated.

"Walter's definitely a known quantity in the division, you're right about that. They like him a lot, and he's wanted to do oncology since his first day of internship. I'm sure you two will find your own way to manage the service. I mean, you don't really have a choice, Shelly. You'll be in charge, and you're gonna have to make it clear to the staff that *you* are their senior fellow. So, maybe don't go telling Dr. Farber that his patients all have cancer…."

He turned toward her desk. "And by the way, if you promise to keep your mouth shut, I can tell you that I'm *plenty* virile enough to keep up with ol' Walter on the procreation matter. Janelle's expecting, but we haven't told anyone. She's due in November, and we're tickled." The joy on his face, planning for a new baby and finally finishing the strenuous medical training, was a balm to Shelly. Ken, though, had had all the sentimentality he could take.

"All right, then. As Burt would say, let's git."

* * *

The dinner for Ken was held at Dr. Farber's country club. The room was open and bright, with hushed wait staff gracious in their whisking away of dirty plates and glasses. A massive table heaved with fresh seafood on

Poised

shaved ice, and the dinner guests helped themselves to shrimp cocktail and oysters. The briny aroma smelled like money to Shelly.

The only open chair was next to Dr. Farber. He barely acknowledged her as she sat, and she hoped her clenched teeth passed for a smile. All her senses jangled on alert for whatever her bosses planned to throw her way.

They toasted Ken, Shelly raising a glass of tonic water as she stepped away to answer a couple pages from the chief resident. They reminisced, Dr. Boldon praised Ken's care and skill, and Dr. Cardinal thanked him for his two years of hard work. Ken made all the appreciative gestures one would expect. The tone was far more subdued than the more raucous party the week before, with the graduating residents and senior fellows. Shelly and Ken had both missed that ceremony while operating late in the hospital. This evening would be the only recognition of Ken's graduation.

Despite the collegial tone, Shelly stayed alert to avoid any sign of being too chummy. She noted the easy way Walter had with them all, including her. She pondered Anita's take on the situation, remembering her saying that men just assumed they belonged, and never begged to be admitted to the club. This exactly fit the bill to her, as the buzz of conversation went on without noticing her absent voice.

"You know what the problem with America is, Shelly?" Dr. Farber's sudden question brought her back to reality.

Oh, no. No, no, no. This is not going to go well.

"I'm almost afraid to ask," she said. The table conversation, loose from cocktails, quieted.

"The Mexicans. They don't learn English and they go on welfare, you know. If it weren't for the Mexicans taking all the good jobs from real Americans, we'd be in much better shape."

Shelly had braced for a different racial slur, and it threw her off her game. What the hell? Those at the table tensed, forks down, napkins to lips. Standing, she smoothed her skirt. There was no air in the room.

"Hmm. So many reasons for our country's troubles, Dr. Farber. I'd have to say, though, people from Mexico wouldn't even make my top hundred."

Shelly knew she couldn't stay to listen to more bigoted remarks from her boss. Her voice quivered as she focused on Ken. "My friend, I wish you the best. You're a gentleman and a scholar," she smiled as she bowed, "and I can't wait to hear about your new job. Give my love to Janelle. And if you all will excuse me," she addressed those around the table. "I'd better go tend to the service. A couple things need my attention. Have a wonderful evening."

She swore she could feel every eye on her back as she walked away, *with purpose,* she told herself. As she strode forward, Shelly narrowly averted walking right into the kitchen, took a sharp turn down an unmarked hallway, and tried to pretend that she meant to leave from the employee's exit all along. She escaped the building into the heavy, humid night air, leaned on the wall, and lit a cigarette as she tried to get oriented enough to find her car.

Shelly ran through the entire night's conversation as she circled the grounds, skirting by glistening golfers coming in for a drink. She found her performance woefully unimpressive. Puny in her defense of Mexican Americans, stupid to have taken the bait of such a question, and horrified about what the next year would hold. She was pretty sure Dr. Farber assumed her abrupt departure was for work, not to register her disgust. What a weakling she was.

She plunged her lanky frame into her car, keeping the door ajar while she smoked and tried to calm down. What did she know? She was white. She had grown up in an entirely white neighborhood and gone to white schools.

That lily-white world had exploded in college, though, when Shelly landed at the Philadelphia airport for the first time and saw people of every skin tone imaginable. She'd reveled in cultural differences she'd never imagined, gravitating to people of all races and walks of life in those years. Most were exceedingly patient with her, answering her dumbass questions, and trying to help her understand how she'd been socialized, along with everyone else.

From the Black student she met in line at the college bookstore laughing at a tin of "flesh-colored" first aid bandages to the Jewish boy explaining how he could tell she wasn't Jewish ("Are you kidding me? You're six feet tall and sound like Norwegian is your first language,") she'd made everyone laugh at how utterly unexposed to the world she'd been.

Shelly's fondest memory, though, was of her dearest male friend Daniel. Over coffee in the Philadelphia airport, hours to kill awaiting their flights, he'd mentioned his letter to the editor in their school paper.

"You wrote about being glad there were some movies with gay characters in the Bi-College Film Series? Yeah, I read it. I think it's great that you'd notice something like that. I mean, I don't even know any gay people on campus."

Daniel looked over his wire-rimmed glasses at her, people rushing around them, announcements blaring over the loudspeakers. "Yes, you do, Shelly."

"Nope," she'd insisted. "I didn't know anyone in high school, either."

Daniel had shaken his head. "You *do* know someone who is gay. Think about what I'm saying."

She'd sat there, staring at Daniel, her feeble brain finally understanding what he meant.

"Are you trying to tell me that you're…?" she'd croaked.

"Yes, my dear, innocent, Nordic ice princess, you have been friends with a gay man for a year. I believe you are the most naïve thing I have ever met in my life, and I still love you."

They'd talked for an hour, Shelly peppering him with question after question, and Daniel trying to explain, counsel, and just generally educate his friend on the issue.

"God, Daniel, I can't thank you enough. You are so good to tolerate me pestering you like this. How can you stand me?"

"Well, you straight people are just so fucking ignorant," he'd answered mildly, having had this conversation hundreds of times in his young life. "If a trusted person can teach you and your unenlightened straight friends, maybe we'll make some progress in this world. Gay people aren't the problem, Shelly. It's straight people who need to get their shit together about us."

"Right," she'd realized aloud.

"Now that you've had your eyes opened, please think, read, and agitate. And go catch your plane. I've got to get to my gate." With a hug and a wink, Daniel was off, leaving Shelly transformed.

Those college years flitted through her mind like a movie as she sat, wilting in the still ninety-degree heat. Her Festiva was parked among Cadillacs and BMWs. Taking stock of her life, nearly a third complete, Shelly was unimpressed. At almost six feet, she tripped on carpeting and walked into country club kitchens. She had no fashion sense, no swagger, no boyfriend. Friends and colleagues had educated her in powerful ways about injustice, but she'd made the puniest argument against a racist remark, then had run away like a child. She felt like an imposter.

Somehow, she felt, Joo-lye the first was unlikely to be much better.

SHORT, RUBY
11/2/66-6/3/95

Beloved mother, daughter, and granddaughter, Ruby left this earthly world too soon. Her loving family grieves this loss, and we trust the Lord has something holy planned for our girl. Our hearts are broken.

Ruby leaves to mourn her son Red, parents Mary Beth and Phil, grandmother Paulette Gibbs, and many cousins, nieces, nephews, aunts, and uncles.

Predeceased by grandparents Lehan Gibbs, George and Grace Short.

Funeral service 11am Tuesday, June 20 at All Praise Methodist Church, 342 Boone Drive, Pastor Frankson officiating. Family will greet friends and relatives after the service with a light lunch. Private graveside service will be at the Wallace Cemetery.

Memorials to Clean Lives Sober House, PO Box 112, Elksville, or to the family for Red's education, are welcomed.

We pray that Ruby is free of pain, and no longer afflicted with earthly woes. We take comfort in her sharing her joy-filled soul with the angels. As a child, she glowed. Please remember her that way.

CHAPTER 13

A Change in Plans

Ken's last week was bittersweet for everyone but Ken. He made no attempt to hide pure relief on his face. He cleaned out his desk, dumping reams of paper out for the shredder. Arlys gave him a little gift bag, telling him he'd been a real joy, and "no trouble at all," while she glanced icily at Shelly. He radiated a maturity from finishing his fellowship. She was sad to see him go and coveted that sense of triumphant completion.

"Why don't you toss that filthy briefcase, Ken? I can have the Archeology Department carbon date it, I suppose, but it looks like it's a hundred years old." Shelly teased her mentor the last evening of work together. She drained the cold coffee in her stained mug without a second thought, watching Ken's last moments in their office with sadness.

"I never told you the story of this briefcase, did I now?" He patted the worn handle and traced the initials. "See the 'BIM' etched there by the lock? That's for Benjamin Isaiah Mackey. My dad. He was a salesman in Chattanooga, and died when I was three. The last picture I have of him was wearing a suit and tie and holding this briefcase."

"Oh, Ken, I'm so sorry—I remember your dad died when you were little. We have that in common, no dad growing up. And here I've been mocking that thing this entire year. Why didn't you tell me to shut up?"

"Naw, that's okay. You know Bernice, the night ward clerk on the Powell? She used to offer to buy me a new one even though she doesn't have two nickels to rub together. She was afraid something was going to crawl out of it when I'd stuff it under her desk." He smiled at the memory.

"Anyway, my dad died in a bad car wreck, and life was tough for my mom after he was gone, so this is kind of special to me. You're probably right, though. I shouldn't bring it to the office in my real job. Might scare the staff," he grinned, picking up his briefcase and preparing to head out for the last time.

He turned to her and said, "Remember this image, Shelly, when it gets hard. For some reason they seem to go after you, and you're not out of here yet. Remember what it looks like for a graduating fellow to walk out this door and go on to an *actual life*. Then put yourself in the picture." He paused. "I've never known a doctor like you. In fact, I look at Briane when she's being a stinker and chuckle to myself that you were probably just like her when you were little."

She shook her head. "I was not nearly as cute as Briane. I had thick octagon glasses and had to wear boy's shoes in the sixth grade, my feet were so big."

"Well, that explains a lot." He laughed but jumped back to his thoughts. "Seriously, though. Keep reminding yourself *this is you* in one year. You were meant to be an oncologist, Shelly. Stick with it, and don't let this place get you down. Go cry in Dr. Hazel's office, or stomp outside for a cigarette, or do whatever it is you do to shake things off. But stick with it, and you'll be walking out of this office with the same relief as me in a year."

"Get out of here, you goof." Shelly stood and waved him out the door. "You're gonna make me cry and I can't have that. Go home and tell Janelle she's a saint to put up with you. And don't say you'll stay in touch because you won't. I just..." Shelly pursed her lips to stay composed, "I just really thank you for not hating me. I mean it, Ken. That would've been too much to bear."

As Ken Mackey walked down the hallway, Shelly pondered how little she really knew of him despite the ridiculous number of hours they'd spent together the past year. Growing up without a father in the sixties made them unique, and she'd only made the link in the last hours of their working relationship. *We don't get close to each other because it'll soon be time to move on.* Ken's desk, now empty, would be Walter's tomorrow. She hoped she could be as good a teacher to him as Ken had been to her.

She sniffed his old white coat, catching both body smells and a faint aftershave. She rifled through his empty drawers, feeling blue and sentimental. Her fingers grasped a yellowed and frayed newspaper clipping left behind way up in the corner. As she read the article, she was reminded that *everyone* has secrets. Ken just kept his exceedingly well. Shelly tucked the paper in her little box with the precious obituaries and made her way to the Powell.

* * *

Since it was June 30th, the new academic year began the next morning. Shelly was thinking about how the new team would work out when she saw Dr. Farber ambling down the hallway of the Powell. She greeted him, whipping out her paper list of the hospital patients so she could update him on his census.

"How's your day going, Dr. Farber?" Shelly's pre-emptive cheerful fellow greeting was an easy habit now. "The service is quiet, and you just have the two post-op patients on the other side of the ward. We sent home your lady with the DVT this morning. Shall I go with you?"

"No, no, that's all right, Shelly. I'll stop in to see them in a minute. I just wanted to talk to you about tomorrow."

"Definitely, sir. Ken briefed me on the second-year fellow's tasks, and Walter'll be up to the job as junior fellow since he's done his whole residency here. It'll be great to have him on board. I'm sure Dr. Cardinal and Dr. Boldon feel the same. I was going to page him shortly, to talk him through the chemo book and everything before tomorrow's morning rounds. At least the year starts on a Saturday; that'll make his transition a little less hectic."

Dr. Farber frowned during her rapid speech, staring off at the ward clerk's desk. Shelly watched as he leaned forward to stretch each calf with a faint groan.

"Now, now, the thing is, Shelly," he stammered, "the thing is, we can't have Walter doing the chemo, now."

Shelly angled her head, her response immediate.

"Oh, yes, we can, Dr. Farber. The first-year fellow *always* does the chemo admits. That's 'The Way.' I even have a little ceremony planned for when I hand him the book."

"Yes, well," he said, evading her eyes and exuding discomfort with his shrugged shoulders and neck twists, "we're going to have you keep taking care of the chemo patients, Shelly, and the rounds, and so on, because Walter is going to be the lab fellow this year. You know the Board changed the length of the fellowship to three years from now on. You stay at two years, of course, but Walter will not be clinical much, this year."

This bombshell hit Shelly, as she tried to understand what he had just said.

"Wait. Dr. Farber, what exactly do you mean by 'not clinical much'? He's not going to be on rounds? Or in the OR? Or helping with clinic? What exactly does 'not clinical much' mean for the service?" She tried to keep incredulity out of her voice, but the idea of running the entire service alone was an impossible concept to take in, in the middle of the hallway, the day before her nirvana of the final year was about to start.

Dr. Cardinal came up to them, smiling, trim and fit in a pressed suit. "How's she taking the news, Ted? Feel like bolting yet, Shelly? Tough deal with this transition to a three-year program. You'll be fine, though, and like always, we'll be here to help. We'll just have to get used to more junior residents in the OR, we talked about that. Being more involved'll be good for us, really. Did you tell her about the class?"

Shelly started to shake her head, as if to clear her ears from the babble she was hearing.

"What class?"

"Well, now, Shelly, don't worry, but you're going to need to take a graduate level course with a paper on something on the health industry," Dr. Farber admitted. "We found a good one for you on medical devices that meets only once a week, starting in September. You just do a little research and then write a fifteen-page paper. I think Walter can round for you on those days, but we really can't have him too involved, here."

"We can't have Walter too involved? I would say that the first year of fellowship is a time to be *very* involved, Dr. Farber." Shelly took a moment to let his words sink in, as if a little time passing, in the middle of the hallway, would make it all go away.

"This is impossible news, I'm going to be honest. With all due respect to you both, running this service is just not a one-person job. I really don't know what else to say. Maybe if I had a little time to prepare, to think this through, I could be more articulate. When are you going to tell Walter?"

They were silent.

Bastards.

"I see. You told him already." Shelly paused, clenching every muscle in her body to hide her rage. "You told him before you told me. Shelly tugged her lab coat down, and took a dramatic breath to project composure she didn't feel. "It appears I have a great deal of work to do, so please excuse me while I gather my thoughts and page Rebecca Lange. She's the chief starting tomorrow."

"Aw, don't feel bad, Shelly! Here, come round with me on my patients. That'll cheer you up," Dr. Cardinal coaxed her along the hall.

Oh, yes, doing more work is surely the sterling antidote to being tortured with too much work. It was all she could do not to scream, and now she couldn't escape. Her mind seemed to freeze, yet words came out of her mouth, as she politely, so politely, gave sign-out to Dr. Cardinal about his patients. They walked into each patient's room, Shelly standing at the doorway, functioning robotically, and rounded on the patients Dr. Cardinal wanted to see.

When this was done, they stood for a moment at a quiet spot down the hall. Shelly spotted the ward clerk gesturing Dr. Boldon down the hall, and he came their way, flashing his teeth at her while buttoning his lab coat.

"Well, I hear we've had some important conversations this afternoon, haven't we?" Brian Boldon put his arm around Shelly's shoulder and pulled her toward him. "This will all be for the best, Shelly, I'm confident in that. All for the best!" She could smell the Listerine on his breath as she worked her way out of his grip.

"We were just covering the details, Brian," Dr. Cardinal said to his boss. He turned back to Shelly and said, "Look, we had no other options. We could only hire one fellow this year," he ticked off the points with his fingers, "we have Walter, and he has to do a lab year. At least you don't have to stay an extra year, and if you can keep improving, you'll graduate next June. We just decided to bite the bullet and make Walter's first year non-clinical. The Board added the extra class, Shelly. That wasn't our idea." His eyes locked onto hers. "It might seem a little unfair to you, though you'll admit we've certainly bent over backwards to help you succeed. So—decision time. Are you in for the long haul?"

The years of anticipation. The brutal pace of the last year. The unnerving slants of subtle distrust from all of them. Was she going to stay?

The anger rose up in her, foul and agonizing. The buildup was nearly unbearable, but the game was played in such a way that it had to be stuffed down. Invisible. She knew the rules now, and had a sense that maybe she held more pieces than she'd realized. As bad as it would be for her to quit, hoping to get a rare position elsewhere as a second-year fellow, the fellowship would clearly suffer if she left.

Did they think she would have a breakdown? Call the Board? Quit? No, those choices were not going to land her in the place she wanted to go. "Go confidently in the direction of your dreams," pealed in her brain and helped her respond.

"Yes, Shelly. What's your decision?" Dr. Boldon was attentive.

"Of *course* I'm in it for the long haul, Dr. Cardinal, Dr. Boldon. I'm afraid there really isn't anything you can do to get rid of me," she said with a furious, innocent smile. "And I can't imagine how you would manage if I chose to leave." It felt exciting to add the veiled threat. "Now, if you have everything you need, I have things to prepare for tomorrow. Have a good day," she said, then turned to stride down the hallway.

She found the ward clerk and asked her to get Rebecca on the phone in the little exam room, where she waited. Tears welled. *Think. Think. What are you going to say to the new chief?*

"Rebecca?" She heard kids in the background. Rebecca was an older resident, married, with a ten-year-old son and an older boy who had moved out to his own place. She must be home already from her last rotation.

"Shelly! I was hoping you'd call. Hang on, I'll close the door." Silence after a latch clicked over the phone. "That's better. My son has a couple friends over, and Lord they are loud. Okay, back to work. I already have sign-out on the service, and I assume we start at six, since it's a Saturday? You'll like the PG-3, Dave Coughlin, I have stories galore about him. Solid, though, and he'll work hard. And I'm pretty sure I interviewed the new intern last fall, seems strong. Her name is Tabitha Rupert, from Vanderbilt. Should be a great team. You hear about Walter yet?"

"Farber just told me. In the fucking hallway, if you can believe that. And then Cardinal and even Boldon came up as reinforcement, I guess, in case I burst into tears or something. Wait—how did *you* know?"

"Walter told me this morning before I left my night shift. He feels bad, Shelly. He knows how brutal the service can be, but they told him he has to stay non-clinical or the program will get dinged. He thought he'd better let the staff tell you, since it's their decision. God, you have to keep the chemo book. Anita said you've been ready to hand that little monster over. I am so sorry."

"Yeah, I had a little speech and everything," Shelly relaxed a little, finally feeling some of her rage dissipating. "I was going to try to find some kazoos and put a ribbon on the book. Good grief," she said. "I'm utterly defeated. Thwarted at every step."

"Not at all, Shelly," Rebecca soothed. "We're going to be fine. You can't be everywhere, so you choose the good cases for yourself, the ones you need for experience. If it hits the fan, remind them that you are running the service with no help, and that there's only so much you can do. And believe me, we will *bring* it from the resident's side. I've already talked to everyone about it. Even if they're not on our service, the other residents are ready to help if they can get away from their rotation. We're going to make you look good!"

"Wow—that's the nicest thing I've heard in a while. Thank you, Rebecca. I'll take all the help you can muster. How'd you know to do this?"

"Everyone will tell you I'm the "old" resident, which is true. I started out as a scrub tech, if you can believe that. As soon as I could, I went to nursing school, and worked as an RN for a few years. Turns out I don't take orders too well, so onto medical school. I can't believe the end is finally in sight—I'll be just as glad to finish off this year as you, I swear. And we're going to do it. No doubt in my mind. I hear *everything* from the nurses, Shelly, and I keep my mouth shut. We're all on your side, so start counting down the days. I'll see you at six!"

* * *

Shelly gathered her things after rounds, saying goodbye to the residents finishing their rotation, thanking them for their hard work and tender patient care. She ordered her usual Olive Garden meal, smoked her way home, and collapsed on the couch, staring into space as the aroma of lasagna filled her little living room.

How in the world was she going to do the impossible? Her house, once a cozy respite, revealed itself as the cheap rental it was, the glare of her standing lamp's halogen bulb bleaching its beige paint and stained carpet. Her whole life had been devoted to learning the art of surgical technique, the mastery of oncologic care, and she felt it slipping as tears trickled down her face.

Silent, beaten, Shelly thought about Rebecca's words. One fellow, same number of cases, chemo admits, complications, radiology rounds, conferences…There was just no way this could be done. She stamped out the cigarette that had been smoldering in the ashtray, left the food where it was, and went to bed. The sheets wrapped her in cool comfort, and the silent ceiling fan lulled her miserable mind to sleep, dreamless, to face the awful truth of the morning.

Chattanooga Daily Times, July 18, 1962

Noted felon Benjamin Mackey was killed in an automobile crash while fleeing authorities. Mackey, 28, had a lengthy record of theft, breaking and entering, and battery. He had been under surveillance by local police for several burglaries he was suspected of conducting in the township, leading to the nickname "The Charmer."

"The officer who was involved in the chase found an opened bottle of liquor, an empty briefcase, some small bags with cash and jewelry, and two Bowie knives in Mackey's car," according to Sgt. Fred Davidson. "We've been tailing this guy for months. He uses a traveling salesman gimmick every time. We've had three witnesses describe the exact same routine. The suspect wears a raincoat and carries a briefcase, acts real official with the lady of the house, then talks her into checking her basement for any items she might want to sell. When she's downstairs, he steals anything small and valuable he can find. Each victim told us that he seemed like a nice, professional guy, very polite, and all that. We finally caught up with him."

Mackey was seen running a red light in downtown Chattanooga. When the patrol car gave chase, lights and sirens on, Mackey sped through town and lost control of his vehicle, hitting a boulevard tree on Mason Avenue. The suspect was declared dead at the scene.

He leaves behind a wife and infant son who live in the area.

CHAPTER 14

Walter

The alarm rattled her out of bed, and she dashed into the shower. It took just a few seconds for the brutal memories to flood back, but her warrior spirit was ready for the self-pity and was having none of it. Viking Valkyrie, or weakling whiner? The choice was made, and with a firm "poised!" Shelly got her coffee ready to tackle her first day as senior fellow.

She sped into work and was lost in thoughts of the upcoming year as she turned the corner to room 201.

"Ladies, gentleman Dave, and...?" Her voice rose when she saw Walter, chatting with the group around the cart in his khaki pants, white shirt, and terrible tie. She noted the freshly pressed white lab coat, embossed, "Walter Dooley, M.D., Fellow, Gyn Onc" on the upper left.

The residents were introducing themselves to Tabitha, the new intern. Shelly said, "Hello. Walter, a word?" She guided him to the mini kitchen where she had found the coffee pot a year earlier. "I wasn't expecting to see you this morning. Farber told me everything yesterday. He said you weren't clinical."

"I just felt so bad, Shelly. I didn't want to leave you in the lurch, so I'll round when I can, and just say it's not keeping me from the lab. I mean, you're going to need my help, there's no doubt."

"Hmm. I think I'll just have to make do, Walter. No other way around it, they made that clear last night. So, let's get rounds done, and we'll make a plan later. Nice lab coat, by the way." Shelly assumed he didn't know that Arlys hadn't even ordered hers until the second week of July.

Shelly guided them around the floor, stopping at each room to allow Rebecca to coax a presentation from the younger residents and students. Shelly knew the patients, none critically ill, so the butterflies in her stomach started to vanish. It felt like the world was perhaps not so grim as the night before. Walter stepped in now and then, confident and bold, with an easy smile here, flattering comment there, as they made their way.

* * *

The weekend was quiet, and Walter came again to Monday's rounds with the same capable grace. Shelly divided up the cases with Rebecca, giving him an awkward glance. "I guess we'll see you around, Walter. Let me know if you need anything. Good luck in the lab." The team went down to the operating room and started the process of prepping patients, looking up lab results, and getting ready for the big week ahead.

As Shelly walked down the hallway to Dr. Farber's room, she did a double take to see Walter scrubbing at the sink with him. "Good morning, Dr. Farber." Shelly nodded to them both.

"I'm here to operate on this patient with you." She was going to elaborate but realized there was nothing she could say that would not lead her to asking why the fuck Walter Dooley was scrubbing her case.

"Well, now, I just thought I'd get Walter involved in this case for the morning, Shelly, since the lab hasn't really gotten him started yet. It'll be good for him, don't you think, Walter?"

The slightest bit of shame shown on Walter's masked face as the suds from his forearms circled the stainless sink's drain. "I'm sure it will, Dr. Farber." He spun from the sink to back into the operating room, never meeting Shelly's glare. Nurse Kit was sitting at her low desk and exchanged a glance with her as the door was closing.

Everyone knew that the senior fellow took Dr. Farber's cases. No matter what, the senior was expected to take care of his patients, and that unspoken rule had never been broken in the first nine months of fellowship, let alone the first bloody day. Shelly was icy with rage, and needed a strategy. She strode down to the rear entrance of Dr. Cardinal's room, saw her chief resident already scrubbed, and decided to enter to see if she could glean some advice.

"Hey, there. You haven't started yet?" Rebecca focused on her incision, hands working.

At that moment Dr. Cardinal came in, hands up, elbows dripping a drop or two of water, and the tech handed him a sterile towel.

"Yes, they have started," Shelly answered. "Dr. Farber and *Dr. Dooley* have started the case in two." She hoped the emphasis showed just the right amount of suppressed fury to get Dr. Cardinal's attention, but he didn't bite. "And it looks like you two have everything handled here. I'll be around, Rebecca. Page me when you're out and we can go over some things."

"Will do."

* * *

Somehow the day flew past, Walter vanished, and Shelly and Rebecca hoped the morning operating room issue had been a fluke. Walter kept showing up on morning rounds, making several of the presentations himself, until Thursday, when he took over the management of one of the patients.

Shelly corrected him mid-sentence. "Sorry, Walter. We're not going to up the ante on the antibiotics in this situation. She's afebrile, the cultures are negative so far, and there's no reason to add that med to her list. We'll observe her for today and reevaluate if she spikes a fever again. Next patient."

"Well, I'd have to take issue with that, Shelly. Um, Dr. Riley. We usually start people on ampicillin/sulbactam in this situation. I think that's the way to go here."

"Walter, *we* are standing right here, and *we* are not going to do that. Let's move on please, Dave. Someone push the cart to the next room."

They eventually got to the last patient on rounds, this one in the ICU. Again, as they conferred on management for the day, Walter stepped in to make the overall medical plan. "I recommend furosemide and extra fluid. This is a common way of managing the volume overload she is experiencing," and he droned on with an educational style that Shelly now recognized. He was a little clone of the men in the department. And he was taking over her service, leading the team as if she were invisible.

"Nope, not going to do that, either Walter. Looks like you and I need to make some ground rules on rounds and decision-making. I'd have done that on Saturday but was under the impression you'd be heading to the lab. Time for Dave to get the orders in and for the rest of us to get to clinic."

"But this is really…" he began.

"Walter, as much as you mean well, I'll treat this patient without a diuretic. I spoke to the ICU attending this morning, and he made it clear he wants us staying out of the volume management. Our role is diet and wound, okay? That's a wrap." She checked her watch. "Off we go, guys. I'm already late."

* * *

As she dashed off to her clinic, she wondered about taking Anita into her confidence. She remembered the comment about missing Ken and finally realized that Walter was waging a turf war with her. Shelly had barely finished seeing the first patient when her pager went off. The buzz alerted her right before the audible chirp, and she looked down to see Arlys' number. She banged her wrist on the corner of the table, jangling her bracelet as she went to answer the call.

Shitdammit ouch! she muttered as she waited for Arlys to pick up.

"Dr. Farber would like to see you in his office, Dr. Riley," Arlys requested. Her honeyed voice always dripped with politeness.

"Sure, Arlys. When should I stop by?" Shelly took the day's next chart from Anita, who stayed close to listen to the call.

"Oh, *now*, darlin'. He wants you here *now*."

The firmness was clear, and Shelly's day became very dark indeed. They knew she would be beyond busy in clinic, and that leaving for a meeting would make patients wait even longer than usual.

"Be right there," Shelly confirmed, sounding as nonchalant and upbeat as she could muster as she slammed the phone down into its cradle. "Dammit, Anita, there's trouble. I've gotta go," she said. "Stall for me, and as soon as I'm on my way back I'll call this extension so you can room the next patient. Tell her I'm sorry for the wait!" she called over her shoulder as she tore down the hall.

She ran up two different stairways, both labeled as locked and alarmed, neither being true. She reached the third-floor office of Dr. Farber in minutes, wiped the sweat off her forehead and presented a cool face to Arlys.

"Shall I go in, Arlys?" she said as she made her way to his office door. *That perfume.*

"Just have a seat, doctor. I'll let him know you are here, and we'll see when he can see you."

Arlys knew those patients would be waiting because of this maneuver. And Shelly knew that it was against the rules of this little war to point that out. So she smiled, sat, and crossed her legs as if she had all the time in the world.

"Thank you, Arlys," she said. She told herself to think clearly and be still so she could react.

A few minutes passed, the spindly red second hand of the wall clock present in every hospital, quietly pulsed the seconds. Finally, Arlys answered her ringing phone, murmured an assent, and stood to let her in Dr. Farber's office.

The door shushed behind her as she crossed the threshold, and she smelled his weak coffee, white with cream. He sat behind his enormous wooden desk, papers and medical files everywhere, with a medal and ribbon framed and hanging prominently on the wall behind him.

She sat where he pointed, the fake leather chair stiff and rarely used.

"I see your gift from being the Society's President," Shelly noted, nodding at the precious memento. "That must have been a hectic year for you."

He smiled, agreeing, "Best year of my life." He pivoted, unwilling to be distracted from the task at hand, "Now, Shelly, how are the patients on the service?"

In that instant, she had clarity. To her knowledge, Dr. Farber had never once called Ken in to his office to talk about the service, even when there were very sick people needing lots of intervention. He had certainly never interrupted Ken's day to chat about specific patients.

Walter.

He proceeded to ask pointed questions about the two patients Walter had challenged her on that morning on rounds. Dr. Farber would never have known the details of those patients' conditions that morning unless Walter had contacted him. Shelly's whole fellowship was teetering between his throne and her fake leather seat. "You're going to have to make it clear to the staff that *you* are their senior fellow," Ken's warning floated in her brain.

She answered him coolly, factually. She reassured him about the patients' conditions and their care, very confident that they were safe and being watched over properly. As he nodded, she decided to strike.

She stood, heart racing, armpits sweaty like her TV idol Dr. Gannon, but for all the wrong reasons. There was no clinical mastery here, rather a battle of wits for her survival in the program. She straightened her lab coat, then stared hard. *You are a badass and you are poised.*

"Dr. Farber, am I the senior fellow?"

"Why, yes, well, you know you are," he stammered.

"Do I have your confidence, sir, in managing our complex and frail patients?"

"Well, uh, certainly, I just wanted to be sure about…" he stood now, uncomfortable with Shelly towering over him.

"Have I given you a single reason to doubt my capability on your service, Dr. Farber? Patient complaints, surgical complications, whispers from the nurses?"

He paused, then shook his head slightly in acquiescence. "No," he admitted, rearranging papers on his desk, then lifting his gaze.

"I didn't think so. Dr. Farber, I have one year left in your program, and I will not spend that year being second guessed by Walter Dooley. Particularly when he is not even officially on the service and is of no help to me in my workload. If you don't want me as your senior fellow, you'd better tell me that now."

She had him. She could see his shock. This level of confrontation in Theodore Farber's life was a once a decade occurrence, she guessed. The surprise of being direct was working in her favor.

He was silent.

"Great. I don't expect to hear any more of Walter Dooley's opinions on how I am running your service. I am *good* at this, Dr. Farber, and he happens to be wrong on both patients. I'm thirty-three years old and have been training for this my whole life. Walter's dear to you, sir, that's fine. But *I* am in charge."

Her voice stayed steady despite sweat working its way down her sides. She turned to leave, satisfied that her point had been resoundingly made. She'd better get out while she could. A thought entered her mind, and she turned back.

"Oh, and Dr. Farber? The senior fellow operates with you. That is 'The Way.' Walter does not take those cases from me."

Boom! She left his office, smiling and calling out, "You have a blessed day, now, Arlys," as she sailed by, a smile on her face and a squish in her pits. She might be smelly with fear, but Shelly had no intention of giving Arlys the tiniest whiff.

CHAPTER 15

Pepper

"Shelly, you like dogs, don't you?" A year was more than enough time for Shelly to have learned that simple questions in her surgical training program were anything but. Bone-crushing fatigue could be tripled by one query from an attending.

"In fact, I'll wager you *love* dogs," Dr. Cardinal persisted, clearly having no intention of dropping the subject.

Shelly had dropped her guard during the tail end of a long but successful operation. Her headlight focused on the surgical field while she ensured the abdomen had no areas of bleeding, and started the closure.

"Dr. Cardinal, nothing good is going to come from answering that question, and you know it, sir." Shelly replied. Her brain was spinning, as the battle of wits began. She was now on high alert. How could he plot her destruction with a question about dogs, she wondered?

"I know I'm going to regret this, but I'll admit to having moderate affection for dogs," Shelly told him in defeat. Now she awaited his next move, and the rest of the surgical team leaned in to hear how this innocuous question was going to lead to Shelly's newest humiliation.

"Good!" he said with satisfaction. "You'll love one of our new puppies. You remember our beagle, Belle—she had her litter a couple months ago. The father, well, he must have been a travelin' man. Black lab, near as we can tell." He cut the last suture and backed up to break scrub. "They're so cute right now. Come over to the farm on Saturday after rounds and pick the one you want."

He started to walk away.

No, no, no. You work fifteen-hour days!

"Dr. Cardinal, I really can't have a puppy right now, sir. It would never get outside! I mean I'm not really ever home, Dr. Cardinal, you know my hours, I just couldn't…"

"You'll figure it out, Shelly. Everyone loves puppies. See you Saturday!"

"And he's outta here," smirked Dave Coughlin, the hilarious PG-3 who was currently keeping Shelly sane. His wife Michelle was a vet, and between stories about her animals and his patients, there was always laughter around Dave.

"Oh, my God. I cannot have a puppy. Can he fire me for not taking a puppy?" Shelly watched everyone in the room chuckle at this new and ridiculous dilemma.

"Shelly, have you had dogs before?" Dave continued to tease. "No offense, but you strike me as the kind of single person who kills plants and grows *pseudomonas* in her bathroom. Do you know the first thing about taking care of a dog?"

"Hey, I resent that! My bathroom is clean. But I have no idea how to take care of a puppy. I can't do this. It isn't fair to the dog."

They closed the abdomen and cleaned the wound while chatting.

"Oh, you're gonna take a dog. Dr. Cardinal decided that before you started the case. It's genius," Dave shook his head. "He continues to torture you while appearing thoughtful and generous." He thought for a moment as they removed the patient's drapes. "Here's my advice. I'll ask Michelle for names of dog walking services. You'll call that stud of an ex-boyfriend of yours and offer him sex if he takes the dog out once a day. It might actually cheer his sorry ass up."

"The sex, or the cute puppy?" Velma piped in.

"Both," Dave continued. "Then those neighbors you said are so nice? That's the third shift. And you, my fearless leader, are not gonna get any sleep for the next eight weeks. You won't care, though, because there's literally nothing cuter than a puppy, and your pitiful existence needs a little joy, I'd say. You rally the troops, and Cardinal's goal, to crush you using an adorable, squirming puppy as a weapon, will fail!"

The hospital duties remained dense, with early morning rounds, surgical cases, and clinics. Shelly pondered the new stressor of adopting a puppy as the week went on. At least the problem presented her with completely different issues from the now-routine abject humiliation, anxiety about hand-eye coordination, or endless suppression of her spirited personality from the robotic one expected of her. This was a new thing to worry about, but it stretched her weary brain with the tiniest quiver of anticipation.

Michelle called her with advice on pet stores and supplies she would need. Robert, with his usual morose tone, agreed to meet the pup and "see what he could do." Shelly got the impression he'd love to have a dog back in his life. Corinne agreed to help, too.

"Pick out one that doesn't bark, Shelly!" she said with a laugh.

Saturday came, and early rounds were brief. The residents coming on fresh for the day knew the patients and could take the handoff fluidly, and the night team's shift had not been so grim as to put a damper on rounds. Soon Shelly was on her way to Dr. Cardinal's farm. She stamped her last cigarette out in the ashtray as she turned onto the gravel road to his place.

The red barn shimmered in the humid late morning light. Dr. Cardinal was in the field next to the house, poking along on one of the tractors Robert had fixed. She pondered fleeing when he noticed her Festiva. He waved Shelly to a parking spot while he shut down the beast and walked over to her.

They spoke about his patients for a few minutes, and Shelly was especially on guard. The farm was the one place where her boss was slightly less inclined to destroy her. This doubled her suspicions.

"Are you ready to meet your new family member? Right over there in the barn. Belle must be feeding them now, or she would've been here to say hello," he said, ambling across the drive. The cool interior of the old barn was a balm to the stickiness outdoors. As her eyes adjusted to the dark, Shelly savored the smells of hay and animal. There were thousands of particles that would stir up her allergies later, but the old barn aroma did her midwestern heart some good.

"You need cows, Dr. Cardinal. My cousins in La Crosse are dairy farmers. I loved the barn cats and milking time."

He laughed at the idea as they came across Belle, lying in the hay on her side with six black pups suckling and mewing. Only about thirteen weeks old, they were fuzzy little balls of cuddle, and Shelly was smitten. Belle, deciding the babes had had enough and craving some attention of her own, shook them off and opened her mouth. With a loud bay, she growled a bit, stretched with her tush in the air, and trotted directly over, as if to determine the newcomer's intentions.

Shelly got low with open arms, and the beagle wiggled to be petted and congratulated.

"Nicely done, Belle," Shelly murmured with approval. "They're a fine effort. Which one doesn't bark?" She spent the next half hour inspecting each one, checking their markings, and generally enjoying the smells and feels of the little wriggling creatures. Shelly eventually settled on a little female with white paws and a white star on her chest. Dr. Cardinal gave her a bag of puppy kibble to start and counseled her about vet appointments and shots. He lugged out a used green dog crate that barely fit into the back of her Festiva.

"Good grief, Dr. Cardinal, how big is this pup going to get?" He shrugged, faking innocence. Shelly drove off, with her new companion yipping and baying in protest.

"Don't forget flea powder," she heard while driving away.

* * *

Oh, my God...Shelly checked in her rearview mirror to see if something was wrong with the little creature, she was howling so loudly. She pulled over, and saw nothing alarming, so she sped to the pet store for supplies. Shelly knew that heat and animals in cars were an absolute no-no, so she scooped up the little wriggly lump and let her lick her entire face.

"Okay, okay," she laughed. "I admit I'm starved for affection, but I know where that tongue has been. Let's get you a leash, okay, lovie? And you need a name!"

Shelly chose a small collar and leash, plus a couple squishy dog toys. As she made her way around the store, a saleswoman caught her.

"Um, Ma'am? You know your pooch is gonna outgrow that collar in a couple days, right?" The woman reached out to scratch the puppy's head. "It looks to be a couple months old, right?"

Shelly put the collar back on the rack. "Do you have time to help me? I have no idea what she needs, except for flea powder." The dog peed all over Shelly's top. "And maybe a new shirt?"

They laughed together. The woman brought over a cart, and counseled her on getting a variety of sizes of collars.

"What color do you think this little girl's gonna want? We've got print and solid, fabric and leather, you name it. And of course, we always have Kentucky blue." She put a couple collars against the dog's black fur as Shelly decided.

Next she reminded her about a vet visit and shots. They landed in the enormous dry food section, and the employee filled her in on the kibble a puppy should have.

"Good grief. There are more choices for puppy food than I have for dinner. Give me your most reliable brand and I'll trust you." Shelly was starting to panic, thinking about fleas and urine and a creature who depended on her for nourishment.

"She's like a little round peppercorn, that pup of yours. Cute as can be! You two are set, I believe. Y'all have a nice day, now," and she waved off Shelly's profuse thanks and went to help another customer.

* * *

Indeed, the pooch needed a double flea bath, and Shelly washed all her clothes in disgust. The puppy mewed and cried when left alone but settled with a firm cuddle on the couch. She examined every inch of the house while Shelly tailed her to avoid accidents on the carpet.

She named her Pepper. The dog destroyed all man-made objects in seconds, resulting in backyard droppings every color of the rainbow. Pepper even managed to consume a bright yellow feather duster when left unattended for the shortest time.

"Hey!" Shelly protested. "What's on your lip?" Pepper cocked her head, her breath gently pushing, then pulling the last of the yellow feathers in and out from the edge of her mouth, with her paws clutching the plastic wand.

"Jesus, Pepper, the neighbors already think I feed you neon dog food. Give me that thing!" Shoes, clothes, and table legs were all fair game for a good chew in those first few months. Shelly found the most indestructible dog toy on the market, laced it with peanut butter, and left Pepper to lick it each morning in her enormous crate.

Shelly fell into an even more sleep-depriving routine, letting her little creature out to do her business at all hours, and finding Robert an immense help. She hired the dog walking service her resident's wife had recommended, which got Pepper outdoors and socialized. Overall, as her resident had predicted, it was the best remedy for her psyche she could have had.

"I talk to the dog continuously, you know," she told Evie on the phone, batting Pepper away from chewing the cord. "The minute I walk in the door until I fall asleep, I'm having an adult conversation with a small dog. It's come to that. I ask her for help with the crossword. I tell her about the latest chemo admit. She's actually a wonderful companion."

Evie laughed, so glad to hear a little happiness in her friend's voice after many difficult months. "Just let me know if she starts to talk back, will you? No problem with the dog walkers?"

"Nope. They leave me a note every day on the consistency of Pepper's stool, the vigor with which her stream watered the neighbor's yard, and the overall maturity of her bark at every damned thing she sees. I look forward to their little notes – they are fast-paced and poetic. Worth every penny I'm paying to have total strangers come into my house and take care of my animal."

"How's Robert seem? Mournful? Beckoning?"

"Funny," Shelly pondered the question. "Not really. I don't get the feeling he has any hopes for getting back together. He seems to be getting through this mid-life crisis on his own. There's no pressure to fix him when he complains. I just let him bitch, and then off he goes. Honestly, Evie, my life is so horrible that I can't possibly cave and take him back."

"Good, good. I'm glad you have a little relief, what with the service so full. I'll let you go—get some sleep and give Pepper a squeeze from San Francisco."

* * *

The hospital duties were at full court press for Shelly. She was grateful for the grand support of her residents, who more than pulled their own weight with the work each day. On a particularly harried afternoon rounds, Dave Coughlin started writing out the chemo orders for the next patient to be seen, newly arrived.

"Coughlin, what are you doing?" Shelly was aghast that he would take on that sacred job.

"I'm just copying them from last time, Shelly. That's all you do, anyway."

The med students chuckled at Dave's audacity with her.

"I do not. Jesus, we have to check her weight, her labs, her tumor markers…"

"I know that doctor, and I have it all done except the doses. What do you think I am, an oncologist? We're gonna have all the details on your chemo patients ready for you, and then you can read them over after rounds after a nice cigarette break outside, confirm the doses and regimen, and be done in half the usual time."

Shelly was amazed. "Ignore the part about the smoking," she told the nursing student while glaring at Dave, who was in full sass mode. "I have no idea what he's talking about."

"It was Tabitha's idea, Shelly. That's how they did it when she was on service as a fourth-year med student, and it worked great. Then you can concentrate on the critical part."

Rebecca smiled. "I told you—we've got your back!"

"Thanks, you guys. Honestly, you're all doing great, and I appreciate it. Somehow, you're getting the work done with precision, but never make the patient feel like a number. That's the most beautiful thing to see. Efficiency with humanity. Looks like we're going to get through this without a junior fellow."

CHAPTER 16

Our Faye

"Let's go on a road trip and see Faye!" Madeline finished her nursing duties for the day, closed the last protocol patient file, and rested her chin on folded arms over Shelly's office carrel.

"I mean it. Let's drive down to Red Rock Falls and see Sissie and Faye. I already called Carrie and she said come. Plus, you're not on call this weekend—I checked."

Shelly ransacked her desk drawer for a snack, pushing aside old newspaper crosswords and matchbooks. "How far a drive is it?" A day away from the hospital would work miracles. "About two hours. We'll leave around eight, they'll feed us like crazy for six hours, then we head home. And we're taking *my* car, not that little toy you drive." Madeline came around to Shelly's cubby. "Say yes!"

Months earlier, Faye had done beautifully after her enormous surgery and qualified for a newly opened clinical chemotherapy trial. Madeline had meticulously reviewed Faye's chart, spending hours on the enrollment. Eventually, she met Faye and Sissie in person, and discovered their many friends and their mighty network of love, food, humor, and tragedy.

Madeline saw Faye every three weeks when she and her posse came up to get the next course of chemo. The other weeks she'd call to go over symptoms, and if Shelly was ever in the office to overhear, she knew when the patient was Faye. Madeline's drawl got heavier, there was always laughter, and instead of a frank discussion of neutrophil counts or CT scan details, Shelly would hear Madeline whisper, "...and then what?" as Faye told one of her mischievous stories about her hometown.

"Well, she's not on active treatment anymore," Shelly brought her thoughts back to Madeline and her proposal. "I don't want to break any rules, here, getting involved with a patient's personal life, but she's actually Dr. Farber's patient, since fellows aren't the doctor of record. It'll be a pretty fall drive, and I'll be gone in less than a year. What the hell! I never have enough time to hear her stories like you do. I'd love to go."

Madeline hooted with pleasure. "It'll be legendary. You just know someone's going to make me those angel biscuits. And there'll be country ham for you. Ooh, Lord. I can't wait!"

* * *

Robert agreed to take the dog for the day, and Shelly smiled to see Pepper's black snout poking out the window of the truck as Robert drove off. Madeline pulled up to Shelly's house in her spotless Camry for the drive to Red Rock Falls. They settled in for the drive and conversation was easy.

"They act regular, but you know they're not, don't you?" Madeline cocked her head at Shelly as she whizzed by truck after semi-truck. "I mean Thelma and her husband run the furniture store, which probably serves everybody in three or four counties. Carrie's the lead auditor in the county, and Glory's husband owns one of the bigger businesses in town with farm equipment and stuff. They're bigwigs in Red Rock Falls…"

"What's that mean?" Shelly focused on the horizon to avoid seeing Madeline's near misses on the highway as much as to enjoy the lush, hilly landscape.

"No liquor. *None*. Glory's daughter got married last summer, and they smuggled in beer at the reception in their back yard. Faye distracted the pastor while Glory's husband backed up the cases into the garage. I could barely breathe from laughing to hear her tell it. She was seriously worried that someone in her church might tattle. Oh, you just wait for the tales you'll hear today."

The drive passed quickly as the women speculated about who would come for the visit, how Faye's treatment had gone, and how breathless Thelma would be.

Poised

Madeline said, "Faye's been an amazing patient, Shelly. Honestly, when I talk to her about her meds, she just sails through the details like she's done this her whole life. She's so strong. I'm in awe of her."

It was easy to find the low-slung brick rambler where Faye and Sissie had lived all their lives. Madeline pulled into the driveway, arching to the back seat to grab her purse filled with greeting cards from the nurses in clinic and the Powell. Shelly slapped her forehead, realizing she had come empty-handed.

"My mom would kill me--I didn't bring anything, Madeline," Shelly moaned.

"Oh, Lord, everybody knows you doctors don't have a clue about normal things like that. They aren't expecting a thing, believe me. It's special enough that you're here."

They passed a mature rosebush along the driveway, blooms so bounteous Shelly had to take a second look to make sure they were real. Fat bees squirmed deep into the yellow blossoms, and the petals' aroma filled her with pleasure as she leaned in. The women stretched their legs on their way to meet Faye on the patio in front of the house. Shelly swam in the sensation of peace, so different from her hectic life.

"Hey, there," Faye beamed as she glided out to meet them.

"Hey, yourself. You've got hair!" Shelly squealed.

"Yes, hair is all the rage this season in Red Rock Falls, so I decided to follow the fashion. Y'all come in. Sissie's been waiting for this ever since you called, I swear. She's on her throne, talking back to *Walker, Texas Ranger* when they use bad language."

Sissie had turned in her recliner to watch them enter, regal upon her perch. The plaid was worn and the ivory doilies on the armrests askew, but it fit the décor of the house. Shelly noticed in seconds how spotless the house was kept.

"Well," Sissie declared, "we're just tickled that y'all could come see us today. The girls have been chirping about it all week." She radiated joy, delighted by the commotion, but her eighty-year-old voice cracked.

Shelly didn't doubt it. She had learned from Madeline that Faye and her friends had an all-for-one-and-one-for-all sensibility. If something unusual like a visit by a surgeon and a research nurse from the city came about, the whole clan would get in on the fun.

The doorbell rang, first of many, Shelly figured, and the procession began.

"Hey, y'all," called Thelma, the talkative one, as she pushed the screen door in with her backside, balancing an armful of fabric. "Y'all are not going to believe this," she started, while setting down her pack and hugging Madeline in one swoop.

"I believe I was going durned near seventy when I passed Leroy the trooper and he didn't do a thing! I was just so excited to get over here, is all. Dr. Riley, welcome to Red Rock Falls! I've got a couple more things in the car—I'll be back!" Out she flew, passing Carrie at the door with a hug.

"Hey, there, Madeline, Dr. Riley," Carrie nodded with a smile as she pressed herself against the screen door to let Thelma's ample body pass. "Angel biscuits, as ordered," she handed a platter to Madeline. "My husband claims they're my best batch yet."

"Angel biscuits, Shelly. I told you someone would make these. I'm about to have flour all over my lips and not even going to care." Madeline brought her dream food into the kitchen. "Thank you, Carrie!" She slid the platter onto the counter Faye had cleared for the feast.

"Did you have a good trip, Dr. Riley?" Carrie gave a light hug to Shelly. "Isn't that a cute top, Madeline? You look darling. Let me go get my brownies and I'll be back. Sissie, I can smell those beautiful pole beans of yours."

"Put 'em on the stove last night. And y'all will have to forgive me—I forgot to put my teeth in," she strained as she rose from her chair. Off Sissie went, barefoot in a flowered housecoat, surprised that her dentures were in the bathroom instead of her mouth. A swirl of running commentary ensued, Faye shaking her head at her beloved mother.

"Lord, Dr. Riley, Sissie's teeth take a tour of this house nearly every day. I swear they're out more than they're in. I've found them in places a pair of dentures shouldn't be found."

Poised

Shelly smiled as she went outdoors to help Carrie gather the rest of her things from the car.

"Faye's been good, Dr. Riley," Carrie confided when she reached her sedan. Her habit was to catch the eye of Shelly or Madeline, away from the others, to let them know whether Faye had been blue, or the trip up for chemo had been hard. If Thelma was the bubbly one, Carrie was the manager, tall and distinguished, constantly assessing the reality of the situation. Shelly noticed Carrie occasionally removed herself from the hectic group, probably her coping mechanism.

"The biggest thing I notice is her spirits are up, and she's in the store quite a bit more. The ladies there say she's *zestier*. That's their word. She's even talking about going to a trade show for new inventory. Those shows take a lot of energy, something she just didn't have during chemo."

They gathered a platter of cut vegetables with a glass container of dip, a paper grocery bag overflowing with a crocheted Afghan, and a little gift-wrapped box that Carrie thrust in Shelly's hands.

"Just a little chocolate from a new store in town, Dr. Riley. They wrap their samplers so nicely I thought you and Maddy could enjoy them on the drive home." She lay the veggie tray on the top of her sedan and sighed. "I think Faye's main concern now is Sissie. She turns eighty-one this year. She's spry and all, but you know people don't get stronger as they age. This little family ends in this house, I'm afraid, and Faye worries what'll happen if she goes before Sissie."

Glory drove up and parked as they chatted. She worked her way out of her car, straining with the weight of a crystal bowl filled with her famous fruit salad. "Hey, Dr. Riley! We're so glad you could come. Doesn't Faye look good with her little fuzzy head?"

"She does," Shelly said. "Sissie's happy to have the gang together."

"Oh, Sissie loves a party. I know that's right. Anything that makes Faye happy is okay with Sissie." Glory pushed her door closed and led the group of three back into the house.

Thelma was in the midst of telling Madeline a story, pointing to the lap quilts she'd made for hospital patients. "…then if their chemo is running while they're in their chair, they won't get cold. Sometimes it's just freezing in those rooms, Madeline. I was like to die the night I stayed over with Faye."

Another five or six women rang the bell and entered, always smiling while balancing their purses and a platter or bowl of their specialty dish. Whether fragrant warm brownies or a casserole dish hinting of gooey cheese and bacon, Shelly couldn't wait to sample every one. Sissie, dentures and all, had ambled back in and claimed her recliner. Within an hour or so of chatting and catching up, the smell of ham warming in the oven permeated the living room, and the eating began in earnest. Glory assembled a flamboyant red punch spiked with pineapple juice and flavored ice cubes in a glass bowl, ladle dangling from the edge. Shelly listened in awe at the buzz of stories, mesmerized by the energy of these dear friends.

They feasted. Salty country ham, deeply pink, followed by fluffy angel biscuits, cheesy potatoes, Sissie's fragrant pole beans in a little stock, flecked with pork, and homemade bread.

Each woman ate bites of food, their plates balanced on their laps as they urged one another to "Tell Dr. Riley about the time…" Faye toured them through the house, and Sissie brought Shelly up and down the rows of her garden.

"Sissie, you plant all this every year? It's huge!" Shelly could imagine this tiny woman roaming up and down the rows, tending her garden in her housecoat, feet bare. Tomatoes, beans, okra, even corn grew in row upon row, the stalks sturdy, and weeds few. "You must harvest like a farmer."

"Well," Sissie agreed with modesty. "I put up quite a bit in the fall. The girls take most of it, and there's some families in my church who like a jar of stewed tomatoes, I'd say. My real pride and joy, though, is my rosebush out front. Did you see it when you came up the driveway?"

"I did, actually. It was so full of blooms. And that yellow!"

"Well, Dr. Riley, I don't know how you look at things," Sissie said as the two women strolled to the front of the house. "You see," Sissie started as they reached the plump blooming bush, lush with buds and open blossoms. Shelly again noted the quivering of the innumerable bees deep in the blooms. "You see, I talk to Jesus all the time."

Shelly blinked and shook her head, caught completely off guard. *How in the world did we go from the rosebush to Jesus?* "I don't follow, Sissie," Shelly admitted, lifting her shoulders to invite more detail.

"Well, I talk to Jesus all the time, but this is where he answered me. About three years ago I was watering the rosebush and asking him all the things I usually ask. Like is my husband Gabe with him in heaven, and what'll happen to Faye, you see? All sorts of things. That morning, though? He answered me."

Shelly waited, while Sissie reached back in that time and space, savoring the moment. "Good grief, Sissie--what did he say?"

Back in the present, Sissie met her gaze.

"Well, he said, 'All is as it should be.' It was so clear to me, then, while I watched the bees in these yellow blooms. It's like the buzz in the blossom reached my very heartbeat, and the rose was the sun. I've never been able to put it in the right words like he did, but ever since that morning, I've felt *everything* is exactly the way it's supposed to be. The good *and* the bad, he was sure to make me know that, especially."

Sissie shook her head, as if unable to make sense of at the majesty of it all, then turned to make her way back to the house.

"It's how I cope with Faye's cancer, you see, Dr. Riley? Now that I've heard that voice, I just look at my rosebush any time I feel the worries about my Faye, and it soothes me, like. That's why it's my pride and joy." She winked. "But sometimes I wonder if Jesus is going to jump out and surprise me in the beans!"

Shelly threw her head back in laughter. "I wouldn't be surprised at all, Sissie! Let me know if he does," Shelly beckoned her in as she held the screen door open.

The room quieted as they came back in. "Well, Dr. Riley?" Faye couldn't wait any longer. "Did you see the Jesus bush? We wondered how long it would take Sissie to get you out there."

"I did indeed, though she caught me by surprise. I was terribly moved by it, to tell you the truth." Shelly breathed in deeply, trying to push away the crushing reality of Faye's dismal prognosis which Sissie's intimate story had triggered. She craved more of the group joy to push the sadness away. "Any chance we could get a tour of Red Rock Falls?"

The living room exploded with agreement and goodbyes. Purses were scooped up and dishes packed for those who had to take their leave. While Sissie and Shelly had been chatting outside, the women had scoured and shined the kitchen, everything back in its place. Within minutes Thelma had shepherded Carrie and Glory into her cavernous van, first moving piles of books, clothes, and bags to make room on the seats. Shelly and Madeline tucked into Faye's station wagon.

"Bye, Madeline! Thanks for coming down, Dr. Riley!" called those not coming on the tour, and Sissie saw them all off, waving from the porch.

"See, Dr. Riley? She took out her teeth," Faye noticed.

"Stop it, now, Faye, I'm too full to laugh anymore," Shelly said.

"All right, are you ready for the grand tour? Red Rock Falls is small, Dr. Riley, but it's one of the best places on earth, I swear. And it'll take all of ten minutes to see every inch. Here we go," Faye watched her rearview mirror as she backed out to follow Thelma. She pointed out the sights as they drove down backroads, through farm fields growing berries and Christmas trees. Faye followed as Thelma put her turn signal on and pulled into a classic rural cemetery, headstones throughout decorated with bold colors and flags.

"How are all the flowers so fresh, Faye?" Shelly was in disbelief at the almost neon colors in the sprays adorning most of the graves.

"Oh, Lord. Just ignore her, Faye." Madeline batted Shelly on the shoulder. "She's a very good doctor and gave you the right chemo and everything. But doctors can be simple and not recognize fake flowers when they're looking right at them," Madeline shook her head. "Is this where your dad is buried, Faye?"

"He is. That must be why Thelma brought us. I haven't been here for a while, actually." The two vehicles emptied out for the women to wander among the graves, Madeline raising her eyebrows at Shelly when they got close enough to see the plastic of the blooms.

"Honestly, all those years of school." Madeline laughed. "Do you recognize these names around your dad, Faye?"

The women nodded. "We know most of these people," answered Glory. "There's Faye's dad, Gabe. We all loved him, didn't we?"

They stood like a choir around the headstone with GABRIEL BERNDT COLGATE etched in marble. His very life was measured between the dates of birth and death. Shelly remembered Ms. Riner, her patient who'd promised to make something of her dash, and recounted the story to the group. They murmured their approval, all hoping their lives were worthy.

"I'm glad to know I'm not the only one who likes cemeteries, ladies," Shelly admitted as they prepared to climb back into Faye's wagon.

"I don't know if we're usual or not, Dr. Riley," Carrie answered for the group, "but a lot of us come here just to sort of say hello, I guess. I go to my mom's grave every year, thereabouts, and pull at the weeds or tidy up someone else's plot. Mostly it's just a couple minutes to remember her and try to think kindly of her. She was a terror, wasn't she Faye? I've spent these years since she's been gone doing my best to rearrange the way I remember her."

Carrie continued, now to Shelly and Madeline, "My mom drank, you see. She drank, she hit, and she read the Bible, in that order. As I got older, I figured the religion part was her desperation to stop the first two. Unfortunately, it didn't much help."

Madeline put an arm around Carrie's shoulder.

Carrie continued. "The good news is that none of us kids drink. We're *afraid* to. So at least this generation put that away." She blinked, giving her head a little shake. "Let's move on, everyone. Sorry to bring that up."

Thelma left the van behind to pick up later, so they all climbed into Faye's wagon. "I don't want to miss a word, y'all. We can all fit in your car, can't we, Faye?" Thelma squished herself into the middle. "I should've left mine at your place." While chatting about more mundane things, everyone happily landed on the topic of Madeline's single status. The group brainstormed, trying to think of young men in town to introduce to her.

"What about Chad, y'all? I know he was a little pitiful for a while, but I heard he's perked up, some." Glory thought this was a reasonable suggestion.

Wails of protest from the others made it clear that Chad would not make the list of potential suitors for their beloved nurse. The decision was finalized when they spotted Chad on the edge of the county road thumbing a lift.

"Now that is literally God speaking, right there, Glory," Faye declared as she pulled into the parking lot of her tidy store. "Chad is out, and we're here."

The Dress was announced from a standing sign large enough to be spotted from the main road. "Sissie and Gabe couldn't decide between *Shop* and *Shoppe* with the fancy extra *'pe'* when they named the place," Faye explained, "so they came up with *The Dress* as a compromise. I've gotten used to it, and Lord knows I'm not about to change it. I'd be called into the county seat!"

"Yes, Ms. Faye, it'll be *The Dress* for eternity." From the shop's threshold smiled one of the most impressive women Shelly had ever seen. About fifty, she stood tall with her shoulders back, and attentive to Faye as the group walked up. Her powerful posture struck Shelly as part bodyguard, part shop employee. "I'm Denean," she said. The fuchsia and navy in her scarf brought flair to her sleeveless grey linen dress. The effect was elegant while her toned upper arms suggested regular exercise. She hugged Faye with the familiarity of a beloved family member. "Madeline," a quick handshake, then "…and you must be Dr. Riley. We're so pleased you could come visit us at *The Dress*. Come right in," and she swept her hand toward the store, drawing the group inside.

Shelly could hear Thelma behind them, "You're not going to believe this, Carrie, but…" and then more hellos all around.

"Denean's been my lifeline, Dr. Riley," Faye nodded to the employee. "She manages the inventory, sells the clothes, and consoles the customers. She does it all. Her specialty is the woman who's gained a bit of weight but doesn't want to try the next size up, isn't it, Denean?"

Denean angled her head and nodded, permitting, "I have a fair amount of experience in that department."

"I love your outfit," Shelly gushed. "I always thought I'd wear clothes that make me more polished, but I have zero style. I'm doomed to stay in my rumpled doctor-in-training outfits," she sighed.

"This store is dazzling, Faye. It makes me need oxygen. I just knew it would be like this!" Madeline was already fanning through a rack of seasonal tops, two draped on her arm while she inspected the rest. "We have to stay a minute, y'all. I need to quick try these on," she told them as another lady approached, asking Denean to see if she could help.

"And this is Barbara, who keeps everything tidy and in its place. She's a whiz with the customers, let me tell you. Barbara can keep up with the wildest shopper in Red Rock Falls. Even if she tried on every outfit in the store, Barbara'll have everything back on the racks before I've rung her up. We're a good team," Denean finished.

"The displays are so clever, Faye! I can see the different styles throughout the store." Shelly admired the jewelry cabinet and glanced at the clothes in the different sections. Madeline bought several items, and Shelly settled on a necklace. When the others dispersed, Denean arranged the pieces while she caught Shelly alone for a word.

"We really do appreciate you coming down, doctor. It means a great deal to us all. You know, Faye's parents started this store, but it's Faye who brought it life. She always thinks of her customers." Denean snapped the case shut. "When she goes to the trade shows, she comes home with ideas for certain people, just nudging them along to a little fresher pattern, or a more flattering cut. Sometimes she buys a piece knowing it'll cheer someone up. In fact, she did that for me, when my husband died. It's the very thing I'm wearing today. We love her in this town. Please," Denean pleaded, "please, you take care of our Faye, won't you?"

Shelly swallowed. "I will, I promise. She's dear to everyone at the hospital, too." Shelly added, "Some people just really make an impression, don't they? Faye is a shining soul."

The driving tour continued, swinging through the business district and past the high school. Shelly tried to push away the reality of Faye's miserable prognosis, aching as she stared out the window at bakeries and diners, the town hardware store, and a butcher shop. When they regrouped at the house, Faye caught Shelly in the kitchen and packed her leftovers for the drive home.

"I've got a wonderful life, Dr. Riley. I'm so glad you had a chance to see my people in action today. Now you know how much I have to live for. We're all so grateful for any extra time the trial meds might give me."

Shelly fought tears while she nodded and fiercely concentrated on the food cartons she packed with her patient. "Everyone at the hospital is grateful too. The nurses, the aides, they all keep asking about you. It's meant so much to be here today," she started to confide when Madeline made her way in.

"We'd better hit the road, Dr. Riley. Rain's coming and I turn into a pumpkin if I'm not in my nightie by nine. We overstayed our welcome—let's get going before they realize we stole all the leftovers!"

Madeline and Shelly showered more thanks for the hospitality and promised to return. A glance at the yellow rosebush reminded Shelly that Sissie and Faye were indeed surrounded by love. The normally effusive Madeline drove them home in near silence, except to assert they'd need to hear more about Carrie's awful mother someday. The quiet trip allowed Shelly to savor the chaos of the day and memorize the stories and action she observed.

"I wonder what they think, Madeline. Do you suppose they realize Faye's cancer's going to come back at some point? They're all just so serene, for God's sake. Sissie's talking to Jesus, Thelma's crocheting lap blankets, and Glory's throwing together sparkling punch. Do they know what's ahead for their friend?"

Madeline drove in silence, then said, "They know, Shelly. They just choose to ignore the future until it's here, I guess. They love Faye, and they put their best face on for her."

"Well, I'd stay in that little town forever if I could. I feel like we just took a bath in love, you know? After all, Sissie said everything's going to work out."

Madeline nodded. "It's not every day you meet people like them. I'm glad we came."

Shelly gazed out the Camry's windows as the scenery became more urban, taking her further from the dreamy Red Rock Falls. *Wouldn't that be grand,* Shelly thought, *if everything really is just the way it's supposed to be?*

FRASER, MARIETTA (née McGraw)
1937-1988

Marietta was called home after a long illness. She died of jaundice and liver disease in the Kentucky SE University Hospital. The doctors did their best, but the Lord had other ideas.

Born to Jefford and Claire McGraw, Marietta grew up on the family farm in Joletta, KY with four brothers and five sisters. She married Ray Fraser at a young age, and their union produced six children: Carrie, Ray, Jr., Peggy, Arden, Hugh, and Betty.

Marietta ran the home with a firm hand and a well-read Bible. Her children were raised with the fear of the Lord. She saw to that. On her deathbed she was sure to tell her children where she would be waiting for them. Well done, faithful servant.

Services Thursday August 18th at the Church of the Redeemer, Red Rock Falls. There will be a luncheon to follow in the church.

Cheryl Bailey

CHAPTER 17

Shelly Meets Aslan

Despite the lack of a first-year fellow, the oncology team had become efficient and strategic. Shelly had called Ken the night she confronted Dr. Farber, hoping for reassurance and a promise he'd call Walter and set him straight. He buckled instead, saying Walter was too good a friend for him to challenge. She was sad to hear the defeat in his voice, as if he'd been expecting the conflict. Ken would side with his friend over her.

She also called Walter, telling him to stay away from rounds. She offered a variety of surgical procedures she'd try out on his anatomy if he ever, "I mean EVER go behind my back to an attending again. Are we clear on this, Walter?" Her satisfaction was delicious as he stammered and deflected on the phone. He got the message and kept his distance.

The medical students abandoned ship the first week of their rotation, stating they'd beg for a reassignment to anything else other than a surgical specialty with such ridiculous hours. The team ran well lean, and Rebecca commanded with capable style. Each doctor knew the patients in detail from the endless hours worked. Shelly shrugged off the insults from Dr. Farber and Cardinal in the operating room the best she could, but she still quaked during evening rounds, when questions could stump her. Boldon added a couple cases and requested Shelly scrub; when the other two protested they'd be without a fellow, Shelly suggested they discuss it with Dr. Boldon himself.

"It's bad enough he asks for me and only me," Shelly told Rebecca. "The other two staff can handle it like grownups, as far as I'm concerned."

They were on the Powell so many hours a day that family members of patients not even on their service greeted the gyn onc team like friends. They started almost all the resuscitations on the floor, which occurred at least once or twice a month, beginning chest compressions until the code team arrived.

In addition to their medical tasks, the social needs of the Powell were managed by Shelly's squad. Dave informed the others when the newly hired medical assistant had a date. Shelly brewed fresh coffee throughout the day. Tabitha flirted with one of the strapping physical therapists, not realizing that her colleagues noticed, and relished, her crush. Rebecca used her rare down time to catch up with a couple nurses on the floor she knew from her prior life as an R.N. Overall, despite fatigue, the team made the best they could of the situation.

* * *

Grateful to escape the already blistering summer morning heat at the usual five-thirty starting time outside Room 201, Shelly groaned as Bernice announced the arrival of the surgical intern on the Gold Surgery service, a medical group separate from Shelly's crew.

"Gold Surgery is on the floor. Dr. Randall from Gold Surgery is on the Powell," her voice carried from the intercom down the hallways.

"He looks like shit, as usual," smirked Dave, the PG-3. "Like he literally just fell out of the bed in the call room. I'll bet his breath smells worse than his pits. His scrubs are more crumpled than the dollar bill you find at the bottom of your jeans pocket when it's gone through the wash. His underwear…"

"That'll do, Dave," Shelly interrupted. "Thanks for the sensory awakening this fine morning. You make a good point, though. We're on this floor day and night, we run their codes, we brew their damned coffee, but *we* never get announced. It goes without saying, we're the best team in the hospital! And seriously, how is it this hot at five thirty in the morning? This weather is not made for humans."

"Have y'all gotten everything off your chests, doctors? Then let's get going," Rebecca clapped Dave on the back while trying not to laugh. "Give us a quick recap of the service."

"Seventeen patients, no real calamities overnight," Dave started. "Six, maybe seven discharges today. Depends on 216's CT from last night—there was no report typed when I checked last night. Three planned chemo admits. Tab wrote 'em up last night. Then OR cases later today. You'll have to tolerate Luca on the Farber case, Shelly, since I've gotta get my wisdom teeth removed."

"Hmm, what kind of performance review do I give a resident who would rather have oral surgery than operate with me?" Shelly eyed him, looking up from a chart.

"Good luck with your surgery, Dave. You expect to be back tomorrow, right?" Rebecca pushed the cart along the corridor to the next room.

He nodded. "I won't take any pain meds in the morning. Michelle had hers out, and she said it's no big deal."

"Well, page me if anything changes. How was your call, Tabitha? How much sleep did you get last night?"

"Not much, I guess," Tabitha yawned. "I feel okay, though. Mostly nuisance pages, and at least I brushed my teeth and changed scrubs!" She pivoted and pointed this out as the disheveled Dr. Randall clumped past them, scratching his side.

"Every time you wake up from another night on call you're grateful there were no disasters, aren't you? It builds a little bit more confidence for when you're a real doctor. Good job." Shelly hoped she was reassuring.

"I'm ready for today, though, that's for sure," Tabitha was quick to add. "I'm fine."

We certainly learn early on to show no weakness, Shelly thought. "Okay, let's roll. Tab, who's first?"

They recounted each patient outside the door with a brief presentation, then all walked in to check incisions and go over the plan for the day. Each doctor kept a paper list in their lab coat, making boxes by the names to check off items they were responsible for that day—path reports, lab results, discharge paperwork—knowing Rebecca would expect updates on the critical items throughout the day.

Everything went so smoothly they applauded themselves at the end of rounds. They'd maneuvered in and out of each room on the circular ward, almost back to the reception area. Shelly glanced at her watch and complimented them. "Less than an hour, and most of the admits ready! Nice job, everyone."

Dave pushed the cart back to the ward secretary's desk, orders flagged on each chart with a red plastic strip, telling her, "Bernice, this team is one magnificently efficient machine and got orders done before your shift ends. We make the Gold Surgery intern look like the wiener that he is. Dr. Riley thinks y'all need to start announcing us in the morning."

"On the loudspeaker! With balloons, or something! C'mon, Bernice, we're here all the time and the Powell never gives us any love," Shelly teased.

"Want me to hide the cart?" Dave offered, half kidding.

Bernice laughed, "I believe y'all are doing just great this rotation. I'll get started on your orders, and Fern can polish them off when she gets here. I've gotta leave on time this morning—otherwise you know I'd stay for y'all. And Dr. Riley, the nurses are real impressed with how you're running your service, with it being just you and this crew. Even your medical students hightailed it outta here, didn't they?"

"Thanks, Bernice. That's nice to hear." She nodded, "Yep, both med students bailed on me. They thought we worked too many hours. Can you imagine?" Shelly shook her head and shrugged.

* * *

Luca was waiting for her in the pre-op area, pacing and taking a page, the long phone cord getting caught on charts and chair edges, generally being a nuisance to those around him.

"Sit down, Luca, you're gonna spill my coffee, and I'm already crabby!" railed anesthesiologist Dr. C. Cole. He was legendary in the OR for having little patience and a foul mouth, but he was the guy to have running the case if things hit the fan. Evidently, no one knew his first name. Even his colleagues called him C.

Shelly wrapped Luca's excess phone cord loosely around his neck and guided him to his seat, putting her first finger to her lips indicating he should idle down and lower his voice. "Sorry about him, Dr. Cole. We have to let him out sometimes or he bites. Any issues with our first case?"

"Well, let's see," C. growled. "Hypertension and poorly controlled diabetes? Check. Obese with a terrible airway? Check. You really know how to make a man's day, Riley."

"We aim to please, Dr. Cole. What's got you so bothered this morning, sir?" *Why am I engaging with this asshole?* she wondered to herself.

"Well, if you must know," he barked, pushing over the metro section of that morning's newspaper. "You goddamned women are already in charge of the world. Do we really need a woman as a three-star General in the Marines?"

Shelly read the text where he'd pointed. "Lt. General Carol Mutter becomes first female three-star officer in Washington, DC…Deputy Chief of staff…" Shelly read aloud. "Okay, I'll go down that garden path with you, Dr. Cole. Why in the world should this Lieutenant General *not* get a promotion?"

"I just told you, dammit. You run everything else. You women could at least let men have a place where we can be men. The Marines, for God's sake. What's next?" He perched on his little rolling stool, scowling face daring her to retort. His ancient OR clogs, covered with the fluids and filth of years working in the operating room, identified C. as a man who cared little about other people's opinion of his physical appearance.

"Well, Dr. Cole," Shelly grinned, "#1, someone invented shoes…" she held up her fingers as she outlined her answer, "…#2 someone invented the Pill, and I guess #3, the kitchen is just too crowded for 'us women.'" She added the emphasis as she dragged Luca up, slack jawed as he watched Dr. Cole laugh despite himself.

"You're all right, Riley, you know that? But I still say there's nothing wrong with barefoot and pregnant, when it comes right down to it." He stared at her, begging for the final retort.

"Well, give it a try, then, Dr. Cole," Shelly encouraged, "and let me know how you like hemorrhoids and breast-feeding." She stood, calling over her shoulder, "I'm going to check in with our patient and get her to the room. Nice chatting with you, as always."

Shelly strode toward the patient care area, pulling the pea-green privacy drapes around her patient's gurney, giving her a warm smile and introducing herself. Luca followed her with glee, rubbing his hands in anticipation of heralding the latest takedown of C. Cole to his fellow residents.

"Strong work, Shelly," Luca whispered. "Now do that to *your* staff."

"Zip it, Luca. Cole is harmless. In fact, I think he likes me to slap him around. This sparring with me is as close as he comes to showing *anyone* respect, even his male colleagues, from what I've seen. Just adds to my theory that we doctors are infantile when it comes to social interaction."

They walked alongside each other in the cold white OR hallway, following the anesthesia resident as she steered the bed into the operating room. She had reassured the patient in the preop suite while she administered a sedative through the IV, resulting in lighthearted, slurred speech as the patient relaxed.

"God, people just look so happy when they get Versed," Shelly sighed. "And they don't remember a thing about preop, which is probably not such a bad thing."

"Maybe Cole can slip you some Versed at the end of your fellowship. Make it all go away like a bad dream," Luca laughed as they tied their surgical masks and headed into the room. Within ten minutes they were scrubbing at the deep OR sinks outside room two, Luca chattering without stop and Shelly daydreaming about the end of fellowship.

He interrupted her reverie with, "So what do you say?"

"Say about what? God, Luca, you talk so much I sort of tune you out. Sorry." Shelly had learned to be brutal when she interacted with Luca. He had the thickest skin imaginable, pondered all feedback precisely at face value, and never took a single thing personally.

"Come camping with Samantha and me. It'll be great. There's this muzzleloader festival coming up that we try to make every year. Well, that and Mardi Gras, we never miss that. And if the Grateful Dead come anywhere near us, we do that, too. Hey! You distracted me!"

Shelly shook her head. "What the hell are muzzleloaders? And camping? I get about three weekends off a year, and you want me to go camping?"

They stopped the water faucets with a quick push of their knees, dripped off for a second or two, and pushed into the OR, back first. Luca was undeterred.

"Well, it's in a really nice state park, for one thing. And it's a combination of stoners and these guys who like to pretend they're living in the 1800s, see? They all wear muslin outfits and cook in big iron pots over a fire. Their kids run through the forest like they were raised by wolves. Even their tents are old-timey." He stood, hands up, elbows bent, while Velma helped Shelly don her sterile gear.

"Sounds great." In her sterile gown Shelly turned to let Kit tie the back and Velma gowned Luca. "I'll look for my corset when I get home and pack my sorghum candy. Seriously, Luca, make a better case." Velma passed the knife into her outstretched hand as she started the surgery.

"Naw, you just ignore the bearded guys. Actually, those forest kids are a little scary, come to think of it…The other part is these groovy, laid-back campers who drum and exchange beads and feathers and stuff. Samantha likes to make necklaces, so she goes to get new supplies from vendors with beads she can't find anywhere else. Maybe you and Pepper can find some burly mountain man who'll give you a tour of his antique tent. "And Shelly?" She kept operating as he exaggerated, *"It's. Not. This. Hospital!"* His triumphant final plea came in a clipped stage whisper.

Shelly laughed. "Let's finish this case, and I'll think about it. Say, Velma?" she turned to her tech. "Dr. Farber isn't here yet, and I'm ready to start the nodes. Let me try a disposable hemaclip. Medium. It'll take me half the time, and maybe that'll drag him into this century. He'll *have* to see how efficient they are."

"You sure about deviating from 'The Way?'" Velma, always ready with the correct instrument, was not encouraging. "I've got the yards of silk ties here, all loaded up for you."

"No, let's try this. I used these for four years in residency with all my attendings, and General Surgery uses them here. I think he'll come along with me on these clips. There's just no downside." Shelly pushed down a shimmer of doubt, as Kit went to find them in the corridor storage.

She and Luca clipped and dissected and removed parcels of nodal tissue off the sturdy pelvic arteries and the thin-walled, dangerous veins.

"Damn, Shelly, you're right. These clips are slick," Luca approved. Kit collected each batch of tissue at her desk, labeling them with the patient's data and cross checking with the team. Velma was quiet.

Without an attending present, the chatter in the OR was looser than usual. Luca kept the room entertained as Shelly continued her work. The random thoughts bouncing around his massive brain lurched from comical to serious and back again, occasionally hitting a medical fact or philosophical note that enlightened them all.

"Mostly, you're full of shit, Luca," Shelly commented as he rambled.

"That's a true statement, Shelly. I still want to know when you take your Onc Boards."

Shelly sighed, "*Now* what're you talking about?"

"The Onc Boards, Shelly. They're every other year, and this should be your year. You'll nail them—won't even need to study, with all the conferences you run."

A tiny stab pierced her gut. "Onc Boards?" she mumbled. "I just did the regular residency testing. I haven't even finished my fellowship yet."

"Yeah, well, I was looking through the Board Requirements Bulletin last night, you know, for a little light reading before bed?" Luca was an absolute animal when it came to his absorption of data. He inhaled everything—medical facts, surgical anatomy, baseball stats, and Board rules all found an equal home in his ample memory. He forgot nothing.

"They offer sub-specialty Boards every other year. Take yours now and you're golden! Otherwise, you'll be in private practice, somewhere up north in an igloo, too busy to study. Hasn't the office signed you up? You gotta take 'em in Dallas, you know."

No, I didn't know, Shelly thought with yet another pang of foreboding. "I'll ask Arlys about it, Luca. Thanks for looking out for me," she nodded.

"No one else seems to," he said with cheer. "Say, can I be primary on Farber's first case tomorrow since Dave'll probably be out with his wisdom teeth and I once again saved your butt?"

"No, you turd," Shelly's shoulders shook from laughing. She was about to unleash a good-natured verbal spanking when Dr. Farber entered the room. His mask loosely covered his face, his brow wrinkled in displeasure as he handed Kit his watch and beeper.

"Shelly, let's keep the OR professional, shall we? How's the case going? Any suspicious nodes you think?"

"No, sir. I think she's got a small IB cancer so we can proceed with the radical portion. I just sent off the last set of nodes and I'm developing the tissue planes now. It all looks good for her, I'd say," Shelly felt great pride at her surgical field, tidy with clips and completely free of blood. The dissection was perfect, and she knew it.

Her attending scrubbed in, making the usual comments to Luca and Velma as he spun to tie up his sterile gown. When he peered into the abdomen, he froze.

"Now, now," his stammer signaling displeasure, "what are these clips?"

Shelly spoke up immediately. "I know you usually use silk ties, Dr. Farber, but I thought I'd show you these hemaclips, just this once. They're so efficient and cut down our OR time by..."

"Take them off." His voice was emotionless, flat. Horrifying.

"But, sir, they'll tear the..."

"Take these clips off right now, Shelly. Velma, have the silk ties ready." Taut with anger, his folksy accent was gone. "You should know better. The ties are to improve your surgical skills, Shelly. I use them for you, so you learn to be gentle with knot-tying and careful on these fragile veins. Anyone can use a clip. I'm surprised you would deviate from 'The Way' just to show me how fast you can be. What a disappointment you've been."

Sick with defeat, Shelly removed the clips off the delicate veins and tried to minimize the tissue damage. She spent the next hour dutifully, furiously doing as she was told. The OR staff stayed silent, accentuating Dr. Farber's criticism of Shelly's every move of her hand, every use of cautery.

He barked with irritation. "You can't remove that without having the stitch immediately available. Doesn't that just make sense?" And later, "The extra operative time is a real problem, Shelly. It adds morbidity with no value. I hope you're learning something from this catastrophe you've caused." Velma stood at her side, instruments ready, while Luca suctioned and adjusted the lighting as she moved through the case. Even Luca, with his utter inability to respect social cues, knew to idle down.

At the end of the surgery, Dr. Farber regarded Velma across the table, saying "Thanks, everyone." He made his signature move of arching his back as he pulled off the overlying gown and gloves, grabbed his things from the nurse, and left the room. Shelly relaxed her shoulders and gasped with relief.

Velma patted her bloody, gloved hand and even held it for a moment in solidarity. "Time to close, doctor. Luca and I can do this. Go get yourself a respiratory treatment."

"I'll take you up on that, Velma. Oh, my God, you were right." She limped away from the sterile field, stiff from hours of standing in one position, hunched over the incision. "I can't believe I added an hour to a four-hour case," she muttered, shaking her head. "The whole time I could have torn a vein—how could he do that?"

Kit came to her and detached her headlamp, clicking its mechanism to loosen it from her forehead. She whispered, "You tried, at least. I've never seen any other fellow try to bring him forward. Remember that, okay?"

Shelly shook her head. "Where did it get me, Kit? He hates me even more. Doesn't trust me. Acts surprised when I use updated techniques in here. No, I've learned my lesson. Shut up, do as I'm told, and graduate. That's the plan." Her voice rang harshly in the tiled operating room.

Luca, ever eavesdropping, added "And go camping with Samantha and me to recharge and meet a mountain man. In one month. Mark her calendar, Kit. Someone's gotta take care of this Nordic giantess. Camping will cure what ails you, Shelly!"

Too furious to manage a smile, she just answered, "You're too much, Luca, as always. I'll see the family if you get the op note and orders done. I'll dictate later. Tell Rebecca I'm off to Farber's office after this case, OK?"

* * *

She schlumped off to give the family the good news of a potentially curative surgery, and with gratitude pushed open the door to one of the innumerable outdoor smoking areas, lighting up the second she felt the fresh air.

"Hey, Doc," greeted her fellow smokers, all nodding and making room for her on the bench.

"Long case? You look woofed," noted one of the housekeepers she knew from her cigarette breaks.

"It shows, eh? No, just the usual. This'll perk me up and I'll get right back at it," she professed a cheer she did not feel. *I'm thirty-three years old and was just humiliated,* she thought. *When do I poof into a grown-up?*

The chatter outside with her comrades helped distract Shelly from Dr. Farber's chastisement. Shelly heard about their families, listened to the usual work gripes, and absorbed the friendly vibe among them. One of the respiratory therapists, a burly man whom Shelly had seen comfort even the most terrified patients, stood to take his leave.

"Whatever it is, Doc, you've got what is takes to beat it. And we both really should quit these damn cancer sticks, ya know," he winked and headed back inside.

Shelly chuckled, stamped out her cigarette with her goodbyes to the group. She whistled as she headed up to Arlys's office, ruminating on Luca's earlier question about Onc Boards. They were the most important tests of her life, since she would need to pass the oral and written Oncology Boards to get a good job and privileges at the hospitals where she wanted to work. She dimly remembered the every-other-year schedule he'd mentioned but hadn't seen any bulletins triggering her to get enrolled. She knew Luca was dead right about taking the tests now, while her fund of knowledge was maximized.

"We don't sign you up for any tests, doctor," Arlys purred. "That's your responsibility, I'm afraid."

Shelly wondered why in the world she was surprised by that yet couldn't resist a poke.

"That's funny, Arlys. I'd have thought my department would *want* to have its fellows Board Certified. In fact, I'd have thought you'd do whatever it took to make that happen."

Arlys shrugged, repeating, "I imagine you've been mailed the bulletins about it. I've not been instructed to sign you up for your Board exam, Dr. Riley. You'll need to take care of that yourself." She smiled at Shelly and the room temperature dropped ten degrees. "Is there anything else?"

Honey, not vinegar, Shelly urged herself to avoid snapping at this sugar-coated scorpion of a secretary. "Yes, Arlys, thanks so much. Could you find the phone number for the Board? I'll call them right now." Without an invitation she sat, crossing her legs to make it clear she would wait for what she needed.

Arlys reached over her desk to the rolodex, flipping the cards until she found the Board. She copied the telephone number on a notecard, handing it to Shelly, impatience shown by the quick withdrawal of her hand.

"Thanks. I'll call them from my office phone since it's long distance." Shelly dashed down to her cubby and made her call, rubbing an unlit cigarette between her fingers under her desk while she sat on hold.

"American Board, how can I help you?"

"Yes, hello!" Startled by the voice after minutes of piped in hold music, Shelly hadn't meant to yelp. "I'm a senior fellow in Kentucky, and I need to sign up for my sub-specialty Boards."

Silence.

"Hello?" Shelly repeated. "I'm calling to get signed up for my Board exam?"

"Well, doctor," the voice was hesitant but warm. "I'm sorry to tell you that the deadline for that test has passed."

Shelly's fingers snapped the unlit cigarette, sending soft bits of tobacco over the carpet.

"No, that can't be. The exam isn't for months. I'm sure there's time!"

"Well, the official application deadline was last Friday, a week and a half ago. There is an extension, but you'd have to pay a hefty fee…"

"I'll pay!" Shelly interrupted. "Of course, I'll pay. I *have* to take that exam. Can you tell me how to go about it? You mentioned an application," she added.

"Doctor, the problem is that the final deadline is tomorrow. That means *everything* must be received here, in Dallas, by tomorrow." Her voice was sympathetic, probably having had to explain this to many young physicians in the past. Her emphasis was clear, though, and Shelly realized she had to act immediately.

Swallow. There was no moisture in her throat to choke down the nausea. "Okay," Shelly said, "I've got a pen and paper. Let me write down your fax number, and I'll give you mine. Then the fee—how can I get the money to you overnight? Money order? I mean, I don't know anything about this, but Western Union or something to wire you the funds?" She looked at her watch. "It's three p.m. here, so I could go to a bank if you tell me how much I owe you…"

"Doctor, I really am sorry," the voice cut in, "but we don't accept faxes. We don't accept cash or money orders." She sounded genuinely sad to give this crushing news.

Shelly stood up, sending the phone base crashing around her desk, nearly emptying a coffee cup's contents all over the papers and trinkets around it. *Shitdammit!*

"I don't understand. How can you not accept a fax? It will be the exact information, just warm paper from your machine, for Pete's sake. It will have everything you need on it."

"Firm rule, I'm afraid. You'll need to get the actual application to this office in Dallas by five p.m. tomorrow. There are just no exceptions. Will you try to get that done, doctor? I can have someone watching for you in the office."

Shelly collapsed back into her chair. "I'm a fellow. I'm in Kentucky. I can't possibly get that to you in time by mail. And I don't even have the application. There's no solution to this?" Shelly swallowed again, desperate that the kind lady would laugh and tell her she was just kidding.

"I do wish I could help you, doctor. If it were up to me, I'd give you more time, but I can't break those rules. If you give me your address, I'll mail you a bulletin that has the date for the exam you'll need to take in two years. Please take care."

Shelly recited her home address like a robot and set the phone in its receiver. She tidied up her desk, stuffing a tissue in her mug to sop up the old coffee, and stared at her nameplate on the top of the cubby.

* * *

Her capacity for pain had been reached, and she was about to lose all semblance of control. Shelly grabbed the edge of the desk for support as she stood to escape the public space, trying the doorknob of Dr. Hazel's office next door. The nurses in her office paid no mind as they continued their phone counseling with patients. No one saw her stumble in.

To her great relief, the cool, dark room was empty. Falling onto the couch, she sobbed in her hands while the humiliation and grief of the last year poured out. She held her head, shaking and gasping as the pain escaped, wiping her nose on her scrubs. As the minutes passed and her gasps mellowed, she concluded that her failure was the department's goal.

And now she'd done it. No Boards, no job. All this colossal expenditure of energy for nothing. Her brave face and sassy determination that they would somehow come around to understand that she was capable? Not going to happen.

Yet even *more* humiliation was possible. Dr. Hazel himself, the lion of the department, chose that moment to walk into his office, switch on the lights, and see Shelly, sniveling like a toad on his sagging couch. Snot on her upper arms, eyes fire engine red, and hiccupping from her sob-fest, she was pathetic.

"Well, hello there, doctor." His gentle greeting was as if he were expecting her there for a long-held appointment, apologetic that he was late. "Some sad news, eh?" He took off his suit coat, draped it on his desk chair, and sat down, ready to hear her tale of woe.

Shelly had never met this man, despite using his office for escape. The main stories she'd heard were about residents coming there for after-hours affection on call.

Gross. She sniffed. This couch.

After his formidable surgical career, Dr. Hazel helped the university with banquets and fundraising. He rarely came to the hospital for clinical events. The radiant light from his desk lamp caught his full face.

He's glowing like an angel, Shelly imagined. I'll have to tell Sissie.

"I'm so sorry to crawl into your office, Dr. Hazel. It's just that, well, I just found out that I missed the deadline for the Boards. Actually, it's tomorrow, but they won't take a fax, and the money can't be wired, and…" she sniffled. "I thought Arlys would take care of something like that. Or would have at least told me. I thought the department would at least *pretend* to want to help me."

Out it came, the snuffling and tears and whining, with Shelly losing all emotional control as she gasped out the story of her last year of training, detail after miserable detail.

Dr. Hazel, a rotund man with little round glasses, sat with gracious ease, allowing Shelly to vent and cry and even rage. As she settled down once again, taking his offer of several tissues to honk her dripping nose and dry her tears, he took off his spectacles and made wiping motions on them, peering through the lens to see if the cleaning was complete.

"I don't doubt it. Not one bit. We have a long way to go in this department, when it comes to recognizing all the skills in our young women physicians. You're something of a pioneer, Shelly. Might I offer a little observation?" His gentle face creased in a smile. "If this exam issue is the worst thing to happen to you in medicine, you are destined for a wonderful career indeed."

His mild commentary, combined with his endless patience listening to the jerky retelling of her woes, deflated Shelly's panic and reassured her beyond his words. A soggier but more composed Shelly managed a smile.

"You think I'll live, eh?"

"You certainly will, young lady," he beamed. "And from what I hear, you will thrive."

The emphasis on a positive image of Shelly saved her soul. She stood, thanking him for helping her gain perspective. He jutted his chin in the direction of an antique wall mirror, a recommendation to tidy up before heading back into the world.

"Take good care of yourself, doctor. Medicine is not for the weak. You've made a few mistakes. Now you seem to have lost the chance to take an exam at the usual time. There are far worse obstacles ahead, with all manner of surgical complications and medical blunders. I'm still haunted by patients who suffered because of my inexpert management. We have to live with those sorrows, and pray they are few. If you learn from this difficult part of your career, you'll only be more prepared for the future. I look forward to hearing wonderful stories from you." Dr. Hazel urged her to re-enter the world with confidence and flair.

"I'm grateful you came into the hospital today," she said, crossing the threshold of Dr. Hazel's inviting office. "Thank you for everything." She exited, feeling like the English kids in *The Lion, The Witch and The Wardrobe* leaving Narnia. *It's nice to know I have Aslan around,* Shelly mused.

She stood up straight. Maybe she had a future after all. At least she knew her enemies now, whether it was Walter tattling to the boss or Arlys keeping her from critical deadlines. *It doesn't really matter if it's benign neglect or outright sabotage.* If graduation and a real job was what she wanted, she'd have to take *and pass* the Boards in two years. Forward was the only direction, even if she tripped now and then.

HALLSTROM, MONIQUE (née Renier)
5/3/38-8/17/95

What a life! Born in Bordeaux, France, Monique "Momo" Renier spent a sweet childhood with her loving family, grateful for recovery from WWII. When her father's international business brought him to the US, the family eventually moved to Chicago, then settled in Rochester, MN.

There she met her love, Kenneth Hallstrom. They married and had three girls, Feline Hammer (Mark, Rochester, MN), Dr. Evie Hallstrom (Dr. Bill Watson, San Francisco, CA), and Bridget Hallstrom (NY, NY). Momo watched over her family, made wonderful tarts and crepes for friends and neighbors, and grew the most amazing garden on the block.

Monique was proud of her girls, and taught them to be fierce and independent. She always made sure there were flowers in the house and music in the air. When people commented on her accent, she'd say, "It's not easy knowing two languages!" and laugh.

We grieve that she is gone, but we feel her in our hearts. And we know she would love to think of her friends having a delicious meal in her honor. Adieu, chére Momo. Arrangements for a service and gathering will be announced later. Private interment.

CHAPTER 18

Baby

"I see you in this class every week, but never on campus," the bearded man whispered to Shelly during the graduate class on medical devices. She'd noticed his interest as each week he managed to squeeze into seats closer to hers, but dismissed potential flirtation with any of these "kids" in her graduate level class. After all, he was probably in his mid-twenties--ten years felt like a generation. She doubted a fling could fit in her schedule.

"I'm a fellow at the hospital," she whispered back. "This is a requirement for me to graduate in June. Now, if you don't mind, we should pay attention." Shelly squared her lanky body to face the professor, feigning interest in his droning voice. She tried to ignore the yummy aroma of the stranger, who had yet to move away.

"I'm Jeremy," he said, a honeyed lilt to his voice.

Oh, yeah, he means business, Shelly thought. *Gonna have to nip this in the bud after class,* though she was distracted to find that even his breath was attractive. *Who has good breath?* she wondered. She struggled to concentrate on the subject matter as the professor paced back and forth, tapping the white board for emphasis.

"Jeremy Finlay, at your service. I'd love to buy you a cup of coffee after class, if you don't have to dash away." A tingling sensation hit Shelly hard, and she shifted her thighs as she toyed with a little innocent flirtation.

"Shh!" scolded the student seated below them, turning to disapprove.

Shelly put her index finger to her lips and nodded to the student, quieting Jeremy for the moment. She prepared for the conversation that she knew would follow as soon as the professor uttered his last word, and he did not disappoint.

"How about it? The student union has terrible coffee and disgusting donuts. What better offer would entice you to take a quick break?"

Oh, she thought, *he's got dimples.* She fought off an impulse to take him home right then. They gathered their notebooks and followed the shuffling students ahead to pass through the only open door.

"You're persistent, I'll give you that," Shelly admitted. "Should I just point out the obvious age difference between us?"

"Well," he drawled, "that's irrelevant, as far as I'm concerned. The *more* obvious thing is you haven't told me your name, and yet here we are, walking to the union together. So I'm gonna try again. I'm Jeremy Finlay, final year, master's program in engineering, at your service." He gave a little bow. "And you are?"

Are you really going to do this? Shelly wondered. With your crazy ass schedule and terrible taste in men and the extra class and no Walter to help and a thesis to submit and…

"Shelly Riley," she thrust her hand out to him, which he took and kissed. Oh, hell, yes, you're going to do all of this. "Gynecologic oncology fellow and keeper of ridiculous work hours. You've got ten minutes, Jeremy, and then I've gotta run."

The light banter continued in earnest as they walked along an inner glass hallway, laughing at each other's choices of pertinent details in their lives.

"I mean, if I only have ten minutes to impress you, I'm only doling out the good stuff, you realize that, right?"

She had to admit, there was plenty of good stuff. *If* he was telling the truth, of course, but her bullshit meter was registering low for this kid from a small town in western Kentucky.

"I'm twenty-six, since you mentioned age, and I took a few years off to work in an engineering firm after college. My boss thought I had enough potential that I should go for the advanced degree. After I paid off some debt and helped my family a little, it was the right time to go back and get my master's degree. They're holding a position for me if I want it."

She sipped her coffee, made undrinkable with his addition of far too much sugar and skim milk. "You're right. Their coffee is horrible. Look, Jeremy," Shelly started to reason with him. "I'm thirty-three. I work a miserable number of hours in the hospital. I come home crabby and mentally exhausted. I pay people to walk my dog. I smoke a pack of Marlboros every day. I have no life—ZERO—outside of work. I just think you're better off with some cute undergraduate who can do fun things with you and, I don't know, listen to the same radio station or something." Her voice trailed off as she watched him drink her in.

"I'm not worried about your hours, and moods can be improved, you know." Jeremy winked. "I'm perfectly happy doing my own thing when you're away. I'm surrounded by this crowd of students," he added. "I'm not cruising for cute undergrads, Shelly."

She checked her watch.

"Jesus, Jeremy, I have to go. Look, I'll take your number, okay? Maybe we can meet for dinner sometime. I've really got to run, though. Thanks for the coffee."

He scribbled something on a piece of notebook paper, as Shelly admired his left-handed grip. Shelly drank in one last heady whiff of this total stranger.

"Tomorrow night at the Dawn Plaza strip mall. I'll treat you to a delicious dinner at this place called The Nectary. It doesn't look like much, but the food is fantastic. I'll be there at six and I'll stay till you come, or until they close, whichever happens first. I hope to see you there," Jeremy stood to let her pass, handing her the paper and allowing his fingers to linger on her wrist.

She paused, cocking her head in admiration. "I wouldn't wait around, Jeremy. I have no idea when I'll be done with rounds." He didn't change expressions, remaining cheery and at ease. "You're a confident little booger, aren't you?"

He laughed. "I was going for mature, sexy, and intriguing," he countered. "But if you meet me tomorrow night, 'confident little booger' will be my style from now on. Go on, now. Work hard!"

She waved to him as she scurried via the faster but steamier outdoor route to the Powell. She knew her off-brand deodorant would activate from the effort in such humidity, but she really was late, and her pager was starting to go off from the residents. She liked it that Jeremy had urged her to work hard, instead of the ubiquitous "Don't work too hard!" she'd heard her whole life. She liked that he was straightforward. Finally, her bullshit meter was silent—no bad vibes.

A car honked as she stepped off the curb without looking.

Great! She thought. *I come this close to graduating and get killed daydreaming about a hot baby boy who probably just wants sex...* She shook her head to shake off her decidedly unprofessional thoughts and grabbed the heavy hospital door to dash up a flight and start afternoon rounds. A pleasant diversion might be just the thing if he wasn't an ax murderer.

"Hey!" A moist Shelly Riley greeted the team, standing at the chart rack, waiting residents confronting her with dramatic checks of their wristwatches.

"Class went late, team. And I'm sweating up a storm 'cause I ran back, *outside,* for your information, so I wouldn't keep you fine people waiting any longer than necessary. For me to actually step outdoors in this heat shows my endless devotion to you all."

They started rounds, catching up on the day's labs and unexpected events, and Shelly managed to fit in some brief teaching while doing her best not to hold up the pace. As they finished, having made it around the entire circle of patient rooms, the team divided the remaining tasks, and Rebecca caught Shelly's eye, moving her back down the hallway apart from the others.

"You're happy," she accused. "Who is he?"

"What are you talking about?" Shelly protested. "I've been away for two hours, and..."

"Shelly, I'm a married woman who still has sex with her husband. I can spot a crush a mile away." Rebecca dragged her into the makeshift office for privacy. "I've watched nurses, students, and residents before, during and after various flings. What's his name?"

Shelly shook her head, amazed that she could be so transparent. "How in the world can you tell? And is Farber going to know?"

Rebecca chuckled. "Farber wouldn't recognize a horny fellow if you came into his OR with a fresh hickey and your bra hanging out of your scrubs. No, it's my intuition. I'm famous for it around here. The residents don't always like it, since I catch them doing things they shouldn't be doing. But you? God, if anyone could use a good roll in the hay, it's you."

Shelly unloaded the recent flirtation, brief though it was. "It's unsettling, really. He's just a kid! God, he smells good."

Rebecca shook her head. "Ooh, boy. You're a goner. He's either a stalker, or a mature young man with wonderful taste. So. Are you gonna meet him tomorrow?"

"I can't believe this, but…Yes, I think I am."

"All right, then. Here's what you're going to do." Rebecca was all business, punching in a pager number while she signed off on the chart she was prepping. "You're not meeting a total stranger in a restaurant, no matter how nice he smells. You will not invite him to your house, nor will you give him your number until I've vetted him. And you will call me if you get the slightest vibe that something isn't right. Got all that?"

The phone rang, which Rebecca answered on the first ring.

"Luca? It's Rebecca. What are you and Samantha doing tomorrow night? Can you happen to be at The Nectary when Shelly meets a blind date?" His massive voice ricocheted in the room as Rebecca held the phone away from her ear. Shelly easily caught Luca's part of the conversation.

"Oh, this stud of a master's student seduced her in class, and I wanna check him out. It's that newish place in the strip mall north of the hospital. He'll be there around six waiting. We've got two cases and I'll finish up rounds for her if it's late. I'll come over there after I swing home. We'll surround him so he knows he's being watched. Okay, then, see you tomorrow. Thanks, Luca," and she hung up.

"There, that's done. If he's a pervert, he'll vanish with so many people able to ID him. If he's not, well, then, Luca and I got a look at the kind of man you go for, I guess," she winked in approval. "Seriously, Shelly. I'm all for meeting new people, but there are enough crazies out there that you've gotta be careful. And no offense, but you *are* a little on the naïve side. Okay—I'm calling it a day, unless you need something else, boss. I'll see you in the A.M." Rebecca shuffled off, grabbing her lab coat from the chair back and fishing out her car keys.

Shelly headed home to her little rental house around seven, grateful to Rebecca for wanting to keep her safe. She received a wild greeting from Pepper, and a "welcome home" from her neighbor Corinne who had popped over to let the dog out. Shelly changed out of her scrubs, reading the dog-walker's assessment of Pepper's production ("mostly full of bird seed today") while slipping into her tennis shoes.

She jangled the leash, "Walk, Peppercorn?" and off they drove to Pike's Creek for a late evening adventure. The walk gave her puppy some more energy-consuming activity, and Shelly some time to ponder the new crush and Rebecca's warnings. She'd never equated a date with danger. She figured her ample height and foul mouth had something to do with it.

Amidst the couples holding hands rollerblading and pairs of joggers, Shelly felt like she was on a Kentucky version of Noah's ark. How it was that she hadn't yet settled with anyone after years of dating?

Once showered and settled in bed with Pepper at her feet, she rang her old med school roomie for advice. The time change to California made her late nights just right for Evie, who had twins to get settled before she collapsed in bed herself. Shelly lit her cigarette as she dialed.

"Evie!" her friend's voice cheered her. "How are you?"

"Oh, Shell, how nice to hear your voice. I've been meaning to call you to tell you…" Evie's voice faltered and cracked. "Mom died, Shell. Mid-August." She paused again. "I still hate saying those words, even though I've said it a hundred times."

"Oh, my God, Ev." Shelly sat up in the bed, swinging her feet down. "What happened? She was so young!" Shelly recalled stories about Evie's very glamorous, oh-so-French mom from their late-night study sessions. She savored the delicious snacks Evie would bring home from holidays spent at home in Rochester, Minnesota, always something elegant with imported tins of *foie gras* or jars of *confitures* from her mom's region in southwestern France.

"We don't know, exactly, but my guess is an aneurysm. Dad went sailing on Lake Pepin during the day, and mom stayed home to putter. She had a headache and just didn't feel up to spending the whole day on the boat, she told him. Plus she was almost done with a huge novel she'd been really into—you know how she loved to read. Dad came home and found her in bed, sitting up, with the book in her lap." Shelly teared up at the image.

"Oh, Shell, I didn't go home at all this summer. She'd only seen the twins a few times. God, if I'd known how little time I'd have her…"

"Nope, Momo would not be having this kind of talk, Ev. No way." Shelly was firm with her friend, thinking of all the stories Evie shared about her mom. Monique Hallstrom was not exactly the doting, maternal type, Shelly had gathered, and had never driven up from Rochester to their Minneapolis apartment in the four years of school. Shelly's mom astounded Evie when she would pop over to their pathetic dwelling with a fresh meal or a frozen lasagna "for later," giving Shelly and Evie big warm hugs as she left.

"She pushed all three of you girls to be independent. Come on, now. She basically kicked you baby birds out of the nest, didn't you tell me?"

Evie sniffed, giggling despite her sorrow.

"I know, I know. She was so unsentimental. When I told her I was pregnant, she told me not to plan on any daycare from her, but to expect 'complete respect for what a good mother I would be.' Even Feline practically never sees her," Evie caught herself in the present tense, "I mean saw her, and they lived two miles from each other. Momo had a certain way about her, and we all felt *so* secure and loved. I know how my patients feel now, when the kids stop by my office after their parent has died. Just lost. I keep wanting to call her."

They kept at it, laughing at Momo stories that Shelly recalled, and Evie told her a couple new ones. "She hated Bill, basically," Evie admitted. "And loved Feline's husband, who's a jerk. Plus, she'd ask us all the time if Bridget was a lesbian, just because she's not married yet."

"Really? Bridget is the straightest female on the planet," Shelly protested. "Now I could see it if she asked about me," Shelly joked.

"Oh, she did, Shell," Evie laughed. "She only stopped when I told her about all the men you slept with. Then she decided you were just secretly French!"

Eventually, Evie begged off to get to bed, and Shelly promised to call her again soon. She ached for her friend's loss, only realizing after hanging up that she hadn't even mentioned Jeremy. *He smells nice, and he made me call Ev,* she thought, as she settled in her bed to sleep.

I'll give him a try, and if he's an ax murderer, I'm pretty sure Rebecca will take care of him.

* * *

The next day flew by, with uneventful rounds and surgery, and blessedly little criticism from Shelly's attendings. She'd dressed in street clothes instead of going to the hospital in scrubs.

Rebecca gave her a nod as Shelly took off down the stairs after evening rounds.

"Cute," Rebecca approved.

She dashed home to let her dog out and reached The Nectary about seven thirty. The curb appeal was unimpressive, a hand painted sign over the door and trash fluttering out of a full garbage can near the entrance. She could hear Luca through the glass, and saw Samantha waving to her to come in.

Inside, the place was darling. Shelly couldn't tell from the décor what type of food would be served there, but the cozy space and savory aroma made Shelly hungry to order anything that could be the source of that smell. The plants were lush, flowing over the rims of their pots, perched on ledges throughout. Each of the small tables had a vintage cotton print covering with mismatched plates and sparkling water glasses. The whole restaurant, which amounted to Luca, Samantha, Jeremy and the two chef-owners, shifted to smile at her as she entered.

"Hello, Shelly!" they all said in unison, laughing when they realized how much prior discussion had just been given away.

Luca started in, "You kept him waiting just long enough. He was getting a little squirmy, there. I'm pretty sure we're gonna let you date him," he concluded as Samantha shook her head.

"Lord, Luca, don't be so obvious. How are you, Shelly? What a coincidence..." Samantha didn't know how far to take the pretense but didn't want to be the one to admit the set-up.

Jeremy took over, standing and greeting her with a smile. "I'm glad you could come, Shelly. And it's been a pleasure getting to meet some of your friends, here. It worked out just great that they happened to come in tonight. I hope they give me the thumbs up."

"Yeah, well, now we know where you live so it would be unwise to make a mess of things with our Shelly. We figured we'd make it clear from the get-go, right? He checks out pretty well, I'd say," Luca concluded, eating the whole time. "And he picked a great place—the pork is fantastic!"

Jeremy led Shelly to a little table along the wall. "I like Helena's artwork above this one," he pointed to the large watercolor hanging near them. "She's the hostess and decorator, and her husband Dwayne cooks. They opened a few months ago, and I've been coming here once a week since I read about them in the paper. Everything on the menu is delicious," he assured her.

Shelly did her best to concentrate on the menu and make small talk. Luca continued to hurl questions their way every few minutes, still unable to tone down his volume despite the cramped quarters. After Helena took their orders, their conversation continued. She learned a bit more about engineering, and Jeremy learned about surgery.

"You *are* charming, I'll admit," Shelly told Jeremy as she dove into the lemon chicken that Helena eventually brought. "And you found a great place to eat. I wish I could sample everything else."

Jeremy persisted. "I haven't dated that many women, Shelly, but for whatever reason I noticed you at the very first class. If you're willing to give me a try, I think we should get to know each other better. No expectations. And because I already think so highly of you, I'll even share my veal." He cut a portion off and placed it on her plate.

When Rebecca walked in with her husband and son around eight thirty, Shelly was embarrassed that the stranger checkout charade had another chapter.

"I'm tired, Momma," the ten-year-old moaned. "Why'd we have to come here so late? Daddy and me ate hours ago."

"'Daddy and I,' Clay. Hush, now," Rebecca gently urged her son inside. "Mommy was hungry, and I heard this was a nice place. We'll just get some takeout and head home, honey. Well, look who's here!" Rebecca feigned surprise as she smiled at Luca and Samantha.

"You don't have to act, Rebecca," Luca boomed. "He already knows we're all checking him out. Seems okay to me, and I got his truck's plates while he was ordering, so…"

Jeremy started to laugh, walking over to Rebecca to introduce himself. "Jeremy Finlay, nice to meet you," and he offered a hand to Rebecca's husband Adam, then to Rebecca. "The place is just full of hospital people tonight."

"I reckon we want to get a look at you to make sure you're not a *preevert* or anything," Adam offered. His ramrod posture was menacing, his raspy cigarette-hoarsened voice added to the package, and the tattoos up and down both arms completed the effect. "That's near as I can tell, anyway. So I'll just have a peek at the menu while Rebecca gives you the third degree, here," and Adam went over to Helena to chat about what was good to order. "And son?" Adam peered at Jeremy with a squint. "My wife seems to have taken a shine to this gal Shelly. That means that if anything happens to her, well, that would be a problem. Hear?"

Jeremy nodded, his face serious, no visible reaction to the threat. "Understood, sir. I intend to be nothing but a gentleman," and he nodded again, this time at the young Clay. "I'd get the cheese quesadilla, if I were you." A wink.

Helena swept in to talk the father and son through food choices for a late snack, as Rebecca engaged with Jeremy. They wandered over to Shelly, head in her hands, laughing in amazement at her friend's bold interrogation.

"Master's program, Shelly said. In engineering?"

"Yes, ma'am. I have my bachelor's from Vanderbilt, and thought I'd try to climb the work ladder a little bit. My boss in Paducah told me the pay scale improves with a more advanced degree. I met Shelly at a master's level class on medical devices."

The third degree continued for a bit, and when Rebecca was satisfied, she put in a quick order to go.

"Jeremy, you seem like a nice young man. Let's keep it that way, you hear. Adam's not medical, by the way. He's a cop, and we're both a pretty good judge of character. Shelly, you may proceed," Rebecca nodded with her motherly permission.

"So, we can stay on the porch swing with our lemonade, Ma?" Shelly inquired.

"Rounds at five-thirty, boss. See you there," Rebecca's waved as she and her family left the café, laden with a bag of decadent fare.

"Bye, Mister Jeremy!" Clay yawned despite the exciting change of routine. "I got the thing you said to get! And the lady put an extra treat in my bag, but I'm not allowed to peek till I get home."

Luca and Samantha rose to leave, too, with Luca observing, "Well, I think you get the picture, right, Jeremy? Your ass is grass, basically, if anything happens to Shelly. Rebecca's husband isn't just a cop, by the way. You saw his flat top? He's a detective, and one bigtime mother…"

"That'll do, honey. Time to go," Samantha grabbed her husband's elbow and ushered him to the door. "Lovely to meet y'all," she called as they left. Helena and Dwayne found work to do in the kitchen.

Peace descended on the restaurant.

"Time to go?" Jeremy's tender voice warmed her heart.

Damn! If he can take that level of questioning… She was jumping in too quick, as usual, and it probably wouldn't work out. But Shelly Riley wanted this man. He had behaved like it was no big deal getting bossed around in a random restaurant by strangers. He gazed at her with the same longing she felt.

Jeremy leaned over the tiny table, brushed Shelly's bangs away, and gave her the most sensual kiss imaginable.

"Baby, I want to do that with you for a good long while," he whispered.

Time to go.

CHAPTER 19

"I Could Whip a Cat!"

"Well, you look radiant enough, I guess," Rebecca smiled at her fellow. "Sleep at all?" She huddled with Shelly away from the others to get a quick update of the night's events.

"Nope," Shelly smiled. "He's a doll, Rebecca. Dreamy. And no alarm bells are going off so far, so I think you can tell Adam to call off the squads following him with bullet proof vests. Oh, and he loved the interrogation by everyone."

Rebecca agreed, "Adam ran his plates when we got home. No priors, so no private detectives. Still," she added, "you call me if anything seems off. I'm a good resource. I'm already pestering Tabitha flirting with the physical therapy kid. Between the two of you, I'm reliving my youth!"

They joined Dave and Tabitha to finish rounds before heading to the operating room. Shelly struggled with the management of a patient currently on the service. Ms. Blossom Miller, now almost two weeks post-op from a big laparotomy, was just not progressing. It was getting to the point where Shelly might have to bring the patient back to surgery to relieve the blockage.

Outside her room, Tabitha updated the team.

"She's still distended, Dr. Riley, and she's spitting mad at how things are going. The NG tube hurts, she can't pass gas, and she wants some answers. I just don't know what to tell her."

The intern took Ms. Miller's condition personally. "Is there anything else we can do?"

Shelly played with her Altoids tin in her lab coat. "Well, folks, what ideas come to mind for Ms. Miller? Tincture of time doesn't seem to be doing the trick. Do you recommend taking her back to the OR?" Shelly wondered if her residents might come up with a strategy.

"Wouldn't that be a mess, Shelly?" Dave shook his head. "I can't imagine that would help at all. These postop bowel obstructions are the worst. You can't predict when their gut will open up, and the patient gets frustrated."

"I saw an attending handle a case like this," Shelly mused, drawing a quick diagram for them on scratch paper. "He ordered an upper GI study—you know, the tech squirts the gastrograffin down the NG tube, and then we bring her back down to Radiology every few hours to see how far the contrast has gone. Sometimes that blows things open. And I do mean blow—the relief can be explosive." She followed the cartoonish path of bowel with her pen and added exclamation points at the end.

Shelly knocked and entered Ms. Miller's room, ready for an earful. "Don't y'all dare come in here without a fix!" she blazed. "I'm plumb done with this place. I'm about to burst if I don't get a good toot TODAY." She glared at Shelly, daring her to come up with reply.

"I'm sorry, Ms. Miller," Shelly agreed, sitting down at the foot of her bed. "I know this is the worst feeling in the world. We keep hoping, day after day, that your bowels will open up. So, here's my plan." She explained the x-ray test to the patient, who had her arms crossed and eyes burning.

"I'll try anything, y'all," Ms. Miller answered, softer this time. "Please, just *do* something. I can't take it no more," tears falling down the sides of her face to the pillow. "I just can't take this no more." Tabitha, so attached to this patient, moved to her bedside and took her hand.

The team left Tabitha and Ms. Miller to chat while they completed rounds. When finished, Shelly made plans for the day in the OR. "Okay, I'm doing that tough case with Farber. It's a bad situation—she was radiated for advanced cervical cancer years ago and has been dealing with partial small bowel obstructions for years. She probably has intestinal loops that are stuck to one another, so food can't move along the way it's supposed to. We'll have to separate every single inch before we close."

"I heard him tell Dr. Cardinal it was a last-ditch effort. This is a super long shot?" Dave washed his hands while the others waited.

"Yep, that's the lady." Shelly handed him a paper towel. "This is one of those times where the cure is worse than the disease. She hasn't eaten well for years, and lately she's lost even more weight. They think it's going to be a big resection. Rebecca, you've got the others covered? I'll either be in there all day, or just a few minutes." Rebecca nodded as Shelly scooted down to the OR.

* * *

Kit held the door to room four open for Shelly. The malnourished woman lay on the bed, abdominal skin prepped and the scrub tech Velma completing the draping. Shelly caught her eye.

"I've got a bad feeling, Velma. This lady's only about eighty-five pounds, and her bowel..." her voice trailed off as Dr. Farber came in, arms up, ready to be gowned. Shelly knew better than to jinx a case, especially with an attending present, and left to scrub.

The two surgeons stood quietly on opposite sides of the patient's body. Shelly used the knife on the skin layer, while Dr. Farber urged her to go millimeter by millimeter to avoid cutting into the adherent intestinal loops stuck directly below. They tried; God knows. In Shelly's young career, it was the worst abdomen she'd seen. They made tiny, incremental progress, eventually getting into the belly cavity, and needing only reinforcing sutures for minor tears in the matted intestinal loops. After working for over two hours in silence, head down in the surgical field, Shelly stated her concerns.

"Dr. Farber, we're not much closer to the area in the deep pelvis. I'm not sure this is fixable."

He shook his head. "I know it's a terrible case, Shelly. But I've followed her for years, and we've tried every possible bowel regimen. She hasn't found a single food that'll nourish her, and she refuses a feeding tube. The pact we made, the two of us, was that I'd do every last thing possible to get her bowel freed up. So that's what I'm going to do. Slow and steady, now. When you get frustrated, focus on a different area, and see if you can make some progress there."

They continued. The OR staff came and went with scheduled breaks, Kit calling out to the waiting room to reassure the family. Dr. Cardinal stopped in and gave Dr. Farber a respite.

"Thanks, Peter. Let me just stretch my back a minute, and I'll be right back in," he thanked his colleague as he backed away from the OR bed.

Once he had left, Dr. Cardinal murmured to Shelly, "How long?"

"I think we're at five hours, Dr. Cardinal. It's futile, really, and I'm worried we're making things worse…" Shelly felt doom settling as she tried repeatedly to free up a loop of small intestine from the raw surfaces it had adhered to from radiotherapy given years ago.

"Any enterotomies yet?" He meant actual punctures through the bowel wall, knowing the more of those, the higher her risk would be postop.

Shelly shook her head no.

"It looks like classic iron pipe bowel here." He pointed at the gleaming dusky spot. "See how pale and stiff it is? That's from microvascular damage over the years. The problem is those changes don't improve. The tissue suffers without oxygen, and the damaged bowel just can't function."

Despite the grim outlook for this patient, Shelly noticed a little thrill at Dr. Cardinal's teaching. He was treating her like he used to treat Ken. Like a junior colleague. It felt wonderful.

As they worked, he occasionally took charge of a little portion, then handed over control to Shelly. They moved right along, until with a sudden lift, after all those hours, the last loop came free.

Velma sighed. "Nicely done, doctors."

Shelly felt a glorious burst of energy, proud to have avoided making a hole in the bowel during so many hours of precarious cutting and unroofing densely adherent tissue planes.

"And yet," Dr. Cardinal nodded toward the field. Dark blood was welling up far faster than she would have expected from a minor bleeder. No, this was a big vessel, and it was *deep*.

She pressed on the area with a sterile lap pad, hoping pressure would block the bleeding.

"How about a second suction and more laps, Velma? Have some clips available, and what suture do you think, Shelly? Some 2-0 silks on a small needle to start. Anesthesia," Dr. Cardinal asked the resident at the head of the bed, "where did we start for a hemoglobin this morning? We may lose a little blood here."

Shelly noted how positively nonchalant Dr. Cardinal behaved, as if he were just in a minor predicament. The hemorrhage continued, faster than she could suction, and as she started to panic, he put his hand on hers to direct the pressure in a different angle. He kept talking to the anesthesia resident. Casual chatter morphed to clear commands, but Dr. Cardinal showed no fear as he worked.

The imperceptible repositioning of the downward pressure made an immediate impact. There was quiet in the room as the anesthesia attending walked in. Dr. C. Cole was pulling up his mask while scanning the various IV lines and the two suction canisters filled with blood, grabbing non-sterile gloves as he approached.

"A little audible blood loss, eh, Peter? She's been under for quite a while. What do you think, a unit to start? I see Flynn is drawing some labs, here. Let's start another IV. Kit, call the blood bank to have them stand by for some stat labs, will you? When was her last antibiotic dose?"

The switch from mundane to near catastrophe flashed the entire room to action, and they all knew their role.

Shelly called to Kit, "I's and O's after you send the labs would be good. It'll help to know how much blood we've lost. Dr. Cole, I think the pressure on the bleeder is buying us some time. When you're ready, we'll let up and see if we can close the tear."

They stabilized the patient with bags of saline and a second IV, adding meds to bring the patient's blood pressure up to more normal values. When they were ready, Dr. Cardinal nodded the go-ahead to Shelly.

"Stitch." She opened her right hand out to Velma. She slowly moved the hand which had been keeping the blood loss at bay while Dr. Cardinal suctioned, keeping the field clear enough to see the damage.

"It's pretty big, Dr. Cardinal," Shelly said. "Maybe you should…" she offered the needle driver to him.

"You've got the better angle, Shelly. I might use a figure of eight in the apex closest to you, and then reevaluate. What do you think?"

What do I think? I think I'm about to shit myself, is what I think. She knew his angle was far better, and he was handing her the responsibility. His confidence in her skill transferred a power to her hand as she reached with the tiny needle…*shitdammit this is far away*…and made the first pass.

"Nice. Now pull up with the least strain possible to keep some tension there. That's right," he encouraged her. "Next pass and then you can tie it. Another stitch ready, hmm, Velma?"

"Yes, Dr. Cardinal," as Velma readied her suture scissors at Shelly's side.

Shelly tied down the first knot, and before cutting the suture, let off the pressure. Blood everywhere. *C'mon, girl, you missed it.*

"That looks much better, Shelly. I think she'll get it with the second stitch, don't you Velma?" He started to whistle the theme from Indiana Jones, suctioning with a light touch and acting like a man on vacation.

"Stitch, Velma," and she a placed a second suture, impossibly far from her eyes, in a tiny rent of an unnamed vein that simply had to be repaired. Failure was not an option, or this patient would die. She tied it down and prayed *please God let this work* as she let off the pressure.

"Looks dry to me, Shelly. How's it going, C? I think Dr. Riley has this under control here. Are you good?"

"I think we're caught up, Peter. Her pressure was pretty saggy there for a bit, but her pulse is down now, and I've got the second unit in as we speak. That was some nice sewing, Riley," he nudged the sterile sheet. "Looked like it was about a mile away. I'd say you've got balls of steel, but…" he cackled.

Shelly, finally able to let down her guard, answered "I imagine you'd prefer we not get in this predicament, right? Instead of showing how good we are in repairing it?" Shelly knew the love-hate relationship between anesthesiologist and surgeon could be strained and figured she might as well admit they had made it difficult for him to care for this fragile patient.

"Hey, shit happens," Dr. Cole said. "You both know what to do when things go south. Maybe Dr. Cardinal will admit you're a great fellow, eh Peter? No complaints from me. I'm going to check on my room next door—I'll be back. Kit, get an ICU bed for this lady, will you?"

As he left, Dr. Cardinal remarked, "That's pretty high praise from C. Cole, Shelly. Let's get a little substrate down in that oozy area and run the bowel. People," he addressed the staff, "I think we're perilously close to being done here."

The adrenalin lasted for the duration of the case. When Dr. Cardinal broke scrub, he told Shelly, "I know you thought we shouldn't bring her to the OR. But if this works, it'll change her life. The key is, I think, that Dr. Farber *made sure* the patient knew this was the longest of long shots. He told her how long the recovery is going to be, and she knew it might just go back to how it was. They have a relationship, see? She tried everything else, she saw other doctors, and she trusted him to try, even knowing the near impossible odds."

Shelly nodded. "I understand, Dr. Cardinal. I appreciate your helping me with the…"

"I didn't do anything, when you think about it. You made the hole, you bought anesthesia time to stabilize her, and then you fixed it. That was your job, and you did it." He paused. "It *was* mighty fine suturing. C. wasn't kidding."

Thanking the rest of the room, Dr. Cardinal noted the clock. "I think I'll spare the team teaching rounds. What do you think, Shelly?" and left before she could reply.

"Woohoo, I'll be damned," Shelly said. "Velma, did you see his eyes twinkling? I might just graduate after all." She didn't even have to mouth "bite me" behind her mask as she finished the abdominal closure.

* * *

Stiff beyond words, she paged Rebecca from PACU and had them start rounds while she did the paperwork. She allowed herself a quick wonder about Jeremy's whereabouts, then shook herself back to earth and limped over to Radiology to check poor Ms. Miller's UGI results.

"It all moved through," the on-call radiologist showed her on the film, "though I'd say it took an extra hour or so from normal transit time. There should be some evidence of relief, I'd say, looking at these images. How does she feel?"

"Don't know yet. I just got out of the OR, and I wanted to know your thoughts before I round on her tonight. She was hunting for bear this morning—pretty miserable ileus for more than a week." Shelly hollered her thanks and headed to the Powell.

As she rounded the corner of the second floor, she saw the team standing around the cart in front of Blossom Miller's room.

"Well?" Shelly couldn't tell from their faces if she was better or not. "Who's gonna present her?"

Tabitha updated the team, face impassive, and ended with, "I think y'all are just going to have to judge for yourselves," as she knocked and opened the patient's door. "Ms. Miller? All right if the team comes in to make rounds and check on you?"

The smell of stool filled the room, and Shelly saw the reflection of the nursing assistant washing her hands in the bathroom. She had a grin on her face, barely outmatched by that of Blossom.

"Well," Ms. Miller said to the flood of young doctors before her. "How's y'all's day been?"

"C'mon, now, Ms. Miller. Our day was fine. The question is how are *you* after that upper GI test?"

Blossom leaned over to Shelly, as if to whisper, and crowed, "I feel so sprightly I could whip a cat!"

The native Kentuckians smiled with her as the assistant chuckled.

"I believe I pooped out all that chalk the nurse squirted down this nose tube, and darned near every meal I missed for the last two weeks. That poor Amy must have helped me clean my bottom a hundred times this afternoon. Thank you, Amy!"

"My pleasure, Ms. Blossom. We were all glad to know you could use the bathroom like you did…" she stepped out of the room as she was drying her hands.

"Wouldn't be surprised if the whole hospital heard me go. Maybe you could feel the vibrations down there in surgery, Dr. Riley? I feel like a new woman, I swear, and I believe I owe you an apology. I've been real crabby, and I'm sorry to have been miserable to y'all. I know y'all were trying to help me."

"I'm still stuck on the part where you said you could whip a cat," Shelly laughed. "I looked at your X-rays with the radiologist just now, and he said your intestines looked open. No obstruction. He asked about how you were feeling, and I told him I was coming up to see. So, Ms. Miller, is it a *good* thing that you could whip a cat?"

"Ooh, yes, Lord!" Blossom reconsidered. "Well, maybe not so good for the cat, you understand. But I feel like my swelling is down, and the tightness is gone, too. See?" Up went her hospital gown, showing a much less distended abdomen from earlier that day. The team examined her healing skin incision, chattering about the test results, and they stayed to congratulate Ms. Miller on her exceptional bowel movements.

The patient's spirits filled Shelly with joy, nearly erasing the last grueling twelve hours in the operating room, and the two weeks spent worrying about Ms. Miller's condition.

"Ma'am, I can't tell you how relieved I am. I was getting ready to reoperate on you if things didn't open up soon."

I feel like I aged ten years today, Shelly thought as she went through the remainder of rounds. She knew medicine took a toll on doctors, and she'd felt twinges of that heaviness in her earlier student and residency years. Still, the ultimate responsibility fell on the staff physician. As a senior fellow, that gravity loomed.

What would I have done if the UGI didn't work? she wondered. *What would I have told the lady I spent twelve hours operating on today? Sorry, ma'am, you'll just have to die of starvation?*

"I don't believe I will ever get that smell out of my nostrils," Dave said, chewing a sandwich remnant in the hallway, licking a mustard smear off his lip. "That must be a huge weight off your shoulders, eh, Shelly?" Dave startled her back to reality. "I'm going to put that upper GI trick away in my noggin in case I ever run into a postop bowel obstruction like Ms. Miller in real life." He stashed the wrapper in the cart and brushed the crumbs off his scrubs. "So, how's the new dude?"

"God, Dave, I can't believe you're eating. And haven't you ever heard of a segue in conversation?" Shelly shook her head. "No wonder no one ever invites us anywhere—doctors are gross. 'The dude's' name is Jeremy, and he's fine, by the way. Let's wrap up and go over the rest of the week so I can see what he's doing."

"Excellent. You know, now that you're dating again, Shelly, I guess we can expect rounds to be a little more streamlined, right?" he gave her a wink and threw his lab coat on the chair, preparing to leave. "See y'all at 5:30," Dave waved to the team as he strode away.

Shelly checked her watch, frowning to see it was nearly nine. Probably no Jeremy sighting in my future, she figured. And probably a little Pepper poop in the living room, since I'm extra late.

* * *

She flew home and tingled as she listened to message after message from Jeremy on her answering machine while Pepper ran throughout her backyard, searching for the perfect place to relieve herself. Shelly collapsed in bed after the briefest of showers but savored the ringtones as she poked in Jeremy's number and heard his voice.

"Baby? Home at last?"

They chatted for an hour, Shelly shuddering herself awake and Pepper shifting in the bed, talking about their respective days. "No regrets with my hours, Jeremy?"

"Oh, I have thousands of regrets, are you kidding? But you warned me, and I promised to be cool, so I await your orders, m'lady. When can the ravishing begin again?"

"Well, if we can wait that long, how's tomorrow? God, I'd tell you to come over right now if I weren't already actually talking to you in my sleep. I'll call you when I'm getting ready to leave the hospital, how's that sound?"

"Dreaming about it already. Sleep tight, baby," he coaxed.

Poised

* * *

Indeed, she did. Their routine quickly became a matter of calls, longing, and hours of bedtime whispers. Pepper loved him, and he took her for walks on the later nights when Shelly was held up. Jeremy met Corinne and Ernie, and although her neighbors were loyal to Robert, they grew to enjoy his company and agreed he was a find.

"When are you going to tell Robert, Shelly?" Corinne walked over with her coffee one weekend morning. "You don't want them to meet up here, by accident, do you?"

"No, no. Of course you're right, it's just that… I don't have the courage to tell him. I'm terrible with relationships, Corinne. I just seem to boomerang from guy to guy. I still feel bad about Robert coming down to Kentucky. He's never been away from his family like this, you know?"

"Want a little advice, hon?" Corinne put her arm around Shelly's shoulder. "Moving away from home was the best thing Robert could've done for himself, and I believe he knows it. I hear him jawing with Ernie, and Ernie lets him go on. Lord, how men talk *around* a thing just to avoid saying what they mean to say. He told me Robert feels like he's grown more in the last year than the rest of his adult life in Massachusetts. He needed a push, is all, and you gave it to him.

"But Shelly?" Corinne took a sip, "tell him in person, all right? Not on the phone. And honey, make it soon. The way you and Jeremy act I believe his truck'll be in the driveway all hours, and that's not a nice way for Robert to find out you have a new beau."

Corinne was a source who kept Shelly grounded and always told her the truth. Shelly appreciated this lovely woman's advice and found a reason to drive over to Robert's apartment with Pepper that morning.

* * *

"How'd you know?" Robert's first words confused her as Pepper tugged on the leash to water a weed cropping up in the asphalt of the apartment lot. "Women's intuition, I've gotta say I believe it now."

Shelly had no idea what he was talking about but encouraged him with a nod. "Go on," she urged.

"Well, this car dealer situation isn't too great. I mean, I like the vehicles, don't get me wrong, but I hate the sales part. That's what you thought all along, isn't it?"

"I just didn't think paperwork and gladhanding were your strong suits. The mechanical stuff you could do all day long and not get bored," Shelly agreed. They found a bench at the park next to the lot and sat.

"Well, I quit. Just yesterday, in fact. I called my sister and told her I was coming back home, and she sounded kinda glad. The gang misses my grumpy personality, she said. 'It's too cheerful without you,'" he mimicked.

Shelly stared at him for a moment, mouth open, surprised, and of course not surprised.

"You're going back to Massachusetts?" Shelly's mind raced as she queried Robert, calculating she'd wait to tell him about Jeremy. "When?"

"Monday. I broke the lease yesterday afternoon, and it won't take me long to pack my crap and hit the road. Want my couch?"

Shelly laughed. "No, Robert, you're on your own with that gross stuff from the previous tenant. Leave 'em where you found 'em. And you don't get Pepper in case you're thinking about mutt kidnapping. I get full custody." They watched as Pepper watered a bike rack. "Seriously, though." Shelly summoned the courage to ask, "Do you regret coming down here?"

He watched the kids playing pickup baseball. "Not one bit. At first, I thought I was a failure. You know me. But not anymore, really. I've got a lot to tell the guys at the plant, and who knows? Maybe I'll like work better now that I know how much sales sucks."

Robert steeled himself with a deep breath. "I would've liked to have had kids with you, Shelly. You would've been a great mom, even if I drive you crazy. I never really told you that." He cleared his throat and shifted on the bench, serious and tender moment over.

"Wow. What a lovely thing to say, Robert. I guess with work and everything I don't give that too much thought. Thank you for that. Really."

"Yeah, well, I'm not too good with emotions, I know." He exhaled a big puff of nerves. "So, if I can't talk you into a couch or a primo Naugahyde Barcalounger, then I'd better get going and get some boxes from U-Haul. I've got a lot to do."

She wiped her eyes as they hugged goodbye. "I'll hope for wonderful things for you, Robert. Meet someone to have babies with you! And give my love to your family. Call me when you get home safe." She backed away, taking one last look at this crabby, handsome northeasterner who had shared her life for so many years. Pepper padded along as they reached the Festiva.

He'll be okay, and so will I. Tears streamed down her face on the ride home, though Shelly was unclear as to what she was crying about. Kids? Marriage? Failed relationships? *All the above, I guess.*

Shelly felt no biologic clock ticking and had *zero* sadness about being single. Yet this serial monogamy she had known her whole adult life—she was starting to wonder when she was going to stumble across a man who could fill in all the blanks for her. She knew it wasn't Robert, and had no real illusions that it was Jeremy, but figured it was only right to try until she got it right. She grinned.

"Let's hit the road, Pepper! The day is a'wastin," and as Pepper wagged and sat shotgun,

Shelly aimed for home, and the handsome, fine smelling Jeremy.

CHAPTER 20

Blooming Desert

"Jeremy, seriously, I don't have time. I've got half an hour to shower and get to the hospital. My big talk is today during M & M. You'll have to meet your own needs, you greedy thing!" Jeremy rolled over, after rubbing on various body parts hoping Shelly would change her mind.

"Understood," he yawned. "Maybe I should set the alarm for earlier, whaddya think?"

"I think if we have sex more often than we already do you might as well just stay inside me and join me for rounds. Seriously, boy, there aren't enough hours in the day to satisfy your cravings," she yelled above the noise of the shower. "Can you let Pepper out quick?"

The morbidity and mortality conference was a monthly event when interesting cases were summarized and then discussed in detail, usually because there were complications. It was at today's M & M where she would make her speech with the slides she and Dr. Cardinal had polished. Afterwards the staff would go over timing and questions, to prepare her for the real deal later next week in Arizona. She couldn't be late this morning. Even clinic had been canceled for her talk.

"Remember I told you about this big conference in Phoenix? I give a speech at a podium, with a microphone, to about a thousand surgeons, and after the last slide the assholes start lining up throughout the room at these strategically placed mikes to pimp me. They love going after the fellows—it satisfies their sense of superiority, I think," Shelly kept up her conversation. As she walked into the bedroom toweling off, she saw Jeremy had fallen asleep.

"Fair enough," she murmured. "It's only five o'clock." She dressed quickly and headed out the door as Pepper jumped up on her side of the bed to snuggle with Jeremy.

"Be good you two," she smiled to herself and headed to the hospital.

When she dashed up the stairwell to the Powell, she worried to see the fire doors to the station closed. She sniffed the air, sure something was wrong. She approached the threshold and cautiously pushed open the door, needing both hands to exert enough force.

"Good morning, boss." Rebecca and the whole team played an enthusiastic "Pomp and Circumstance" on kazoos. "Yah, yada yah yaaah, yaaah, yah, yada yah yah." Tabitha pranced around the cart filled with patient charts, while Alita threw rose petals around her feet, bowing nearly to the floor.

Next she heard Bernice announce over the intercom, "Dr. Riley is on the Powell. Dr. Shelly Riley, Senior Gyn Onc Fellow, has now entered the Powell, y'all!"

After another round of acoustically awful serenading, they all gestured her onto the Powell Cancer Center, making a pathway by holding the charts in an overhead arch. Shelly shook with laughter as she thanked each doctor and nurse for their efforts, ending with a big hug for Bernice when they arrived at her reception desk.

"Now this is what I'm talking about!" Shelly told the ward clerk. "It's about danged time we got a little attention on Oncology. The rose petals were a nice touch, Bernice."

"Dr. Riley, you'll never see us fuss like this over Gold Surgery. Not in a million years," the night nurse Alita reminded her. "We love y'all, even if you work too hard. And we figured it was about time somebody told y'all that!"

"I'm touched. It's been a rough year, I admit, but I'm grateful to all of you for having my back. All right! It's a new day, this is my service, and we are going to unwind. Dave, push the cart over to 236 – we're going counterclockwise for a while. Second floor Powell universe is wound too tight."

* * *

Poised

The team settled down after protests at the vast disruption of tradition, made lightning rounds, and planned out the day so Shelly could rehearse her talk a bit in private. She grabbed the gray plastic holder, filled with her treasured slides that she had carefully arranged, and scooted down her favorite staircase. Downstairs and across from the cafeteria, Shelly entered the empty auditorium and found the slide projector. She turned the machine on as she clicked the carousel in place.

They were all upside down.

Shelly grabbed each slide and reoriented it as quickly as she could, checking the huge hospital clock across from her, hung just to taunt her with how little time she had left before the entire department would start streaming in. Flustered, she put the first couple slides in backwards, though right side up, and cursed again until she got the proper fit.

The projector's fan whirred as the little machine sent off its electrical smell, the bulb heating each plastic slide as she sped through the talk. She pushed the clumsy lever to advance the next slide, but hoped to use a control from the podium, so headed there to investigate. The doors in back opened and the first M & M attendees wandered in.

Most were exhausted interns and residents, wiping their faces from a free drug rep breakfast or gulping their umpteenth coffee of the day, chatting as they found their usual seats. Laughs and loud conversations filtered down to Shelly as she searched everywhere on the podium for a control or pointer. *There's gotta be a phone extension for an AV guy...*

Dr. Boldon came down to greet her. With his usual flash unnaturally sparkly and white teeth, he started, "Gosh, Shelly, we're going to need to push your talk back a bit today, I'm afraid. There was a big complication on a consult last week discuss, and Medicine wants to go over some of the details this morning. The Head of Internal Medicine called me last night—his Chief Resident is going to present."

Shelly stared at her boss. "Um, Dr. Boldon, the conference in Arizona is next week. Don't you think I should give it at least once for all of you so you can make sure it's ready? This is my only chance to practice, and I'll be representing the whole hospital."

"Peter said it was great, Shelly. I'm confident in your delivery. Maybe you can do it over dinner with me one of these nights?" Dr. Boldon moved past Shelly to greet a man approaching. He was impeccable in his pressed white lab coat, aftershave reeking a mile away, pomade slicking down his thinning grey combover. Shelly hated him on sight.

"Brian, thanks for this. We've simply got to get this point across to your team about coagulopathy and sepsis. It's a critical topic, and my Chief has spent hours on his presentation. We'll be bringing it to Washington, DC this month and I want him to get as much exposure as possible before he presents it there. He's what you might call high-strung."

"Fred, you know my Senior fellow, don't you? Shelly Riley, this is Fred Cunningham, the Head of Medicine. He's the reason you're not doing your talk, I'm afraid. You'll have to make it up to Dr. Riley, Fred. She's got a big talk to give too, you know." Dr. Boldon continued to smile, all while stating in clear terms that he had just thrown Shelly under the bus for some resident in a different department.

"Whose slides are in the projector?" a nasal voice called from the AV room through the open window. "I'm taking them out!" was followed by a fit of coughing.

Shelly stared at Dr. Boldon, then Dr. Cunningham, wondering if they in any way could read the disgust she felt for them in her face. "Excuse me while I rescue my slides," Shelly told them as she took the carpeted steps two at a time. She would beat the crap out of the sniveling Medicine resident if he so much as scratched one slide.

Taking the carousel from his hands, "That's mine, thank you. How long's your talk today?"

"Well, about forty-five minutes, if I pace myself. I've got a stopwatch and I pinch myself to slow down every third slide. That's why my wrist is red, see?" He was sweaty, coughing with a deep hack from his chest, and scared to death.

Shelly followed his gesture. "Yes. Don't pinch so hard, okay? You're breaking the skin. It's bad enough you have a terrible cold. Try taking a deeper breath than usual, or looking at the screen for a second. Pretend the whole presentation is just *you* telling *me* some interesting things. I'll be in front, to your left. I'm sure you'll be good."

This kid just stole your rehearsal time—and you're giving him a pep talk? Shelly shook her head as she headed down into the now darkened auditorium. *He's gonna suck.*

Which he did. Mightily. The young doctor knew his material, but the dull delivery was mind-numbing. His nose was running, and he had to ask for a tissue partway through his talk. It was not uncommon to hear light snores during other lectures, since the audience was all sleep deprived. This M&M caused a particularly fine slumber, slide after tedious slide in the dark room providing just the ambience for a morning nap. Shelly nodded with encouragement, and applauded when he finished.

Shelly gathered her team after his talk, and they agreed to sit and listen to her go through a dry run, hoping no one had reserved the auditorium over the next hour. As the crowd exited, Shelly nestled her carousel in the slide projector and headed back to the podium. She was hyperaware of her surroundings, seeing each audience member and noting many of the residents from other departments who had initially stood to leave, pushed back into their seats with curiosity.

"Dr. Williamson, Dr. Gilbert, members of the Advisory Committee, noted panelists, and fellow Society Members. On behalf of the University of Southern Kentucky, I am so pleased to present a novel portion of our decades of work in pelvic sonography, entitled "Cystic parameters of..." Shelly drew on her years of acting in high school and college plays, countless band and choir concerts and auditions to deliver the talk with pizazz. She brought the audience through her slides, pointing out important images here, encircling significant data points there, at times stepping to the podium's side to engage.

"Are there any questions from the audience?" Shelly swept her gaze to spot any outstretched hands. "Seeing none, I thank you all for your kind attention."

Rebecca, Dave, and Tabitha leapt to their feet, whistling and hooting appreciation. The rest of the audience politely clapped and started to exit, for real this time. Dr. Cardinal made his way down from where he'd stood in back the whole time.

"That seemed fine, Shelly," he told her. "I'm pleased with the slides—there's nothing worse than tiny little graphs and illegible words. You're ready."

Shelly thanked him, still peeved at missing out on the whole crowd, but glad to have had a chance to run through all the slides. She waved the resident team on to their tasks to get more feedback from Dr. Cardinal. That left them in the empty lecture hall, stray paper plates and half eaten bagels strewn throughout.

"I'm worried about the audience questions," Shelly told him. "They might ask anything. How do I prepare for that? I've seen them really go after people."

"The obnoxious ones tend to leave the fellows alone. They wait for someone they've been competing with for years and try to show them up." Dr. Cardinal added, "Our university doesn't really have any spats like that, I'm happy to say. They tend not to mess with Dr. Farber's guys."

Shelly thought back to Dr. Farber's framed medal noting his year of presidency in the Society. That was worth something, she realized, and his influence might offer her a little protection. "Well, I appreciate your walking me through the right greeting and all. I couldn't have finished the paper without you. I want us *all* to look good." Shelly wondered if they'd turned some imaginary corner in her training. *Maybe he doesn't hate me so much, after that big case. After running the service alone all year. After Pepper. After this national talk.*

"That's the goal. You'd better check with Arlys to be sure the flight and registration are all handled. A vigorous presentation will draw the right kind of attention." Dr. Cardinal strode out the side door, leaving Shelly clutching the precious slide carousel and watching his back.

* * *

"Hey, Arlys. Dr. Cardinal asked to verify my flight and registration. My talk is Monday morning, and I need to stay at the conference hotel, since there are practice rooms and chances for early meetings for anyone giving a talk."

"Yes, doctor. I've booked you to arrive Sunday. I was just about to copy everything and put the tickets on your desk. Have you arranged call coverage?"

"Yep, Walter is it, since he's 'not clinical' and all." Shelly loved using this phrase whenever she could squeeze it in. "He'll have his chance next year, and it turns out he's been to this conference every year during his residency. It's so nice he's able to help out this time around, isn't it?" Shelly smiled at Arlys and sailed down the hall to go over charts and chat with Madeline.

"Well, y'all just break every leg you can, now. And take some pictures of the desert for me, will you? I've always wanted to see it!" Madeline was glad for her friend to have a positive, even exciting event for once.

"Look at this brochure, Madeline. There's a tour the afternoon after my talk—should I splurge and spend the twenty bucks on it? 'The Desert in Bloom,' see? It sounds cool, and since the stress of the presentation will be over, I thought it'd be a good way to celebrate."

"Hell, yes. When exactly do you think you are going to be in a blooming desert again? Good lord, I really don't know how you've made it this far. Dream a little, Shelly. Life is short! Oh, and Faye says hi. She's feeling strong and comes back in a couple weeks. I hope she has a good CA 125."

* * *

The days flew, and Shelly took a moment to tumble around with Jeremy, play with Pepper and pack an item or two in her suitcase. Her presentation was on her mind every minute.

"Baby, I don't believe those are mutterings of desire I'm hearing," Jeremy chided her. "Are you talking to yourself? I am trying mightily to bring your delight to a new level, but I get the feeling we might be here a while."

Shelly agreed, raising herself on an elbow to see him better. "Sorry, you're right. I'm thinking about my relief when I'm walking down those steps back into the audience after my talk. As always, I appreciate the effort," she wrapped her legs around him to draw him close. "You're terribly good at this, you know," she told him.

She and Jeremy had developed a warmth in their activities aside from the wonderful sex. The affection they had for one another made them very honest about most everything they encountered as a couple. He was great with Pepper, showing Shelly when it was safe to let the dog off leash to explore in a little deserted area near the rental house. He won over her neighbors as well as Mona and Henry, her hospital friends. So why did she feel so…bored?

Lying together, he caressed her cheek. "After your trip to Phoenix, I really want to bring you home to meet my folks, Shelly. They ask about you all the time, and it's not too long a trip. We could make it in a weekend, no doubt. They think I'm imagining you," his eyes squinted the way she liked.

"Hmm, nice idea, Jeremy, but there's really no time before I'm done. I've got that camping thing with Luca and Samantha the weekend you had to study for finals, remember?" She hadn't given much thought to her graduation, and where Jeremy fit in her life after fellowship. *Shouldn't I be thinking about him after I leave Kentucky?*

"We'll figure it out, I'm sure. Sweet dreams, baby. Kiss me in the morning before you go," he reassured her and nuzzled in for sleep.

* * *

The excitement for the annual meeting rose in Shelly's department. Very few Kentucky fellows had been selected to present, so despite their treatment of her, the men on staff were certainly rooting for a good performance. Luca caught up with her a few days before her trip. The two leaned on the front desk of the second floor Powell and chatted.

"Mostly they just don't want me to fuck up," she admitted to Luca, "but it does feel kind of nice to have a little positive feedback lately."

"If you keep doing twice the usual work with no complications, I'm not sure how they can keep biting on you," Luca mused. "I'm not on your service anymore, so I'm not in the loop. Maybe they're getting used to a chain-smoking female after all this time."

"I don't chain smoke, Luca," she protested. "Just absolutely every spare second I have, which is only a pack a day."

"You know, they won't care that you smoke at the Muzzle Loaders convention. There's so much pot you'll look like a schoolgirl or something with plain old tobacco. Just not in the tent, right?"

"Of course. You guys really don't mind getting all the gear and food? I feel guilty about just tagging along like this." Shelly had told them about her utter lack of camping experience, and Samantha had planned the whole weekend for three.

"Nah, Samantha will figure out costs to the penny, and she'll tell you what you owe. We'd be packing all the stuff for the two of us, so it's no trouble to add extra for you. Jeremy's staying back with Pepper?"

"Yep, and wondering what he's going to do without sex for two days. It'll be good for us to have a couple breaks with the conference and then camping. He'll survive, some disgusting way. Anyway—I'll give you a call when I get back from Arizona. Wish me luck!"

* * *

Her trip to Phoenix was easy, and her excitement built as she registered as a "SPEAKER," her badge flowing with a blue fabric ribbon. She fell back on her hotel bed, arms and legs outstretched, praying for a capable yet mesmerizing talk.

She searched for the special room reserved for speakers to prepare, bringing her container of slides and her notes. She whispered through her talk a couple of times, trying to ignore two equally nervous doctors in other sections of the room. Though it wasn't a competition, she gauged their slides and style as they, too, zipped through the presentation they had memorized. She decided she'd be fine after the second run through. She'd practice once more in the morning, then would go to the auditorium and sit in the front row to be announced. Her pager went off to the Pathology Department while she was sitting, so she reached for a phone hooked up for long distance in the Speakers' room.

"Hello? Dr. Riley here, I was paged," Shelly said with authority, as the others peeked at her during their practice.

"Chris Steele, here, Dr. Riley. You know—your favorite pathologist? Just calling to wish you luck on your talk. I know you'll nail it. Next time, though, get those maniacs in your department to put some pathology in your next thesis. I would've loved to work on a project with you."

"Oh, my gosh, how nice of you to call, Dr. Steele! That gives me a boost, believe me. The talk is first thing in the morning, so until then, I'm on edge," she admitted in a whisper, not wanting the others to hear.

"Nonsense. Just imagine 'em in their underpants. You've heard that advice. Or naked, but that would be foul, I imagine. No, old underpants is just the strategy. Shoulders back, smile, and take that stage! See you when you get back. Gotta run," and with that he was off the line.

* * *

Shelly spent the rest of her time in her room, ordering room service for the first time. Although she tossed in her bed, fresh with linens she could only dream about owning, she slept deeply and woke with purpose. Her nerves jangled as she showered and dressed. Precious slides guarded with both arms, she hustled to the prep room and did another brief run through. Coffee forbidden in case of an errant spill, Shelly made her way to the front few rows in the ballroom, cringing at the freezing room temperature. She waited her turn, imagining herself at the podium.

"Are you Dr. Riley?" A young woman in a suit crouched beside Shelly, as she checked her clipboard.

Shelly nodded and whispered, "Yes, I think I'm on after the next speaker."

"Correct. There'll be a pointer at the podium for you, and I can take your slides and get them ready. Be sure to wait after your talk in case there are questions. The review planned by Dr. Hanlon from NYU isn't going to happen—she couldn't leave the hospital, so you'll just wait for questions, then come back to your seat, instead of staying on stage with the panel. Good luck!"

Shit... That means more time for audience questions instead of soft lobs from a friendly reviewer. Shelly knew there could always be changes before a performance, so she did what she could to put it out of her head and concentrate on that first greeting slide and a big smile.

"Thank you for that presentation, Dr. Han. Next, from the University of Southern Kentucky, Dr. Shelly Riley will present…" Shelly rose as soon as the thanks started, knowing silence was deadly. She'd be ready to start as soon as her own introduction was complete. Authority flowed through her as she adjusted the microphone to her level. She placed her paper copy of the speech quietly on the podium to keep the audience from hearing rustling and grabbed the laser pointer. After verifying her first slide was on the screen, she turned to face her audience, breathed deep and gave a full-on grin.

"Dr. Williamson, Dr. Gilbert…" and she was off. At times, Shelly sensed her speech had become pressured, so she forced herself to stop for a breath. She couldn't see a soul due to the lights beaming on her, but she absorbed the energy of the packed crowd and fed it right back.

"Again, many thanks on behalf of my department to the program committee for allowing me to present our data. Are there any questions?" As Shelly shaded her eyes from the lights to see if there were any takers at the microphones nestled in among the aisles, she saw only one short man step forward. She nodded, "Yes, sir?"

"I wonder if you can comment on the ultra-sonographer's qualifications. What if one tech measures totally out of the range of the others? It would destroy your entire premise."

Shelly was ready. "Yes, I addressed that earlier in the presentation." She quickly rifled through her papers. "Could you put up slide #14 again for me, please?" A moment passed, then the slide titled "Interobserver differences in Sonogram Measurements" flashed on the screen. "As you can see, the published differences among thousands of various readings from multiple medical centers is quite small. Negligible, you could say."

The man nodded. "Thank you. Good job."

There were no others. Shelly assembled her papers, thanked the audience again, and watched every step as she made her way back to her seat. Relief over finishing the talk unscathed drenched her with joy. After the plenary session ended, she caught sight of Dr. Devlin and Dr. Alain Lacombe, the third of her former surgical mentors from Springfield, walking toward her. Like all conference attendees, they sported an ID tag on a lanyard, and carried a canvas bag covered with various logos from surgical instruments and textbook companies. Classic dorks.

"Well done, well done," Dr. Lacombe called to her, grabbing her hands and giving the Montreal "kiss-kiss" on each cheek. "I missed you last year, but Rhonda said you were surviving. Now this? You blew it off the field!"

"You mean she hit it out of the pahk, Alain. Wrong metaphor, but we get the idea." Dr. Devlin turned to her, hands clasped to her chest with pleasure.

"Splendid, Shelly, just splendid. Kirk hated to miss it, but I'll fill him in on every word. You did us proud." Rhonda Devlin had been strict, even unforgiving, during residency, but Shelly remembered that she was quick to praise a young doctor who met her standards.

"You think they liked it, really? It was a simple thesis--too simple, I thought." Shelly basked as they strolled, the three of them, toward the back of the ballroom. The crowds of attendees squeezed through the one open door, no one thinking to tether open the second one and allow more bodies to pass.

"Well, Di Amato didn't think so. You know that's the short guy who asked you the ultrasound question, don't you? You spanked him!" Dr. Lacombe identified the famous surgeon from California.

She gulped. "That was Di Amato? Like the textbook?"

Rhonda Devlin laughed. "One and the same. You handled him ably, and he admired you for it. I heard him say 'good job,' didn't you Alain? I wouldn't guess many people get that praise from him, though I've heard he's a nice man."

Shelly was stunned to hear the man whom she'd rather flippantly answered was one of the most famous surgeons in her field. "Was I okay in that? Respectful, I mean?"

"Oh, good grief, yes. He puts his pants on one leg at a time, just like the rest of us mortals. You were great. Now. Dinner tonight? I have a tour of the blooming desert till five, but we'd love to take you out after that, Shelly." Dr. Devlin hugged her, an entirely unexpected display of affection. "I was quite delighted by your talk."

"That means so much to me, Dr. Devlin. Really. And I'm on the tour, too! I figured it'd be wonderful to get outside after all the stress of presenting. We can catch up there." Shelly dashed to retrieve her slides, nodding with thanks for the many compliments strangers lobbed her way as she exited, and found a furtive space to grab a quick cigarette before heading back to the rest of the morning session.

Hmmm...the blooming desert. Harsh, no sustenance, yet the flowers find a way to survive, and even show off a little. Me, too?

JOSTEN, CLARETTA ANNE
Born March 12, 1909
Died May 1, 1996

Claretta "Corky" Josten has waltzed into her heavenly Father's home, and probably snuck a few fireworks in her pocket for the trip. Born into a large family in Blushing County, her parents Felix and Elizabeth plus most of her brothers and sisters were waiting at the gate to welcome her in.

Corky loved her husband Merle, her kids Sara Ann and Clive, and her cherished grandchildren. They mourn her passing, as does her one remaining sister Inez, but they know that Corky is raising the roof, meeting up with old friends and just generally carrying on in heaven the way she did on earth. She had a green thumb, which was one of the many ways she supported her family. She loved to cook, making stews and roasts out of all the game Clive would bring, and homemade bread was her specialty. We love you, Mom.

Services Thursday 1 p.m. at the Church of the Nazarene. The family welcomes you for lunch after church.

CHAPTER 21

Elk Sausage

Afternoon clinic was winding down for Shelly, with only a couple patients left to see. Her monstrous, impossible senior year was ending. She remembered Ken's face as he left their fellows' office last June, and she had a glimmer of hope that she would feel the same.

Her nurse Anita caught her gazing into space, cautioning her, "You're not in the clear yet, Dr. Riley. Two to go, and Mrs. Heslie is roomed."

"I was dreaming of graduation, Anita. I was thinking I might actually survive the oncology service fellowship of Southern Kentucky with both buttocks relatively intact. And I might even have a job in the Twin Cities! I met the doctor in person at the conference. We must've talked for an hour, and he seems great. It's just him in a solo private practice, so he's biting to get some relief. If you'd have asked me the odds last year, I would have thought they were pretty low."

"Oh, we all knew you'd graduate, Dr. Riley. I just wish you didn't get quite so abused in the process, is all. Now, which Sunday works best for you to come to my church before you move away?"

"You're serious, aren't you?" Shelly stopped to think. "Would it be okay if Jeremy came, too?"

"Of course he's welcome! I'd love it. Best you both eat your Wheaties, though. Our service lasts about two to three hours. If you come on Father's Day, the Men's Choir will be singing. You may change your mind about moving home to Minnesota once you hear them. It's powerful, Dr. Riley, like a mighty engine when they get going. Can we plan on that?"

"It's a deal, and I can't wait. Thank you, Anita, for inviting me. I feel honored."

While Shelly marked the church address in her pocket calendar in her lab coat, the clinic receptionist came to the back area, searching for her.

"There you are! Dr. Riley, there's a man here to see you. A, uh, a *big* man, bushy beard, overalls. Won't take no for an answer. He said his name is Clive, and he, well, he wouldn't tell me anymore than that. 'Only Dr. Riley' he said. To tell you the truth he kindly scared me."

"Clive? I don't know a Clive. Well, let him come on back here quick. I've still got a couple patients to see."

As Clive made his way through the back clinic doors, Shelly broke into a grin. At about six-foot-six, with a red-grey beard down to his chest, sporting denim overalls, he was a character hard to forget.

"I remember you!" she exclaimed, and he rushed to give her a crushing bear hug, lifting her off the floor. "You're Ms. Josten's son, aren't you?"

"Yes, ma'am, I'm Clive Josten, her youngest. Sara Ann's a heap older than me, and I do get a charge outta reminding her of that whenever I can." His smile was sad, and Shelly realized he probably had bad news for her.

"Are you going to tell me something about your mom? Something I don't want to hear?" His mother had been pure delight, teaching her intern how to harvest marijuana, and regaling the team with anecdotes about the many adventures she had had during her long life. She was quite the character, but in her eighties, Shelly remembered, and hadn't wanted any heroic measures for her recurrent cancer. Her bowel function had been precarious, and she just wanted to spend her time at home with family.

"I am. Dr. Riley, I'm sad to tell you that Momma died on May Day. She knew it was her time, and we had lots of laughs with her once she got out of the hospital. It was peaceful, really, like she hoped. She scolded us all not to cry, but…" he choked as he tried to hold his tears in. "She was the best mother in the world, I mean that. Funny as all get out, I think y'all doctors noticed that, even when she didn't feel too good. But she was real special to us kids. Always looking out for us. And Lord could she cook."

Shelly was sniffling now, loving the fuller picture of a dear patient. "We loved her, Clive. She made us laugh, and she took a liking to my youngest doctor, Dr. Edsel. Remember him? Big guy? Well, *puny* next to you, but..."

They both chuckled through the tears.

Clive cleared his throat and heaved a sigh. "I won't keep you and Ms. Anita, 'cause I know y'all are busy." He took a massive package out of a bag and thumped it on the desk. "This here's for taking such good care of my momma," he nodded at the cylinder, wrapped in white paper.

"I can't even guess, Clive. What'd you bring?"

"Elk sausage, Dr. Riley. It's a real treat, that is. I had a trip out west before she got sick, and we were lucky to get a big elk out there. The whole family wants you to know that we appreciated what you tried to do. How you treated our momma like she was your own. I hope you like it," his enormous work boots chipping at a random paper scrap on the floor.

"That's the tenderest thing I've ever heard, Clive. Will you give our regards to your family from the team here? I'll tell all the nurses on the Powell that you came in, and of course I'll let them know about your mom." She walked him out to the reception area and got another bear hug from the grateful son.

Dr. Cardinal walked past the package as Shelly was reading through her next patient's chart. "Elk sausage from Ms. Josten's son," Shelly started on the story. "She was an older lady, patient of Dr. Farber's, from the mountains. Taught Dick Edsel how to concentrate THC from..."

"Elk, eh?" Dr. Cardinal interrupted. "Lot of parasites in elk," he told her as he made his way to his half of the clinic space.

Deflated, Shelly picked up the bundle of sausage, then glanced at Anita.

"Oh, Dr. Riley," she comforted her, shaking her head. "They just have to poke at you, don't they? Can't just leave well enough alone." With that she insisted Shelly move on and examine her last few patients.

"Come on, then, let's get these ladies seen."

***

Shelly told and retold the story in her head, and then bounced it off Jeremy at home. "Maybe he didn't mean to sour it for me. I don't know." They sat out back on lawn chairs so Pepper could romp, and Shelly could smoke. She was miserable with paranoia that all three of her supposed mentors were still hoping for her downfall.

"Seems to me that no matter how well you perform, they find a way to do something that eats at you," Jeremy commented. "But nothing you could prove. They call it gaslighting, you know. I learned about it in psych, and I remember it because my friend's dad did it to him all the time. As soon as the prof went over the definition, Ricky's face came to me. Jeez, the stuff he told me…" He shook his head.

"Gaslighting? I've never heard of it. What's it mean?"

"Well, my psychology textbook's at home, but it's basically when one person tells you you're stupid, or eat too much, or smell, or whatever, over and over, to make you feel bad. The key is that the thing they pick on isn't true. At first you know that. After enough time, though, the bad guy gaslights you so well that you start to believe it. It's sick, really."

"What'd the dad do to your friend Ricky?"

Jeremy scratched Pepper's head. "It's not a pleasant story, baby."

Shelly watched him. "It might help me cope with this whole thing. I'd like to hear it, Jeremy." She nodded at him to continue.

"Well, he was a little husky, you might say. Big frame, maybe a little overweight when we were in high school. Not unhealthy, though, and he played football, so being a little beefy was okay. His dad, though. God, he just railed on Ricky all the time about how much he ate, and how he'd never get a girl being pudgy and all. *Called* him Pudge. Ricky hated it."

"He sounds mean. He didn't hit him?"

"No, that's the sneaky part of gaslighting. Nothing physical. Nothing provable. Ricky started to believe his dad and would say defeatist things like "I'll never have a girlfriend" or "I'm such a whale I don't know why you even hang out with me." Jeremy's eyes squinted at the memories and shook his head. "And he was just the nicest guy," he finished.

"Where's Ricky now? I'd like to meet him, if you think he'd be up for chatting about something personal with someone he doesn't even know, that is."

Jeremy stood up, nearly spilling the can of Old Style on the cement patio. He ran his hand through his hair, took a deep breath, and faced her.

"Baby, he's gone. He shot himself. Ricky shot himself when we were juniors in high school." He slugged down the rest of his beer and sighed. "I've always wondered how I could've been a better friend to him. You know, convinced him his dad was an asshole or something."

She gasped at the sudden reveal. "Oh, Jeremy, I'm sorry. I didn't mean to bring up something so awful. And teen years are an especially terrible time of life for all of you to deal with a friend's suicide."

"Yep, we were miserable, everyone in my friend group. And you know, his dad just acted like he had nothing to do with it. It was sickening." Jeremy reached into his wallet, pulling out a frayed newspaper clipping. "…'doting parents,' it says." He handed the years old obituary notice over to her, the final notice of his high school friend's short life.

"That's burned me up all these years. He wasn't doting. He was cruel. And Ricky's mom, well she just sorta vanished after he died. I went over there a couple times after the funeral, and she was still in a housecoat at 4 pm. She was so depressed she could barely look at me. I couldn't stand it, so I stopped going."

Shelly read the news clipping with an arm around Jeremy.

"It's so cold, isn't it? I mean, it's way plainer than the obituary of a 17-year-old should be. There should be more love, somehow. I guess parents must be so shocked after a suicide they just go through the motions. Horrible." She handed the obituary back, and he folded it with care.

"Anyway, I feel like gaslighting is what your workplace bosses are doing to you. You're a wonderful person, and I'm sure you're a good doctor, too. You wouldn't think of hurting yourself, would you baby?" Jeremy's face was lined with the worry that comes with experience.

"Suicide? God, no! *Homicide,* maybe,'" Shelly laughed. "I've got my eyes on graduation, Jeremy. I'm ready to be an actual grownup doctor!"

He smiled at her and took her hands. "That's my feisty girl. I have every confidence in you and sounds like so do all the nurses and residents. Use the evidence in front of you to fight off the mind games. That's my advice, at least. Data's an engineer's friend. Now, you'd better get packed for your mountain man camping, and I'd better get back to studying." He hugged her tight. "I'm glad I told you about Ricky. That was a long time ago, but it still hurts."

Shelly pondered that terrible story as she packed. Clearly, she had to keep her mental contests in perspective, learn every damned thing she could as a fellow, and graduate. She'd just have to face the fact that not everyone liked her, let alone loved her. Which drove her crazy.

* * *

Finished with work at the hospital, Shelly had packed for the camping weekend and changed into jeans and a long-sleeved shirt with tennis shoes for the ride. Luca was waiting in the lobby, chatting at twice the normal volume with the hospital greeter, a trim older man with some sort of uniform that identified him as retired military. She gathered he was charming him with an anecdote about post-call fatigue.

"I have no idea how I get home, half the time. Just find myself pulling into my driveway. Anyway, my wife'll drive tonight. She'll tune in some terrible pop station and I'll be asleep before we reach city limits."

Shelly tapped him on the shoulder. "Ready, Luca!"

"Oh, hey, Shelly," he boomed, louder still, if possible. "Let's git, then, if you've got your stuff. We'll be putting up the tent in the dark tonight. That's always fun. See ya, Carl!" he gave a little salute as they swung through the side door of the hospital to Samantha awaiting them in the main entrance drive-up.

"Yep, I hear *104.5 on the FM Dial, Smooth as Silk* already on," Luca gave his best impression of a radio DJ while swinging up the back hatch for Shelly's bag. "Want to sit next to Samantha for the ride and keep her awake while I pass out? Hey, wifey, thanks for picking us up here," he kissed Samantha through her open window.

"Fellows are never as sleep deprived as residents, that's for sure," he informed Shelly over the top of the car. "Except you've got the new beau, now, eh? How're you two gonna survive a weekend apart?" He clambered into the backseat, kicking off his clogs as he settled in.

"Luca, let the woman get a word in, honestly," Samantha decreased the radio volume and leaned to smooch Shelly's cheek from the driver's seat. "How're you, Shelly? Ready for our adventure?" They settled into an easy chat about life and work as Samantha eased them out of town and onto more rural roads. "It's about two hours to the campgrounds, give or take. I don't generally stop unless there's a need. Y'all just let me know."

Samantha needed no guidance with the route. "We've been here five years in a row. I just love to get away, to tell you the truth. Beautiful forest, lots of nice people, and bathrooms and showers on site. You camp much at home?"

"Nope—I've never even put up a tent."

"Hmm. This isn't super rustic, so I think you'll be fine. There are wheelbarrows to move our stuff to our campsite, and putting up the tent's easy, even in the dark. We love the food from all these cool vendors. Most of them make old timey foods that you might've found in the 1800's, like meat on skewers and stews. You'll see the real serious campers cooking everything in huge pots over the fire. Those folks mean business, right down to the clothes."

Luca snored in the back seat and Samantha drove the two-lane paved roads with skill, chatting about her job in the insurance company in town, and how many kids she thought they'd have once Luca was out of his residency. "My girlfriends kept trying to get me to break up with Luca in college. They finally agreed we were perfect for one another. He's the toughie, and I'm the softie. We like the same odd things too."

"Like the Grateful Dead?" Shelly asked.

"Yep, Grateful Dead and Mardi Gras are our big obsessions. And this muzzleloaders convention which I believe…" she turned the wheel onto a dirt road, barely marked with a wooden arrow stuck in the shoulder of the road, "we're about to enter! Luca, hon, time to wake up!"

The exhausted resident sat bolt upright at Samantha's words. "We're here?"

"Wow, Luca. Samantha and I have been talking in a normal tone of voice for two hours while you slept. How'd you wake up to that?"

He laughed. "Sam's voice is my alarm clock, honestly. If she says the words 'wake up' from the kitchen, I swear I hear it in the bedroom. I gotta pee. How close are we, babe?"

Samantha pulled into the camping area, slowing down to pay the entrance fee and chat with the ranger. Soon they were parked and unloading their gear onto a couple wheeled carts. They were nestled inside their tent in no time, munching on granola bars and drinking beer.

"You think of everything, Samantha!" Shelly drank with the gratitude of someone finally relinquished, even if just for a day or two, from an onerous burden.

"See what I mean, Shelly?" Luca laid on his sleeping bag, head propped up on his sack of clothes. "Who cares where we are—we're not at work, they can't page us, and we're surrounded by good folks. It doesn't get any better, I'm telling you."

"Oh, yes it does," Samantha reminded him. "The first coffee in the morning. That's my favorite part of camping. I'm not a huge fan of the sleeping on the ground, but I do love the camp stove and the delicious smell of coffee outdoors. We'll have to see what you like best, Shelly."

They were soon asleep, soothed by the sound of nighttime creatures and the feel of a breeze through the tent's screened windows. Shelly heard various voices throughout the night, and an occasional loud laugh or call. Though anticipating freshly brewed coffee, the aroma Shelly woke to was Luca's flatulence in the enclosed tent.

Shelly scrambled to escape the foul smell. She tried her best not to disturb her hosts, slowly unzipping the screen door of the tent and looking for the bathroom and shower building Samantha had told her about.

It was a glorious morning, birds chirping, and a small number of people milling around campfires or little propane stoves. A man with a huge white beard, dark pants, buckskin boots and a hip length, coarse linen tunic wandered to the bathrooms. Shelly brushed her teeth and ran her fingers through her now tangled hair. Forgetting her brush didn't strike her as much of an issue, since everyone was pretending to be back in the 1800s.

She wandered the area, and saw a smattering of modern tents like theirs and a section of the reenactors, with ivory colored cotton/muslin tents, staked with rough metal spikes and ropes. She noted the heavy iron pots hung over the firepits, grateful Jeremy didn't have a similar hobby.

* * *

When she reached her tent, Samantha was crouched over the little stove and a pot of water nearly boiling atop the tripod. "Hey, there, Shelly! Coffee's near ready." Her concoction was a combination of Nescafe, powdered milk, and a store-bought instant mocha powder, stirred in a "secret recipe" to deliver caffeine without too much sugar. "You find the facilities?"

"Yep. And this is delicious," Shelly approved, sipping and sitting down on a log at the site. "No need for my espresso pot."

When Luca eventually exited the tent, yawning at the same volume he used to talk, the day was truly ready to begin for everyone around them. "Morning, babe," he boomed to Samantha, giving her a smooch as she offered him a clean mug and the powdered mix.

"Help yourself, hon. There's more than enough hot water."

"You sleep good, Shelly? I was out as soon as I lay down. Man, I don't even remember moving stuff in, that's how tired I was. I feel great now! Ready to roll. I definitely want to hit that place that makes the buckwheat pancakes. Y'all hungry? I've gotta check out the men's room—I'll be right back."

"Boy, as soon as his eyes open his brain connects to his mouth, doesn't it?" Shelly marveled at just how energized Luca was at all times.

Samantha's eye twinkled with love. "He's alert, I agree. Always in the present moment, no matter what we're doing. More so if he likes the event. We'll give you a walking tour after he gets back. There's a pancake place that uses old-timey sorghum syrup. Sometimes they have wild rice pancakes from their Wisconsin rendezvous. These vendors go all over the country for these little festivals."

They wandered around for the morning, eating their fill of cakes and syrup, admiring the various items for sale, and generally winding down from hyper work mode to rendezvous time.

That took Shelly a few hours.

"Luca, do you have a hard time relaxing at a place like this?"

He considered the question. "Well, I *have* thought about hospital stuff a few times already this morning, if that's what you mean. My presentation at next week's M&M is on my mind. I wonder how I did on the national exam last month. Oh, and I don't know if I remembered to tell Carmen one of the key labs on a lady in my sign-out yesterday. I guess I don't exactly bliss out right off the bat. That's life, right?"

"That's *no* life, my dear ones," Samantha corrected him. "Y'all really have a hard time decompressing. I've watched you from a distance all these years, and all you think about is medicine. No matter what the social situation, you start talking about the hospital, or the OR, or some gross thing you saw in clinic."

"I think it's because we don't really start doing our actual job until we're almost thirty," Shelly offered as they found a communal firepit. "I'm finally operating and giving chemo to the patients I'm going to be treating for my real career. Most people start their first job out of college. There are so many years of buildup to when our professional job starts, we're super enthusiastic about all of it."

"Well, look around at these people. They have the leather boots and floppy hats in the 1800s style, right? They research their favorite era. They read books about the food and the clothes, and save their money to buy more authentic gear at these rendezvous." Samantha sat next to her husband. "They have *a life* outside of their work. Y'all need other interests, I'd say."

"Yeah, well, the beard wouldn't work in the OR, my love," Luca told Samantha. "And I don't really like guns. I'm just here for the beef jerky and the camping. You find your beads, and Shelly and I will try to avoid shop talk for the next day, I swear."

Shelly laughed. "I brought a book, and I'm going to try to think of anything but the hospital, too. You're good for us, Samantha. Rein us in when you have to!"

* * *

They spent the day surrounded by children running barefoot and people who really belonged in 1796, not 1996. The aromas from the wood campfires and the pots simmering over them were enticing. The aromas of some of the burliest mountain men, less so. Shelly couldn't really believe the extent to which these folks were play acting. So much effort, for pretend. The women mostly wore simple calico dresses, long hair swept back, legs bare.

The men, though. They went all out, with pouches dangling at the waist, leather belts cinching their tunics with a brass buckle, and oh, the beautiful leather boots, draped with fringe, sometimes beaded. Old, young, all were obsessed with a time long ago. *Clive would look exactly right, here,* Shelly mused, *but I'll bet he could outshoot all these guys.*

* * *

When they packed up the next afternoon, Shelly thanked her friends for an eye-opening weekend.

"I can't thank you all enough. I probably won't be buying my own calico dress, you understand. Samantha, my favorite part was watching you two, getting along and working together." Shelly was surprised at the catch in her voice. "You've shown me a healthy relationship. I'm not sure I've ever had one."

As they wheeled their items to the car, Luca commented, "It's all about the right person, Shelly. I could never be this happy if it weren't for Samantha. Gotta be the right fit. You think Jeremy's the one for you?"

No.

"Well, I'm not sure I'd say he's exactly the one I envision marrying. He's a really great person, I just don't know if we're meant to be together for the whole 'better or worse' stuff. Really, he's as nice a guy as I could ever hope to meet."

"I'd say that answer is just a plain 'no,' Shelly," Luca said.

"I agree with Luca, Shelly. That was a lot of empty talking there. The guy for you is out there, I'm sure." Samantha grabbed Luca by the waist and hugged him tight. "And it'll have been worth the wait."

DESMA, RICHARD DEAN "Ricky"
Born January 17, 1971
Passed March 20, 1988

Taken from his family too soon. Ricky was a fine boy who enjoyed football and horses. He rode his bike to the horse farms to watch them take care of the animals and put them through their paces.

Ricky had nice friends. They liked nothing better than an early day out of school so they could be together on their bikes.

He leaves behind doting parents Charles and Lainie Desma, plus little sister Connie. He will be missed by all his aunts, uncles, and cousins, too.

Wake Thursday, March 24 from 6-8pm at Paducah Heights Funeral Home, Grand Avenue. Funeral Friday, March 25. Private graveside burial.

CHAPTER 22

Hoo, boy!

With less than a month between her fellowship and official career adulthood, Shelly stayed alert around the three attendings, but dared to imagine herself finishing with success. She'd grown fond of the operating room staff and Dr. Steele in Pathology. She wrote cards to the housekeeper on the Powell who'd always had a moment to chat with her, and to Bernice, the night ward clerk who'd been her first contact that dawn nearly two years ago.

She'd unwound them from the decades-long rut by starting rounds at Room 236, the opposite end of the circle. She'd started joke of the day on morning rounds, with mostly groans resulting. Now and then a resident had an idea to streamline their process, and if at all possible she tried to use it. Shelly felt her brain, creativity, and energy had been stifled for two years. It was time for them all to reset, and Shelly was digging deep to remember her authentic personality.

One June afternoon, she saw her former resident Patricia Quinn walking down the hallway, shaking her head and moving her lips as if having a conversation with herself.

Shelly greeted her, "Hey, Patricia! Ready for graduation?"

"Oh, Shelly, I'm grateful to see you. Have you heard?" Patricia's eyes filled with tears.

"What in the world happened to make you so sad?" Shelly reached to comfort her.

Patricia had the heart of a lioness, and rarely had Shelly met a person whose convictions and actions meshed as completely. She was a gem, and it was shocking to see her so undone, especially before her graduation.

Patricia gathered herself and drew Shelly to an alcove away from other eyes and ears. "It's terrible, Shelly. I'm just so confused." Her voice trailed as she wept. "Dr. Boldon, you know, the department chair? He's getting a divorce."

Shelly cocked her head. "No offense, Patricia, but why's that so terrible? Lots of people get divorced."

Patricia sniffled. "His wife's divorcing him because he's been having an affair, Shelly. With his twenty-year-old office nursing assistant. And she is..." She blinked and swallowed. "She is pregnant." Her shoulders shook. "I just want to wail over it. He's born again like me, Shelly. And this behavior, well, it's just not allowed. He's supposed to be stronger than that against temptation. He's supposed to lead his marriage and be a fierce protector of his family!"

Shelly remembered Dr. Cardinal crowing in the OR about his church officially declaring the man the head of the household. She could see that Patricia was one thousand percent in support of this and had just had her worldview demolished by those age-old human failures of lust, poor judgement, and infidelity.

She put her arms around the young woman's shoulder and let her whimper. "It's a painfully common story, Patricia. You know that, deep down. It's just that you're such a solid, dear person you can't imagine all the yucky people out here in the world. And right in your church. How'd you find this out?"

"It was quite a scene this morning, Shelly. Dr. Boldon's wife came into clinic with two huge suitcases. Marched into the lobby, shoulders back, and her face set like she was about to kill somebody. She walked into the back and started screaming the second she saw him. I mean bellowing, Shelly. Opened one of the suitcases and dumped his clothes on the floor. Lord, his underwear and all. The whole time he was trying to shush her, saying, 'Now, Lizzie, just hold on now. I can explain if you just stop this foolishness...'"

Patricia shook her head. Paused. "And then the girl came out of a room. She had a chart in one arm and was helping a patient to the bathroom with her other. Oh, Shelly. When she saw Mrs. Boldon? It was just crushing. She stood there for a second, and then kept walking with her patient and passed right through the two of them. Then she stopped, turned her head around and said, clear as day, 'Well, I'm keeping this baby, and neither of you can stop me.' And off she went. I thought the whole clinic was going to explode. *I'm* going to explode!"

She shuddered with sobs. "I asked for the rest of the day off, and I'm going home to be with my parents, Shelly. They'll know what to do," she asserted as she wiped her face and pulled tight her lab coat.

"Boldon should know better, for goodness' sake, and he *certainly* shouldn't be leading the department. You can't have sex with an employee who depends on you for her job, for one thing. And the infidelity's disgusting. That sounds like a good idea to talk to your folks, Patricia. Drive safely." She waved as the young woman walked away, head down and still brushing away tears.

* * *

Shelly was stunned at how shaken Patricia had been, and how personally she'd taken the failings of her department head. *He's just another asshole*, Shelly thought, making her way to the Powell. The story fit Shelly's suspicions of him to a tee.

Dr. Cardinal called from the hallway, "Shelly, wait up." He made a show of a slow jog to catch up to her. "Now, there's been a little altercation this morning," he started.

"Is that what you'd call it, Dr. Cardinal? A department head having sex with an underling is against hospital bylaws, I'm guessing, and totally inappropriate, I'm sure you agree. Not to mention it's really icky. I can't say I blame his wife."

"Well, don't be so quick to judge, now, that's what I wanted to tell you. We need to be a forgiving people, here, and support him in this difficult time. He's truly in pain, I can tell you."

Shelly realized that he wasn't joking. "You're entirely serious, aren't you?" Shelly stared him down. *Fuck this. You only have a month left.* "Dr. Cardinal, forgive him all you want. Pray with him. Do whatever you care to in your church. But this is a hospital, with tons of women employees. We don't deserve to be toyed with and then tossed out when an affair is discovered by a furious wife." Shelly felt her face flush but continued. "That nursing assistant is twenty years old. Boldon's a predator and needs to step down. That's all there is to it. He should probably be fired, to tell you the truth."

"Now, that's what I wanted to talk to you about. I can't have you getting the residents all excited about this. It's a private matter between a good man and his wife, and..."

"C'mon, Dr. Cardinal," Shelly raged. "A forty-five-year-old married staff physician having unprotected sex with a twenty-year-old employee is *not* a good man. And I believe Mrs. Boldon took the 'private matter' issue out of play this morning, wouldn't you say?" Shelly turned her back to storm off, then paused, adrenalin surging. *I'm gonna regret this.*

"You've had issues with me since I arrived here. You poked and prodded and tried to break me. You called me a baby killer. You implied I have no moral compass because I don't chime in when you talk about your religious views. Favored Walter over me, in every situation."

Pacing now, her voice shook with anger, and as people walked past them in the hallway, she took the volume down to a hiss. "Might I point out that I've quietly taken *everything* you dished out, without a word of complaint?"

"Wait, now, about Walter..." Dr. Cardinal tried to interject.

Shelly continued as if he hadn't spoken. "But with all that, I never doubted your moral character. I always believed you loved Melissa and your kids. I'd couldn't imagine you cheating on her. So, you can't tell me, with all your devotion to the Bible, that Dr. Boldon gets to go on his merry way with all his titles after pulling a move like this. If so, I think you missed a couple important passages in that book you love so much." Peter Cardinal rocked on his heels, avoiding Shelly's eyes.

Livid, Shelly added, "You know, 'hate the sin, love the sinner' works in church, Dr. Cardinal." Her breath was coming in ragged spurts and she trembled. She gestured at the space with her arms wide,

"But this is a secular institution, with hiring practices and rules to protect people. Your colleague has done a very bad thing. The women in this department aren't going to stand behind him, I promise you that. What remains to be seen is if the *men* do the right thing by urging him to step down."

She strode away, escaping into her favorite hospital stairway to deny Dr. Cardinal a retort. Shelly was astounded at the endless shit men could get away with and still expect favors and exceptions to be made for them. *Why'd he come running to me, of all people?* she wondered. She was the most vulnerable of all of them in the department. She had been cowering at their mercy for two years, after all, powerless.

Shelly stopped in the hospital stairway, shivering at the sudden revelation.

"Now just do that in your own department" from Luca, referencing her tete-a-tete with C. Cole.

"If you don't want me as your senior fellow, you need to tell me that now," when Walter had gone tattling to Dr. Farber on her supposed incompetence.

Now her latest confrontation with Dr. Cardinal, finally having the guts to tell him to do the right thing.

Of course she had power.

The stairwell door opened one floor up, followed by Luca's booming, "Shelly, you in here?"

Shelly laughed, "Down a flight, Luca, come get me!" recalling the day she confided in him that she considered this stairway her second office, since no one else used it. She felt enveloped in the spirits of fellows past, sitting on a step and gazing at the little sparkles in the greenish linoleum. It helped her think.

"Hoo, boy, you're not gonna believe what just happened!" Luca plopped down next to her, throwing his head back in glee. "There hasn't been this big a shitstorm in our department in, like, ever. You hear about Boldon's wife barging into clinic and dumping his clothes?"

"I ran into Patricia. She was really shaken up by the whole scene."

"The clincher was when Ginny Mae, that's the nursing assistant, comes out with 'I'm keeping the baby' and walks right between them. The patient on her arm had to walk right through Brian Boldon's underpants to get to the bathroom!

"So now Mrs. Boldon is just purple. She can't believe the girl her husband impregnated walked right past her, see? The wife's voice gets real low, kind of ominous, and she says, 'You'll never work again. I'm contacting the Medical Board. I'm contacting the hospital's Board of Trustees. And I'm calling the pastor. You have soiled your name for good this time. I will not have you soiling mine.' Hoo, boy, you should have seen her! Now I know what people mean when they say someone's eyes were blazing. She could have lit our campfire, she was that pissed."

"Good recap, Luca. You were there?"

"Lord, yes, and I wouldn't have missed it for the world. Right afterwards I looked up university policy on relationships in the workplace, and I'm pretty sure this counts as sexual harassment. Look," he held out a thick blue spiral bound book of medical staff bylaws. "'There shall be no personal relationships among employees with a reporting or similar work close work tie'…blah, blah, blah."

Luca turned to a dog-eared page. "Plus this: 'Employees cannot have a personal or family relationship when they are responsible for a performance review, compensation, or approval of travel or expenses.' That should seal the deal since he's Ginny Mae's boss. But you know what else got me? Mrs. Boldon said 'this time' like there have been others. So I snooped around with the clinic nurses. Turns out this is *not* our beloved department head's first affair. The first one was with a patient, and that's a big no-no."

"Oh, my God. The man's rotten. You know, Cardinal came looking for me to tell me the department had to forgive him. That he was in so much pain. I couldn't believe it. He specifically told me not to get the residents riled up. What do you make of that?"

Luca's eyes gleamed. "What do I make of that? That the man understands we'll follow you anywhere, and that if you speak out against his buddy, his buddy will go down. They've tried to break you for two years, Shelly, and you just keep showing up! You have the most senior status as fellow. They're scared of you. Hell, you only have three weeks left. What are they gonna do—fire you?"

Shelly thought a moment.

"I could draft a letter from the residents and fellows, saying we've lost confidence in his leadership, and feel he should step down as Department Head. 'In light of recent events...' type thing. You think we could get a couple signatures?"

"Shelly, I guarantee that *everyone* will sign it. Well, except Walter. He's already acting like a mini-Dr. Cardinal. And Patricia might feel a little conflicted, I guess. But, hell, yeah, we'll sign it today. There's a typewriter in the resident's room. Oh, and guess who took typing in high school?"

"There's no way you could sit still long enough to type a memo, Luca," Shelly protested.

"Not me! No, our little bubba Dick Edsel. Those linebacker fingers of his will pound out whatever you write. I'll ask Rebecca who we should send it to. For sure Farber. The President of the hospital, I guess? Chief of Medical Staff, the Board, and the other department faculty, so they know what we think. Bernice'll get me some nice paper, so it looks official. After rounds?"

Shelly nodded. "It's already outlined in my head. I'll meet you in the resident's room in about an hour. Anything to eat in there?"

Luca cackled as he bounded up the first couple steps, "Probably. We'll pool our cafeteria tickets and get as much as we can. Better tell Jeremy to let the dog out, cuz you're gonna be late tonight!"

* * *

Rounds flew, and Shelly took a legal pad from the ward clerk's desk to write her rough draft in the stairwell. The nurses were in clumps along the hallways, talking quietly in groups of three or so, some shaking their heads, others listening, mesmerized.

Shelly paged Mona, her "fellow-fellow," as they called themselves, who confirmed her whole division had heard the news. She would sign the letter, as would her junior fellow, Jim Coolidge.

"I'm proud of Jim, really," Mona told her. "He just about blew a gasket when he heard, and said, 'Men like that give the rest of us a bad reputation. I hope he loses his job, the stupid bastard!' I've never heard Jim swear before. I hope that's how every man in the department reacts, don't you?"

Shelly scribbled away, thinking of the main point she wanted to make crystal clear: subordinates depended on bosses for job security, which paid for rent and food. *Stick to the facts,* she muttered to herself as she made the final paragraph firmer. *Keep it short and resolute so they take us seriously.*

She dashed off to the residents' room, where nearly every intern and resident had convened. Wild with energy, they hooted when Shelly plugged in the access code and swept open the door. The aroma of cafeteria foods filled her nostrils, and she immediately dug into the nearest plate shoved her way.

"Thanks, you guys. I'm starving!" As she read the rough draft aloud, the group listened while inhaling their food, then chimed in with suggestions. They agreed to the wording quickly, and Dick sat down to type the final version on heavy letterhead paper. He handed it to Shelly to proofread when finished.

"Nice work, Dick. No typos, and it fits on one page. I say we sign it and make copies for the others like Luca suggested. Is everyone on board?"

The young physicians murmured their assent, some looking to others for validation, a couple boldly avowing, "Hell, yes!"

"I'd like to tell you all something, if I could," Shelly took a deep breath to change the subject, and the room went silent. "You know I'm leaving in a few weeks…"

"The Nordic Queen heads back to the hinterland, we know. We're gonna miss that nasal voice something fierce, Shelly!"

"Shut up, Coughlin." Dick Edsel scolded him. Mona stood and gave her a quick hug.

"As I was saying. I'm gonna miss you all, and I want to thank you for your hard work this year on the oncology service. You really made the difference, with me working solo." Her voice cracked as she swallowed. "You helped our patients like you can't even believe. Thanks for that, everyone. I couldn't have survived without you." Shelly nodded directly at Rebecca.

"Now, about this matter. I know it's outrageous, and it's almost impossible not to gossip about something this dramatic. But please--be careful with your words once you leave this room.

"Every single person in this hospital is gonna know about this. Boldon's reputation will tank, but Dr. Cardinal will go to bat for him. There may be others, and they may play rough. People get desperate when their career's at stake. So don't slander him. Don't get into the weeds about it with the nurses and other hospital employees. And be nice to Ginny Mae. She has a hell of an ordeal ahead of her, and who knows how much trouble she's going to get from Boldon. Be…" Shelly reached for the right advice. "Be poised."

The residents were still, and many nodded in recognition of Velma's word. They took turns signing their illegible signatures with their free pharmaceutical pens. When the last resident finally placed the letter on the table next to the typewriter, Rebecca offered to copy the original and deliver them by hand the next day to all the residents who were post-call and excused from work.

Luca wondered, "If Boldon steps down as Department Head, who's gonna take his place?"

Shelly left them to hash out the remaining details of what would happen to their department. It mattered to them all since a scandal could harm a school's reputation and therefore their academic futures. She listened to the hum of those earnest voices as she made her way out of the hospital that evening. She trusted them all to be firm in their convictions. She drove home guilty to feel excited to tell Jeremy about the latest scandal, and already pondering if her outburst to Dr. Cardinal would have consequences.

June 4, 1996

To Whom It May Concern:

We, the residents and fellows of the University of Southern Kentucky, learned today that Dr. Brian Boldon, Department Head, had an extramarital affair and impregnated his clinic nursing assistant. Dr. Boldon is her boss and immediate supervisor. Dr. Boldon's wife confronted him in the clinic today, a dramatic, ugly scene witnessed by many residents, staff, and patients.

Please be advised that we consider Dr. Boldon's personal behavior unprofessional and unbecoming of a Department Head. According to the University of Southern Kentucky's Hospital bylaws, sexual harassment of employees is against item 3) a (ii). It is also against employment policy since the nursing assistant is Dr. Boldon's employee.

We take our medical education very seriously, having worked and studied for decades to learn our specialty. The department's reputation affects our current education and our careers. Poor, unethical leadership puts the training program on shaky ground with accreditation by the American Board of Medical Examiners.

Therefore, we have lost confidence in Dr. Brian Boldon. He has squandered his right to be regarded as a leader and teacher. We respectfully ask that he step down as Department Head immediately.

Sincerely,

CHAPTER 23

Amen

"Let's go, Jeremy. It'll take us twenty minutes to get there, and I don't want to walk in late. We'll stick out enough as it is."

"All set. I was just letting Pepper out one more time." Jeremy appraised his girlfriend and smiled. "You look stunning! Very appropriate for church, but beautiful. Am I okay?" He turned, striking an elaborate pose to demonstrate his suit and polished shoes. His dark brown hair and beard were immaculate.

"Perfect." Shelly hugged him tightly. "And you smell like heaven, also very appropriate for church. Let's hit it."

They made their way to Anita's church, following her directions and driving right to the building. A line of five older Black men, each in an elegant suit, greeted them with warm smiles and outstretched hands.

"Welcome to Bethany, y'all! So glad to see you this fine morning." Shelly and Jeremy walked through the entryway, holding hands as they gazed at the magnitude of the sanctuary. Already nearly half filled, the sacred space was massive, walls painted a buttery hue that complemented the polished brown pews.

"Jesus, Jeremy, the place is huge," Shelly whispered. "I'm not sure I'll be able to even find Anita with all these people."

"She'll find us, baby, and you might want to watch your language," Jeremy shook his head at Shelly's inability to avoid the occasional slip of the tongue. Sure enough, Shelly noticed Anita ahead, waving and gesturing for them to come down a few pews.

"Dr. Riley, I'm so tickled you could come. And you must be Jeremy. Welcome to Bethany, Jeremy, and thank you for bringing my favorite fellow to my favorite place in the world." Anita glowed with pleasure as she scooted to gather in her young guests. She introduced her son Calvin, and explained her husband was getting robed to sing in the Father's Day Men's choir.

"My dad can really sing!" young Calvin assured them, leaning over his mom, and squirming with excitement. "And when I'm a teenager I'm gonna be in the choir, too."

"Anita, you have to tell us if we're doing something wrong, okay? I don't want to embarrass you," Shelly admitted her worry.

"Dr. Riley, it's just church. We sing, we pray, and we sing some more. I'm sure it's like your church at home."

"Yeah, um, Anita, I can pretty much guarantee this is not going to be like my Episcopal church at home," taking a few tissues from a young usher offering them pew by pew. "For one thing, no one needs tissues at my place. And there are maybe eighty people at the service I used to go to. There's got to be three hundred people here!"

She nodded, "We're full today because of Father's Day. I'd say maybe fifty fewer on a regular Sunday. Okay, here we go, Dr. Riley. This is the choir I told you about. I'll point out Ray if I can."

And the beauty unfolded. The front of the church contained an electric keyboard facing an acoustic piano, both with players who nodded to one another indicating they were ready to start. An amplified bass guitar and drummer accompanied. A quiet chord shivered in the sanctuary, offering a cue to the congregation that the service was beginning, and the voices hushed and quickly silenced.

And then.

As the melody became clearer, Shelly heard a low roar behind her. Men of all ages, resplendent in purple choir robes, came down both edges of the church, and two by two down the center aisle, deep voices stirring and powerful.

"The baritones," Anita whispered. "Ray's a tenor, and I think I see him set to come down the middle." Soon those higher voices sounded above, the tenors taking the melody and soaring as they processed. Music now surrounded the entire congregation. Anita nodded as her husband Ray walked past them, stepping in time with the music and giving a wink to Calvin as he passed.

The incredible harmony washed over Shelly again and again, sending chills along her spine and arms. She dabbed her eyes, filled with emotion she couldn't explain. Soon the choir had taken its place on the risers in the front of the church, and the pastor had made his way to the wooden pulpit during the processional. He greeted the congregation as a trusted friend and colleague, and many responded in kind. There were readings, more music, and a sermon.

"We appreciate our amazing men's choir on this Father's Day, do we not?" Pastor Mattson addressed the church. Applause and adoration followed for the musical enrichment of the service. "Are there any announcements?"

One older woman in the front stood to thank the many people who had visited her during a recent hospital stay, and for the rest who had brought food. The congregation murmured and blessed her when she explained her condition, and gratefully filled them in that she was on the mend. Another woman, older still, rose just to say, "Good morning to all my Bethany sisters and brothers. I'm ninety-five this week, and I feel I owe the Lord thanksgiving and praise for this long life!" Jubilation followed from the parishioners as her friends helped her sit back. Others stood to give an update on building repairs and committee reports. One reported the death of a relative in another state. By the nodding heads in the congregation, Shelly guessed there were many who knew the situation, and perhaps the person. The mood was relaxed and patient, and all were attentive.

"Any visitors to our church this fine Father's Day?" The pastor faced his parishioners.

Did Shelly just imagine that literally every single face turned to regard her and Jeremy?

No, she did not. Anita stood, taking Shelly's elbow with her.

"I'd appreciate my Bethany family's welcome to my co-worker at the hospital, Dr. Shelly Riley, and her friend Jeremy. I have known Dr. Riley for two years, now, and I'm so pleased to bring her to my favorite place on earth. Dr. Riley, these people are family to me," Anita told her as she swept her arm to indicate everyone in sight. "Now they'll be family to you."

Immediately calls of "That's right!" and "Welcome, welcome!" came to Shelly and Jeremy. Blushing furiously, they nodded their thanks, turning and greeting those behind them as well as on the sides. Others followed suit, introducing various friends and relatives in town for Father's Day and visiting the church, and enthusiastic calls followed for them, too.

As the service ended, a multitude of friendly faces smiled at Shelly, stopping to chat and express their hope that she enjoyed the service. "Everyone knows you, Anita," Shelly told her as they headed downstairs for lunch.

"Everyone knows everyone, Dr. Riley. It's like a small town, and we're *all* up in each other's business. That's the strength of the church community, as far as I'm concerned. If anyone from Bethany sees Calvin doing something he shouldn't be doing, I'll get twenty calls about it before he even gets home," she laughed.

"Well, I certainly see why you love it here. It's filled with joy. And the music!"

Anita nodded, "I knew you'd appreciate the choir. They work so hard--Ray rehearses constantly before a big event like this, on top of the full choir rehearsals they go to. We really pride ourselves on our music program."

"It shapes the service, doesn't it?" Shelly agreed. "Powerful. What about you, Jeremy?"

Jeremy had been quiet, leaving the conversation to Anita and Shelly while taking it all in.

"Well, I was thinking the whole time that I've never in my life been in a Black church, and I've been asking myself why that is."

"Young man, there's a saying that ten in the morning on Sunday is the most segregated time of the week in America," Pastor Mattson's booming voice added from the steps behind them. "As much as I'd like to see us all mingle, the Black church has been a real sanctuary for generations. Still, I hope you two liked what you witnessed today," he smiled. "And I know you're going to like what you're about to taste! Anita, have you filled them in on the Father's Day spread?"

"I decided to let it speak for itself, Pastor Mattson. Thank you for your sermon today, and for getting the word out on the blood pressure screening at the hospital," she added.

They made their way, along with the hundreds of others, into the parish hall. The aromas of spices and fresh bread were enticing, and the assembly line of youngsters ushering in people, helping their elders, and pouring milk and water refills at tables impressed Shelly.

"Quite the production, Anita!" Jeremy admired.

"All home-made. Usually, the men clean up at luncheons, but it's their day today, so we had the teens take over," she explained.

They dished up the delicacies, choosing from a multitude of platters heaped with corn bread and rolls, country ham and fried chicken, greens, macaroni and cheese, pickles and olives, Jello, fruit, and vegetable sticks. Shelly spied Anita's turkey tetrazzini in the mix. Cakes, cookies, and bars loaded down another table in the corner. She wondered at her great luck to have been included in this delicious southern meal, noting the similarities to Faye's friends pulling out all the stops to feed a crowd. Aproned women were ready to switch the serving bowls as soon as the bottom of one peeked out. The unmistakable sense of bounty added to the festivities. If church upstairs had been formal and respectful, this ambiance was cheery, relaxed, and loud.

"More joy!" Shelly exclaimed in delight. "Seriously, Anita, this is the most wonderful morning. I can't thank you enough for sharing this with us. I'll never forget it."

"I'm never going to miss an opportunity to show off this excellence, Shelly. I knew you'd be able to appreciate it, and I'm glad you could come before you leave me for good," Anita's eyes filled. "It's been a wonderful two years being your nurse. I admire your grit. They ran you through the gauntlet, and you made it!"

Shelly knew this was high praise indeed. Anita had twenty years of experience, and in her wisdom kept quiet and did her job to perfection. She didn't feed the rumor mill, but she didn't miss a thing.

Jeremy and Shelly made their way outside, full from the experience of the service and the feast. "I would never have had the chance to be in that worship space without you, baby," Jeremy said quietly as he maneuvered his truck out of the lot. "It made me think about a lot of things I haven't pondered before now."

"Well, it's Anita you owe. She made this happen because it mattered to her, and she wouldn't take no for an answer. I'm glad it made you think—that's exactly what she wanted to happen. I can't wait to tell my mom about yet another approach to church. I've gotta admit, these churches I've attended here couldn't be more different than the one I grew up in in Minnesota, but they're all aiming for the same thing. Makes *me* think, too, Jeremy, and I'd say that's great."

***

Shelly had been packing intermittently, with a moving service coming to complete the task the last weekend before she left Kentucky. She worked a full day Friday, had the resident and fellow graduation party that night, and had to completely vacate the house Sunday morning. Jeremy planned to drive with all his belongings to his mom's house in Paducah that day.

Jeremy and Shelly had a cordial agreement to see how things went for the first month apart. He planned to drive up to Minnesota and visit for a week or two to see how they felt together again. Both realized that it had been a fun time, but neither really wanted to relocate.

Shelly had avoided any real plans about their future, and her ridiculous schedule provided cover.

Aside from the usual workday tasks, Shelly's only obligation was the big department party. There was no gathering of just the gyn onc faculty at Dr. Farber's club, as they had done for Ken and Brent before her. "There is a good deal of construction, doctor, so it won't be possible this year," Arlys had claimed.

"I understand, Arlys. It must be *so* hard to find a suitable place for five people to have a nice dinner out," Shelly had replied, hoping the saccharine in her voice was equal. The insult of no recognition by her division stung, but she was relieved to avoid artifice at this point.

None of the faculty had made any mention of the situation with Dr. Boldon, nor had they mentioned the letter which she had signed. Arlys left a note on her desk reminding her to leave her beeper on her desk. Dr. Farber had told her with a cool smile, "Well, it looks like you did it, Shelly. It wasn't all bad, right?"

Her last day of actual work was unremarkable, really. Rounds at 5:30 a.m., this time with Walter so he knew the service for the weekend. She indicated he should follow her to the cubby where the coffee so they could talk privately.

Shelly quietly handed the chemo book over to him, saying, "Walter, I've kept this up well, so you have the most current dates of chemo and tumor markers. I wish you the best with writing the chemo orders. You'll need to talk with the oncology pharmacist to review your orders for the first month and check out dose changes with them and the staff. Here you go." She choked back her emotions as she saw the last of the chemo book. *So many names, so many lives, and my God, so many deaths.* Walter took the book without a word.

A weight lifted off Shelly's back as the little black spiral book she had maintained for two solid years was no longer her domain. "It's like having a bunion removed," she tried to joke. "I didn't like it, but it was part of me. It's weird to have it gone."

Before they went back to the rounding team, Shelly impulsively added, "You know, Walter, it'll be up to you to bring them forward. I know you're a believer in 'The Way' and all, but you've gotta think for yourself. Believe it or not, I had some good ideas, and I'll bet you'll have some, too. They'll listen to you, Walter." She didn't wait for him to answer, reaching the group and saying, "Okay—one last time!" As Walter asked questions along rounds, her hackles were no longer raised. As she regarded him along the corridor, she wondered if he'd look back and wish he hadn't been such a dick. She gave him a massive smile. *Probably not.*

They pushed the cart around the bend and talked about the new first year fellow, a man from Vanderbilt whom Shelly hadn't met when he came for his interview. Walter had already talked to his team which started fresh on Monday, including Luca as his chief resident.

Joo-lye the first. Shelly thought. And I won't be here.

She made her goodbyes as she walked off the Powell one last time, looking back over her shoulder, and remembering some of the more intense conversations she had experienced on that floor.

Blossom, feeling so good she could whip a cat. Maxine, strutting in leopard skin. Paulette, loving her family and church. Kristi, practically ripping out her own IV to watch her beloved Ham catching a football. Irina, sobbing at her impending death. And of course, Faye.

Lively, sparkling, funny, competent, loyal, smart, hilarious, and so beloved, Faye.

Countless others swirled in her memory, causing Shelly to shiver. Infected wounds. Scared faces under thin crumpled bedsheets. Frowns of surgical pain. Terrible hospital food. Gasping, rattly breaths for those on their way to the next place. God, how Shelly stuffed all that suffering down. She headed to her desk and cleared out the pens and items she wanted to keep, taking care with the little box of obituaries. She'd checked in that week with Dr. Steele, who had made her laugh, as usual. She'd left a note on Dr. Hazel's desk thanking him for his guidance.

Arlys had left for the day. Shelly took a deep whiff of the stale perfume knowing she would recoil at that scent for the rest of her days. Such a shame there'd been no time for a fond farewell.

Shelly Riley took her last steps toward the door, remembering Ken's words to her, "Remember what it looks like for a graduating fellow to walk out this door," as he'd left for his new life only a year before. Sneaking one last peek into Dr. Hazel's office, she breathed deep of that comforting smell. *Goodbye, old couch,* she saluted, *you've got plenty of use ahead.* She turned and touched the office carrels for the last time. Seeing no one, Shelly gave a huge whoop of joy.

Bite me.

* * *

She drove her little Festiva home to get showered and changed for the party, finding Jeremy ready for her with a bottle of cheap champagne and two coffee cups that hadn't been packed away yet.

"How'd it feel to leave?" He popped the cork and poured, spilling foam everywhere on the counter. Pepper yipped and cowered at the sound.

"Unbelievable, I guess. As in, I literally don't believe I've done it. I'm sure it'll hit me sooner or later, but I'm still a little on the paranoid side."

They wore the same outfits they'd worn to Anita's church, arriving at the venue just as the piped-in music for the reception was ending. They each grabbed a glass of terrible red wine and gobbled a couple cheese cubes and headed into the ballroom area.

Round tables covered with confetti strewn white linens filled the room. Salads were at each seat, and nametags as well. Rebecca waved, her husband sitting with ramrod posture as if he'd rather be anywhere but there. Doctors Farber and Cardinal, without their wives, were at a table of their own, not talking. She didn't see Dr. Boldon, but the rest of the attendings from the department were there, as were all the residents except those on call at the hospital.

She and Jeremy found their table with Mona, also graduating from her infertility fellowship. Shelly was happy to be seated with Luca and Samantha. They stood as she approached and started clapping. The remaining tables of residents turned to see, and gradually joined in, standing and applauding Shelly. Luca whistled between his fingers, yelling, "Here she is!" Samantha elbowed him to shush.

Shelly's right hand went over her heart and she met as many eyes as she could, mouthing "thank you." She was touched beyond words. At last, she and Jeremy sat, and the emcee took the microphone at the podium.

"Well, well. A standing ovation for the oncology service? Very impressive. And now, let's get started on the roast. Eat your salads while we show the video of your PG-3s making fun of you, and then the wait staff will clear the plates and bring your entrées when the real show begins!"

The amateur video was hilarious, and even Jeremy laughed at the images of bone-tired residents in various stages of waking up, drinking coffee, and laughing with their peers and the hospital staff. Shelly and Mona were in a couple of the shots.

I don't remember people taking photos, she thought as the memories of her years there overflowed. The video documented the overwhelming exhaustion they had all experienced.

The individual roasts were precious, really, with each chief resident having a third year come to the podium to start the storytelling. Every doctor had any number of embarrassing incidents, bad relationships, or horribly funny baby pictures to keep the crowd in stitches. She loved watching her former chiefs laughing at themselves, agreeing with some of the jokes and protesting others, all the while knowing there was really nothing anyone could do to hurt them anymore. Each gladly took their diploma, a mint julep glass inscribed with their name, and a very nice chair with the university logo and crest on its back. The emcee made a lovely speech for Mona with similar gifts.

Next the chiefs gathered at the podium and another photo was shown. Black and white, it was a toddler with a thin white tee shirt, sitting otherwise naked on a potty with a ducky head.

It was Shelly, age eighteen months. Her mouth dropped as the presentation continued. Each resident took a turn roasting Shelly, showing photo after photo of her with a bowl haircut, dreadful aviator glasses, droopy long brown hair, and an especially miserable high school shot of her sitting in front of the fireplace with her flute on her lap.

Mona leaned over and said, "They found your mother's number and asked for the worst pictures she could find!" Shelly was crying with laughter as they made silly comments about her supposed childhood in an igloo, her terrible nicotine habit, tsk, tsk, her cheap but functional Festiva, her foul mouth, and her little dog Pepper.

The last picture was flattering, taken of her and Jeremy as they went out a month earlier.

Jeremy squeezed her shoulder and whispered, "That was from me. It's my favorite picture of us." Rebecca took the microphone.

"Dr. Shelly Riley, you barreled down here two years ago, in a toy car that didn't even have air conditioning. Angie knew you couldn't understand a word she said your first month. You'd sneak away for a Marlboro and come back to rounds with an Altoid in your mouth, thinking no one knew you smoked. You made us deviate from the decades of starting rounds at room 201 to the opposite end of the Powell, so we could 'unwind.' You asked for instruments we hadn't heard of in the OR, swore like a sailor if the staff weren't in hearing range, and started dating a total stranger in a graduate class. We had to vet him to make sure he wasn't an ax murderer. So far, so good."

Jeremy saluted Rebecca as the crowd laughed.

"And with all your crazy traits, Northern accent, and tobacco breath, we fell for you. We fell hard."

The room became silent.

"You carried burdens asked of no one else. You lost the support of a first-year fellow. You took on an extra graduate level class thrown at you by the Board. You finished your thesis and presented it at the national conference. Even your precious practice session was stolen by a Medicine resident. You missed the Board exam deadline. And of course, you maintained the dreaded chemo book for a full two years."

Her staff physicians were staring intently at Rebecca now, whereas everyone else watched Shelly. Walter deeply investigated his shoes.

Rebecca swallowed. "Well, we residents would like to honor you with a new award, Shelly. We know you're heading back home to Minnesota, and your state's motto is 'Étoile du Nord,' star of the north."

"I was the one who looked that up, by the way," Luca offered.

Rebecca pulled out a primitive papier-mâché star from the podium's shelf, and announced, "You never wavered in your support for us residents, Shelly. You taught us to put the patients first, to try to think about what our language or our actions could do to best help them. You showed emotion with the patients with the worst diseases and laughed with them when things were going well. We never saw you flinch when they would ask how long you thought they had to live." Rebecca composed herself.

"We hereby name you the *North Star* for 1996, and we're pretty sure you're the only gyn onc fellow who's ever going to get this!" The room exploded with laughter and applause, as the chiefs gestured for her to come up and get the gaudy ornament. Shelly hugged each one, and then came to Walter. Ramrod straight, she held out her hand and nodded her head once. He took her hand and gave it a shake. "Good luck, Shelly. I really mean that." They both smiled. She turned to the rest of the audience, waved her North Star above her head with a grin, and said into the mic, "Thanks to you all. Now I need a cigarette!"

The emcee came back to wind down the proceedings, wish them a lovely night and send them on their way. Then he said, "For those residents remaining in the program, I wanted to let you know that there'll be a small change in leadership for the academic year starting July first. Dr. Boldon has decided to pursue private practice at another location and will be stepping down as Department Head. He has planned this career change for some time and wishes you all well. Dr. Farber will lead us as interim, and the department has opened the search for candidates. Good night, all!" And with that, he winked at Shelly, and walked off the stage.

After an inadvertent gasp, the residents were eager to get outside so they could chatter about the news and make their own goodbyes. Hugs. Tears. Bittersweet and tender farewells. Shelly walked over to the table where her bosses stood to leave.

"Goodbye, Dr. Cardinal. Dr. Farber. Thank you for my training. I'll certainly do everything I can during my career to make the university proud. And I'll let you know when I pass my Boards!" She shook each one's hand as they offered general congratulations. She felt like she should wash after stepping away.

Outside at last, Jeremy twirled her around and around in the parking lot while she giggled and squealed. "I did it! I survived, Jeremy, I actually survived! This is what triumph feels like!"

Shelly's relief was overwhelming, having escaped her purgatory. Life was going to be grand. No more gaslighting. No more imposter syndrome. No more second and third guessing herself. She was embarking on new, grand adventures, and watched the scenery on the ride home with nostalgia. Entering her little rental house, she knew she'd retain her fond memories, but felt alive with the spirit of moving on.

COLGATE, FAYE
6/8/1950 – 6/30/1996

Our marvelous Faye passed on to be with the angels in heaven after surgery and treatment for ovarian cancer. Surviving is her mother Sissie. Faye was a miraculous, funny, and powerful spirit. She lived in Red Rock Falls her whole life, graduating from the Falls High School and getting her bachelor's degree at Kentucky State.

She owned and ran the town's beloved clothing store "The Dress" for over fifteen years, keeping it prosperous and popular. It was a well-respected place to work, especially given Faye's expertise and management.

Faye had the most wonderful friends a person could ever hope for. They have each promised to watch over Sissie. Carrie, Thelma, and Glory helped Faye and Sissie when chemo schedules and office appointments made life hectic. They mourn her like a sister, as do so many others. The whole town will miss our Faye. We will never find another soul as perfect.

Services this Saturday, 7/6/96, at 11am. Pastor Randy will officiate, and there will be a luncheon to follow.

CHAPTER 24

I'll Be in Bliss

The answering machine blinked with multiple messages, alarming Shelly as she and Jeremy fell through the front door. The insistent red light jolted her from the tranquil ride home.

"Gosh, we've only been gone a couple hours, baby. How could you get that many calls?"

"I was thinking the same thing. Especially since everyone I know was at the party. Can you let Pepper out while I listen?" Shelly tossed her purse on the dining room table, sat down with the memo pad by the phone, and gave Pepper a quick nuzzle.

BEEP. "Dr. Bailey, I'm sorry to call you at home, but Madeline gave me your number. This is Carrie, down in Red Rock Falls. I wonder if you could give a call? No matter how late, really. I'd appreciate it. My number is…" Shelly jotted the telephone number. *Maybe the gang wants to give a quick goodbye. That's so nice.*

BEEP. "Hey, it's Madeline." Shelly heard her blow her nose. "Where are you? I figured you'd be packing like mad. Call me right back." Shelly scribbled "Maddie" on the memo pad and reached for her address book to find her number.

BEEP. "Um, Dr. Riley, I'm so sorry to pester you, but if you would call me back as soon as you get this, well, that would be wonderful. I know it's your last night in Kentucky, and I need to reach you. Here's the number again…"

BEEP. Muffled voices and a click.

Jeremy came in from the back yard, Pepper following at his heels. "Who were all the calls?"

"Madeline called once, and then Carrie, one of the ladies from Red River Falls, called twice. The last one didn't leave a message." Shelly looked at her watch. "She said to call back no matter what time it is, but I don't know. It's almost midnight. What do you think?"

"They probably want to say goodbye—I'd give her a ring. I'll be in bed."

Shelly nodded, fingers turning her rotary dial to the number Carrie had left. It was picked up on the first ring. "Quiet y'all, it might be her," Shelly recognized the familiar voice and thought she heard Thelma chattering in the background. "Hello?"

"Carrie, it's Dr. Riley. I took you seriously when you said no matter the time…"

"Dr. Riley. I can't thank you enough for calling back. We've had such a time, I hardly know where to start. You see, well…" Carrie's voice faltered and she gave a little sob. "Faye's gone, Dr. Riley. She just collapsed this afternoon at the store, and the doctors couldn't get her back. Oh, my God, I can't believe I'm saying these words."

Shelly took a sharp breath in and grabbed the edge of the table. "Wait. That can't be. I just saw her CBC, and when we visited you all she was fine. I mean, she was in remission. She's only forty-six years old! This can't be." Shelly's hand trembled as she reached to light a cigarette.

Carrie's voice quivered. "It's been a nightmare, Dr. Riley. This is Faye's number I gave you, because we're all here watching over Sissie to make sure she gets to bed. The doctors think it was a blood clot to the lung. They called it--wait I wrote it down here--they called it a "saddle embolism" that just totally blocked off both sides of the lung. Oh, Lord, it was merciful for her, but…we are just lost."

Shelly listened to the details in miserable silence. She could envision the medical scene, the frantic efforts to revive her dear patient, the futility of respiratory attempts to get oxygen flowing with such a massive block. Shelly felt nauseated, and lurched to lean over the kitchen sink. She exhaled and stubbed out the cigarette. "Carrie, was she ever conscious?"

"Just for such a short time. She grabbed the nurse's hand in the ER and said, 'Tell them I'll be in bliss, will you? I'll be in bliss.' That's what the doctor told us when he came out to talk to us. Denean had called me at the school as soon as the ambulance left, and we were there within minutes. She was gone before any of us could see her." Carrie sobbed on the phone, passing the receiver to Thelma.

"Oh, Dr. Riley, we just had to tell you before you left. We didn't want you to hear it weeks later, and we knew you'd be on the road tomorrow, so when we called Madeline she gave us your number. Were we right to call?" Thelma's speech was even more pressured than usual. "It's so hard to believe she could be gone so fast. I saw her a couple days ago and she looked great. She had a follow-up appointment with Dr. Farber next week, so she had her labs drawn ahead of time."

"Now I know why Madeline left me a message tonight, too," Shelly answered. "I appreciate you all so much, and I'll think of you and Sissie during this awful time. I'm just so sorry," Shelly choked, tears flowing and shoulders shuddering. "I'm sorry I couldn't fix it for her."

Jeremy was at her side by now, smelling the smoke and realizing Shelly was still on the phone. He rubbed her back as she hung up.

"You hit the nail on the head, baby." He soothed her as she bawled. "Y'all feel personally responsible when you lose a patient, like it was your fault. That's not how it goes, though. Cancer kills people, I'm afraid. Unless you made a mistake on the chemo dose or screwed up her surgery, it's not your fault that she wasn't cured."

Shelly nodded, blowing her nose in misery. "I know I can't cure everyone. Of course I do. Still, Faye was so young. So healthy. What in the world happened? And what if I missed something? I've gotta call Madeline," she reached for another cigarette and found the number.

Madeline also answered on the first ring.

"Oh, my land, Shelly." Madeline had been crying, and that set off another minute of tears and gasps from them both. When she could catch her breath, she added, "Her tumor marker was up, Shelly. I saw it before I left work today. I think she was recurring, and that's why she threw that pulmonary embolus," Madeline blew her nose, the honk blasting over the phone line.

Shelly nodded. "Well, at least that makes a little more sense to me. I just couldn't understand how she could die so suddenly, during remission. Poor Sissie." The two commiserated for another half hour, and Madeline promised to keep Shelly informed as the friends in Red Rock Falls would grieve and mourn the loss of their dear friend Faye Colgate.

Shelly remembered Faye telling her she didn't expect to have a long life, as she told Madeline. "I'm going to hold onto that," Shelly said. "She was happy, she loved her mom and her friends, and she wasn't afraid. She wanted us to think of her in bliss, and so I will."

Shelly's night, having begun with triumph over obstacles and promise of a better future, ended with Shelly wiping her nose and wallowing in despair over her patient's sudden death. She kept shaking her head, as if she could force the news to another day, another year, but the heaviness followed her from room to room. The last day of her fellowship, Shelly Riley finally felt the burden of real loss in medicine and realized she was starting her life in her chosen field with death. Whether bliss, or heaven, or eternal nothingness, she was going to lose patients for the rest of her life. *Better figure this out,* she thought to herself.

* * *

She slept fitfully, her mind racing from Faye's death to packing up to leaving Jeremy and starting a new chapter. Shelly was awake as the bedroom became light with the dawn. She slipped out of bed to shower, cleaning her smeared mascara off her cheeks as her shampoo ran down her face and back. Toweling off, Pepper at her feet, she gazed upon Jeremy.

What am I thinking? I don't love him, I'm not going to marry him anymore than I thought I was going to marry Robert. What's the matter with me? Shelly shook her head, knowing that as nice a man as he was, there was no future for the two of them. She could either repeat the Robert situation or be direct. She dressed quietly, let the dog out, and made her last coffee. The packers rang the doorbell as she finished washing her mug and found the box she would place it in.

"Jeremy, up and at 'em! Movers are here," she called into the bedroom, making sure he stirred enough to be awake. Shelly walked the packing team, a dad and his daughter, through the remainder of the house, instructing them what to pack and where to put the boxes.

She stepped out her back screen door, lit a cigarette, and soaked in the memories of her home for the past two years. Her shed in better shape than she'd found it, her lovely neighbors, the chestnuts, and all the late nights she'd simply collapsed in bed after a huge day and a quick shower. She'd miss the people, she'd miss her patients, but Lord Almighty was she ever glad to be getting out of there. She smiled to herself, as Jeremy slid the screen to join her.

"What's making you smile, Shelly?"

"I'm ready to go, Jeremy. I'm ready to start my new life. I can't wait." She took both his hands. "And Jeremy, you and I are going to go ahead, to see whatever awaits, on our own separate paths. You're a wonderful man, you've been a great boyfriend, but I don't see us together long term, and I want to be honest. You deserve that." She stubbed out the cigarette and checked his face for a reaction.

"You've decided our future just now? The day you're leaving? I mean, do I get a say in this?" Jeremy's tone was mild, but he stared at Shelly hard and crossed his arms. "I thought we'd agreed that I'd drive up to see you in a month or two and we'd take stock of things then. Change of plans because…?" his voice inflected, awaiting a better explanation.

She heaved a big sigh. "I just spent two years stifling my voice, stuffing down my emotions, and feeling like absolute shit. I'm almost thirty-five years old, for crying out loud, and I'm still scared to say what I actually think! It's time for me to grow up. I like you Jeremy, very much. You're thoughtful and kind. But I'm never going to marry you, and for me, that means my move is a natural end to our romance. Believe me, you're going to find someone fabulous, and when you look back you'll be glad you're free to pursue her."

Jeremy stared into the yard, petting Pepper and shaking his head. "Well, I guess if one person feels this way, there's not much use in the other one fighting about it. It's a little abrupt, if you want my opinion."

He took a big breath in. "I guess that's my exit cue, Shelly. Can I..." He paused, trying to think through his next steps. "Can I call you, at least?"

"You have my mom's number, and that's where I'll be until I find my own place. And Jeremy, as sudden as this is, it's the right thing to do. I'm positive. Follow your dreams and be glad for what we had, okay?"

Jeremy was too surprised to register much of a reaction. "I guess there's no other choice, is there? Be well, Shelly. I'll think of you, up there in your igloo," he said with a tiny smile. "Take good care of Pepper, and stay in touch, now."

Back inside, Jeremy gathered his things. He packed up his truck and headed out of the driveway—and Shelly's life—with a wave and a toot of his horn. All Shelly felt, watching him leave, was relief and freedom. She had no idea how the need to end the relationship had become so clear. She hadn't a clue where the guts to call it off, clean and sudden, had originated. She just knew that her life was finally beginning, past trauma and patient losses being part of the story, and she had to start it alone. She would grieve Faye, she'd remember Jeremy fondly, and she'd still smart about the abuse of the last two years, but the future was bright. Blue skies ahead!

The phone rang as she walked back into the house. It was one of her colleagues in the Twin Cities whom she'd known well during medical school. They made small talk, the old friend telling Shelly how eager the community was for Shelly to establish her clinic quickly.

"I had to call you as soon as I heard you were coming back home to practice. I'm thrilled. Your specialty is in such short supply up here. Are you joining the U?" meaning the University of Minnesota.

"Nope. I'm joining a solo guy in private practice—Dr. Eddie Barbare. I'll have an office in Edina and one in Minneapolis, I guess. It's all still a little vague." Silence on the other end.

A little too much silence.

"Oh, my God. You're joining him?"

Acknowledgements

From medical colleague Lisa Erickson in the Abbott Northwestern Hospital Doctor's Lounge urging me to write this story to my writing group friends Meagh Decker, Megan Smith Genetzky, Anna Henderson, Tariq Samad, and Tom Sebanc who patiently workshopped chapter after chapter, lots of souls helped me get this book into your hands. A year-long writing class at The Loft by author and teacher Peter Geye motivated me to complete and revise this book. I'm confident we remain Peter's favorite writing cohort.

My Bryn Mawr College classmates Naomi Thomson, Julia Kuhn Mikell, and Katie McKenzie, all with careers in science and health, were powerful beta readers of the completed text. Not only did they give good feedback, but they deeply understood the story and encouraged me to persist. A Bryn Mawr friend in the industry, Claire Kirch, answered my timid questions about the imperatives in publishing with gentleness and good cheer. Anassa Kata!

My friends in the League of Women Voters Saint Paul, Diane Hellekson and Claudia Dieter, read the novel from an entirely non-medical perspective and offered critical, detailed insight—I warned them in advance about the f-bombs.

It was an exciting day to meet Ian Leask at Calumet Editions, and with Gary Lindberg and Josh Weber they made my dream come true. Editor Susan Thurston Hamerski reassured me when I asked, over and over, if this work was good, or if it was actually exceedingly terrible and she was just being nice. In addition to her psychotherapy she expertly streamlined this text and made me a better writer.

I wrote this book in a meditation space at St. Christopher's Episcopal Church in Roseville, Minnesota, when my kids were in Sunday school. I wrote it in the early morning hours at my cabin when everyone was still asleep. I wrote it at night in my little home office, usually with my two mixed breed dogs sleeping in their corners. With a weekly three-hour check-in, I always wanted to hit my word count goal and not disappoint Peter; he told us at the start of class that if we stayed on his schedule, we would each produce a novel. I'm grateful to have had these gifts of a teacher plus space and solitude while raising two sons and maintaining a very busy gynecological oncology practice in Minneapolis.

I'm also grateful for the support from my husband, Dan, my two sons, Jackson and Sam, and my mom Cynthia, who listened for years to my literary hopes. Big props to Libby Shindorf for crafting a sweet one-page sheet outlining Poised: A Patient Love Story to give to potential readers. I appreciate family and friends asking when they could buy my book, keeping the goal in sight for me. Thanks to my fellow readers in the Merriam Park book club and the League of Women Voters Saint Paul morning book club for asking about my progress and giving kind encouragement. Jeanette Anderson in the Abbott Northwestern Credentialing Department (who knows where ALL the bodies are buried) helped me on sexual harassment policies.

Despite policies and public outcry and decades of women in medicine, we still have so much work to do in medical and science education to shake off sexism. Memories of my past medical school classmates, residents, and fellows throughout my medical training are sprinkled and fictionalized in this text. Those years were always strenuous, but often exhilarating, and our relationships will last a lifetime. To my beloved mentors, Drs. Julia Donovan, and Michel Prefontaine at Baystate Medical Center, I appreciated your superb surgical technique and your fervent support of my career. As for my fiercest advocate, Dr. John Powell, I'm so glad he knew I had finished this novel before his death. I honor and thank you all.

Finally, this is a patient love story. Early in my private practice career I read Rachel Naomi Remen's powerful books (*Kitchen Table*

Wisdom, My Grandfather's Blessings) and attended several of her talks. Years ago, when pregnant with Jackson, I traveled to her location in Northern California for a course she ran on healing the healer. (They were entirely vegetarian, so I didn't mention the meat stick I packed…) She saw her patients and her medical colleagues in much the same light, as utterly imperfect humans. We all search for meaning, and disease is often a part of life. She remains a role model as a physician and writer.

    I so adored my patients. I admired their fierceness when fighting cancer, or hilarity when describing various physical indignities, or tenderness when asking about my kids in the midst of one last recurrence. God they were strong. And funny. And scared. And simple. And brave. And just so generous to me with their time and emotional intelligence. I learned and stretched and grew every day I was their doctor. I will forever be thankful for finding the best career in the world, and I hope I gave the service and affection those women deserved. My nurse Helen Flynn kept the whole thing afloat; we made a good team for our beloved patients facing the toughest times of their lives. In this book, I aimed to shower the women I've cared for in the past, many of whom are long gone, with all the attention and gratitude we doctors wish we could better express in our daily interactions. The patients are the whole reason we spend ten plus years in training, why we take call, why we get up in the morning.

    This is their story.

About the Author

Author Cheryl Bailey is a retired gynecologic oncologist who writes and makes music in her hometown of Saint Paul, Minnesota. Previously published short stories can be found in the Autumn 2022 ("Love, Frank" nominated for "Best American Short Stories") and Spring 2024 ("People are Dumb") issues of the narrative medicine journal *Intima: A Journal of Narrative Medicine* and was a community columnist for the Saint Paul Pioneer Press.

Other work includes the Minnesota Board of Medical Practice (President, 2024) and the Board of the Saint Paul League of Women Voters. Cheryl sings in the Mill City Singers and plays the flute in the Saint Paul JCC orchestra. She lives with her extended family and dogs in Union Park. Memories of her patients resonate with her still, years after retiring, and spurred her to write this novel.

Made in the USA
Monee, IL
02 December 2024